ATLANTIC OCEAN

South Georgia

South Orkney Islands

Antarctica

Drake Passage

Area of Main Map

WEDDELL SEA

South Pole

0 — 1000 Miles

THE
UNVEILING

Also by Quan Barry

Fiction
When I'm Gone, Look for Me in the East
We Ride Upon Sticks
She Weeps Each Time You're Born

Poetry
Auction
Loose Strife
Water Puppets
Controvertibles
Asylum

Plays
The Mytilenean Debate

THE UNVEILING

A NOVEL

QUAN BARRY

Grove Press
New York

Copyright © 2025 by Quan Barry
Map © 2025 by Keith Chaffer

Image on page 181: University of Virginia Special Collections

"WAR PIGS." Words and Music by Frank Iommi, John Osbourne, William Ward, and Terence Butler. (c) Copyright 1970 (Renewed) and 1974 (Renewed) Westminster Music Ltd., London, England. TRO - Essex Music International, Inc., New York, controls all publication rights for the USA and Canada. International Copyright Secured Made in USA. All Rights Reserved Including Public Performance For Profit. Used by Permission.

All rights reserved. No part of this book may be reproduced in any form or by any electronic or mechanical means, including information storage and retrieval systems, without permission in writing from the publisher, except by a reviewer, who may quote brief passages in a review. Scanning, uploading, and electronic distribution of this book or the facilitation of such without the permission of the publisher is prohibited. Please purchase only authorized electronic editions, and do not participate in or encourage electronic piracy of copyrighted materials. Your support of the author's rights is appreciated. Any member of educational institutions wishing to photocopy part or all of the work for classroom use, or anthology, should send inquiries to Grove Atlantic, 154 West 14th Street, New York, NY 10011 or permissions@groveatlantic.com.

Any use of this publication to train generative artificial intelligence ("AI") technologies is expressly prohibited. The author and publisher reserve all rights to license uses of this work for generative AI training and development of machine learning language models.

FIRST EDITION

Printed in the United States of America

This book is set in 10.8-pt. Janson Text by Alpha Design & Composition of Pittsfield NH.

First Grove Atlantic hardcover edition: October 2025

Library of Congress Cataloging-in-Publication data is available for this title.

ISBN 978-0-8021-6535-0
eISBN 978-0-8021-6536-7

Grove Press
an imprint of Grove Atlantic
154 West 14th Street
New York, NY 10011

Distributed by Publishers Group West

groveatlantic.com

25 26 27 28   10 9 8 7 6 5 4 3 2 1

For my parents
who chose me

The Negro is a sort of seventh son, born with a veil, and gifted with second-sight in this American world—a world which yields him no self-consciousness, but only lets him see himself through the revelation of the other world. It is a peculiar sensation, this double-consciousness, this sense of always looking at one's self through the eyes of others, of measuring one's soul by the tape of a world that looks on in amused contempt and pity.

—W.E.B. Du Bois

CHRISTMAS EVE

Finally the lot of them were assembled in the zodiac, their kayaks and gear loaded onto two support boats. Like eggs, Striker thought, a baker's dozen. Instantly she could hear Riley's retort. *You better hope one of you ain't cracked.*

A passenger was waving at them from one of the upper decks. Since coming through the Drake Passage, the man and his foot-long telephoto had become a fixture near the bridge, the man a birder from New England and on the hunt for some rare Antarctic tern. It seemed like a pointless way to spend your days, but whatever. Striker's last male friend had been a part-time paparazzo, so who was she to judge?

The birder trained his lens on the group. "Look up here!" he shouted.

"Say 'waiver,'" said Percy, and the adults laughed. "This'll be the photo we give the search party," the guide quipped, but only a handful of them laughed this time.

Striker felt her neck burning as if someone were pointing a magnifying glass at her. She turned around. But of course! There was that creepy little kid sitting at the back of the boat, nestled in among her dads. The kid was watching Striker, her eyes dark spear points. From what Striker had picked up in passing, Lucy was about seven, maybe eight, a small nine tops. While boarding the *Yegorov*, her scrum of dads let slip that they'd decided to take this trip anyway, even after their Eastern European nanny, who spoke the consonant-crazy language of Lucy's native country, got called home to visit a sick relative for the holidays.

"We offered to double her pay," said the youngest of the dads after Lucy knocked over a whole row of suitcases domino-style, "but money ain't what it used to be." The guy couldn't shut up about it, regaling anyone who would listen with the tale of how three years ago Frank and Hector had adopted Lucy from an orphanage in one of the former Soviet republics. Then six months ago, Frank had divorced Hector and married Abbott though Hector was still very much in the picture. "We think she has autism," the dad whisper-yelled by way of explanation as the suitcases toppled over. *Sorry!*

Ten minutes before boarding the zodiac for the kayak outing, Striker had the misfortune of running into Lucy alone by the stairs to the launch platform as the kid stood waiting for the rest of the group to suit up. It was like meeting a child in a horror movie. The way those children stare long and hard without blinking, an eerie innocence blanketing their faces.

Striker couldn't recall which former republic had spawned the child, the kid the very definition of ethnically ambiguous, her skin a toasted brown, her softly almond eyes reminiscent of the Eastern steppes. The little girl reminded her of that actor who played Pharaoh in *The Ten Commandments*, his ever-shifting claims to Mongolian, Russian, French ancestry. Like him, the kid could pass as native on practically any continent. Well, any one except *this*.

"Lucy, right?" Striker said. She tried to dial up the casualness in her voice. The child simply gaped, her face frozen. Striker found herself scrambling for something to say. Usually she was okay with awkward silences. Watching people squirm could be fun. But this was a whole new level of unease. The feeling as if earwigs were exploring the surface of her body, searching for a way in. "Happy early birthday. Mine's tomorrow too," she'd finally managed to squeeze out. "You ready to rumble?"

It wasn't the kind of thing one usually said to a small child, but so what? When Striker was a kid, she'd hungered for the moments when adults spoke to her as if she were one of them. Each time it happened, she felt she'd been gifted with a glimpse into the inner sanctum.

"Ready to rumble ready to rumble," said Lucy. The little girl remained immobile, a kind of recording device, her eyes full of seeing but no one was home.

Striker realized something was seriously off. "I'm Striker," she said, recovering her composure. "Nice to meet you." It was a strategy she'd perfected on the streets of New York. When talking to someone whose electrical box had blown a fuse, just act normal.

"I'm Striker I'm Striker," said the little girl.

Striker nodded, happy to play along. "Have a nice day, kid," she said. Already she was turning toward the stairs down to the zodiac, eager to make her exit.

Lucy continued to stare, her dark eyes fiery. "*I'm* Striker," the child said one last time. The way she emphasized the pronoun. Her voice down a full octave. "Have a nice death."

Striker blinked hard, trying to clear her vision. She hadn't made a mistake. The thing had been hiding under the little girl's ponytail, but now it crawled out from behind the child's curtain of dark hair. The kid remained nonplused. She stood softly stroking it, glaring at Striker as if daring her to mention it.

Sitting upright on the little girl's shoulder was a full-grown rat like something out of a New York City sewer.

People are going *ham* over their emotional support animals, Striker thought. Didn't somebody recently try to board a plane with a peacock? This had to be what this was, right? Some flea-infested emotional support animal her dads had managed to smuggle onboard. Technically we're in international waters, she concluded. I guess anything goes.

Then something landed on Striker's shoulder.

Startled, she dropped her paddle. The oar clattering at her feet. She couldn't turn around fast enough.

A pair of eyes were sizing her up. Take a picture, she thought, it'll last longer. She might be the only one onboard, but geez.

She was standing face-to-face with one of the dads.

At first the man seemed frazzled, exasperated at having to go in search of his child, who once again wasn't where she was supposed to be. But once he saw Striker, he began to act all friendly-like. White people acting friendly made Striker anything but. The appearance of the dad sobered her up, for the moment the child's alarming pronouncement forgotten. She was about to nudge the kid in the ribs and say something snarky that showed her age, like "Look out, here comes Wrangler," but Lucy had already disappeared.

Striker scowled at the man's hand still locked on her shoulder. Gently he patted her arm before letting go, apparently proving he was one of the good guys. His kid had given him the slip yet again, but Striker could tell he had decided to make the most of this encounter.

"Any chance you were just talking to my daughter?" he asked.

Up close the man looked faintly brown but in a different way than his child. Striker couldn't tell if it was genetic or the result of a booth. Knowing her luck it was genetic, the man scoping out possible onboard allies in case something went down. They both knew the score. Excluding housekeeping, it was a boatful of white people and her and this guy plus his antisocial kid. It was a smart move on his part. Striker took another look just to be sure. Yeah, the dude was brown all right but probably not brown enough to keep a running tally. She sure as hell did. Every room, every plane, every restaurant and bar, every nook and cranny, Striker forever sailing in and taking inventory. It was crazy. In a few decades, the country would be a rainbow majority, yet there were still entire swaths of life where hers was the only brown face not pushing a broom. She always wondered if the other people in whatever theater or museum or airport lounge even noticed that the folks manning the Hudson News kiosk looked nothing like them. Recently it seemed like every few weeks some Dick and Jane would tell her a story about the time they'd been the only white people at Sylvia's up on Malcolm X and how *alive* it made them feel, Dick and Jane beyond grateful for the chance to *finally* experience being in the minority even if it only lasted until a tour bus pulled up out front.

Tales of white life in the urban jungle always left Striker fighting the urge to twirl her finger in the air and whistle. *Whoop-de-doo.*

She bent over and picked up her paddle. Any time she was around parents and children who didn't racially match, a tightness stormed in her stomach. Good luck, kid, she'd always think. You're gonna need it.

"I wouldn't call it talking," she said, hoping it would end there. "Clam lips on that one."

"Her other dads think she's on the spectrum," the man sighed. "I dunno. Could be some form of attachment syndrome. We don't really know how much time she spent in the orphanage."

Whoa, Striker thought. I have a two-drink minimum if you want me to listen to your life story. She didn't stick around to hear more. White people and people who were light enough to pass had a way of floating through the world in search of alliances. Unfortunately for this guy, Striker preferred going it alone.

She knew Riley would understand. It was why they were besties. Being ally-less had its benefits. It meant you didn't have to make war on anyone if someone attacked Japan. We are the very dictionary definition of resilient, Riley would say. White people need to back the fuck up and stop pushing that ally shit on us just because it makes them feel useful.

Yeah, everyone knows the worst thing that could ever happen had already happened to Black folk. White people and people who looked white were starting to wake up and smell the proverbial coffee. Striker's one Native friend Halyn rolling her eyes anytime someone mentioned global warming. "Don't talk to me about the apocalypse," Halyn would say. "Been there, done that." Halyn raising an eyebrow in Striker's direction, the two of them sharing a look without needing to say a single word.

For a second time that morning, Striker turned and headed toward the stairs down to the waiting zodiac. The storm massing in her stomach only seemed to be ramping up. It wasn't the first time since boarding the *Yegorov* two days ago in Ushuaia, the southernmost city on the planet, and steaming through the mad waves of the Drake Passage that Striker was having a funny feeling about cruising around what she'd mentally dubbed the ass of the world. You shouldn't be here—God made Antarctica inaccessible for a reason, Riley would've said. Riley was always the first to tell her what she didn't want to hear, Riley never afraid to beat a dead horse. People like us don't go to places like that, her friend had told her, seriously, where are we in the histories? and Striker had countered with *it's for work plus I'm turning forty so just chillax, it'll be—*

The birder with the giant camera was still standing on deck trying to get the kayakers to look up. Just then a shadow swept overhead. The air stank like the breeze over a garbage dump. There was a loud crash and a thud followed by the sound of feet running from all directions. Striker looked to where the man had been standing.

At first the birder appeared fine, just shocked. Then a red line began to snake down from the new groove gouged in the middle of his face, the man's nose broken, the cartilage visible, a few feathers stuck to the blood on his skin.

"What the hell?" said one of the dads.

The man's camera was lying at his feet, the telephoto lens smashed beyond repair. Too bad. His homeowners wouldn't cover it. From her line of work, Striker knew a thing or two about cameras. She priced the lens alone just north a cool 15Gs.

Something huge and white was flopping around screaming in the broken glass. Ruby drops of blood evenly spraying the scene. "It flew straight into my camera," the man blubbered. "It came out of nowhere." The ship doctor with the unforgiving buzzcut had already materialized and was leading him away, the doctor's hand tightly cuffing the man's wrist in case he suddenly fell apart.

Several members of the crew, mostly from housekeeping, stood crossing themselves. One of them worked his way through the crowd and knelt beside the thrashing creature, the bird convulsing as if an electric current were being pumped through it.

Striker couldn't get over the span of it, the creature the length of a compact car. During one of the lectures the onboard ornithologist told them that an albatross can travel distances equivalent to circumnavigating the globe in forty-six days, living upward of seventy years. The expert said that the superstition about killing an albatross originated with Coleridge's *Rime of the Ancient Mariner*, and that prior to the nineteenth century, the albatross was believed to be the vessel that housed the souls of sailors lost at sea. According to the ornithologist, the curse of the Ancient Mariner didn't stop famed British explorer Ernest Shackleton from eating a nestful of albatross chicks when he and his men made landfall on South Georgia Island after a harrowing eight-hundred-mile voyage in a twenty-two-foot boat, the men gleefully adding the baby birds to their hoosh. The woman closed her talk with an excerpt, the reading almost comical thanks to her wobbly Katharine Hepburn–like voice.

> *And I had done a hellish thing,*
> *And it would work 'em woe;*
> *For all averred, I had killed the bird*
> *That made the breeze to blow.*

Lying there on deck, the creature's wings formed an inside-out umbrella. Striker shuddered. There was so much bad luck spewing in the air. Accidentally or not, this magnificent bird's body was broken, its limbs pointing in nonsensical directions. Someone was going to pay for this. The bad luck had to fall somewhere. Shackleton and the entire crew of the *Endurance* may have made it back to England, but a few years later during yet another expedition to the white continent, Sir Ernest had dropped dead of a sudden heart attack. The curse of the albatross would not be denied. The guy was only forty-seven years old. A voice bubbled up from out of the Sunday mornings of Striker's childhood:

> *Then answered all the people and said,*
> *His blood be on us, and on our children.*

The worker cupped the bird's head in his hands and twisted. The thing shrieked. He twisted again. It shrieked louder, its cries unearthly. With each twist you could hear the bones breaking, then breaking more, like wringing a dishcloth full of chalk. The man stood up and put the heel of his rubber boot on the crown of its skull before thinking better of it. "Someone throw me a rag," he called. Within seconds something white went sailing through the air. The man took his foot off the albatross and laid the towel over its head. He stood back up and closed his eyes. Striker thought that was a nice touch. Closing your eyes could get you through anything. Closing her eyes had gotten her through forty long ones and would hopefully get her through at least forty more. The problem with Antarctica was the twenty-four-hour sun. Even with your eyes closed the light made it hard to keep out the stuff you wanted to keep out. Stuff like this.

Mercifully, Percy hit the starter and the zodiac's engine roared to life, drowning out the sound of the worker stomping on the small head, the gray matter shooting out in all directions. Even over the noise of the engine, Striker thought she could hear the sickening crunch, feel the sensation of the skull splintering, the hot smell of the bird's brains coating the air.

Lucy turned excitedly to her brown father. "Throw me a rag," she said, "throw me a rag." A small gray face peeked out from the top of her dry suit, the creature's head as if sprouting from her throat.

"Not now, honey," the man said distractedly, his eyes locked on the mayhem on deck. Slowly the child turned and trained her empty stare on Striker.

> *I pass, like night, from land to land;*
> *I have strange powers of speech;*
> *That moment that his face I see,*
> *I know the man that must hear me:*
> *To him my tale I teach.*

"Throw me a rag," the little girl commanded.

Striker found herself searching around for something, anything to toss, but then the brown dad handed his daughter a piece of gum, and the little girl settled down. The other fathers just sat there wide-eyed like they might throw up. The summer air once again bright and scentless.

On the short ride out to the island, they did introductions. The Tech Titan's husband concluded his by proudly pointing to one of the support boats trailing in their wake. "The wife and I brought our own gear," Kevin said. "Luckily our kayaks are also red." As a location scout, Striker knew a thing or two about transportation costs. The couple could've bought all-new gear, top-of-the-line, for the same amount it probably ran them to ship their boats down to the bottom of the world. Rich people gonna rich, Riley would've said.

"Taylor loves this kind of stuff," Kevin added. He gazed at the Tech Titan as if her very existence powered the universe, his eyes practically fluttering. "She paddles out to Alcatraz at least once a week."

Striker guessed the battered and dented kayak was the woman's boat. Even at a distance it looked like it had seen its fair share of hairy moments. The man's had a shiny patina glossing its sides, the thing fresh out of the wrapper.

"You're in paradise right now, aren't you, hun?" Kevin said. His wife looked at him blankly as if battling not to roll her eyes.

Lean out, honey, Striker thought. She smiled inwardly, looking forward to whatever marital fireworks might be on the horizon. In her book, marriage was like buying a gun or dispensing pharmaceuticals—you needed a license for it, plus in most states there was a three-day waiting period. Judging from the married couples Striker knew, three days wasn't nearly long enough.

Despite his wife's obvious disinterest, Kevin kept his adoration on high beams. He rested a gloved hand on Taylor's knee and took off his sunglasses, presumably so everyone could see the bountiful love radiating from his sockets. Didn't anybody else sense what it was costing him to keep that sappy smile spackled on his face? A body could fake conjugal bliss only so long before cracking.

"And what do *you* do?" la Grande Dame asked Kevin, the arch front and center in her voice.

Striker couldn't look away from the Dame's luscious head of silvery hair, her perfectly beveled bob reflective like polished steel, one wing of her hair falling enticingly over her eyes. La Grande Dame and her husband the Baron of Industry Who Had Never Worked a Day in His Life and Had the Hands to Prove It were the last two people on earth Striker had ever expected to see in dry suits. The image did not disappoint. Jane and Robert Foley were well preserved, though the Baron skewed a bit on the frail side. Decked out in the gear necessary for kayaking in Antarctica, the couple reminded Striker of Kodiak bears dancing around in tutus. The black lycra spray skirts girding their waists were undoubtedly the most undignified pieces of clothing the pair had ever donned. Rumor had it that the week before the trip, the Baron had had his valet fly down a case of Château Margaux. The first night onboard, the entire dining room had watched as the Baron and the Dame sipped from a bottle costing on the higher end of four figures, more than most of the crew earned all season. The Margaux gleamed dark and menstrual in the glass, an emerald the size of a grape adorning the Dame's finger. Perhaps unsurprisingly, the Baron and the Dame would be riding in two separate tandems and not together. Striker hadn't seen it listed as an option in the *Yegorov* activity book, but the Foleys were each to be ferried about in the glacial waters of the Weddell Sea by one of the Russian crew.

Striker snuck another peek at la Grande Dame and her silver hair shiny as a pith helmet. Yeah, this chick was bona fide trouble, her vibe a complicated scent reeking of unbridled arrogance and a carefully cultivated aloofness. As if for confirmation, the Dame tipped her head from side to side, touching each shoulder, the bones cracking in her neck, the sound like a small whip flaying the air. Yeah, Striker had chosen the right nickname for this one. There was something else off about her, something about the manufactured nature of her smile, but Striker had already been staring at the old woman for too long. Whatever it was would come to her sooner or later. For now, she made a mental note to steer clear of the old bird and her titanium helmet.

"I'm a consultant," Kevin said, answering the Dame's question. Nobody asked in what. If you dug around for specifics, he seemed like the type to launch into some corporate mumbo-jumbo designed to make you feel stupid for needing to ask the follow-up question: what does *that* mean?

"Nice work if you can get it," said Billy Bob, the father of the Texas bunch.

"Amen to that," said Billy Bob's wife, Bobbi Sue.

To be fair, the petite blond with the dark eyebrows didn't *really* say this. Since encountering the pair at the breakfast buffet and secretly dubbing them Billy Bob and Bobbi Sue, Striker would periodically put words in their mouths to go along with the characters she'd created. Now as she learned their real names, she decided to stick with the ones she'd already christened them with. It just made things easier.

Billy Bob and Bobbi Sue had two kids. Any time Striker made eye contact with the girl, the teen began rapidly blinking. Striker liked to think it was some kind of Morse code, the kid begging for help. When they went around the group and introduced themselves, the girl said her name was Anders, her pronouns they/them.

"Anna also answers to her given name and she/hers," interjected Bobbi Sue. "Isn't that right, Anna?"

Striker was surprised by the brief whiff of compassion that surged in her chest. The parents were probably hoping that by offering as little resistance to "Anders" as their Texan hearts could muster, the sooner Anders would get shelved. But if Striker had to guess based on the look of things, Anders was there to stay.

Anders' little brother was a towheaded kid named Mikey who was somewhere around Lucy's age. Striker could already tell that in the days ahead, Mikey and Lucy would not become fast friends. Mikey was a golden retriever, Lucy a Persian. That these kids were even *allowed* out on the Southern Ocean seemed like a bad idea. The night before in the sauna, Percy had explained to Striker how young kids got to kayak. Company rules said you had to be at least thirteen, but it happened all the time. Rich families paying an extra "calamity fee" above the $1500 it already cost to be part of the kayaking expedition. The parents forking it over and promising that their kids would be in a tandem with one of them at all times.

What else Percy tell you in the sauna? Even ten thousand miles away, Striker could imagine Riley thirsting for the gory details.

It was a recent enough encounter that she was still basking in it. Honestly, they'd kept the conversing to a minimum. It was a twelve-day trip. They both knew it and worked fast. When they first entered the sauna, he'd pretended to be insulted when she asked if he was Australian. "I'm a Kiwi through and through," he said. She'd nodded, secretly thinking *even better*. He'd joked that the little girl with three dads had mastered the space-time continuum. He said it while running a finger up Striker's thigh. "Kid's everywhere at once," he murmured, kissing her neck. She could barely see him through the steam. "Don't tell anyone but someone drowned in the plunge pool two seasons back." He'd nodded at the small, windowless room next to the sauna where the water sat dark as oil. "Maintenance must have left the metal safety door open," he explained. "Kid was only ten years old." Striker felt her body tighten, her breath becoming labored as though something were swelling inside her throat. Percy continued. "Worst part is we had six days left in the trip. Definitely not a lot of fun." His thumb snagged on her medical alert bracelet as he ran his index finger down the inside of her arm. "You sick?" he asked. "Anything I should know?"

In the heat of the sauna, she could feel the sweat running down her skin, her body raining. She traced Percy's nipple with her finger, told him the medical alert bracelet was a gag gift her best friend had given her for Christmas, the inscription a private joke between the two of them. "So what's it say?" he said, drawing her wrist toward his face, but she pulled her hand away and put it on his—

In the zodiac, the two married dads sat pawing anxiously at their dry bag. "The seal's not *tight*," said the one wearing aviators.

"Yes it is," countered the youngest of the three. He looked younger than the other dads by a solid decade, maybe two.

"Guys," said the faintly brown dad who'd introduced himself as Hector. He patted the air with his hand, the international signal for *keep it down*. Striker had already forgotten the names of the other dads, but she knew she'd remember Hector's plus the fact that he was some kind of environmental lawyer. After all these years her default setting remained set to automatically retain the deets of brown folks she encountered. Not that it had ever done her any good.

When it was her turn to introduce herself, Striker felt a sudden dip in the temperature, the day preternaturally quiet. Was it her imagination, or were the adults leaning in, eager to hear her every word?

This was a new phenomenon Striker had noticed ever since 2020 when pandemonium broke out in the streets. A certain breed of white people attempting to make space. Acting like you had their ear. Like they actually *cared* what you had to say. Like they appreciated you and believed every single word about your personal story and were forever sorry for anything they might have ever said or done or thought or worn or interpretive danced that you found offensive. She thought of the summer she'd spent in the posh coastal town on the northern cape. Everywhere she went, the people doing a double take, startled to see someone of her complexion. Once they recovered, they'd offer her a hearty hello and beam for all they were worth, desperate to convey their message: *Dear Human of Color, please know I am your friend.*

"So what, you'd rather be run outta town?" Riley had said when she'd told her.

"It's just creepy is all." Striker didn't tell her friend that she'd kept expecting someone to challenge her right to be there, like the Florida teen who got killed on his way home from the corner store with a bag of Skittles tucked in his jeans.

Floating in the zodiac, the group sat gazing at her, unblinking like fish. She didn't even know where to begin. 2020 had made everything worse. This breed of white people was becoming trickier than ever to read as they gripped their cards closer to their chests. Why did Gen Z not get this? If white people became inscrutable, then how would folks like her know how to act around them, how genuine you could be? No, she needed white folks to keep their caveman ways front and center. When they did, it made her feel safe. She knew where she stood.

"I'm Striker," she finally said, "I'm in the industry," and left it at that. She saw the youngest dad whisper to his husband, *porn?* She smiled but didn't disabuse him of this, thankful there was at least one white person in the group she could still read.

Bobbi Sue took the smile as a signal. She nudged her son.

"Happy birthday, Veronique!" said little Texas Mikey in a voice sweet as cane sugar. "Have a beautiful *Yegorov* day!"

The adults laughed. Less than three days into their Antarctic adventure and the kid had already drunk the *Yegorov* Kool-Aid.

"Thanks," said Striker, "but the guy on the intercom this morning got it wrong. A: I go by Striker. And B: technically my birthday's tomorrow. On Christmas." She nodded toward Lucy and her dads. "As is Lucy's," she added.

"Tomorrow she'll be ten," said the quietest of the dads.

"And I'll be four times that," said Striker.

"Bet there's a lot of living under that belt," said the Baron. Kevin laughed, his wife sighing.

"Happy birthday, happy birthday," said Lucy. "Happy birthday porn."

The goodwill they'd all been riding popped, the fountain of awkwardness once again flowing freely. Only la Grande Dame remained impervious to it. The old woman sat openly staring at Striker, this most exotic of creatures—a Black tourist on a high-end vacation. Most likely the old girl had never seen her kind before.

The Dame smiled stiffly. "Who did you hurt to get here?" she asked.

"*Excuse* me?" said Striker.

"I said, how long was the flight to get here?"

"Oh," said Striker. She unclenched her fists. "It's a little over eleven hours from JFK to Buenos Aires."

"Interesting," said the old woman, satisfied, but by what, Striker couldn't guess.

And so their tour group was a lucky thirteen in number.

Striker watched the *Yegorov* grow smaller in the distance. She wanted to ask Percy how the crew would dispose of the albatross. Would it be thrown overboard or put to sea in a more gracious manner? She hoped the damn thing wasn't an omen. In Antarctica, there had to be countless ways to die. Death by air, death by fire, death by icy waters, death by earth gaping open or crushing you. There was also the one she feared most—death by fellow man suffering from cabin fever. During the pandemic, she'd been thankful she lived alone.

The broken bird with its ten-foot wingspan already seemed long forgotten by the others. The past few years Striker had grown more and more shocked by white people's willingness to push their luck. With her white friends, she was careful never to mention the few superstitions she held sacrosanct, but with Riley, she never had to explain why she wouldn't put her purse down on the floor in a restaurant. She just hoped someone from housekeeping had lit some sage in the spot where the bird died. She'd ask Percy about it once they got back. He'd laugh, but so what? In her book, white people could stand to be a little more in awe of the inexplicable.

Like the night before at dinner when the first mate offered a toast. *To both Christmas and summer in the Weddell Sea,* he shouted. Throughout the dining room people raising their water glasses high in the air. What she'd learned while scouting a location in the Balkans. Toasting with water was bad luck. It was just one step up from toasting with an empty glass. In most cultures, such toasts were said to result in bankruptcy or some other disaster.

It didn't matter if it was summer in the southern hemisphere. Normally summer was a season of barbeques and easy living. But Antarctica was the continent with no margin for error. A place demanding you respect it and what it could do to you in the blink of an eye. Yeah, the Antarctic summer was more than happy to kill you even if it was Christmas. Had any of them *really* thought this through? Being a full hemisphere away from help? And worst-case scenario, would your body be repatriated or would you be left there in the snow and ice among the scavengers, the birds with their tearing feet, or worse yet, would your corpse be stashed away somewhere in the craggy landscape where nothing ever rots, every frozen thing frozen forever?

These white people didn't seem to know the half of it. If you can help it, don't tempt fate. All around the room, the music of water glasses merrily clinking. Judging from the symphony of sound, Riley would've nudged her in the ribs and said half-jokingly that with all that bad luck being generated, someone, maybe multiple someones, was bound to die.

No thank you, thought Striker. I'm here to do a job and go home and not hurt anybody. She'd kept her palms planted flat on the table. For a brief instant, she thought she smelled something sickly, like a moldering piece of fruit, but she decided someone had simply let the baked Alaska flame a little too long.

"Remember," said Percy, as he steered the zodiac out into the waters ringing Paulet Island. "Don't get any closer to an iceberg than twice its height."

Striker adjusted her sunglasses for the umpteenth time. She knew it wouldn't do any good. Looking at this golden man was like looking directly at the sun. His handsomeness was too much for mortal eyes even if there was a sloppy gob of neon-pink oxide slathered on his face. It was like drawing a fig leaf on Michelangelo's *David*. Why ruin an object's best feature?

You mean his second *best feature*, Riley would've cackled.

At breakfast Striker had already been fantasizing about the steamy new trouble she and their intrepid kayak leader might cook up later that night after the eggnog and off-key carols. Regardless of his bright pink nose, there was no hiding the chiseled planes of his face, his perfect jaw chainsaw rugged. Only la Grande Dame seemed able to hold her gaze on him without breaking into a fit of pre-adolescent giggles. The youngest of the dads was the worst, the way he would reach over and tap Percy on his iron forearm with a finger, coyly asking what kind of penguin they had seen, gentoo or chinstrap? Striker felt bad for the dad. He was doomed to spend the whole trip alternating between thirsting and then trying to convince his husband he wasn't. Good luck with that.

For now, their collective fantasizing would have to suffice, as Percy was in the middle of a factoid dump. "Antarctica's bigger than China and India combined," he said. "It accounts for sixty-one percent of the earth's freshwater but technically it's a desert with less than seven inches of annual precipitation. Cold *and* dry means nothing here ever decomposes."

"So this is the land of eternal youth?" joked the youngest dad.

"Maybe," said Percy. "In 2017, scientists found a hundred-year-old fruitcake in an explorer's hut that they claim is still edible."

"I wouldn't wanna be the intern charged with finding out," said the middle dad.

"It was still lying around because somebody was using it as a doorstop," said Billy Bob.

"If the *magnetic* pole is eighteen hundred miles from the *geographic* pole, will we get a chance to see it?" squeaked the Tech Titan hopefully. Striker could already envision next year's Christmas card featuring Taylor and hubby dearest holding a handmade sign reading MERRY CHRISTMAS FROM THE ENDS OF THE EARTH.

Percy shook his head. "The magnetic pole's on the other side closer to Tasmania, plus it's always shifting."

"What about the pole of inaccessibility?" asked Taylor, not ready to give up on her dream of the ultimate envy-inducing holiday card.

"What does *that* mean?" yawned la Grande Dame.

"It's just the spot on the mainland furthest from the sea," explained Percy. "And no, we'll be nowhere near it." He moved on to ice safety. Striker couldn't believe there was so much to say. She found herself tuning out, trying to remember if she'd put film in the Holga, shut her refrigerator door tight. "And if the ice calves, you could get hit," Percy concluded, wrapping up his spiel. "Or the wave action from the spray could tip you." He made a low whistling noise. "It'd be game over before you could even think *my bad*, so just steer clear." They nodded dutifully, the youngest dad practically crossing his heart and hoping to die if he strayed from doing exactly as directed. "Any questions?"

"What time's cocktail hour?" asked la Grande Dame.

Percy laughed. "We haven't even had lunch yet."

"Your point being?" said the Dame.

Damn! Someone's living her best life, Striker thought.

"I don't know what time *you* usually cheers," Percy said, careful to keep his voice light and neutral, "but we'll head back in a little after noon. Does that work?"

The Dame nodded but retained her air of patrician skepticism.

The Tech Titan raised her hand. "We have emergency plans in place in case of unforeseen variables, correct?" Each time Taylor spoke, her voice was higher than Striker anticipated, like she'd taken a hit off a helium balloon. No wonder her husband Kevin carried himself like a man who had ground his molars down to nubs. A voice that stratospheric could drive anyone nuts.

"Correct," said Percy. He left it at that, beaming his 240-watt smile at the group. Like the Dame, the Tech Titan also looked as if she wasn't buying what Percy was selling, but Kevin managed to get her to stand down by signaling that mama's little baby needed his neck seal rechecked. Taylor sighed and gave Kevin's zipper a good, hard yank. As an extra bonus, she took off one of her gloves and licked her finger, wiped something imperceptible off his face.

That is what a three-day waiting period gets you, Riley would've said.

"But in case of emergency, Texans first, right Coach?" guffawed Billy Bob. Since nobody laughed, Striker could only conclude she'd just imagined him saying it.

Soon it was her turn to shove off from the support boat. Getting in the kayak was a much easier process than it looked. Various beefy Russians held your boat tight against the zodiac. It was just a matter of stepping over and in. Once she sat down, someone handed her a paddle. He gave her a small salute, which might have been a signal for *all clear* or else was some sort of friendly detente between their countries.

"One more point," said Percy. "Anything goes down, you can survive a full fifteen minutes in a dry suit in water this cold."

"Is that supposed to be reassuring?" asked the youngest dad, feigning alarm.

"All I'm saying is fifteen minutes is plenty of time for someone to get to you," said Percy. "So don't panic."

"Easier said than done," mused Taylor, giving her husband a healthy dose of side-eye.

Striker took a deep breath. Tomorrow she'd be forty. It was true. There was a lot of living under this belt. She was about to push off into the unending blue. Then the lead Russian holding her boat in place reached out and tucked the small gold cross hanging around her neck back inside her dry suit.

"It's just an old keepsake," she explained. "Doesn't mean a thing."

He grinned and winked conspiratorially. "Scared?" he asked.

She was pretty sure this one was named Vadim. During the pre-launch orientation, she had watched as he introduced himself to la Grande Dame as the crew member who would be piloting her kayak. The old woman had barely acknowledged him. Too bad for her, Striker thought. The guy looked like a serious player, what the youngs called DTF. Down To Fuck. He sported a shaved head and had the half-lidded eyes of someone who'd seen it all. The flirtation was obvious in his voice. Striker shot him a long, cool look. Back home everyone had told her to enjoy herself on this trip of a lifetime. Well, *almost* everyone. Riley had brought it up one night while out with friends after Striker had announced she was heading to Antarctica.

"Is it just me or do y'all think that's crazy?" Riley had asked the group. When nobody took up the gauntlet, she charged ahead. "Personally? I'm a hard hell to the no on everything polar," she said. "I mean, who do you think a polar bear's gonna go for first?" She raised an eyebrow and peered around the table.

"There are no polar bears in Antarctica," said Striker. "No walruses either."

"Whatever," said Riley. "I'm just telling you for your own good. Cold, ice, white people as far as the eye can see? Hands down, that's my worst nightmare."

Everyone laughed, including their two white friends, Scarlett and Casey. Then the group got into it, each sharing what scared them the most. At first there were the usual suspects—the dark, spiders, clowns with big feet, the city after 2 a.m. Three drinks in their answers became more interesting. One person talked about the time she got lost coming home from the grocery store, a place she came and went from almost daily, yet suddenly nothing seemed familiar, her heart racing as she tried to make sense of it, relocate herself in time and space. Casey said she had a fear of not knowing why certain things happened. She named a movie filled with inexplicable moments, a series of bizarre occurrences.

"Lame," pronounced Riley.

"Hear me out. It's deeper than a fear of the unknown," Casey insisted. "It's a fear of not having answers."

Scarlett tried backing her up. "I remember as a kid being scared shitless by 'The Lottery,'" she said.

"You were scared of *Powerball*?" said Riley, raising both eyebrows in disbelief.

"No, the short story by Shirley Jackson," Scarlett clarified. "You never find out where the town is or why they started stoning people once a year just for kicks."

"Exactly," said Casey. "If you knew *why* they did it, it might not be so creepy."

"Like that woman last year who stabbed her three-year-old out of the blue," said Scarlett. "There were no signs of psychosis or anything. She had a nanny, for Chrissake. They still don't know why she did it."

"No offense but that all sounds like some white people bullshit, needing answers and stuff," yawned Riley. "Note to self: you are not entitled to reasons. When Job asked God why He was picking on him, didn't God tell him to go fuck himself?"

"I'm terrified of hurting someone," offered a woman at one end of the table.

"Girl, you broke that man's heart," Riley said.

"I mean *physically*." She explained that a friend of a friend of her sister's had killed someone in a car accident. "She hit a child," the woman said. "A *child*. How do you keep living after that?" A silence fell over the table.

"What about you?" Riley finally asked.

"Me?" said Striker. She found herself ransacking her brain for something to say, something easy, like choking to death while eating junk food alone in her apartment. "I dunno," she said. "How about squirrels?"

"Squirrels?" Riley said.

"Ever seen one loose in a house?"

Around the table people nodded, similarly creeped out by the thought.

The group moved on. Striker felt herself relax. Why put it into words if you didn't have to?

Her greatest fear was of losing her mind. One day just waking up and having no idea who or where or what anything was, the way the world worked, your mind wiped clean of its owner's manual, reduced to static on a TV, the rainforest setting on a white noise machine. Yeah, mos def that was the winning ticket. Or was it? Striker let herself linger on the question a beat too long. *Shizer.* It was one thing to lose your mind, to become forgetful or not recognize people. It was a whole other level to go full frontal insane, for reality to turn topsy-turvy, your perception of the world suddenly unreliable. A small shiver rippled through her heart. Bingo! Becoming insane was hands down her biggest fear. For the past few decades, how many times had she secretly entertained the possibility that that ship had already sailed?

She turned to the Russian holding her kayak in place and threw back her shoulders, squared herself. "*Honey*," she said, stressing the word, which she coolly tossed in his lap not as a come-on but as a diminutive used when addressing a child. "It's called tenacity."

Suddenly the world seemed to shift a few degrees, everything slightly unbalanced. Striker had the sensation she was floating in a tandem and that somebody was seated behind her. She could feel a ghostliness just over her shoulder, the heat of someone's rancid breath soughing on her neck.

But that was *crazy*. Nobody was watching her from beyond the veil. She had paid for a single boat, and a single boat was what she was floating in. There was no echo lingering in the air, no frisson left behind like the moment after a person exits a room. Just to be sure, she sat for a moment studying her surroundings.

Straight ahead in the distance two icebergs bobbed along. There was something unsettling about their position relative to the horizon. Quickly she looked away.

The things had been glaring at her, a pair of salt-white eyes.

Told you so, Riley would've said. You don't belong here.

But this is the one place on earth where I shouldn't have to deal with that, Striker thought. She was as far away from her life as a human being could physically get. Isn't that why we stay in motion, she mused. So we don't have to mess with all the junk orbiting around inside our heads?

She was at the start of a journey costing tens of thousands of dollars. Happily, someone else was footing the bill. She let that lucky fact bolster her. Yeah, not today, Satan. She gripped her paddle and pushed off into the icy unknown.

The *Yegorov* floated reassuringly in the distance. The two support boats hung back a few hundred yards, probably told to remain out of camera shot. Striker was surprised by how glassy and flat the ocean stayed, placid like water in the tropics. She wondered if this was a fluke or normal for this time of year. If this was the norm, it would make finding suitable locations for the movie she was scouting that much easier.

Striker wasn't the world's greatest kayaker but today she didn't need to be. Percy had said he'd only ever take them out in the good stuff, never anything too choppy. It made sense. There were kids in the mix.

"And trust me," he'd added. "We may be in Antarctica but there's plenty of good stuff down here."

Two summers ago Striker had scouted for a Viking flick up in the Norwegian fjords. She'd learned the hard way that the key to kayaking for long periods of time was to relax, not grip the paddle too tightly. At the end of her first day of touring, she'd barely been able to open her hands.

Today as she paddled away from the zodiac, she tried to employ proper technique like she'd learned in Norway. Inside the front of the boat, she nestled her toes on the foot pads. Gently pushing on something with your feet helped engage your core. Ideally that was where all the action took place. Making kayaking all about your arms spelled trouble. She also knew you should never just pull with the arm actively stroking the water but always push equally on the paddle with the opposite arm, pushing and pulling simultaneously. It made a big difference. Unfortunately she still hadn't mastered how to keep her shoulders from aching. Probably it would help if she were taller and sitting further up above the water. This outing was only supposed to last an hour. She figured she could handle anything for that long, come what may.

For the first ten minutes the group splashed sloppily about, drunk on beauty. In this alien realm, Striker was happy to let her Leica do the talking. The beauty was overpowering, like floating inside a sapphire. Every conceivable shade of blue on display, rendering the icebergs whiter than white.

The group spread out but even a hundred feet apart you could easily hear your neighbor talking. Striker put her paddle down for whole minutes at a time to shoot the landscape. There was no wind or current to carry her elsewhere. Percy explained they were at the tip of the Antarctic Peninsula and that the peninsula was part of a chain of volcanic islands that stretched north across the tempestuous four-hundred-mile-wide Drake Passage all the way up to the Andes in Tierra del Fuego.

"Enjoy the day, folks," he called out to the group. "It's Christmas Eve, and the support team tells me it's a balmy fifty-two degrees out here."

"Unbelievable," squealed Taylor.

"Yeah but *unbelievable* is bad, isn't it," said Anders. When Percy gave the teen a small nod, the kid turned to their mom. "See, I *told* you," they hissed, but Bobbi Sue ignored whatever her teenager was getting at and paddled on ahead.

"Take good care of your sunnies," Percy said, using the British expression. "After a season down here, the early explorers would often go sun blind." He explained that the men wore smoked pieces of glass tied into cloth goggles. Little did they know the dark glass caused their pupils to dilate, letting in more UV radiation, the men slowly losing their sight. The unfortunates without goggles could become temporarily blind in a single afternoon from the light reflecting off the ice and burning their retina.

Striker sat studying a bergy bit the size of a garage. "The Formation of Ice" had been one of the numerous onboard lectures the *Yegorov* offered as a way to pass the time between Argentina and the peninsula. Striker had attended most of them. Back in New York, she'd need to show she'd done her homework.

During the lecture, the ice expert had looked a little green. Striker couldn't tell if it was the lighting or the previous night's crossing of the Drake. It took him a while to get the AV running. Once it was up, he explained that when ice first forms on the ocean, it's called grease ice because it looks like grease on the water. "Grease ice forms pancake ice," he said, pulling up a video. The water did indeed appear oily, a slick film glossing its surface as gelid circles of water jostled about like human cells. "Pancake ice forms field ice. Field ice looks like the crushed stuff you get in a drink." He rattled off a list: black ice, brash ice, jade ice, young ice, pack ice, all the way up to bergy bits, which, despite the name, were the size of houses. Growlers were among the most ancient, some hundreds, even thousands of years old. They formed at the base of icebergs when the weight of the ice compressed on itself, squeezing out all of the oxygen and absorbing the red end of the spectrum until the ice turned a brilliant translucent blue and broke off. Most growlers were the size of cars.

His final video was so beautiful, Striker pulled out her phone and began recording. "When the part under the water gets eroded enough, the iceberg becomes top-heavy. Eventually it flips over. The bottom becomes the top," he said. "Then you can see what was below the waterline." In the video the blue thing drifted merrily along, its top fluted and scalloped, hand-crafted by the waters of time, the ice delicate yet frilly like icing on a wedding cake.

Now surrounded by it, the ice reminded Striker of summer clouds. The way each piece slowly revealed its true self to the eye of the beholder—that one a horse, that one a barn, that one a man in a rowboat lost and desperate on the Southern Sea. And the water surrounding each berg was a brilliant aquamarine as the sunlight reflected off the ice submerged below the waterline, the water ringing each iceberg the coolest blue like the jeweled waters of the Caribbean.

You had to admit: that would look good on film. *Damn* good. Maybe even *award-season* good. Everywhere, this blue mise-en-scene as if strangled, deprived of air. Already she was imagining the arguments she'd make to the producer for assembling a polar crew. Audiences had a right to see this place before it melted. If you wanted to get the best performances out of the actors, you had to bring them to the source. Think DiCaprio in that angry bear movie. You couldn't make a biopic about Shackleton, one of the greatest leaders of men in the twentieth century, in a water tank on a soundstage in Burbank. Plus, think of the press they'd get. They'd barely need to run an Oscar campaign.

Back home she'd need to keep researching, writing up reports on everything from weather, transport, and energy sources to shelter, food, and insurance. What it would cost to fly down an entire shooting unit, or if it was more efficient to go with a few folks and a handheld. There would be long, involved talks with the financiers about how much the film would have to gross to make it all worthwhile. Fortunately those conversations were above her pay grade.

If the production did indeed send a full unit to Antarctica, Gabor, the principal cinematographer, would spend the entire shoot complaining about the cold. My lenses, he'd moan. Anti-fogger no good. Get me special lens made from tears of baby. Yeah, he'd milk it for all it was worth, the hardship, the horror, his novelistic Czech sense of drama on full display right up until the moment he bagged his third Oscar. There was so much beauty down here, all you had to do was point and shoot. Any dolt could get it on film. It was exactly what the director was looking for, but pulling off filming this far south would be a herculean undertaking. It would cost someone an arm and a leg. Before she'd left on the flight down to Buenos Aires, the producer had called her up, slyly hinting that she should enjoy herself but not come back with too many workable location shots. "I'm not made out of money," said the man practically made out of money.

Only three days ago she'd been standing on a train platform waiting for the F while watching a woman throw bits of donut to a rat down on the rails. And now this, a landscape without cars and exhaust and litter, people pushing and shoving. The distant island they were heading to was carpeted with small specks like pepper. Hundreds of penguins zipped about on the island's rocky crags, little black birds in their feathery tuxedoes visible as far as the eye could see. She floated past an iceberg, its sheer sides ten feet tall, the snow stained pink with guano, proving their stubby little legs could navigate even the steepest terrain.

As the group closed in on the island, the glassy waters surrounding Paulet subtly shifted in color. The shade wasn't exactly cobalt, more like bice, something a celebrity might name their kid. The head designer Margo would practically shit herself. Bice was Margo's ideal color. Slatey yet bright, a color you could play up in moments of joy, then turn around and temper when the violins rolled in. The design team would take one look at Striker's images and begin salivating.

"Is that the mainland?" Taylor shouted from a few hundred feet in the lead, pointing at what appeared to be a white mountain in the distance.

"No, that's a tabular iceberg that split off from B-15, one of the first real monster bergs scientists began tracking," said Percy.

"You sunk my battleship," called out the youngest dad.

Percy ignored him. "B-15 broke off the Ross Ice Shelf back in 2000. Originally it was three hundred by forty kilometers, or about the size of Jamaica."

"Ya, mon," said the young dad.

Percy continued unfazed. "Think about it. B-15 contained enough water to fill Lake Michigan," he said, "but most aren't that big."

To Striker, the white mass in the distance looked vast enough to be the prison barge on which the world's dead were put to sea. She lowered her camera. Over the next ten days, there were bound to be other magical locations, other chances to capture the one image that would launch a thousand union crew members south. Later just for fun she'd shoot a couple of rolls using her Holga. Digital was her primary tool, but there was a magic to film. She felt a small thrill each time she got an envelope of photos back from the developer. Nowadays it cost a small fortune, but nine times out of ten the shots you weren't sure would turn out proved to be the best of the bunch.

"You couldn't ask for a better day," called Bobbi Sue from her side of paradise.

"That's true on every level, hun," replied Billy Bob.

"Yeah, because consumerism vis-à-vis climate change is melting the poles," lectured their teen, "making both the Arctic and Antarctica more accessible to increased fossil fuel extraction."

Shizer, thought Striker. Who brought along the president of the junior Marxists society? Anders trailed along in their parents' wake, the grimness of their being radiating out in every direction. "It don't get no better than this," Striker imagined Billy Bob telling his first born as he raised an Old Milwaukee in his fist.

Precisely! It was Christmas Eve day. They were in Antarctica paddling around on the Southern Ocean as flocks? schools? shoals? of penguins skimmed effortlessly over the water. Teen angst aside, it was all pretty cool.

Percy was pointing at something on the island. The Tech Titan and her husband were still visible in the distance, Lucy and her dads trailing behind, the Dame and the Baron peacefully bringing up the rear thanks to their beefy Russian muscle. The red of the groups' boats was a stark contrast to the colors of the landscape, their yellow dry suits flaming suns.

Suddenly there was a roar and a thundering crash. Striker wasn't the only one who jumped at the noise. Percy whipped his head around, scanning the landscape. The support boats zoomed into the frame. A series of hands shot into the air, each one pointing, Percy's radio crackling with voices. Finally they all agreed on the source.

Several hundred yards away an iceberg had calved, the berg the size of an apartment building. Striker could see where a large chunk of ice had hit the water, the iridescent spray still clouding the air, a rainbow spangling the day.

The kayakers watched as the wave action raced toward them. For the first ten seconds it looked like it would never reach them. Toward the end they could see how fast the water was still moving, how big the initial wave must have been.

"We're okay," Percy called. They were far enough away that by the time it hit, they bobbed about pleasantly, merely children playing in a bathtub. Like its more famous sister Time, Distance also heals all wounds, Striker thought. She was kicking herself for not getting it on film. By the time she'd heard the crack, the ice had already come down, breaking off the berg as if sparked by a controlled explosion.

"See what I mean?" said Percy. "You gotta give nature her space."

"Like a woman," muttered Kevin.

"I thought you said that was rare," said the Baron from his position at the front of his tandem. There was something imperial about his posture that called the Ptolemies to mind, the way he leaned back in his seat plus the fact that he hadn't bothered to bring a paddle, leaving his tandem mate Alexei to do all the work.

"Ten years ago I could go weeks and weeks without seeing an iceberg calve. Now? It's practically on the hour." Percy started to say more, then decided against it.

Anders raised a hand. "Could the earth's increased tilt affect the seasons down here?"

The youngest dad began singing in a growly voice reminiscent of Eartha Kitt. "I feel the earth. Move. Under my feet."

The teen remained undeterred. "We're drawing too much water out of the planet's aquifers," they explained. "It's disrupting the rotation of the planet."

"For the time being, things here are copacetic," said Percy, but he was obviously blowing off the question. "Now let's go check out the island," he added.

Anders scowled. Give the guy a break, kid, Striker thought. Somebody that easy on the eyes can't be expected to know *everything*.

The kayakers followed their guide into land, the youngest dad practically glued to his hip. The distant iceberg now missing half its face. The thing openly staring at them as if to say *j'accuse!*

Without too much effort, the group paddled into shore. Paulet Island was only a mile in diameter but within that mile there was a lot going on. Vadim and Alexei stayed with the boats, the two of them getting a break from playing gondolier to the Dame and the Baron. When Percy wasn't looking, Vadim pulled out a cigarette and a beat-up lighter. He noticed Striker looking and grinned. Someone paved paradise, dropped in a parking lot, she thought. She wondered if the landscape inspired any awe in the two men or if this day out was just part of the grind called making a living.

The beach was a long, stony strip of land running hundreds of feet along the ocean. It was an easy spot to come aground, the coarse brown sand teeming with wildlife. Everywhere the various local species vied for space as they sunned themselves in the Antarctic summer. Carefully the group picked their way among the smorgasbord of creatures lying on the shore, animals with no aversions to humans as there weren't ever enough people around to grow wary of.

Texas Mikey asked the first question. "Who owns this place?"

Striker thought it was a funny question coming from a kid, but his parents oooed and aaahed as if their child were some pint-sized Carl Sagan. Mikey smiled angelically then picked up a rock. Bobbi

Sue paused her adoration long enough to ease it out of her son's hand before he could chuck it at the wildlife. A hundred years ago the first men to set foot here had probably done the same thing in a need to draw blood and feel all-powerful, only their moms weren't around to stop them.

"In 1959, a dozen nations signed a treaty stating that Antarctica should only be used for science and that nobody owns it—it belongs to everyone." Percy waved a hand over the landscape like a game show hostess showing off a new car. "Antarctica is the only landmass ever discovered by Anglo-Europeans with no native inhabitants."

"What about *them*?" said the Baron, pointing at a pair of penguins who were staring quizzically at the tourists.

"I meant no native *people*," Percy clarified.

"Don't be dumb, Robert," said the Dame.

Percy continued. "The other pole was a vastly different story," he said. "The first two men to the North Pole, Peary and Henson, even fathered children with Inuit women."

"Then I guess they weren't the first men there," remarked Taylor.

"Wasn't Matthew Henson African American?" asked Anders.

Percy nodded. Striker didn't know why the teen had posed the question. It seemed clear they already knew the answer. She couldn't help but think the teen had asked it for her sake. Like hey, Black person! Did I mention I'm an ally?

"I thought there was an American base somewhere down here," said Lucy's brown dad.

"There is on the mainland," Percy said. He explained that several countries had Antarctic research stations, some even making territorial claims, but at the end of the day, all claims were nonbinding and unenforceable. "You Yanks will be interested to know—"

"We're *all* Yanks," said Anders sadly.

"—that the US makes no territorial claim to any part of Antarctica, which some foreign governments interpret as an underhanded claim on the whole continent."

"USA! USA!" chanted Kevin.

"More than a hundred years ago, things were a lot different," said Percy. "Hunters from all over the globe sailed down to places like the Shetland Islands or South Georgia and decimated the fur seal populations." He pointed at a group of seals lying on the sand. "Look at those guys," he said. "They're easy targets. Last century, a single boat could wipe out a ten-thousand-plus seal colony in under a week."

Anders delivered a one-word pronouncement on the history of the fur trade. "Greed."

"Rubbish," said the Baron. "It's called ingenuity."

"How does wearing fur make the world a better place?" asked the teen.

"It makes the *ladies* of the world more pleasing to the eye," said the Baron, at which point Bobbi Sue ushered her child along.

"We're still allowed to wear *vintage* fur, right?" whispered the youngest dad to his husband.

A baby fur seal lay picturesquely on a rock as though it were school photo day, its eyes perfectly circular, like something straight out of a Japanese comic book. It was obvious Texas Mikey would've given anything to pet the little fuzzball, but Percy shook his head and reiterated his speech about cross-species contamination and protecting the ecosystem. He went on to explain the difference between a Weddell and a fur seal. To Striker, the distinction between flipper length and muzzle shape felt nitpicky.

She was surprised by the abject pettiness of these animals, groups of them acting every bit like human sunbathers as they tossed and turned, throwing sand at their neighbors to dissuade them from putting up an umbrella, the crabeater seals glistening in their silver pelts like mammoth anchovies.

"Look at that." The youngest dad pointed at a quivering mound.

"It's like Jabba the Hutt but with flippers," marveled Kevin.

The group stood mesmerized as the beast slugged its way down the beach. Percy warned them to always give the elephant seals their space. A bull male like this one could weigh more than four tons, he said, often crushing younger seal pups as they hauled themselves around on shore, sometimes inadvertently, sometimes on purpose. Striker watched as the mammoth creature lumbered about, moving its tremendous body by undulating along as if doing the '80s dance move the Worm, its tumescent nose like some kind of misplaced genital.

"Give that one an extra wide berth," Percy repeated. "The big guy might be in the mood for some lovin', which makes him super dangerous."

"Who doesn't like it *rough*?" growled the youngest dad. Bobbi Sue shot him a look, but the dad just smiled.

"Sure, you can outrun him," continued Percy, "but you don't want to rile him up. Last year a tourist had his leg broken in multiple places." He winced at the memory. "And if an elephant seal starts rolling over again and again," he warned, "get outta there. That means it's pissed."

"Carry on and Godspeed with the fornication, my good man," said the Baron, nodding at the elephant seal as he passed by. Striker couldn't tell which was the hornier species, the marine animals or them. The presence of the youngest dad made it a tough call.

But if Paulet Island belonged to anyone, it was the penguins. The island was home to a massive Adélie rookery, thousands of birds constructing threadbare nests consisting of a few pitiful rocks on which they laid their speckled eggs. The luckier ones among the newly hatched fledglings had their small gray heads stuffed up their parents' throats, the adult birds regurgitating a white paste that would help their offspring grow quickly in the Antarctic summer, everywhere the adults standing around gagging on their young.

There's a metaphor here, thought Striker, but lucky for me, I'm not a poet.

She picked her way among the rocks, the landscape stained with the fishy stench of penguin guano. The smell was unbearable. If she breathed too deeply, she was afraid it would coat her nose and throat and stay with her for the rest of the outing, the vulcanized rubber of her dry suit permanently fumigated by it. Most of the group put on a brave face. Only la Grande Dame openly pinched her nostrils shut as she strolled about like the queen of England reviewing the troops. Downwind of the colony, loose feathers billowed in the breeze, a gentle snow.

"Oh my god," said one of Lucy's non-brown dads, waving his hand in front of his face. "I feel like someone's boa got caught in a fan."

Striker had to hand it to the little critters. She was impressed by their mobility. The stubby little birds were all over the place. On the beach, on the rocky outcrops, on the slopes of the tiniest volcano that rose a few hundred feet in the air, a stony pimple smack dab in the middle of the island. Even far inland, the landscape was rife with rivers of birds coming and going like trails of ants hundreds of feet from the water, their shabby nests located on the most unforgiving terrain.

As if reading her mind, Percy explained that waterfront real estate was at a premium, and that the unlucky birds who had arrived late for the breeding season were forced to build their nests up in the hills closer to their enemies. Because the penguin chicks were starting to hatch, the air was filled with clouds of skua, large brown birds with hooked beaks, the better to tear apart small fluffy creatures. Percy's voice clicked into nature boy mode. He explained that the skua made their home in the cliffs, the birds a dark presence forever watching for the weak, the unattended, the ones who would go easily without much of a fight.

"Paulet Island's actually a dormant cinder cone volcano," he said. "The whole Antarctic peninsula's a series of volcanic islands. In a couple of days, we'll sail inside the most famous caldera, Deception Island." He pointed to Paulet Island's small cone rising in the distance. "A caldera forms when a volcano erupts and then the cone collapses. Basically it's a fancy word for the crater. Around these parts, if the cone collapses low enough and the volcano was mostly undersea, the ocean floods in." He explained that cinder cone volcanos were the most common type of volcano and also the smallest. Generally their slopes ran 30° to 40° and consisted of cinders, also known as scoria, which were loose rocks ejected from the volcanic vent when an eruption occurred.

"But don't worry, this one's not dangerous," he said. "You're standing on one of the safest spots in the entire world."

"So what's the most dangerous animal down here?" asked Kevin. He looked like he was researching something dark, a chain of black thought bubbles rising from his forehead.

"Man," said Anders in a small voice.

"Don't I know it," said Lucy's infatuated dad.

"The largest native animal on Antarctica is a one-centimeter wingless midge," said Mikey, reciting the factoid from memory as if performing his lines in a Christmas pageant. Striker had seen the same show on the Discovery Channel. Regardless Bobbi Sue beamed proudly.

"That's true on land, but in the water orca are definitely the most dangerous," said Percy, "though no worries—we won't see them up close."

"I was promised whales," soliloquized the Baron. Everything he said was delivered as though the guy were holding forth with himself, the Baron the star in his own biopic.

"Chill," said Percy. The brown-skinned father of Lucy laughed. Striker also laughed but on the inside. It was probably the only time the word *chill* would ever be directed at the Baron. "You'll see whales," Percy said. "This morning there was a pod of humpbacks off the starboard side."

"At what time exactly?" asked the Baron.

"Whale time," said Percy. The brown-skinned dad laughed again, enjoying the show. "Anyway, the second most dangerous species down here is the leopard seal," Percy continued. "You see them now and then but not very often."

"I thought you said the wind is the most dangerous thing down here," said Anders. Bobbi Sue nodded encouragingly, happy that at the very least her older child was listening despite the ear pods practically glued in their ears.

"Well yeah," Percy conceded. He reiterated that katabatic winds form hundreds of miles away as the air current sweeps down off the Andes. Once over the Southern Ocean, there was nothing to stop them as they gained speed and intensity in their push toward Antarctica.

"Doesn't katabatic mean 'from below'?" asked Anders.

"Affirmative," said Percy.

"Like hell winds?" asked the quietest dad.

"Katabatics can form anywhere you have unimpeded wind sweeping down a landscape. Trust me," Percy added. "If we run into some, you won't even know what hit you." He snapped his fingers as if to demonstrate.

"Well that's hella reassuring," said the youngest dad.

"But we don't have to worry about that now," screeched Taylor to Anders. "The algorithms put that at one in a million. So we're good."

Anders didn't seem any less angsty at the news. They were a teenager. Striker figured angsty was their default setting.

"We're more than good," said Percy. "The katabatics are pretty much unheard of this time of year. Mawson Station clocked some *six months back* as high as 150 miles an hour. Never say never—that's why we have you sign those indemnity forms, but this is summer. We're fine."

Little Mikey wasn't going to let the idea of disaster go that easy. "Any tunnels down here?" he asked.

"You mean dug in the ice?" said Percy.

"More like *burrowed*," said Mikey. The three dads looked at each other, for once glad it wasn't their kid everyone was staring at. "A long time ago, these big bubbles of ectoplasm called *shoggoths* built cities here in Antarctica for their overlords," the kid said, the excitement palpable in his voice. Striker couldn't help but notice both Bobbi Sue and Anders shaking their heads at the exact same speed.

"Sweet pea," said Bobbi Sue. "Remember what we said about all that being make-believe?"

"My boy and I like us some Lovecraft," explained Billy Bob rather sheepishly.

"A *what* craft?" said the Baron.

"H. P. Lovecraft," said Billy Bob. "The sci-fi writer."

"And raging racist," murmured Anders.

"But Mom," pleaded Mikey. "The *shoggoths* are shape-shifters. They can *do* whatever they want, *be* whatever they want." He looked to his father for help, but Billy Bob was too busy making placating eyes at Bobbi Sue. "Right this second they could even be walking among—"

"Michael Samuel Reeves. Stop," said his mother.

"You're talking about *At the Mountains of Madness*," said the quietest dad. Bobbi Sue threw up her hands. The Dame tsked-tsked sympathetically. Men and their monsters! They always had to be chasing something. The dad continued. "That's the one where the guy goes insane from something he sees in the ice."

"Spoiler alert," chimed his husband.

The quiet dad ignored him. "It's a pretty cool story," he concluded, smiling at Mikey. "Just for your sake, I hope we stumble on some *shoggoths*."

"Well," said Percy, "there are some pretty famous ice tunnels at McMurdo, but those babies were built with chainsaws and are mostly just full of pipes." He shrugged. "Now and then early explorers dug larders in the ice to store fresh meat, but that's about it."

"Still, this would be a great place to house a few alien corpses," said Billy Bob, his apology tour apparently over, Bobbi Sue and Anders once again performing their synchronized headshaking. "I just mean it's cold enough and plenty remote."

"Moving on," commanded la Grande Dame.

Striker could tell Percy was more than happy to comply. He pointed at a pile of rocks a few hundred feet from shore. "Let's go check out how things would look if something *really* went wrong."

"That's what I came for," said the Dame. She cranked her neck from side to side, the sound like cracking walnuts, and headed out first as if she knew the way.

They trekked to the spot. It only took a few minutes. You could see the ruins from the water. It was gravelly though a faint path ran up from the beach. In the distance there were penguins waddling up and down the hillside. Patches of old snow glittered on the ground, a few icy slicks gleaming where the snow had melted and then refrozen. La Grande Dame plowed ahead in the lead, Lucy and her fathers in the back. The string of them like a line of ducks in their yellow dry suits. It was difficult to walk, their hiking boots encased in the dry suits' legs. Lucy gave her brown dad the stink eye when he offered to pick her up and carry her.

The shelter wasn't even as big as Striker's New York City living room. All that was left was its foundation and a partial wall. "This is a historical site," said Percy. He explained that the two raised platforms made of stones heaped inside the ruin were ten-person beds. Striker tried to imagine spending a long, dark winter hunkered down at the ass of the world with twenty other people shoulder to shoulder in the unrelenting cold. It was crazy what human beings could survive. At least they'd had an amazing view. The waters of the Southern Ocean gleamed, studded with blindingly white ice, the view stretching on for more than fifty miles, maybe a hundred, maybe more. "Everything here's protected," Percy concluded.

By what, thought Striker. There were no docents slouching around, no red velvet ropes, no security cameras. Just a plaque nailed to a post explaining the importance of this hole carved in the ground and lined with rocks, here and there a piece of old-timey trash preserved by nothing more than the cold. Case in point, a trio of Adélie penguins were standing around on the collapsed roof like hourly workers out on a smoke break, a few more wandering in and out of the shelter.

Striker had read about this place in the prospectus. In 1903 the first Swedish crew to explore Antarctica wintered in this very spot after their ship got crushed in the sea ice. The expedition was led by Otto Nordenskøld, who survived the Antarctic winds only to get creamed by a bus back in Gothenburg. Years before Nordenskøld's death, he and the other survivors of the lost ship dug a small foundation in the hillside, then made a simple shelter using the island's rocks. Striker imagined the men supplementing their diet with penguin stroganoff and penguin oscar and penguin bolognese and omelets made from their endless supply of fresh Adélie eggs.

"Some of the expeditions brought animals with them," said Percy. "The Norwegian Amundsen was smart. He used dogs. Scott?" Percy shook his head. "He went with ponies. Either way, both dog and pony ended up in the hoosh."

"What's hoosh?" asked Mikey.

"It's an Inuit word," replied Percy, leaving the meat of the question hanging in the air. No one else stepped up to the plate as nobody wanted to be the grinch that tells a kid man's best friend is sometimes also man's main course.

"Back then what kind of people would sign on to an expedition?" asked Billy Bob. There wasn't much to see, but he was going to town anyway with his camera.

"I assume they came down here in the name of science," said Taylor.

"Gimme a break," said Kevin. "They were convicts and killers. They came down here to escape."

"Where'd you get that from?" asked Percy. "They were military men with commissions and sailors enlisted in the navy."

"So they *did* have a chain of command," said Billy Bob. He seemed weirdly pleased by the news. "Folks like Shackleton and Scott must have been the big dogs."

"The expedition commander was definitely the boss," said Percy, "but under certain circumstances, the ship's doctor could become the de facto leader."

Billy Bob perked up even more, the muscle flexing in his jaw. "Because the power to save lives trumps all."

"Exactly," said Percy. "Things go south, it's the doctor who's handing out rations, deciding who gets the last vial of morphine."

"That must have been fun," said the Dame. "Having your life depend on a man with a god complex."

"What if someone went nuts?" said Kevin. "Like, what would happen if the *good doctor* was the one who lost his marbles?"

It dawned on Striker from the way Taylor kept rolling her eyes that she and Kevin were in Antarctica to save their marriage. It was one of the oldest tricks in the book, second only to having another baby. Travel somewhere exotic and hope a little vacation magic might cause you to fall back in love with the putz you were legally shackled to.

"You mean what would happen if the doctor went insane," repeated Percy. Striker could tell he was eager to get off the worst-case scenario train. In a place like Antarctica, it was probably a train with no end. "Well I suppose they had protocols" was all he said.

"What about women?" asked Anders.

"What *about* women?" said Percy.

"Were there women down here?"

"Excellent question," said Taylor.

Percy adjusted his sunglasses. "It's well documented that in the late 1800s women would sometimes dress up as men in order to sign on to a whaling ship to be with their lovers," he said. "But there's no proof any woman overwintered on the continent among the early expeditions."

"But that doesn't mean they *didn't*, right?" said Anders.

"How would you pull that off?" mused the Dame. "Women have specific—"

"Demands," interjected the Baron.

"Any babies born down here?" asked Kevin.

"Honey." The exasperation was evident in Taylor's voice. "The man just said there's no proof women overwintered on Antarctica."

"I'm not *deaf*," said Kevin. "But I still say some of those early explorers were bad hombres. I mean who else would sign on?" Striker was wondering where he was going with this. "Let's face facts. We all know how much women *love* bad boys." Ah! The subtext hung plainly in the air. "No, I wouldn't put it past some goggly-eyed lass to follow her man down here. Bad boys get all the loving." He gave his wife a look that could drill through steel.

"Listen," said Percy, cutting to the heart of the matter. "You know what one of the first questions any prospective sailor was asked by the expedition leader?"

"Boxers or briefs?" said the youngest dad. Striker was surprised she still found him funny.

"Nope," said Percy. "'Can you sing or dance?'"

"My people," hallelujahed the dad.

"Seriously," said Percy. "They needed the crew to be highly sociable folks with sunny dispositions. You don't sail down to the ends of the earth with depressives and misanthropes."

"Well maybe *you* don't," said the Baron cryptically.

"You think they're still down here?" asked Kevin.

"Honey," repeated Taylor in a tone of voice Striker could tell she used a lot.

"No, I mean it," he said. The guy was definitely goading his wife. "Ghosts, spirits, angry sailors pissed off at their countrymen for abandoning them. They could be floating around somewhere."

"Why don't you overwinter in Antarctica and let us know who you run into?" said Percy.

"If this ice is anything like the ice in our Sub-Zero," said Billy Bob, "then it absorbs every smell, every flavor." He patted his son on the head, rested his hand there, the kid a banister. "Betcha there are some tall tales down here just waiting to be thawed out."

The conversation was beginning to make Striker feel like she was back in elementary school touring around some musty historical site. The kids daring each other to ask the guide questions like *did anyone ever die right here?* I am too old for this, she thought. She left the group standing by the ragged hole and began to wander around.

Overhead the day throbbed blue and cloudless. Striker stepped cautiously, careful not to twist an ankle. Admittedly it was a little freaky. This island probably looked exactly the same as it had a hundred-plus years ago when Nordenskøld and his half-starved men dragged themselves up on this stony beach. To think there was a comfortable berth just offshore waiting for her to come lay her head, the ship resplendent with a sauna where, deep in the pale blue night, consenting adults might play steamy reindeer games together. What a difference a century makes, Striker thought.

Suddenly the wind shifted. The air smelled of rot. Striker was less than fifty feet from the ruin but the world had gone silent. She could no longer hear Percy explaining the area's history to the group. I must be upwind, she thought. In the silence she had become the last person on earth, every other living being wiped out of existence. Even the penguin rookery seemed still.

She stopped and peered around. She couldn't see the others. They were probably gathered behind the shelter's one remaining wall, the youngest dad asking some stupid question just to make Percy look at him. Either that or they'd abandoned her and paddled back to the *Yegorov*, forgetting all about her. White people were like that. Out of sight, out of mind. Ha ha. Striker turned back to her wandering, but the strange tingling on the back of her neck was intensifying, the feeling that something was tracking her every move.

Quickly she whipped around in a circle.

The world stayed silent. She was still alone. Weird. It was probably just a case of the Antarctic creeps. In one scene in *90° South*,

Shackleton and two of his men had a bad case of extra man syndrome as they tromped over South Georgia looking for rescue. The screenwriter had explained that it could happen anytime, anywhere, though it was most likely under periods of extreme duress. People reporting the sensation that another person was with them. "There's even a line about it in *The Waste Land*," the writer had said. "'Who is it that walks always beside you?'" The writer was desperate to save the scene, afraid the director would cut it before they'd even started filming. Striker tried to imagine being so stressed that you conjured up a companion out of thin air.

That's when she saw them. Winding haphazardly up the beach.

From what she'd seen, the penguins left shallow marks in the snow, their prints as if stamped by a three-pronged fork. But these tracks were different.

The footprints were more like hands. A child's hands. Hands that had been seriously disfigured. Striker felt the discomfit spread up her throat. At best it meant some weird-ass bird was slinking around Antarctica. At worst—she wouldn't let herself come up with other possibilities. A morbid wave of fascination drew her on.

The thing was lying in a patch of snow at the end of the trail. The rock's bluish-red hue startling, a color she'd never seen before. Somehow the two primary colors were fused yet it was only one color and without a hint of purple, a shade she could only describe as blue-red. The other rocks were dark and flat like pieces of slate. Even without the trail of baffling footprints leading to it, there was no way she could have missed it.

She flipped the rock over with her foot. The air rushed out of her lungs. It was hard to tell what she was looking at. Was it simply scratched up from the natural wear and tear of Antarctica, or had a human hand consciously done this? And why did the engraving seem so familiar, like some sinister logo or religious symbol, something Judas Iscariot might have etched in the trunk of the tree before he hung himself?

Striker closed her eyes. Sometimes voluntary blindness was the best way to go. She thought of the time at a county fair when her sister Ama had handled a tarantula. *Just pet it, Ronnie,* Ama had cooed as the tiny beast sat cupped in her palm. *It's like a handful of eyelashes.* How Striker had squeezed her eyes shut, then willed herself to run a finger down one of the creature's many legs, her frightened heart beating like a bird's. Her sister was right. The spider was softer than anything she had ever touched.

And now she was standing in the silence of a rocky beach in Antarctica. In some ways it felt as if no time had passed. Just do it, you big chicken, she thought. She kept her eyes closed and edged forward, kicked the weird rock back over, hiding the odd symbol. A jolt shot through her foot. Sound rushed back into the world, her lungs once again filling with air. Already it seemed like some dumb overreaction on her part, her mind intent on scaring itself silly. Still, she couldn't help but scurry back to the others.

She was glad no one else had seen her, especially that creepy little kid. She thought of the night out with Riley and their friends and all that talk about what scared them the most. Riley had said her number-one fear was the fear of looking.

"Looking?" someone asked, incredulous.

"Yeah," said Riley. "You can't just *tell* yourself there's no monster under the bed. You actually gotta get down on your hands and knees and *look*. That shit's scary as hell."

"Scopophobia is the fear of being seen," said the only doctor in the group. "Schizophrenics often have it. But I don't think there's a fear of just *seeing*."

"Ommetaphobia is the fear of eyes," said Striker. She couldn't remember how she knew this.

"That's gotta suck," said Riley. "But everyone's got something they don't wanna see. You ask me, there should be a name for that."

"There is," said one of the women. "It's called denial."

The waiter came around and announced last call. The group began ordering one more drink for—

Striker came around a bend just in time to hear Texas Mikey ask, "Did the crew get rescued?"

"They did, but only after ten months." Percy pointed to a tower of rocks piled on a hilltop. "They built that cairn so passing ships would know there were people here." He explained that there were historical preservation spots like this all over the peninsula, huts built by early explorers, many with roofs and fireplaces, the foodstuff still visible along with tools and survival supplies left behind in the men's happiness to be rescued. "It's important we leave these places the same way we found them."

"Fireplaces," said the Tech Titan. "What were they burning?"

"Often it was the actual wood of their ship," said Percy. "Sometimes they rendered the fat from the animals they killed. We know from some of their surviving journals that a male elephant seal could keep a cabin lit for weeks at a time."

"Always the male," said Kevin.

"Think of the stink," said la Grande Dame.

"But think of the stories you'd have to tell," said Striker, slipping back among the group. It was her first contribution to the conversation. La Grande Dame threw her a look that seemed to ask who had given her permission to speak.

"These folks here got lucky," said Billy Bob, pointing at the hole in the ground. "They made it out. But what about all the other parties stuck on these islands? Any of them make it home?"

Percy sucked in his cheeks, steadying himself to deliver the bad news. "Some did, a lot didn't," he said. "You got your starvation, your hypothermia. Explorers even died from scurvy, which is not one of the more pleasant ways to go."

"Do tell," said the Dame, intrigued at last by something Percy had to say.

"Scurvy causes severe joint pain. Your gums get dark and spongy, your teeth fall out, then old wounds start to reopen."

"*Reopen?*"

Without being asked, Billy Bob decided to field this one. "Any time you injure yourself, the body repairs the injury site with collagen that it then has to keep producing in perpetuity in order to keep the wound sealed," he said. "Without vitamin C, the body stops making collagen. No vitamin C, no more collagen. No more collagen, and old wounds lose their adhesion and start opening back up."

The Texan obviously had some kind of medical training. Striker wasn't sure if this made her feel better or worse.

Now that the gruesome cat was out of the bag, the group let loose.

"Is it true your teeth can shatter just from the cold?" asked the quietest dad.

"You mean because of that show on Netflix?" said Percy.

The dad nodded. "There's an episode where the guy's teeth explode out of his mouth like bullets." The brown dad shook his head, embarrassed by the question. "What?" said the quiet dad. "The show's based on real life."

"A hundred years ago sailors probably had crap teeth to begin with," said Percy. "In extreme temps I could *maybe* believe it's possible for severely compromised enamel to crack."

"What about cannibalism?" asked Kevin, ratcheting up the gore factor.

Percy made a face. "There's always a bit of that in the histories, but you don't have to get that dramatic. First, you got your basic bargain-brand accidents, like falling down a crevice, or worse, getting scalded by a geothermal vent."

"Cool," said Mikey.

"Definitely *not* cool," said Percy. "Remember these islands are volcanic. There's all kinds of seismic activity going on. It's rare, but

Antarctica has a million tricks up her sleeve. Earthquake, avalanche, poisonous gases." He peered theatrically around at the group. "Not to mention your run-of-the-mill human nature."

"What's *that* supposed to mean?" asked la Grande Dame.

You could see Percy deciding which fork in the road to take; was he going to go dark or keep it Disney? "I'm sure you can imagine," he said. "Men in tight quarters with nothing to do."

"I know what they do in *prison*," said the Baron. "You mean *that*?"

"I would *think* if you wanted to have a chance of surviving down here, you'd have to cooperate," said Taylor. Kevin stood beside his wife and nodded.

La Grande Dame threw her head back, braying with laughter.

"I'm with her," said one of the dads.

"What's so funny about cooperating?" asked Taylor.

"Nothing," said the Dame, regaining her composure. "I've just seen my fair share of *men*."

"Here here!" sang a second father.

Now it was the Baron's turn to nod. Striker couldn't figure out if he was agreeing with his wife's assessment of 50% of the population, or if he was admitting that he himself was indeed a rapscallion who wouldn't lift a finger should the going get tough.

"Let's just say Antarctica in the early 1900s wasn't for the faint of heart," said Percy. "When expeditions got stranded, their number-one enemy was mayhem. Squabbles escalating. Someone ending up with their head bashed in. Men sailing off the deep end." Percy decided to take the dark fork after all. "After a few months of solid night, some of the more *sensitive* ones often decided to take the off-ramp." He looked around to see if the detour was too much.

"You mean suicide," offered Kevin.

Striker hadn't thought of that one. Death by your own hand.

"Suicide suicide," sang Lucy in her monotone. The way she said it, it sounded like a dare.

Percy shrugged. "These islands are *littered* with bodies," he said. "One of these days, thanks to global warming, the ice will cough 'em all back up." From his tone of voice, he seemed to be implying he was only the messenger, don't blame him. "Mark my words," he said. "Soon even the suicides will get their moment in the sun."

"Happily, some of us will be long gone by the time that happens," said the Baron. Anders scowled at the old man but kept quiet.

"No, really," said Percy. "Nothing stays put down here. The ice is constantly shifting as it slides toward the ocean. It's like a conveyor belt. More than a hundred years ago, Robert Scott's body was interred in the ice. A century later, it's very possible his body has been carried out to sea, that the earth itself has given him a proper seaman's burial."

"How poetic," yawned the Dame.

Kevin couldn't seem to let it go. "How did people off themselves down here? What was the number-one method?"

"Really, honey?" said his wife.

The Baron also seemed to lean in, eager for the answer. Striker could tell Percy was regretting bringing it up.

"Exposure. The most famous example is Seaman Oates."

The youngest dad tittered.

"Oates was with Scott on the final push to the pole. Guy probably already had a serious brain injury from falling down a crevasse." Percy took a long swig from his water bottle. "Anyway, he knew he was holding the group back. He gets up one morning, says he's going out and he may be some time, then walks out of the tent. That's it."

"Suicide!" shouted Lucy in what was clearly some sort of outburst. Did the kid have Tourette's? One of the dads put his hands on her shoulders but the child twisted free.

"Yeah," said Percy. He tried to lighten the mood. "All I can say is, do me a solid and try not to die down here. You wouldn't believe the paperwork."

Suddenly the Baron let out a womanly shriek. Something came crashing down out of the sky. A fishy stench filled the air.

"Bird attack!" yelled the youngest of Lucy's dads.

The group scattered as a single skua began divebombing them, the bird everywhere at once. Within seconds the Baron was halfway down the beach. Kevin took to hiding behind the stony ruin, leaving his wife exposed. Even Percy seemed caught off guard. The Dame simply sat down in the middle of the commotion and made herself lower than the rest of the group excluding the youngest dad, who was splayed flat on the ground while covering his head. Only Billy Bob stood swinging at the sky. Later Striker would notice that his dry suit had a series of even slashes running down both forearms.

Then the day filled with frenzy as other skua joined the attack, the birds' wingspans nothing to sneeze at, hooked beaks mini scimitars. It was a scene straight out of Hitchcock, the sky roiling above their heads. There was nothing else to do but run.

In the chaos, nobody noticed Lucy slip down into the preservation site and pull something out of the rubble, then zip it up in one of her pockets. Nobody, that is, but Striker. She watched as Lucy scrambled back up out of the hole, her face stony like she hadn't just been pawing around a World UNESCO heritage site. Silently the child patted her front pocket.

Striker had seen what the child pilfered. She was surprised the kid had even known what it was. Or maybe she didn't.

It was an old tuning fork, the kind you gently rapped on something to make it vibrate and give you a pitch. The object elongated like a Y. The dull metal flashing in the daylight.

What happens on Paulet Island, stays on Paulet Island, kid, thought Striker. *Now it's my turn. When I do something bad, you keep it zipped. Capiche?*

You mean like the stuff you did in the sauna with Percy? He's married, you know.

Says who, thought Striker, *nobody's put a ring on it.*

Lucy didn't bat an eye. *What'd Ama used to say? You only see what you wanna see.*

You keep her name out of your mouth, child, but then Striker was running away from the skua along with everyone else.

Later, when she had time to reflect on it, Striker chastised herself. Fun is fun, she thought, but girl, keep it together. Her little inner dialogues were a crutch, these imaginary conversations that kept her entertained during life's duller moments, but here she was in Antarctica, *goddammit!* You'd think Antarctica would be entertainment enough.

They slouched their way back to the boats, their sheepish hearts racing. Some of them were ashamed of having ceded ground to a bunch of creatures weighing less than four pounds; others were already imagining how they'd spin the tale once they got home, telling friends and coworkers they'd bravely fought off a flock of Antarctica's most bloodthirsty predators, were lucky they hadn't lost an eye or worse in the war.

Something about the bird attack launched Kevin on another hypothetical foray into cannibalism. He was trying to convince the youngest dad that technically you could eat human flesh and nobody had to die. The human body had plenty to spare.

"How *exactly* would that work?" asked the dad. He sounded skeptical but open to the possibility.

"I'm starting to think you guys didn't have enough for breakfast," said Percy.

"Stephen King's got a story in *Night Shift*," said Kevin, "about a doctor stranded on a desert isle with nothing but a mountain of cocaine."

"It's in *Skeleton Crew*," corrected the middle dad. "And it's heroin."

"Don't encourage him," said Taylor.

But her husband kept on with his thought experiment. "The guy starts amputating parts of himself bit by bit," Kevin explained. "He stays alive—"

"Stop!" Taylor shrieked.

"In 1961, Leonid Rogozov surgically removed his own appendix," said little Mikey brightly. "Isn't that right, Dad?"

Jesus, thought Striker. Kid's some kind of Rain Man.

"You nailed it, son," said Billy Bob. He patted his child on the head. "Rogozov was part of a twelve-man Soviet team sent down here to build a research station. He was the only doctor in the group when he came down with appendicitis."

"My dad could take out his own appendix if he had to," said Mikey. It was the weirdest flex Striker had ever heard.

"That's enough," said Bobbi Sue, the finality evident in her voice. "Now let's enjoy the scenery."

They all let it go, chastised. When a mom speaks, people listen, Striker thought.

For the second time that morning, they passed the libidinous elephant seal, the guy still slugging around the beach hungry for some action, his smaller seal cousins still whapping each other with their flippers, everywhere the Adélie penguins shuffling like little Charlie Chaplins out for some air.

Percy was off talking to the support boats on his walkie-talkie. He had his back to them. An Adélie hitched up to Taylor as she was getting in her kayak. The bird was out of synch with the others, its movements twitchy, the area around its eyes red and inflamed. Everything about it just seemed wrong.

"Aw, look at this little guy," Taylor cooed in her octave-above-middle-C voice. "Honey," she called to her husband. "Get a picture of me and my new friend." She crouched down to fit her and the penguin in the frame.

"Smile," called the youngest of the dads. The bird turned its raggedy head toward Taylor and opened its beak. "No, with your eyes," cracked the dad, just as the creature emitted what sounded like a wet cough.

"Whew," said Taylor, waving a hand in front of her face. "Somebody needs a breath mint." The bird began thrashing itself against her.

"Hilarious," said Kevin. "The little guy's in love with you. It's trying to get a leg over." Bobbi Sue shot him a disapproving look. "What?" he said. "It's nature."

"I'm not sure that's what's going on," said Striker. She was sitting in her kayak and had already snapped her spray skirt in place, locking herself in.

The bird turned and made a beeline for her boat. Striker realized she'd been breathing out of her mouth this whole time to avoid the stink of the penguin rookery. She felt her sinuses unexpectedly fill with the stench of trash.

The Adélie hopped up on the front of her kayak. Up close it smelled of rot, of drowned things left beached on the sand. It was staring her right in the eye, gazing from beyond time and space. Striker couldn't breathe. The greasy smell of shit glazed everything.

The bird knew absolutely. It knew about the things she herself didn't dare to know. The disparate memories she still couldn't piece together even decades later. Like the hole in time in the room under the stairs. The trail of bloody breadcrumbs. The sound of children singing, something dripping in the water in the toilet bowl. Striker's throat closing up like a flower. The dreadful door swelling open then shut, blocking the rest out.

The Adélie unlocked its beak. Striker couldn't help but peer inside. She was trapped. There was nowhere else to look. The moment like being down on your hands and knees by the side of the bed, then lifting the edge of the blanket and peering into the monstrous dark.

Redness as far as she could see, a fiery hell housed inside the small bird. For an instant there was nothing else in existence besides this eternal burning. She could have reached out and touched the void, probed it with her fingers, but once you handle damnation, there is no going back. She knew this was only a preview, an intimation of the journey ahead. The next time she encountered the void, it would be the only road forward. It would swallow her whole and take its time breaking her down into nothing.

She threw both arms over her face.

From the bird's mouth the stench of acid and death and fish, things that burn. A red chum spraying from its gullet. Even with her hands up, Striker felt it land on her lips, a hot mist.

Percy kicked the bird off the kayak. He picked up a rock. Striker heard the sharp crunch as he crushed its head. She kept her arms locked over her face.

"You okay?" he said. He was breathing hard.

She lowered her arms in time to see him pull a plastic bag from his backpack and quickly stuff the bird's body in it. She checked herself.

There were no red droplets stippling the sleeves of her dry suit. She had imagined it. The day once again blue and white, everywhere the terrible everyday smell of the rookery.

"Little critter wasn't right in the head," said Percy, as he sealed up the bag.

"But I'd imagine down here you gotta be on the lookout for disease," said Hector, Lucy's brown father. "A bird flu could wipe out thirty thousand birds in under a week. Not to mention what it could do to your guests."

"That'd be bad for business," said la Grande Dame, cracking her neck.

"You think it was sick and not lovelorn?" said the Baron.

"Same difference," said the youngest dad, but you could tell his heart wasn't in it.

"There's no bird flu down here," said Percy. "It's too cold."

"You mean it *used* to be," said Anders under their breath.

Percy looked Striker over. "You're okay," he stated as a matter of indisputable fact. Striker could only nod. She wished it were that easy. Overhead, the Antarctic sun like a spotlight.

They shoved off, defeated. It was a quarter past noon. Overhead the sun sat a few degrees beyond vertical. As they were only a day or two past the southern solstice, Striker wasn't sure if the sun would remain fixed in the sky for the next week or if this far from the pole it inched along as the day progressed without ever slipping below the horizon, the sky forever some shade of blue.

Except for the commotion at the very end, it had been a pretty decent first outing. They were promised mulled wine with lunch. Some of them could already feel the warmth of their cashmere-lined slippers. Striker was anxious to get back. After the incident with the penguin, she was craving a long shower. The smell of hot trash was an added reminder that she needed to take her meds. It had been too long, plus the Antarctic air might be triggering. *Just take the damn things already*, Riley kept telling her in the first few months after Striker got the prescription. *Who cares if the doctor said you're one of the lucky ones—why be a hero?*

"Congratulations," said Percy as the group paddled back toward the support boats. "You survived. We'll try to head out at least once a day if the weather's good."

Little Mikey pointed at something in the distance. "What's that?"

"My boy's got eagle eyes," said Billy Bob. "Someday he's gonna see a wide receiver open at fifty yards."

Percy lifted his binoculars to his face. He gasped. "Careful now," he whispered. "Follow me. We don't want to spook it."

They formed a ragged line behind him. The support boats killed their engines. You could see something happening, some kind of struggle, the sound traveling over the water. He took them to within twenty feet.

Striker couldn't believe the size of its teeth, the prehistoric menace of its bullet-shaped head. The thing didn't seem to care if they were watching. If anything, it ramped up the show.

The unlucky penguin was fluttering its flippers, determined to live, but even if it got away, at this point it would be pretty messed up, just another Adélie burger served up for someone. A few scavengers floated overhead, waiting to see what would happen.

Finally the leopard seal finished the deal. The Adélie hung limp in its terrible jaws. *Bon appetit!* thought Striker. Percy was pointing to the spot where the leopard seal went under, the Adélie grasped in the seal's ripping teeth, the kind of teeth you don't expect on an animal with the word *seal* in its name. A seal is supposed to be cheerful and fun, a red-and-white-striped ball balanced on the end of its perky black nose. But this is pure uncut nature, baby, life unvarnished and serrated. Percy is telling them you don't see this every day up close and personal, a leopard seal breaking its prey's back by savaging it on the water, the way a dog will sometimes get hold of a rope and smack it from side to side on the ground, beating the thing to death, the penguin a chew toy. Then a flash of light fills the sky, the air like a city sidewalk heaped with trash, the heavens roaring as if on fire and there isn't time for Striker to close her eyes—she's doomed to watch someone's kayak fly up and smash Percy in the back of the head, yes, that Percy, indestructible Percy, golden Percy who crewed for New Zealand in the last Olympics, Percy of the broad chest and muscled neck, Percy of the other night in the sauna who did this thing with his index finger until she screamed, Percy who was telling them to put down their goddam phones and *really* look, to have a true and direct experience of the moment, *please mates, this is gaga!* the front of his face reiterating that the leopard seal is the area's number-two predator and then something in his eyes registers as wrong, his skull caving in, letting the light in, the day tossed in a blender, and Striker doesn't really remember the rest, won't remember the rest even though she is a being who loves turbulence, the feel of your stomach flipping, going so far as to seek it out, that sensation of being unmoored, centerless *drop down on your hands and knees, girlfriend* and yet after the rest is over and she finds herself on the other side of this, even then she might refuse to acknowledge it *this place ain't gonna give you a choice* because even with your eyes closed thanks to the 24-hour Antarctic sun, the worst can

The Unveiling

The Unveiling

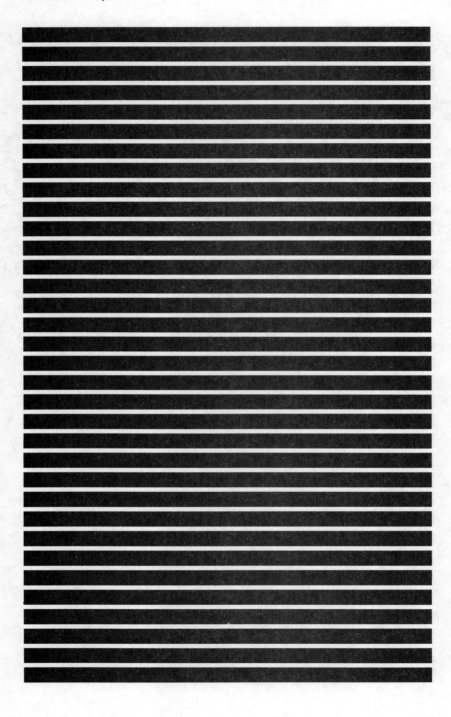

The Unveiling

do I have to

The Unveiling | 65

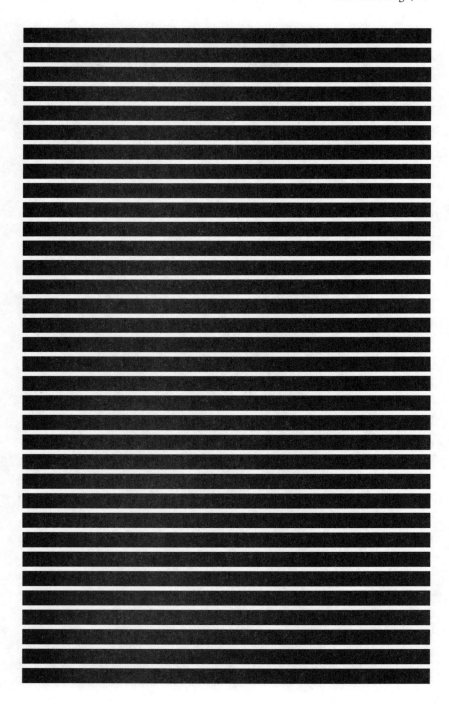

No better time than the present to check under the bed

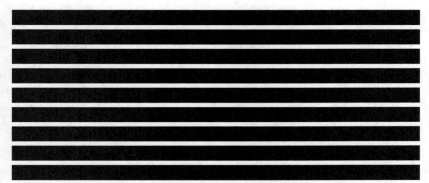

read 12:14 p.m. Overhead the sun sat slightly off center. Under normal circumstances the setting would have been heavenly. Instead, she had to swallow an urge to scream.

She was floating on the Southern Ocean, thirteen million square miles of bone-chilling blue. She could see all the way to the horizon, out to the very edge of the world. It was disorienting. Each time she gazed over the endless water, weights and counterweights deep inside her shifted out of synch.

"Hello," she shouted. "Anybody out there?"

Come out, come out, wherever you are!

No answer. Just a silence so deep it hurt her ears. Where had she experienced a quiet like this before?

That's right. At that start-up in Midtown with an inner room that cost a few million. The room billed itself as the quietest spot on earth. It was designed as a space where architects and builders could come try out different materials, experiment with ceiling heights, windows, brick thickness, HVACs. Striker once spent thirty minutes tousling with one of the company founders on the rubber floor suspended over a series of sound-absorbent panels. The founder had talked her into it by saying it was a one-of-a-kind rush, the heart audible with every thrust, an aliveness you had to experience to believe, like jumping out of a plane without a parachute or snorting a line of coke all the way from New York to Mexico. He'd put his hand over her mouth. Within seconds a terrible silence blossomed inside her head, the feeling of being a hundred feet underwater, her ears starting to pop. That's true silence, he said. A grave wouldn't be that quiet.

And now the whole blue world had become that deathly silent room in Midtown. Striker imagined the scene from the air. Miles and miles of ocean studded with roving belts of ice. And somewhere in all that vastness, she would appear as the tiniest spark of yellow, the redness of her kayak like the flame of a single candle burning in an empty stadium, the vacant sky leering at her, this lowly speck of dust hungering for something, anything to hold on to.

Nobody has ever been this alone, she thought. The ocean surrounding her boat was a glassy blank free of ice, the water smooth as steel. It probably had something to do with the currents. She could only hope some lonely iceberg would drift her way, a companion to keep her mind from shattering.

"Percy? Jane?" she yelled. Weird. Why, of everyone in existence, would she call for the old woman with the helmet of silvery hair?

It didn't matter. With every second, she could feel herself disappearing. The air smelled brisk like early spring. A faint breeze stirred the water, drops raining off her paddle each time she lifted it. For a dizzying instant, she couldn't even recollect the specifics of her own face. To make it all worse, her sunglasses were gone.

"Hello," she screamed. "I'm here, I'm right—"

An unexpected sourness filled her mouth, the taste like sucking on dirty coins. What if somebody *is* out there, she thought, just not anybody I want to know? She peered around at the incalculable nothingness. Everywhere the water gleamed an unnatural blue.

Striker remembered an expert on the *Yegorov* claiming the oceans were the last unexplored realms. Was this the reason humans were content to let the sea remain a mystery? Subconsciously it reminds us we're expendable, she thought, microscopic flotsam roiling in the gut of the universe. If you were tired enough, a message like that could be comforting. *Might as well give up*, it said. *No one will blame you.* She pushed the thought down and went back to searching for signs of rescue.

"This can't be happening," she whispered. She had no proof hers wasn't the only human consciousness left on the planet. She recalled a philosophy class she'd taken as an undergrad. The professor admitting that the greatest questions of philosophy still had yet to be solved. Who are we? Is there a god? How do we know who we are without others around to reflect our personhood back at us? In the middle of the talk, she began to panic, her breath growing ragged as the blood pounded in her throat.

What would it feel like to be dead?

In the lecture hall, she could hear someone hyperventilating. She knew the one struggling to breathe was her. Something small and dark was stirring behind her ribs. She worried she might scream.

It was nonsensical, like dividing by zero. Whether you acknowledged it or not, every human had the capacity to transform in a flash from everything into nothing, the whole human race acting like that moment would never arrive. There will come a time not of my choosing, she thought, and on that day this power to blink out of existence will be fulfilled. She'd grabbed her things and rushed out into the noise of the city. It was only there she could breathe again.

The polar light bounced around unimpeded. Striker shielded her eyes with her hand. Could the sun *already* be damaging her vision? Even a pair of cloth goggles like the kind Percy had described would've been better than nothing. From horizon to horizon, the indifference of Antarctica swallowing her whole.

I have to get out of here. It was dawning on her that agoraphobia was the flip side of claustrophobia. The same feeling of being obliterated either by too much space or not enough of it. How long did it take the dead to realize they were dead? What part of her would even perceive the difference?

Desperately she scanned the landscape. Her gaze raking the emptiness until her vision burned. She could hear a voice begging *please*. The earth was pummeling her with her own insignificance. Finally her eyes snagged on something.

A band of icebergs was migrating her way. Her mouth flooded with hope. Beyond them she might find the others or maybe with a little luck the *Yegorov*. She might even run into one of those giant cruise ships with five thousand passengers, the ship floating like a white city.

If there was nothing beyond the ice but more emptiness, there was a strong possibility she would zero out. *Don't take your ass past go. Do not collect $200.* Already an inner void was rooting in her chest. The feeling like falling off a cliff. Arms pinwheeling through space. She placed her feet on the footrests in the front of her boat and locked her eyes on where she was headed.

"Wait for me," she begged.

It was like sailing on glass. Each stroke of her paddle sent her flying. She knew she was making remarkable time. Already she could see the distant icebergs zooming up to meet her. Any tiredness had drained from her body. She had never felt so alive, so purposeful, arms driving her kayak over the silky water. This is what the earth will smell like without life, she thought. It was beyond pristine. She could hear someone breathing hard, their heartbeat filling the universe.

Striker couldn't be sure how long it took to reach the ice. If it was ten minutes or ten years. When she finally arrived, the unbridled panic she'd been experiencing suddenly flooded with awe.

It was like drifting through a sculpture garden.

The icebergs ranged in height from a few feet to more than thirty. The scale of their size struck her as relatable and human, unlike the alien vastness she'd encountered out on the open sea. All around her the ocean glittered, the ice immaculate. One slipped past shaped like a giant heart, both lobes ethereal and pearly. Her own heart surged. It's a sign, she thought. Just get to the other side. She began working her way through.

Within minutes she remembered the time she'd gone into the dunes while on location in the Sahara. She had wanted to see to the edge of the desert, but with each one she crested, there was another dune blocking her view. Dune after dune after dune. The desert light starting to change. The certainty growing that she was the last woman on earth. Eventually one of the crew came racing over the sands on an ATV. She waved him down and almost cried when he stopped.

Overhead the Antarctic sun burned feverishly. At least she didn't have to worry about night falling. Percy had said it was 52°. Sweat trickled down her back. She was already realizing how quickly the light could burn your retina. If it did, she would see only white, the day an appalling blank. Her backside was starting to ache. She considered slipping off her life jacket and sliding it under her bum, but it would take too much time and every second mattered. I bet everyone's waiting on the other side of this, she thought. I'm coming. Please don't leave without me.

Striker paddled toward a small, tabular berg shaped like a mausoleum. *It's just your size!* She tried not to dwell on it, but the longer she stared, the clearer the vision became. There were the mausoleum's doors flanked by decorative columns, a series of gargoyles scowling from the roof. She couldn't help envisioning herself entombed in it, mind cast outside time. The fear of dividing by zero began to creep up her throat. She paddled harder.

Of course you're a nervous Nellie. This place wants to eat you alive.

She searched the ice, hoping for another glimpse of the enormous heart. Any friendly face was better than nothing. When she finally spotted it, it looked misshapen. The heart's left lobe sagged as it slogged along.

Everywhere she turned the white world sat watching. Icebergs like sentinels, silent as wraiths. In the near-total quiet her ears popped, the feeling like being entombed deep underwater. What earlier that day had seemed delightful now felt imposing. It was the perfect scenario to trigger a case of extra man syndrome. She imagined the ghostly figure cloaked in furs gliding by Shackleton's side during his ascent on South Georgia. His mind on the verge of breaking.

Out of the corner of her eye, she sensed something creeping up behind her. "Just what I need," she said out loud, desperate for a laugh. "Another backseat driver telling me to make a left." Slowly she turned to look.

The water gleamed, polished as glass. The way it glistened made her shudder.

See? Nothing is following me, she told herself, though her heart wouldn't stop trembling.

Then the ocean began to swirl.

It's just currents, she mused. Warm air, cold water colliding. All the same she ramped up her pace but only just a little. Paddling like a bat out of hell would've been a signal to whatever was out there, like running away from a bear. The skin tightened on the back of her neck.

A sudden thunderclap shook the day. Please let me be far enough away from it, she thought. In the distance she could see where the gutted lobe of the deformed heart had broken off and crashed into the water. Within seconds waves slammed her kayak. In the tumult, a massive slab of ice rose straight up out of the ocean, blocking her path. Slobber dripped from the iceberg's fangs, the tips of its icy hackles glittering.

Urgently Striker squeezed her eyes shut and paddled backward. It's just a trick of the light. There is no hungry wolf looking to crush my throat. Stop thinking like a five-year-old. She took a deep breath.

"When I open my eyes, it'll all just be ice again." Cautiously she took another look.

The wolf was gone.

It was only then Striker noticed the thirty-foot wall of ice keeping pace with her kayak. Where a pair of eyes should be, two blurry hollows glared. The iceberg looked disproportioned, top-heavy. The slightest breeze could send it toppling. The waves would swamp her boat, lungs flooded with seawater. She spun around in all directions, eager to retreat a safe distance. But retreat was impossible.

She was surrounded by it. 360° of ice. Everywhere icebergs trapping her like an animal in a pen. The air turned frosty. Echoes began to form. She could feel the day rip open, a presence entering through the tear. (Or did it seep out of the ice?) Something had taken a seat behind her. Its breath chilled her neck. *Look*, a voice rasped in her ear. It's just the wind, she told herself. All the same, she leaned over the side of her kayak and peered into the deep.

A face stared back.

Even at the edge of sanity, she recognized herself in the water. Brown eyes bulging with fear. She spit the coppery taste flooding her mouth into the ocean. Her spit hit the reflection smack dab in the middle of its forehead.

A hand shot up out of the sea. It waved, fingers wrinkled and bloodless.

Striker screamed and stabbed at the water with her paddle, kept stabbing, trying to push her way through.

The ice barely moved.

"Don't be stupid," she whispered. "It was only a mangled penguin."

Guess again.

Percy had claimed Antarctica was riddled with bodies, that someday even the suicides would have their moment in the sun. It was a place where nothing ever decomposes. History lurking beneath the surface. She imagined Seaman Oates reappearing from his long white walk, skin charred from the sun and cold. His blackened hand wordlessly beckoning her to join him.

From underneath the water something knocked on the bottom of her boat. Two slow taps, then two fast. Her mind went blank. The tiny hairs on the back of her neck came alive.

God be troubling the water.

Between two towering icebergs she spied a sliver of blue. She knew it could be a trap. Once inside, the ice might shift, crushing her in its terrible jaws. What other choice did she have?

Striker shot into the narrow sliver just in time to hear the top-heavy iceberg topple over. Everywhere the thunder of ice colliding. Even as she sped away, a familiar tingle warmed the back of her neck, the feeling of an ever-present gaze watching as she fled.

The wind picked up but remained gentle. Her shoulders ached, backside numb. She was drifting toward a magnificent blue arch, loose pieces of ice straggling behind it like a ragtag army. Despite Antarctica suddenly turning on her, Striker couldn't help but admire the frozen archway. Once it had probably been a solid ball of ice. Over geological epochs the ocean had carved out the sphere's interior, creating this spectacular formation. The same elements at work that had sculpted the desert monoliths in Monument Valley. Wind and endless time.

A cry pierced the silence. Her stomach dropped. She sat listening, willing her ears wide open. She could hear voices growing closer. There was something eerie about their timbre, the cries as if a crowd of people were moaning.

"Hullo!" someone called. It wasn't all in her mind. Somebody was out there. Even in her wildest dreams she never would have conjured up a voice with such a flat midwestern vowel.

Striker flexed her tired fingers. She took up her paddle and started toward it. "I'm coming," she shouted. "Where are you?"

The blue arch was still visible in the distance when the other kayaks came into view. Among the whiteness the red burned like drops of blood. A pang of regret detonated in her chest. She'd been hoping for anyone else, even that freaky kid and her light brown dad, but you get what you get. Their matching old-person Him and Her sunglasses flashing like shields covering half their faces.

"Well hullo there," boomed the Baron.

"A better greeting might be, what the hell happened and where is the *Yegorov*?" said Striker. She knew she sounded angry but in truth relief was flooding her every synapse.

"You say potato, I say po-tah-to," shrugged the Baron.

"Are you for *real*?" she said.

"Of course we're real," pooh-poohed the Dame. "Why wouldn't we be?"

This is *not* happening, Striker told herself for the millionth time. She blinked hard, trying to reset her vision. Jane and Robert Foley sat floating before her looking pretty much as they had earlier that morning—two rich geezers in vulcanized rubber, their expressions as though waiting for someone to bring them a highball. How could they be so *chill*? Weren't they petrified by the idea that this carnival ride might lead straight to hell?

Still, she had to admit the couple's nonchalance was a pleasant surprise. Who, us worry? they seemed to be saying. It meant everyone's favorite primetime villains weren't in panic mode. Maybe they truly believed they would never die. From what Striker had seen in Hollywood, copious amounts of money could do that. Yeah, the old lady and her old man were giving Striker permission to treat this as just another inconvenience caused by bad luck and an incompetent butler. Like your luggage getting lost at LaGuardia or a valet bringing you the wrong Mercedes. Okay then, thought Striker. I'm down to ride. Wouldn't be the first time in her life sarcasm had saved the day.

"What time's cocktail hour?" she said.

La Grande Dame gave her the tiniest of nods, metaphorically tapping a sword on each of her shoulders. Pact sealed. We shall carry on, tallyho, the old gal seemed to say, and treat it all as farce.

In the back of each of their tandems, the Russian crew member assigned to shuttle the couple around the Weddell Sea were in bad shape. The guy in the Baron's was dead. Striker could tell from the angle of Alexei's neck and the stillness of his body. Otherwise he looked fine. No blood, no visible bones. She tried to recall something, anything, just a single human detail about him but she had to admit the guy hadn't made much of an impression.

"What happened to him?"

"Cardiac arrest, I assume," said la Grande Dame. "Poor beastie took a kayak directly between the shoulder blades at maximum speed."

Despite their newly minted agreement, Striker was still surprised by the old lady's calm. She and her husband seemed totally cool floating around the Southern Ocean with a dead body in tow. Then again, Striker considered the tonal alternative: total *hysteria*. Yeah, no thank you.

"He's weighing down my boat," complained the Baron. His neoprene hat had blown off, his white hair crazy and tufted around his bald head, a tonsured dandelion.

"You should be grateful," said Striker. "The extra weight could've been what kept you from tipping."

"Well, his services are no longer required."

The Baron's use of the passive voice made Striker shudder. Despite the pact, was it too late for her to turn around and paddle like hell, leaving these two jackals to their own devices?

"How'd you manage to stay together in all that killer wind?" she asked.

"What wind?" said the Baron.

"What do you mean?" said Striker. "The wind that blew us all to kingdom come."

The two old people looked at each other. "That is not what we experienced," the Baron slowly said. His wife gave a small nod. "Now," he said. "What about me and my weight problem?"

Striker chalked their weirdness up to shock. It *was* puzzling. One second they were all watching the leopard seal go to town on the Adélie, and the next Percy's head had caved in. Once they all got rescued, there'd be plenty of time to sort it out. For now, the very dead Alexei was indeed misbalancing the Baron's kayak. The Baron himself was riding high up out of the water, but the back of his boat was floating only inches above the waterline, in danger of being swamped.

"Right now there's not much we can do about it," said Striker. "Plus the guy deserves to get back to his people."

"Fantastic," said the Baron.

"It's like when you have a bruise and the doctor tells you not to press it," she said. "Just don't turn around."

"*Don't turn around?*" said the Baron incredulously. "I *literally* have the Grim Reaper sitting over my shoulder."

You're a man in what, your *eighties*, thought Striker, how's this any different from everyday life?

"Forgive my husband," said la Grande Dame. "He has a hard time staying on point." The Baron smiled, a naughty child caught red-handed with his grubby paws in the safety-deposit box. "To answer your earlier question, at the start of the festivities—" Striker winced at her use of the word. "Vadim and Alexei grabbed each other's paddles. They made a brace between our boats."

Now Striker could tell what was wrong with Vadim. He was passed out in the back of the Dame's kayak. The poor guy's arms looked longer than normal, like something you'd see in a cartoon after a mail-order contraption goes *kablooey*, both his shoulders dislocated, his arms inert pieces of rubber tubing.

"So what's your plan?" she asked.

"Veronique," said la Grande Dame wearily, Striker a caterer who had put a tray down on the wrong table. "My husband is eighty years old."

She was about to throw a witty riposte back at the old gal—like, *so you're saying he's had a long life, no heroic measures needed?*—but something caught her eye.

Nestled front and center among the old woman's bottom teeth were two metal studs. Studs like that were almost always titanium, one of the strongest elements on earth, the two little posts implanted in her gums so that fake teeth could be screwed onto them later.

Striker tried not to stare but there was something vampiric about it. A few years back she had watched the long, slow process as a famous director got outfitted with a whole new set of choppers. It didn't look like a lot of fun. Usually you were tarted up with some temporary teeth you could pop in and out while you waited for your gums to heal. The temporaries kept people from having to stare at your ravaged mouth. Who knew what the Dame's story was? Maybe the old lady had accidentally swallowed hers in the midst of those lethal winds. Or maybe she just didn't give a shit what people thought.

"I'm seventy-nine for four more months," whined the Baron. "She likes to age me up."

Striker shook her head, the spell broken. Whether she liked it or not, she now knew more about these two and their internal dynamics than she cared to. She filed it all away among the million and one details she was jotting down internally. Someday she might need to bust open one of these unimportant nuggets in order to save her own life. Which is why all she said as she paddled over and threw the Baron the rope at the back of her kayak was, "Don't call me Veronique."

Bobbi Sue and Anders were the next to float in. They didn't even need to paddle. A gentle breeze ushered the pair through the maze of ice toward the small troupe of survivors. Bobbi Sue's skin gleamed white as if she were made out of cartilage, her lips the same blue as any growler.

"My baby," she moaned on repeat, periodically correcting herself and whimpering, "my babies." She was shivering in a way that went down deep beyond the bone, her whole skeleton rattling. Just looking at her made Striker's own body temperature plummet several degrees, the woman translucent as skim milk.

"Don't worry. We were only supposed to be gone an hour," groused la Grande Dame. "Someone must be looking for us by now."

"I wouldn't count on it," said Striker. She checked her watch, frowned, then rummaged through her dry bag and pulled out her phone. Just like her watch, it read 12:14 p.m. *Shizer*. What did she expect? The two were synched. The crazy winds had messed up her devices. "The *Yegorov*'s probably used to groups coming in late because of folks snapping too many selfies."

"Remind me never to book a trip with you," said la Grande Dame.

"My babies," Bobbi Sue repeated.

"Mom," said Anders. Though they didn't say it, the teen's tone implied *pull yourself together*. For once, the kid didn't seem angsty or resentful. Of the lot of them, Anders' reaction was the most by-the-book. The kid was obviously scared and needed their mother now more than ever, but from the look of things, some serious role reversal was going on. Anders had become the parent, Bobbi Sue the sullen teen.

Only one word came to mind. *Hysteria*. Striker had never liked it. What woman did? The ancient Greeks believed the uterus could come loose and wander aimlessly around in a woman's body like a laser pointer at a concert. The ancients blamed every type of unsavory feminine behavior on it. Wandering uterus my ass, Striker thought, as she watched Bobbi Sue begin to slap her own forehead in what could only be frustration. If the ancients were right, then Bobbi Sue's uterus was currently located in her frontal sinus.

"For what it's worth," whispered the Baron, "I might suggest the occasional full-throated slap across the face is an underused remedy." He glanced around to see if anyone might second his medical opinion. His wife rolled her eyes—at his uselessness or the suggestion itself, Striker couldn't be sure.

"Nobody's slapping anyone," she said. But if it comes to that, *I'll* be the one doing the slapping. "Listen, the *Yegorov* wouldn't sail into an ice field. It'll be easier to get our bearings out in open water."

"Or this ice is protecting us," mused la Grande Dame.

"From what?" said Striker.

The Dame tipped her head in the direction of the sea beyond the blue arch. "From whatever might be out there."

"Go ahead," said the Baron gleefully. "Tell everyone what you saw."

"I'm already regretting telling *you*," she said.

"You're talking about those killer winds, right?" said Striker.

"Katabatic," said Anders.

"My guess is it's yet another symptom of global warming," said Striker. "It's probably never happened before."

"Goody goody," said the Baron.

"That is *not* what I was referring to," said la Grande Dame.

"Then what?"

The Dame fell silent.

"Well *I* for one believe Mr. Leopard Seal had him some hangry friends," said the Baron.

Striker and Anders both looked at each other disbelievingly. Did the old guy just say *hangry*?

"Orca," Bobbi Sue managed to stutter.

"No, it was a rogue wave," said Anders.

The Dame remained quiet. Inexplicably she slipped off a glove and began inspecting her giant emerald, the thing dark as kelp. Something in the way she twisted the jewel round and round as if screwing it into her finger told Striker that for now it was best if the old woman kept her theories to herself.

"I lost my earbuds, but I still have my binoculars," offered Anders.

"Awesome," said Striker, "but all this ice is blocking anyone from seeing us. If folks want to stay put, be my guest," she said, "but I'm heading out, and once I'm out, I ain't coming back."

"Unless you have to," murmured the Dame.

Striker ignored her. "Who's with me?"

Anders nudged their mother's kayak with their paddle. "Mom? Mom," they said. "We gotta go."

"My baby."

"Dad and Mikey are fine, Mom," Anders said. "Mikey's always been lucky. The wave probably carried them back to the boat. Mikey's probably guzzling a hot chocolate right this instant."

"He most *certainly* is not," said the Baron. "I saw what happened to those two."

"Really?" said Striker.

The Baron fell silent. For once, other people seemed to register in his consciousness. You could see it happening in real time. The old man's gaze searching for purchase.

"Admittedly, the eye can be a trickster," he finally offered. "I'm sure the little man is indeed enjoying his *cocoa*." He said the word as if he'd never pronounced it in all his born days. "Wherever he is," he added, sotto voce.

Bobbi Sue accepted the gesture with a small nod. "My babies," she concurred, her husband and son's survival now a matter of settled law. "My beautiful babies."

"All right then," said Striker. "Everyone tie up. You." She pointed at Anders. "You might have to pull her." Anders nodded and tied their boat to their mother's. "And you." She pointed to a spot where la Grande Dame could add a second rope to her husband's kayak.

"The metaphor becomes life," opined the Dame.

You married him, lady, but Striker had already made a note to herself to stay the hell out of their marital head games. "We doing this?" she said.

Suddenly the very dead Alexei sat up straight in the back of the Baron's tandem. Striker gasped. The skin on the back of her neck burned as if someone were flaying it with nettles.

Alexei stared aimlessly around the group until his eyes met hers. Striker tried to look away but her head felt locked in a vice, eyes glued open. He grinned. There was madness in his gaze. "Prizrak," he whispered. A sunbeam shone through a ragged piece of ice, casting a spotlight on him, his skin illumed an airless blue. "Prizrak."

The word rattled inside Striker's skull like a lone die. With a wink, the Russian slumped back down into nothingness. The ice shifted, the spotlight doused.

Striker had heard it loud and clear. The hair was still standing up on her forearms. It wasn't pain in his voice, the pain of a man who had given his all so that some rich bastard wouldn't have to break a sweat.

It was dread.

"Just our luck," said the Baron, "another Cossack who doesn't speak English."

"Keep it to yourself," barked Striker.

"Excuse me?" said the Baron.

His confusion coupled with the bewilderment on the faces of the others made her realize the whole exchange had probably taken place inside her head. She looked at the dead Alexei slumped in the back of the old guy's tandem, this man-sized sack of potatoes in a yellow dry suit.

C'mon, Ronnie, keep it together.

"Might I suggest," Striker said quietly, "we keep our speculation about what happened to ourselves till we're back onboard."

"Aye-aye, captain," said the Baron. He made a sloppy salute.

Fuck you, Striker thought. It was just her luck to be carting around the monocle guy from *Monopoly* and his Botox-faced moll. But given everything she had ever done in this life, she probably deserved nothing less.

It was strange. Just minutes ago the magnificent blue archway had been on the other side of the ice field. Now here it was perfectly positioned right in front of their boats, like a balloon backdrop at a prom. Striker chalked it up to currents, maybe a riptide. With one mighty stroke apiece, she and la Grande Dame sailed under the massive structure and out into the open sea, the Baron trailing silently in their wake. Striker could feel where drops of ice melt had landed on her cheeks. The moment like a baptism, the universe softly raining on her, rinsing the gunk off.

They were paddling out in the open. The ocean was choppier than before but nothing too terrible. Kayaking really was the next best thing to walking on water. To think only a layer of fiberglass separated her from the deep blue sea. She glanced around to see how the others were holding up. Nobody looked tired. Anders' arms were practically a blur as they towed their mom. It had to be the adrenaline. Striker herself felt like she'd mainlined something, pupils big as dimes.

Nothing gets your mojo working like a little certain death.

It would have been a truly gorgeous outing except for all that other stuff. Panoramas like this were the reason tourists traveled to Antarctica. The silence of the ice, the sense of drifting outside time, the beauty of every shade of blue. Towing the Baron and the dead Alexei wasn't even a problem as Striker lost herself in the magnificence of the landscape.

It reminded her of the heaven of her childhood. The way the nun who taught the religious instruction class Tuesday nights in the basement of Our Lady would describe it, the old woman with the glassy eyes of a true believer. No hunger, no cold, just peace, everything white, infinite and eternal, no need to speak. (But what about the *people*, Striker always thought. What color were they?) She almost expected to see the dead crowding around on the ice, the dearly departed barefoot and robed in soft white tunics.

She had never really thought about heaven until all those hours she was forced to spend in the damp basement of Our Lady, an army of dehumidifiers running full blast year-round. Mabel had never used the word. Instead, her grandmother spoke of making that final trip across the River Jordan to a land of good food, good music, rest, a little justice. Mabel sitting in the broke-down chair in the tiny apartment on Clark that Ama liked to pick the stuffing out of, shoving it in her mouth when Mabel wasn't looking. Mabel with her feet in a dented bucket filled with water and salts. What her grandmother believed. All people—the good *and* the bad—would one day make that journey across the water, find a place to finally sit down and catch their breath. It wasn't about being worthy. It was about having served your time on earth.

Striker took hold of her Leica. Might as well, she thought. Her sunglasses were gone but she still had her camera. She pressed the power button, kept pressing it. The shutter wouldn't open. *Shizer.* Maybe it was the temperature, the Leica finnicky even in good weather. Early in her career she had learned to always bring a Holga along. She pulled the cheap plastic camera out of her dry bag and snapped a few shots. It had been with her on every scouting trip for the last two decades. As long as she didn't drop it, the thing would never die.

"If I'd *known* we were still sightseeing, I would've brought my popcorn," said la Grande Dame.

Striker recapped the lens. The jibe made her think the old lady wasn't as old as she'd budgeted. The Dame was one of those chicks who could run anywhere from fifty to Jane Fonda. Either way, she was probably right. By now the cavalry had likely been called. Help was speeding their way. A sailor named Grigorii might wrap Striker up tight in one of those tinfoil blankets, use other means later that night to properly warm her. Grigorii with olive skin and green eyes. In a first-world sense, they were all too rich to die.

Damn, girl! Is that what you learned on Zinnia Trace?

"Red boats, yellow dry suits, they'll find us within the hour," Striker said. "In this landscape we're hard to miss."

"Elaborate," said the Baron. After a full minute of silence, he added, "Please."

"They'll launch a plane from McMurdo or one of the other research stations," Striker said. "What's the Argentinian one?"

"Esperanza," said Anders. "It means 'hope' in Spanish."

"Yeah, that. They might even use drones."

"Assuming nothing also happened to them," said Bobbi Sue blankly.

"I see something," said Anders. The teen had been tooling around with their binoculars.

"Is it the ship?" asked la Grande Dame.

"Is it your brother?" asked Bobbi Sue.

"It's an island," said Anders. "Could be Paulet."

"Can I take a look?" The teen handed Striker the binoculars. She was surprised by their heft. They felt like military issue, heavy enough to kill a man, a pair of binoculars built for Armageddon. Through them you could probably see up to a mile away, maybe more. Maybe all the way back into the distant past where everything gleamed 20-20, crystal clear. Past-Striker standing on the forward bow of the *Yegorov* waving her arms in the air and jumping up and down, warning Present-Striker not to push off.

She took a nice long look. There was indeed an island visible in the distance. It appeared bigger than Paulet and more rugged, a volcano rising up in the air, but the cone looked intact, not like the one on Paulet where one of the sides had caved in. Also unlike Paulet, this volcano was positioned in the center of the island and not closer to the shoreline.

"Well?" asked the Baron.

"It's an island all right." Striker scanned the ocean, searching for the tiniest reflection on the water. The *Yegorov* had to be out there. Their group hadn't just materialized out of thin air and landed here smack dab in the middle of nowhere. A couple of hours ago they'd been passengers on what was once a Russian expeditionary research ship turned tourist venture now based out of Turkmenistan. They'd each paid an extra few thousand dollars on top of the $25,000 base price to channel their inner marine biologist and pretend they belonged out here on the big blue southern sea—wasn't *that* what happened?

"May I?" asked la Grande Dame.

Before giving up the binoculars, Striker deferred to Anders, who shrugged. "Knock yourself out."

The old woman took them in both hands and twisted the main focal ring, then began twirling other parts Striker hadn't realized were adjustable.

"You a birder?" asked the teen.

"As a matter of fact, I am."

"You here to see an emperor?"

"Emperor penguins breed mostly in the interior of the continent," la Grande Dame explained. "The chances of seeing one here on the peninsula are basically zero." She continued to study the landscape, periodically adjusting the various focal rings. Suddenly she sat up straight, a pointer dog signaling a grouse. "There," she said. She handed the binoculars back to Striker.

"What am I looking at?"

"People," said la Grande Dame.

"Where?" said Striker. Already she could feel an uneasiness working its way through her limbs. She peered through the binoculars. Two red kayaks were pulled up on the shore.

"More people means more mouths to feed," said the Baron.

"Who has any food?" said Anders.

"I'm merely pointing out the repercussions of increasing our numbers," he replied.

Yeah, thought Striker. Mo' money, mo' problems. Unless these new people had a satellite phone, more players in your hunger games didn't necessarily make for a good time.

"Do *you* have any food?" Anders asked the Baron.

The old man dipped a gloved hand in the water. He appeared to be writing something, possibly taking a tally of his enemies. "Your mommy wouldn't want you to have what I have," he said, doing his best to sound avuncular but failing miserably. "Though I'd be happy to share."

Just then a loud crash rattled the landscape. Striker almost dropped the binoculars.

"Are we far enough away?" said Anders.

It was hard to tell. Already Striker could see a spot where the ocean was angry from a few tons of ice hitting the water, the swell growing more and more ferocious as it raced toward them at upward of 50 mph.

Mesmerized, they sat and watched.

The wave wasn't getting any smaller.

"Paddle!" Striker shouted. She put her weight into it, lunging at the water with her oar. Instantly she felt her kayak lurch forward and then just as quickly snap back. The rope went taut between her boat and the Baron's, his kayak seemingly loaded with bricks. It would take precious seconds to stop and cut the old man loose, time she didn't have.

Striker paddled for all she was worth. It was as if a hurricane had arisen at sea. Everywhere the day roaring. Waves slammed her boat. She felt herself starting to tip. Oh god! She had never learned to roll. Last year before heading to Norway she'd taken a few lessons at a public pool in the Bronx. She'd assured the instructor she didn't need to learn how to flip, that she wouldn't be shooting any rapids where she was headed. *Please god!* She was almost completely sideways. The ocean raced past under her shoulder. She closed her eyes and braced for it.

Suddenly her boat snapped upright. Frigid water splashed her face but her spray skirt held. The Dame was by her side, a gloved hand steadying her kayak. Then the old woman let go and went back to paddling. The group kept up their sprint. The world slowly quieted. Finally Striker felt it was safe to turn around and look.

The sea lay flat as concrete, calm as milk. She collapsed in her boat, breathing hard as if she'd just run a marathon.

"You okay?" asked Anders.

Striker looked around. The others seemed fine, perfectly unperturbed. The Baron picking at something underneath his fingernails.

Her heart was still rattling the bars of her ribcage, the blood sluicing through her veins. She ignored the question and lifted the teen's binoculars to her face, scanned the island one more time as she struggled to catch her breath.

There. On the shore. Twinkling among a group of penguins and the occasional Weddell seal. A tiny being in a bright yellow dry suit stood facing the ocean. A small gray oblong hunched on the little girl's shoulder. The oblong's teeth glinting.

"Well I'll be damned," said Striker.

"What is it?" said the Baron.

"Nothing," she said.

She wasn't sure why she didn't tell the others that creepy kid was standing onshore with a full-grown rat perched on her shoulder. Something in her gut said don't, so she didn't, not a word.

That instant across a half mile of ocean, the child looked up. The thing on her shoulder did too. Together they met Striker's gaze. Striker was never one to read lips, but sometimes you get a feeling. You can just tell. She could practically hear the little girl's affectless voice.

"Ready to rumble you ready to rumble."

The kid held something up in the light as if gripping a sword. Striker adjusted the focus. It was the tuning fork the child had pilfered from the ruined shelter on Paulet. The little girl smiled wide, then tapped the fork against her front teeth. Striker jumped, almost dropping the binoculars in the ocean for the second time. The note rang in the air. She knew not to ask if anyone else could hear it. The sound clanged on and on in her head.

A pitch-perfect concert A.

"What's going on?" asked Bobbi Sue, her teeth chattering. "Is it Mikey?"

Striker realized where she'd seen someone shaking like that. It was the albatross with the ten-foot wingspan, the broken creature convulsing on the deck of the *Yegorov* as though zapped with an electrical current. That's what Bobbi Sue looked like. Her body conducting a million volts.

"It's nothing," she replied. "We're almost there. There'll be safety in numbers," she lied.

"Safety in numbers, madness in crowds," cooed la Grande Dame.

Before Striker handed the binoculars back to Anders, she took one last look at the island. She wasn't surprised.

Lucy and her little gray friend were nowhere in sight.

The group floated offshore surveying the beach. After the mad sprint, Striker's arms felt like jelly. The others acted like they were on a leisurely outing. If anything, the Dame seemed revitalized, her internal engine all revved up. Striker was just grateful for land. She recalled a documentary she'd once helped find interview locations. A bearded academic standing on a wooden pier in Bangor explained that early explorers in wooden ships would sail around a cape for days, sometimes weeks, the men searching for spacious harbors with aquamarine waters where they could row ashore in their flimsy dinghies without worry of being smashed to pieces on the rocks.

"Once they found a suitable harbor, their next worry was the natives," said the scholar. A stupid little grin played over the man's face. The guy was clearly hungry to tell the story of first encounters, bloodlust twinkling in his eyes, but the director didn't ask him to elaborate. At least this island was making it easy for them, the beach peppered with penguins. Thank god for small, feathery favors. If need be, they could kill any of these natives with a rock.

From her vantage point Striker studied the pair of kayaks beached on the shore. Had whoever landed here first reasoned it out or just gotten lucky? All you had to do was follow Mother Nature's lead. Most rookeries were situated in spots with handy water access. It was prime real estate. At the far end of the coastline, a rocky promontory erupted where the island curved, a series of sea-level ridges quickly staggering upward into towering cliffs. The setup couldn't have been better. The rocky bluffs protected the beach from strong winds.

Look at me, Percy, Striker thought. I'm thinking like a naturalist. Location location location.

"What are we waiting for?" called la Grande Dame.

Why you asking me, Striker thought, but she pointed toward a spot where the land gently sloped down into the water, the rocks worn smooth from thousands of penguin feet. She took a deep breath. It was this island or bust. Their only alternative was the endless sea. When Antarctica turned on them, hadn't the early explorers abandoned their ships in order to make their fortune on solid earth?

One if by land, death if by sea.

Striker flashed the group a thumbs-up. They began to paddle in. Already she could smell something in the air, like garbage spilling out of a dumpster. More likely it was the ammonia tang of fifty thousand free-range creatures. How long would it be before she stopped noticing?

The natives gave way as the party came ashore. Unlike on Paulet, every species of penguin seemed to be wobbling around on this island. The Adélie and the gentoo were the most similar in appearance, the birds conventionally penguin-looking, nothing strange or out of place. It was the exact opposite with the rockhoppers, the smallest of the various species, a fringe of flamboyant blond feathers framing their faces like '90s actors with bleached tips. The chinstraps had a black line running horizontally over their throats. To Striker, it seemed like a bad evolutionary move as it was basically a dotted line showing hungry predators exactly where to cut.

Whoever was already there had beached their kayaks end to end, creating a long red line on the rocky shore. It was a smart move. Someone was thinking ahead, the boats maximally positioned to be seen. Hopefully it wouldn't take long. What little sand there was gleamed, dark and sparkling, volcanic in origin. The only footprints were webbed.

Striker detached her spray skirt. It had only been a few hours since she'd strolled around on the decks of the *Yegorov*. For the foreseeable future, she expected to feel like she was still on the water, the earth rolling beneath her feet. Once, after a ten-day cruise, for a solid week she'd had the sensation of floating weightlessly every time she crawled into bed. It was amazing what water could make you believe. Water was the original trickster.

"One small step," she whispered as she clambered out, "one giant—"

Her foot touched sand. A sudden blast of cold shook the day. A chorus of voices whirled around her as if she were standing in a glass box at a carnival, the box swirling with words. What do you want, she thought, but they were all speaking at once, voices softly burbling like water.

That same night out over drinks with Riley and their friends, one of the women in the group had told the story of a premonition she'd had the first time she met her now husband.

"Don't tell me," said Riley. "Birds suddenly appeared."

"Nope to that," said Imani. "I had a vision of me lying on a tile floor, like in a mall or something. Dead. Marcus was holding my hand." Concerned gasps rippled around the table. "That's why I now only shop online," she said.

"You think you're gonna die at the Galleria?" Riley asked.

"Why push it?" Imani replied.

"Who here thinks she's fixating on the wrong thing?" asked Riley. "Your being dead probably had nothing to do with the *place*. More likely it had to do with who you were *with*."

Riley was obviously only half kidding. Fortunately, the waiter appeared with their appetizers and in—

The vortex of voices died out as quickly as it had arisen. One word hung in the bright Antarctic air before the breeze carried it away.

Help.

It's just the wind again, Striker thought. If she stopped to listen every time it kicked up, she'd be standing around all day with drool trickling from her mouth, her head stuffed with gibberish.

Anders was staring at her, the teen's eyes narrowed and wary. "Time to get to work," Striker said, eager to move on. She untied her kayak from the Baron's. "Everyone add your boat to the lineup. Let's cover this whole beach in red." It wasn't cold, the air still hovering above fifty, but all the same she did ten jumping jacks, ten squats. She knew that the temperature could change on a dime. When the real Antarctica appeared, a thousand squats wouldn't be enough to warm her.

"Ah, the thin red line," said the Baron. He remained seated. "A line that must be respected at all costs."

"What are you yammering on about?" she asked, instantly regretting it.

"The thin red line is the line between sanity and insanity."

Jesus Christ. Five minutes in and already the guy was acting like they'd been snowed in for the winter at the Overlook Hotel. Still, the old guy wasn't wrong. You could either go off the deep end or keep it together. But why present people with options?

"Who do you think beat us here?" asked la Grande Dame, ignoring her husband.

"It's probably the people from San Francisco," said Anders.

"Mikey! Jim! It's Mommy!" yelled Bobbi Sue. The lady was already off on her own planet.

"Mom, it's not them," said Anders in a small voice.

The kid was perceptive. They glanced around for help. In the moment, Striker felt cowardly and looked away, already tired at the prospect of having to constantly wrangle Bobbi Sue's uterus back to a fixed position. The thin red line was indeed *thin* in that one. It was not a line Striker was eager to navigate.

Anders, on the other hand, was still with the program. That counted for something. The teen read the lay of the land same as Striker. It was obvious who was there. The position of the boats stretched along the shore was likely the work of the Tech Titan, Taylor like a world-class pool player who never makes a shot without thinking about the next shot to come. If you want to win at pool, you have to set yourself up, leave yourself with a play, otherwise it's game over. Striker had a hard time imagining any of the dads strategizing like that, well, except for the brown dad—he seemed to have a clue—but these boats weren't tandems. That meant that like Mikey and Jim, Lucy and Hector were also out of the running.

Striker took a closer look. One of the kayaks was high-end glossy, like it had never seen the ocean, the other battered from paddling to the moon and back. Yup. It was Taylor and Kevin. She wasn't sure if that was good or bad.

In the back of la Grande Dame's tandem, Vadim remained out cold. A chinstrap stood staring at him. The penguin tipping its head from side to side, waiting for him to wake up and come out and play. Sorry, little fellow, Striker thought. Your boy's playing days are long over.

Striker had once dated the consultant on a weekly hospital drama. One episode had mirrored a real-life surfing accident the consultant had suffered at Manly Beach in New South Wales, the consultant's shoulder coming out of the socket when a first-time surfer smashed into him. The gist of the episode was the main character had taken a much-needed vacation to California far away from the Windy City, but the second he landed at LAX, he ran headfirst into every conceivable medical emergency possible—dislocation, gunshot wound, not one but *two* women going into labor, even a horse in need of treatment. While filming the surfing accident, Striker learned that the longer a limb is dislocated, the harder it is to get back in the socket. The consultant said that in his case, it took three male doctors plus two assistants, a whole bunch of morphine, and a scalpel to guide his shoulder back into place, a ragged scar now patterning his scapular. The skin shiny as if once upon a time he'd had a wing growing there but somebody ripped it off.

"We move him, he's gonna be in a world of hurt," Anders said as they stood studying Vadim. Striker sighed. It wasn't what she wanted to hear. "Health class, first aid," the teen added.

"I don't doubt you," she said.

All Striker could dredge up from health class was how to stabilize someone's neck if you were prepping to perform CPR on them. Place one hand on their forehead, lift the chin with the other. Everything else she'd learned about chest compressions and alternate breathing was wrong now too. You could kill somebody with all the wrong things she knew. Yeah, why were these people deferring to her? What the hell did she know about wilderness survival? She was Black. Antarctica was not the land of her people.

"So what do we do, Doc?"

"Keep him warm, I guess," said Anders, "and as pain-free as possible. People can survive an initial trauma and then die from the pain." The kid glanced over at their mother, who was running up and down the beach, her face both twisted and ecstatic, hopeful as she called out to her husband and son, the small animals lying in the sun oblivious to the screams of this pale beast. "Where do you think the others are?"

"Can't be far. These dry suits weren't made for hiking."

"Is that smoke?" The Baron pointed to a nearby ridge. He was still sitting in the front of his kayak, the very dead Alexei just over his shoulder.

"I see it, but I don't smell anything," said Striker.

"Me neither," said Anders.

"Fingers crossed it's steam." Just saying it made her feel hopeful. Steam meant heat, meant water, meant surviving for as long as their fat reserves might hold out.

"Anna, why don't you stay here with your mom?" said la Grande Dame. "Veronique and I will go have a look-see."

"It's Anders," said Striker. She figured the old lady should get at least one of their names right.

"Sarah said she answers to Anna," replied the Dame.

"Whatever," said the teen.

Striker was saddened to see them back down so fast. She made a mental note to tell them later that you can't give in or the world will run right over you, and being the universe's roadkill wasn't anyone's idea of fun. Of all people she should know.

What are you talking about? You were always the first to merge. That's what you called it. Merging.

"Here." Anders handed Striker the binoculars.

"Okay. Call us if you need us. Sound should travel pretty easy around here."

"If the wind's in your favor," said the Baron.

"And *you*," she said to him. "You should get out of your boat, get your circulation going."

"Whatever you say, Chief."

Too much more of this *chief* talk and she'd never be able to pass the conch to someone else. Someone who spoke in graphs, someone who was used to crunching numbers, someone like the Tech Titan, her little girl voice be damned. Yeah, Taylor would make an excellent leader, what with her algorithms and her weekly jaunts over to Alcatraz. Striker imagined standing in front of the group and explaining that she was resigning her post effective immediately as unelected problem solver to spend more time with family. Oh, and by the way—heeeeere's Taylor! She could already picture herself with her feet soaking in an old, dented bucket like the one Mabel had on Clark Street. Good food, good music, rest, a little justice.

In the Baron's case, Striker couldn't tell if he was mocking her with the captain-my-captain act or if the old man was more than happy to take orders. If it turned out the old guy was the kind of geezer who got off on being bossed around by strong women, so help her god she'd find a way to ram a kayak into the back of his head while he was standing right there on land. Hadn't Percy said something or other about the number-one cause of death among stranded explorers being general mayhem? It wasn't too hard to believe.

By the time we return, the Baron better be a useful member of society, she thought as she walked away with the Dame, their destination the highest possible peak. Otherwise, come Christmas Day, I take zero responsibility for whatever happens to him.

Striker glanced at her wrist. 12:14 p.m. She'd never realized she was so addicted to time. Likely two hours had passed since no more Percy though who could tell? The sun sat merrily twinkling in the exact same spot in the sky since they'd pushed off from the *Yegorov*. Everywhere bits of feathers drifted in the air, the day reverse snowing as the wind kicked fluff up off the ground. Striker waved a hand in front of her face, a windshield wiper.

The top of the volcano sparkled fiercely. "Up there the world should be our oyster," she said.

Without looking, la Grande Dame cinched the seals around her wrists. "I find oysters to be too much work," she replied, one eyebrow coyly arched.

Chick's like a movie villain popping a new clip in a Glock, Striker thought.

You starting to dig this lady?

No, she wouldn't go that far, just the Dame's cool-as-a-cucumber routine was infectious. The old girl had glided through the past few hours with the air of a woman in a plush white bathrobe wandering around a spa in search of the steam room. Yeah, nobody was keeping Striker from growing hysterical more than la Grande Dame and her chemically ironed face. Remind me never to play poker with this ho, she thought. In a game of pickup basketball, in descending order, she'd pick the Dame, Anders, the Baron, then Bobbi Sue but only if she had to. She just hoped her favorite villain kept in mind they were all on the same team.

"I bet we'll be able to see a hundred miles out," she said. "The *Yegorov*'s gotta be out there."

"One would think." For a moment the sunlight caught in the Dame's teeth, a silvery ray sparking in her mouth.

Striker could hear the doubt in her traveling companion's voice. The thought had also crossed her mind. If katabatic winds could lift a kayak and send it crashing through the back of a man's skull easy as breaking an egg, then what kind of damage might they inflict on a sixty something-year-old Russian icebreaker that had seen better days?

Right now she had bigger fish to fry than thinking about the wind. Hiking in a dry suit was proving ridiculous—*it's like mountaineering in footie pajamas*—but the thought of spotting the *Yegorov* propelled her on. That plus la Grande Dame was an excellent goad. Even swaddled in a dry suit, the Dame had the body of a dancer, one of those people who'd jumped on the yoga train back in the '70s and had kept it up ever since.

Be honest now. Lady's got a helluva rack on her.

Too true. At dinner the night before, Striker had noticed several men in the dining room checking her out. The old girl's obvious surgical enhancements made for a strange but compelling contrast. White hair, D cup. *Damn!* Milk might do a body good but not as good as unlimited resources. The rich were becoming ageless.

Beyond the beach the land flattened out as it stretched to the foot of the volcano. It was fast becoming apparent that unlike Paulet, this island was big enough to house secrets. The baldness of the ground made you feel like you should be able to see everything at once, but in reality there were innumerable ridges and hills texturing the area, places where a person could tuck herself into the landscape in order to get out of the path of the wind and cold.

Even beyond the beach they encountered the occasional penguin, sometimes clusters of them, the birds plodding along in both directions. It was amazing the way they navigated the terrain. Nothing stopped them. What business could they have so far from the sea? The penguins remained unflustered and steadfast no matter how rocky the landscape, little black-and-white commuters. Now and then one of them would stop and study the two women, then toddle on.

Overhead the sun was still slightly off-center when she and the Dame arrived at the foot of the volcano. It wasn't big but they were both surprised by its steepness, the cone with enough buttes and escarpments to prevent them from seeing the summit. Who knew what was up there? Unlike the flat terrain, the cone was covered in a layer of unbroken white. It wasn't deep but as they climbed, they encountered icy slicks where the snow had melted and then refrozen. It made for tough going. Striker felt lucky for the stony patches where the ground was exposed. The rocky terrain gave her purchase on what was proving to be a beautiful yet treacherous location.

They were almost to the rim when they stumbled on it. "Well well well," said la Grande Dame. It was the understatement of the year.

Striker had eaten breakfast hours ago but she could still feel the vomit rising. "Goddam. Can't we go five minutes without an emergency?"

"I think at this point, five minutes won't make a difference," said the Dame, calm as ever.

"What are you talking about?" snapped Striker. "Somebody needs help."

The blood spatter glistened on the snow like an abstract painting.

"*Needed*," said la Grande Dame. She pointed at something with her foot.

The rock was the perfect size and shape to do damage, jagged on one side yet small enough to fit comfortably in the palm of an angry hand. Striker bent down for a closer look.

Something was stuck to it. Something pink and wet and gooey like raw chicken. Just the littlest slab of flesh. Strands of hair were crusted along the rock's ragged edge, the strands auburn and shiny. And underneath the hair was a substance she had never seen before. The gunk gray yet fatty like pâté.

Admittedly it was slick where they were standing. It wouldn't take much to slip and fall. Between the cold and the fear since the accident, hunger starting to arise, the body uncontrollably shaking to stay warm. Especially bodies with little to no extra meat on the bones. These poor ass-less white women. Their legs going rubbery on the way up the volcano, blood sugar dropping. Wanting to stop but pushing forward out of fear, every minute precious in the race to be seen. The legs giving out, the dizziness overwhelming, slipping on a patch of ice where you didn't expect there to be ice because this is supposed to be summer, goddammit, the season of barbeques and fireworks and white-people sunburns. Everyone knows once the head starts bleeding, good luck getting it to stop. The heart like an oil rig pumping pumping no matter what. Sometimes the littlest nick on the scalp and it's on. Striker had never seen so much of the red stuff (or had she?) and yet it was only the beginning.

On the far edge of the spatter, a rut lay gouged in the snow. The furrow running off into the distance. The rut the width of a person. And in the middle of the rut right where a head should be was a bright red smear.

Somebody was dragging a body up the volcano.

"Goddammit," whispered Striker, but what else was there to do but push on? Down below on the beach the thin red line of kayaks like a warning.

It took them a second to realize they'd reached the top. The moment was anticlimactic. No matter where you went, the earth stopped going up. No more ground to climb. Simple as that.

"Guess we're here," said Striker.

"I guess we are," said the Dame.

Striker turned and gazed down the slope of the volcano, past the beach and out onto the ocean, all while trying not to fixate on the trail of blood that had led them there. She wished she'd brought her

Holga. They say no matter how rough shit got, Van Gogh took his brushes with him everywhere. Dude was onto something. You never knew when you might hit the jackpot. Miles and miles of beautiful emptiness, the water and the sky the same bright blue, the snow a soft periwinkle as it reflected the light, the ice and its infinite facets sparkling.

The crater was wider than she'd expected. On the inside she could make out standing pools of water, the empty sky reflected in their perfect mirrors. A colony of small white birds had built nests along a lumpy interior shelf. Thank god for animals. The colony meant the wispy white clouds coming out of the crater were indeed steam, nothing poisonous. Striker let herself relax.

Down on the beach the penguin rookery was still teeming with life, little black specks like fleas shuffling in and out of the ocean. Even from way up there the eye snagged on the kayaks. You couldn't miss them. A bright red line drawn along the shore for anyone to spot.

Striker raised the binoculars to her face. "Come on," she muttered, as she combed through the sea of birds. She felt a panic dawning in her chest. "Not now."

La Grande Dame stood waiting her turn. "What is it?"

Striker handed her the binoculars. "They're gone," she said. "No Anders, your husband, the crazy Texas lady. Even Vadim." She found herself clenching and unclenching her fists. "This isn't Disneyland," she said. "We don't need any more people getting hurt."

The Dame adjusted yet another secret focal ring. "My husband is a man of nine lives," she said. Striker imagined a cat stretching in a patch of sunlight, the cat wearing a maroon smoking jacket and lapping milk from a martini glass. "If the others are with him, they're fine—I guarantee it—they're *better* than fine. That man has a nose for pleasure," said the old girl. She lowered the binoculars and headed off along the bright red trail around the rim.

Striker found herself following in the Dame's footsteps, grumbling all the way. Once in the lower village on Christopher Street,

Riley had gifted her a tarot reading. While laying out the cards, the medium had claimed nothing ever happens to us unless our higher mind acquiesces. *When the darkness comes, you gotta ask yourself what you're meant to learn from it,* said the medium in a thick Brooklyn accent. The afternoon had been entertaining. In the days and weeks that followed, she and Riley had laughed and laughed about it, asking each other anytime a plan went sideways why their higher minds were letting this fuckery go down. Now schlepping along the top of a sleeping volcano while following a bloody path through the summer snow, she couldn't help but wonder who was greenlighting this shit.

Striker was surprised she and the Dame hadn't noticed them before. On the far side of the crater, a forest of stones rose skyward, from a distance their forms improbably human. It made sense. If you wanted to catch some passing ship's eye, build this, each one silent and daunting. After twelve, Striker lost count.

Her first thoughts were of Stonehenge and the days when mankind worshipped the sun. The knot in her belly tightened. She couldn't tell if it was due to the bloody path twisting toward this city of rocks or the rocks themselves, their auras calling to mind the era of human sacrifice.

As she approached the first one, the skin of her neck began to tingle. An eeriness hung over the spot, a feeling of being watched. Long ago someone had stood right where she was standing. Someone who was hungry and cold and despairing as the days grew shorter until the light went out, the darkness heavy and permanent. In their desperation, some hand had stacked them high, higher still, rock upon rock, growing the cairns as big as they could so that a ship far out at sea might see these stony figures and realize there were people living here against their will.

The cairns were scattered along the rim. How had the builders erected structures so immense, the tallest one stretching more than sixty feet, tall as an oak? She had seen cairns before in places like

Mongolia, Buddhist countries where travelers would leave a rock on an area's highest spot as a request to the sky god for safe passage. Those cairns were simply heaps of rocks, small man-made hills. But these structures were more like totems. Stones balanced one on top of the other in a giant, precarious tower. Without cement, there was no room for error. For the past hundred years, she wondered what had kept them from toppling.

At least on a place like Easter Island, you could tell where those giant heads were staring, their eyes fixed on a faraway spot out in the ocean, the heads carved with discernible features. But cairns by definition are faceless, though here it didn't seem to matter. Everywhere Striker turned, their stony gaze as if following her.

In the center the tallest one stood flanked by two smaller but equally massive pilings. Already she couldn't help but imagine a family. The biggest, Mama, was the protector of the clan. Baby was built entirely of blood-red rocks, the cairn deeply oxidized while Daddy sat a little lower on the rim, Daddy's rocks black and pointy and gnashing.

Striker realized she was holding her breath. It was silly. These cairns had been standing like this for more than a century. Still, it couldn't hurt to tiptoe past. It was a paradox, each structure solid yet delicate, stony needles precariously balanced. She imagined one crashing down simply from the tremor of her feet on the earth. What had Percy said about giving nature her space? Carefully she picked her way through the forest of stone.

The first one she noticed was carved on the boulder at the base of the mama cairn. The rock speckled with silica and glittering a perplexing blue-red.

A sinister feeling spread through her gut. She craned her neck and gazed up the column of rocks. Even from the ground, she could see another stone gleaming at the very top, the stone a mesmerizing blue-red. She knew if she were a bird and could fly up for a look, she would find the same puzzling symbol. The emblem weirdly familiar, like a face in a grainy photo of someone she should recognize but didn't.

The same mark was gouged on other blue-red stones stacked in other cairns. Some of the carvings were shallow, others deep like the earth's first scars.

The feeling of unease ignited. In Machu Picchu she had learned about ancient symbols the Inca believed were portals to distant realities. Her guide had explained the symbols were like primitive QR codes. All you had to do was gaze at them with a clean and honest heart, and instantly you would be transported to a kingdom of peace. But if your heart was imperfect and dirty, then you looked on the symbols at your own peril. There was no telling what kind of hellhole you might end up in. You could even end up dead.

Perhaps the most disconcerting feature of these strange marks was their perfection. Their lines preternaturally straight, angles crisp as if scored by a laser.

"May I never meet the soul who carved these," she whispered as she slipped past yet another perilous tower of rocks.

She was almost out of the shadow of the cairns when she spotted a small cabin built a few hundred feet down on the side of the volcano. Striker hardly had time to register the miracle of the hut when she saw a figure in yellow working their way toward the shelter. The figure advancing and busy busy busy. Something in yellow lying still at their feet.

Someone was dragging a body toward the cabin.

Suddenly the figure glanced up. A good ten seconds passed. Finally the person waved their arms in the air.

"Help, help me!" the man yelled. He collapsed on his knees, the sound of his crying floating over the snow. "My wife fell. I think she'd dead."

It was Kevin. He of the black thought balloons. As she surveyed the scene, Striker could have sworn she heard music drifting on the wind. A Christmas carol playing on a distant organ, the song joyless and flat.

Why had she wanted to come down here on behalf of a production about a band of early twentieth century white men who got stuck in the ice? Was the survival story of Ernest Shackleton and the men of the *Endurance* worth all this?

Tell the truth, Ronnie. It's no coincidence it's Christmas and somebody's dead.

It was a free trip to Antarctica, she thought. Was that so wrong?

But la Grande Dame and her yoga legs was already sweeping past her, following the bloody trail toward the man and what was once his wife.

The body lay in the snow. The three of them huddled around it as if it were a campfire. What were they waiting for? Taylor looked dead. On film, the dead appeared to be made of ash, their pupils without color. Taylor was the same bloodless gray but her deadness went deeper than that. You could see it in the slackness of her face. All the light had drained out of the lantern, her inner fire burned up. There was no longer any *there* there, nothing to fan back into flame.

"We need a mirror," said Kevin. "The dry suit makes it hard to tell."

Striker herself was having a hard time looking. No, what the dead need is some privacy, she thought. That's why we close the casket, bury it up tight in the cold, hard ground, seal it away in a mausoleum, set fire to it, then walk away.

Or in your case, run.

"Oh for Chrissake," said la Grande Dame. She slipped off one of her gloves and bent over, gripped Taylor's neck in her fingers, and began squeezing. The emerald on her finger threw green sparkles on the snow like a disco ball. At one point, the Dame felt around on her own neck for comparison. Finally she gave up. "My hands are numb," she said. "I can't feel my own pulse."

"That's because you're one of the walking dead," said Striker. When nobody reacted, she breathed a little easier.

"I don't know what happened," whimpered Kevin.

"Just take it from the top," said Striker. Her last long-term contract had been on one of the ubiquitous network cop shows. Each week the po-po asked random bystanders to give it to them straight from the top. On TV at least, The Top gave people structure, a way into the story. "Where were you headed?"

"Up here, same as you," said Kevin. He sounded like one of the weekly bystanders from the show. A man searching his memories for anything important, desperate to convince the fuzz he was only out walking his dog and had nothing to do with whatever was lying under those trash bags. "Taylor wanted to see if we could spot the boat."

Striker went straight for the jugular, no time for good cop/bad cop. She probably should've eased into it. Hell, it was Christmas Eve.

"Who else is here?"

"What do you mean?"

"Anyone else here?" she repeated, thinking of the little stony-faced girl and her emotional support rat. "Anyone who could vouch for your story?"

Kevin didn't seem shocked by the insinuation. He took a deep breath. "It was just us," he said. "After the sub breached—"

"The *what*?" said la Grande Dame.

"*I* thought it was a nuclear submarine," he said. "Taylor thought it was shaped more like a submersible."

Striker let herself recall the main actor who played the sergeant on the cop show. The sound of his voice like a handsaw cutting through wood. Two seasons back they'd had a dalliance going, sneaking off to his trailer while his double did blocking. The actor liked it on the floor Greco-Roman style. All season long Striker's skinned elbows burning every time she took a shower.

"The sub surfaced, shit went haywire, we ended up here, then Taylor said we should trek up to the top and look for the ship." Kevin stopped for a moment, glancing out at the breathtaking vista as he collected his thoughts.

You mean stalling for time while he gets his shit together, Riley would've said.

"We were hiking to the top," he continued, his voice going shrill. (Ooo, a *man* could sound shrill. Striker found herself growing excited by the prospect.) "But we didn't have the right gear," he said, as he started to blubber. "You need hiking sticks, the right shoes, water, energy bars."

Fleece. GPS. A satellite phone. Sherpas.

"Next thing I know, Taylor slipped, went down hard. There was blood, so much blood. That's the last thing I remember. The rest is a blank. Like I got *roofied*. Guess I'm in shock," he said.

Silently the two women caught each other's eyes. A lot was said in that glance.

Guy's a coward. Mashing his wife's head on a rock like the rock's a lemon juicer doesn't seem like his style.

Agreed. He's more the type to use poison.

Plus, if he was ever hoping to be rescued, she would've been his best bet to get out of here. Alone, little Lord Fauntleroy's a popsicle within the hour.

Was that an actual historical person?

Can you stay on track?

Roofied? What's up with that?

Agreed, it's creepy.

Wait, in this thread, which one of us is which?

"Okay," said Striker. "For now, where should we stick her?" Once it was out of her mouth, she realized it wouldn't kill her to show a little sympathy. The guy's wife was dead.

At least he wasn't down on the beach shaking each penguin that wobbled past by the shoulders and demanding, "Where are they, what have you done with them?" his uterus crammed into his amygdala.

There wasn't much more to discuss. In an hour or two the *Yegorov* would find them, the kayaks a line of stoplights on the beach. The *Yegorov* would deploy a throng of big strapping Russians to come striding up the volcano. Striker would finally be free to stop thinking, stop making decisions, stop fighting whatever inner darkness was rising to the surface. One of the Russians might even fold her in his arms later that night. Grigorii of the green eyes. After all, it was Christmas Eve. She and Grigorii could pretend they were Joseph and Mary, his teen bride, following a shining star toward paradise. Why the hell not?

You know why not.

A plan was hatched. They would put Taylor in the cabin. Kevin and the Dame would head down to the beach and get the others. Without a watch, she couldn't be sure, but Striker put it at a twenty-minute walk back to the penguin rookery. She didn't see any reason why she should go. The Dame was in killer shape—for her, twenty minutes there and back would be a walk in the park. Kevin said he needed to get some things from his dry bag. The way he said it, hurrying over the phrase *some things* while trying to act casual.

"What *kinda* things?" Striker asked, imagining a needle and a piece of rubber tubing, both of his inner arms stained black and blue.

"Just stuff," he said. She could practically see the dark clouds racing behind his eyes. She had known guys like this in her past. The best route forward was to give him just enough rope and then wait it out.

"Whatever," she said. "Let's just get this done."

The door to the hut was secured with a rusted bolt that hadn't moved in a hundred years. The women watched as Kevin toggled it in place, trying to get it to slide open. After a few minutes Striker lost interest and turned to examine the shelter. Unlike the one on Paulet, this one was a small cabin made of wood. The chimney was built with stones, some of which had fallen out, creating a patchwork of holes in the side, allowing the inner dark to pour out into the day.

"Let me," said the Dame, stepping forward.

"No, I almost got it," said Kevin. The Dame rolled her eyes. Striker wandered off to do more reconnaissance.

The shelter was roughly twenty by thirty, the materials obviously scavenged from the survivors' ship. The surface of the hut appeared feathery as huge flakes of wood splintered off. At the other shelter on Paulet, she had sensed a heaviness blanketing the air, a stasis like walking through the eye of a storm. But up here the stillness went further. The silence was suffocating, as if the living had been driven out. Maybe it was due to the distance between this hut and the penguin rookery, the isolation total. Striker had sensed the same feeling once walking through an abandoned village on the outskirts of Chernobyl. Children's toys abandoned in the yards, clothes hanging on the line. The sense that humans are impermanent. The resulting quiet smothering in its vastness.

Finally the bolt slid open. "Got it," Kevin said. Beads of sweat sparkled on his brow. He gripped the iron bar soldered to the door where normally a doorknob would be and pulled. Nothing happened. He kept pulling. Striker had to hand it to the guy. He was pulling for all he was worth. This wasn't about him forcing open some hundred-year-old door. It was about him establishing himself, proving his strength in front of women, being the alpha male when every other marker definitively stated he was a beta at best. For a moment she felt bad for him. The guy was gonna pull his freaking arms off.

"Lemme know when you're in," she said, and disappeared around a corner.

The cabin's only door was on the leeward side facing the volcano. It was a smart move, protecting the door from the winds that would whip up the side of the cone. The outward-facing side of the hut had the million-dollar view. Two tiny windows looked out toward the Southern Ocean. The panes rattled in the breeze, the glass encrusted with grime. Striker reached out and worked a finger under one of the frames.

Girl, why you bugging? Riley would've asked in the dated lingo she used to annoy her friend.

"Cuz we may need a place to crash." Carefully Striker slipped more fingers under the wood, trying to pry it loose. She could hear the Dame and Kevin grunting on the other side of the cabin, the door not wanting to budge.

Once you in, ain't no going back, Riley would've said.

Striker stopped in her tracks. She remembered her friend's fear of peering under the bed, of seeking out the thing that goes bump in the night.

What if they were still in there? What if these castaways stranded at the ass of the world had been among the unlucky ones who were never rescued? What if something was slumbering inside these four walls? A cabin full of bones, or worse, a cabin full of bodies that had never decomposed, their dead eyes forever open and waiting in the dark?

Something flashed in one of the windows. Striker's breath caught in her throat. *What is going on?* She squeezed her eyes shut and didn't move. Finally she exhaled and took another look.

It was still there.

Reflected in the filthy glass was a face. Its skin was shrunken and tight, strips of it hanging off the bone like old wallpaper, skull dotted with ratty twists. Both lips were gone, teeth permanently exposed in a mad grin. Striker violently shook her head, but the terrible vision remained. *Please, anything but this.* She knew without a doubt it was her own face, eyes lidless and bulging, each iris white as salt. Was it a premonition of what the island would reduce her to? She glanced in the other dirty pane.

A stranger stared back. It was obvious he was starving. The gauntness of his face gave his features a delicateness, every bone visible, the scalp of his badly shaved head nicked and scabby. Striker sensed he was much younger than the creases gouged in his forehead would suggest, eyes sunken and bruised. A weak grin rippled over his cracked lips. Slowly he opened his mouth. Several teeth were missing. The rest appeared loose, gums inflamed. The remaining teeth coated with blood.

"My god is godly," the man whispered, voice soft and painfully hoarse. "Doctor says in Him, all things are possible."

Suddenly both windows blew open out toward the sea, as if a strong gust of wind had originated from inside the cabin.

Riley would've said this is the part where you turn around and march your Black ass back down the volcano, the whole way down holding a palm up in front of your face and telling the world to talk to the hand. Instead, Striker placed both palms on the windowsill. She could only describe it as a compulsion. The way she would come home to her apartment late at night and throw open the door to the bedroom closet before crawling in bed. Sometimes it was better to just get it over with and look. It gave you the upper hand plus it kept stuff from creeping up on you later.

Guess I'm really doing this.

Thankfully there was a table pushed up against the wall. She wriggled through and sat on its edge. She could hear Kevin and the Dame still working on the door. "I'm in," she said, her voice barely a whisper. Nobody's set foot in this place for a hundred years, she thought. She imagined a beautiful princess lying asleep in a glass coffin, the realm growing thorny and wretched around her.

She put a foot down on the floor. Instantly her knees weakened.

It was like riding the New York City subway during rush hour. The sensation of being packed in tight, of standing shoulder to shoulder, the air heavy with the heat of bodies, their exhalations. She was all alone in a cabin at the bottom of the world yet it felt like the room was crammed full of people.

Stop being silly, she told herself. There's no one here.

Even with the windows open it was darker than she'd anticipated but something was shimmering in the far corner. Slowly she approached the spot.

A steady hiss was pouring out of a hole in the floor, the air faintly glowing. The constancy of the sound like white noise. She edged closer, hand outstretched in a dream. Soft tendrils of light floated up into the air.

Suddenly she heard a shuffling.

The sound was stilted. Its gait asymmetrical as it lurched toward her. Something was creeping across the wooden slats, dragging itself closer. The room cast in darkness except for the small square of light pouring through the open window and the long, misshapen shadows thrown up from the hole in the floor.

The thing was almost at her feet. The sound of its breathing ragged and labored, a sound she had heard once long ago. The sound of life fighting for life. Pulling itself into the tiny swatch of sunlight and forcing her to acknowledge it, take its bloodiness up into her arms.

Just then the door flew open.

"What is *that*?" asked la Grande Dame. The old girl didn't sound scared so much as awed.

"Poor little guy," said Kevin. "Wish I had my dry bag with me."

It must have wriggled in through one of the holes in the chimney. The creature searching and searching for the perfect spot. It was probably one of the last to come ashore. Then finding this place, warm and dark and tucked away from the skua with their tearing feet. Who knew how long it had been shuffling around in the dark? The same stones that had shifted and created a way in had likely shifted again and blocked the way out. And so it was left dragging itself around the room, smearing its guano on the wooden floor until there was nothing left inside it. The golden egg it had laid in the corner all but forgotten.

Already Kevin is striding forth holding something old and iron overhead. But Kevin is no Percy. When he attempts to bring it down on the small, feathery skull, he misses, striking the thing in the body, its shriek wet and both sorrowful and angry. He tries to hit it again, but it's a moving target, the light pitiful, Kevin pitiful, both Striker and the Dame shaking their heads, the Dame frowning, Striker wondering why he doesn't just herd the poor creature *outside*—if the *Yegorov* doesn't come soon, they may have to sleep in here—wondering what it is he's really beating to death, some poor penguin that stumbled into a hundred-year-old cabin and couldn't get out, or something darker and harder to kill, a part of himself he wishes were different.

In the end, the best-laid plans of mice and Kevin.

The penguin manages to duck his blows. Striker can hear it scampering about in terror. The sound of its breathing frenetic. Kevin never lets up, but the creature somehow finds a way out, disappearing back into the chimney mottled with holes and out into the daylight where it's free to waddle back down the volcano to the safety of its kind.

Or not.

Bird or no bird, they stuck to their plan, dragging the body into the shelter. It might have been easier with just her and the Dame. After the debacle with the penguin, Kevin's only contribution was getting in the way and criticizing their progress.

In life, Taylor couldn't have weighed more than a buck and a quarter, but in death, it felt like the two women were shuttling a block of pure ice thousands of miles across the tundra. Lucky for them the cold had stopped the bleeding. There was only a light pink smear left in places where the back of Taylor's head kissed the snow. Like lip gloss, Striker thought. She wondered if the Dame had anticipated this on her Antarctic bingo card. *Sheltering a dead body*.

She remembered the story the *Yegorov*'s historian had told about the discovery of Robert Scott's corpse by his crew seven months after he and his four companions had failed to return. One of the men present at the interment later described the eerie sound of Scott's icy arm snapping as the men worked to free his journal from his frozen grip. Striker was grateful *this* body wasn't anywhere near cold enough for that. The lip gloss pinking the ice was bad enough.

Once Taylor the Tech Titan was inside the shelter, it began to seem like a bad idea. Under the hole cut in the floor, the jagged vent gleamed like an ember, issuing a stream of warm air. The glow was mesmerizing, the flickering like starlight, the hut balmy, even tropical.

For a second time, Striker stood by the hole and held out her hand. "Must be from the volcano," she said. "This could change everything."

"*Vittles* would change everything," said la Grande Dame.

Vittles? It sounded like a word the Baron would use.

"We should leave the body outside," suggested Kevin. "It's too hot in here."

Striker found his use of the word *body* odd. "But we just managed to bring her in," she said.

"Anyway," said la Grande Dame, "we saw it on Paulet. Our friends the skua are relentless."

Striker hadn't considered that. The thought of the birds with their hooked beaks made her queasy. The disgust in Kevin's face also signaled that yeah, inside was better.

Carefully they arranged Taylor on the floor furthest from the vent. Kevin took a moment to rummage through his wife's pockets. He came away with a small key, the kind used for luggage. He made a show of kissing her on the forehead.

"Back soon, my love," he said before pulling a ratty blanket up over her face.

The three of them went back outside to what was beginning to feel like the roof of the world. Down below the penguins were still living their best lives. It was absolutely bonkers, Striker thought, that an unsophisticated little bird could survive in one of the world's most punishing terrains but the odds were fifty-fifty for the species with the opposable thumbs. Riley would've said that was why she wasn't against dating short men. Striker could hear her friend's voice, Riley taking her to church. *Sometimes God packs a lot in a little.*

Before Kevin and the Dame headed back down to the beach, Striker decided to take one last stab at it. While it's fresh in our minds, she thought. She figured it couldn't hurt.

"I *told* you," said Kevin. "We were walking. It was slippery. She fell. Boom. Like dead weight. Didn't hold out her hand or anything. Just boom. Down."

"She fell or she slipped?"

"What's the difference?" He was getting suspicious, closing himself off.

"I'm trying to picture it, is all. It must have been awful for you."

"It was," he said. After a few moments, he added, "She slipped. Yeah, *slipped*. That's the right word. Her feet shot out from under her."

"I thought you said you were in the lead." Was the Dame also having a hard time imagining Taylor following her husband anywhere?

"I didn't actually *see* what happened, but she must have slipped. I heard it. I turned around. I saw her lying there twitching. The snow already—" He stood searching for the right word. "Reddening."

"We found a loose rock nearby. It had hair on it."

"So? The rocks were icy."

"It's kinda weird. The rock wasn't in the spot where she fell. It was a few feet away."

"I dunno. I moved her, so maybe the snow stopped the bleeding and stuff?"

"There were definitely gobs of—" She caught herself. "There was a lot of trauma on the snow. Just not on the rocks where you said she fell."

"I don't know!" he shouted. Striker thought if she'd been a man, he would've taken a swing at her. It was possible he still would. "My wife is dead! You happy?"

"No, are you?"

Overhead, a skua was circling on the winds. After a few turns it came down and landed on a rock. Striker noticed it had only one eye. The remaining eye locked on her like a scope.

Kevin and la Grande Dame were also staring. Had she *really* just asked if he was happy his wife was dead? Sometimes you need other people to help you regulate yourself. When other people shut down or don't engage or start to act crazy, you can't tell when you yourself are out of line. When you've said something you shouldn't have said. When you've done something you can never walk back.

The skua began preening its feathers, its missing eye red like a coil on a stove. You and me both, honey, it seemed to say. You and me both.

Kevin used the silence to turn the tables. "You gonna be okay up here?" he asked, twirling the key he'd lifted off his wife's body. Striker could hear it in the timbre of his voice, his words pitched wide and innocent to demonstrate no hard feelings.

Don't be trifling, Riley would've said. *Nobody knows mind games better than us.* It was clear Kevin was trying to plant a seed, implying that all alone up there with a dead body, Striker would be anything but okay. Losing your highly successful wife who was a giant in her industry was proving to be a helluva boner. Since coming ashore, the guy had grown several inches, his chest newly puffed out like a silverback gorilla.

"Don't worry about me," Striker said. She aimed her arrow low. "Just make sure you stay upright out there on the slopes."

La Grande Dame's eyes lit up full tilt. "I'll make sure he makes it down and back *intact*," she said. The way the old girl held the word. The three of them knew it was an allusion to his manly bits. "Toodles," said the Dame, scratching the air with her fingers, a rich woman's wave goodbye. She turned and set off down the slope. For an instant Kevin scowled at Striker before storming off.

This isn't over.

Promises promises.

Striker watched them disappear down the volcano. Back inside the cabin, she left the door wide open, but even with the radiance shooting up out of the earth, it felt darker than she would've liked.

Okay. Tidy up and take stock. See if there's anything useful. Avoid the corner with the thing laid out under the ratty blanket. Don't even look at it.

It was clear the hut had been around more than ten decades. She could tell from the stamp on the crate containing the Victrola. 1908. Percy had said the First World War marked the close of the golden age of polar exploration, which had started before the turn of the century. That put this place anywhere from 120 to 140 years old. What else had Percy told them? There had been whalers further north on South Georgia going back to the time of the Civil War, the whalers destroying that island's fur seal colonies before moving on. It was possible some of those men could have sailed further south, some even becoming stranded in the very room where she was standing.

Luckily there were no signs of decay. The cabin was sturdy, any gaps in the wooden boards covered with ticking. From the look of things entire walls had been transported from the crew's foundering ship, the panels dark, blackened by the oily smoke of fatty marine animals. The space was crammed with the comforts of home, the ship fully scavenged before it was abandoned and left to be crushed in the ice. On the wall opposite the chimney was a huge cast-iron stove. It probably weighed a ton. That the men had wrestled it all the way up the volcano was beyond amazing. Even after more than a century, there was no doubt in Striker's mind it would heat up the instant someone stuffed it full of wood and tossed in a match.

In the corner closest to the chimney, two mattresses sat on iron bed stands, one of them probably the captain's. A handful of hammocks hung from nearby hooks. During one of the lectures onboard the *Yegorov*, a historian had explained that any given expedition might number upwards of fifty men though the sailors would often be left for the season at the whaling stations on the northernmost islands while the explorers headed further south into the ice.

Large wooden crates sat heaped on the floor, their stamps faded but legible. Tate and Lyle, Day and Martin Shoe Polish, Spratt's Dog Biscuits, Keiller's Orange Marmalade, Bovril, Superior Chocolate Powder. Several crates still contained their contents. She bent down and pulled out a packet. The biscuits were practically calcified. Same for the coffee and sugar. A little hot water might soften them up. Nothing had gone bad, just hardened.

In the far corner leaned a series of shelves loaded with baskets full of utensils, early twentieth century kitchenware, much of it tin. There were buckets and jugs, towels and rags, everything one would need to set up house, even a microscope sitting on a wooden case, a glass slide wedged under the lens. She wondered how the men had stayed busy tucked up on the side of a volcano. How many winters they had fought to remain upbeat in the face of the interminable Antarctic night. The *Yegorov*'s onboard historian had mentioned that the doomed Franklin expedition had carried three thousand books with them during their arctic journey in search of the Northwest Passage. She imagined some poor soul's reading glasses breaking just days into his trip like in that *Twilight Zone* episode starring Burgess Meredith.

Striker gave the room a last long look. There was zero chance a person with a uterus could've kept herself hidden in such close quarters. And if, by the skin of her teeth, some lovesick woman had managed to pull off the unimaginable, her relationship with her lover would have rapidly deteriorated. There was no privacy, nowhere to sneak off to. The woman would've been just another one of the dirty, smelly, starving boys. Where was the fun in that?

Something lay tossed under a chair, maybe a rag. Striker wouldn't have given it a second thought except that crumpled up in the fabric were two strange pebbles that glinted in the weak light. Even without knowing what it was, it looked like nothing she wanted to touch. She grabbed a fork from one of the baskets and speared it with the tines.

It was a mask, the leather thin and still pliable. Someone had painstakingly glued a sparse path of red hair around the chin. Slits were cut for the eyes and nose though their narrowness gave the mask a sinister look. Striker poked at the mouth hole with her finger. *Shizer.* What she had thought were pebbles were actual teeth. Two yellow incisors sewn into the leather with twine and jutting out of the mouth like small tusks. The mask was heavily soiled. The stains didn't seem dark enough to be soot, the spots more rust colored. She felt her stomach tense.

She had seen a mask like this before on the set of that turgid period flick she had scouted in Scotland about Charles I. The people who wore them were called Covenanters. They were Scotsmen who refused to bow to the English Catholic Church. Covenanter priests would hold secret outdoor masses for those who dared to attend upon pain of death. The ones who were caught were killed in gruesome ways that often involved the exposing of their entrails. Some of the outlaw priests traveled from town to town incognito, their faces obscured by elaborate masks adorned with human features. To Striker, none of it made sense. If anything, the strange masks only rendered the wearer more conspicuous.

There had been a brief talk on the *Yegerov* about the kind of clothing the early explorers wore. Most were made of wool and furs, some canvas. It all sounded pretty miserable. Striker wondered if maybe the men had also worn leather masks to protect their faces from the elements. The lecturer had mentioned that the Inuit often shielded their eyes by cutting slits in slats of wood that they would then peer through.

Personally I'd rather be burnt to a crisp than wear that thing.

Even on the end of a fork, the mask evinced a dark power. The eye slits staring from beyond time. Striker followed its gaze across the room to a small ax leaning upright in the corner. She tossed the mask aside and went to see if the blade had dulled. The cabin didn't have any discernible armory. It was probably just as easy to use a knife or a club to do your killing, a gun's firing mechanism unreliable in extreme cold. She reached down and picked up the ax by the—

Instantly she jumped back as though she'd brushed a live wire.

That wasn't real, she told herself. It couldn't be. She stood panting in the quiet, waiting for her heart to slow.

In a flash she had seen the room in the glow of lantern light. The floorboards and walls, even the ceiling spattered with blood. There had been a terrible smell, something on the cusp of death, the sound of men openly vomiting.

Her heart was pounding but she had to know. A higher power was pulling the strings. She watched as her hand reached down and picked up the ax again—

<< Striker is shouting orders, her voice thick with a Highland brogue. Something clings to her face, the object clammy like a second skin, her vision lessened as if peering at the world from between two fingers. A terrible sourness fills her mouth but she disregards it as she addresses the room, instructing those assembled that the saw has been lost in the grotto and the matter is urgent, *aye, we need tae get it aff noo, lads*. A body lies screaming on the table. Shouting *it's just my three fingers*, but she counters *the deadness might weel be ower the three*. The man on the table fights with every ounce of his strength until he is hit on the head with a mallet and the gruesome surgery begins, some of the men holding the patient down, others gripping the arm, three of the man's fingertips the color of ash, skin black as charcoal, the hand itself also a bloodless yellow, the flesh no longer spongy but flaccid like unrisen dough, and the smell in the room is beyond sickening, a smell of dead flesh and burning animal fat and unwashed bodies pushed to their limits and Striker never falters as she raises the blade overhead, God's commandant here on earth, the ax coming down on the patient's wrist but it's not quite through, the

blood spurting in the greasy air like syrup as she soldiers on steadfast and righteous, *naked I came frae o' ma mither's belly, an' naked I'll go bak thare,* the stout blade rising for a second >>

Striker let go, the ax clattering on the floor.

Her doctors suspected it was a type of migraine. They said it was possible to experience the aura that precedes the event without encountering the subsequent pain. For most migraine sufferers, the aura involved sensitivity to light and sound, flashing circles dancing in the air, sometimes smells. From the darkness of her walled anchorage, the thirteenth century mystic Hildegard von Bingen had described seeing a shining city on a hill followed by hours of stabbing pain. The doctors told Striker she should consider herself lucky. Debilitating headache wasn't one of her symptoms. Instead, she would be strolling around minding her own business when, without warning, she'd smell rotten food mixed with the greasy smell of shit. Then time would pass without her perceiving it and she'd come back to herself in a different location.

In New York it was easy enough to manage. She didn't drive, and every time it happened, what she called "Dark Striker" (*it's me but without the lights on*) carried on perfectly fine, never stepping into traffic or off a subway platform into the path of a screaming train. Dark Striker was mostly just disconcerting. Like the time she'd landed in bed with a Broadway dancer—she could tell the brother had moves! The two of them were just at the start of the festivities when the smell of rotten food filled the sheets, and the next thing she knew he was lying beside her, his hand rubbing her shoulder as he fell into a happy sleep.

The first inklings of her heightened sensitivity started in childhood that first summer on Zinnia Trace. She was six when Trish and Doug called the fire department after Striker blacked out and came to twenty feet up a tree. What happened, she later asked. Trish's eyes filled with tears. It wasn't unusual for Trish to cry. She'd been crying all summer. But this time she seemed truly hopeless. "I dunno," Trish said. "You just went dark."

And now along with the blackouts she was having visions. Moments when she would touch some unassuming object and its story would spool into her. Out of her army of doctors, Striker only told her gynecologist a simplified version of what was happening. "You're a woman on the cusp of forty and perimenopausal," the woman had said. "It's possible your symptoms have shifted." The other doctors would have looked for darker reasons, recommended upping her meds.

The first vision hit in the subway a week after Labor Day. A silk scarf lay on the platform, the fabric a beautiful burnt orange. She had picked it up, thinking a woman heading for the stairs had dropped it. Instantly she was standing in a room, low music on in the background. A man was walking toward her in his boxers, pulling her into his arms. Playfully she was running the scarf over his face. Then the man was laying her down on the bed. Striker could sense an inner reluctance, a pang of fear as the woman handed over control, but she felt the woman push beyond it, a soft *baby, yes* playing on her lips, the fear slowly morphing into the thrill of the unknown, the adrenaline rush that comes with arousal, the man pulling her arms over her head, tying her hands to the bedpost with the scarf, the woman's heart thundering as he—

Striker had never told the doctors about the things she heard, afraid that such symptoms would tip their diagnosis from the realm of the relatively benign over into the hell of crazy. She could never predict when it would happen, but some days she would hear a baby howling, its cries muffled as if coming through a wall. At other times her head filled with the breathy notes of an organ playing holiday music or the percussive thump of a beating heart. Through the years, she had simply done as women do. She had learned to live with it.

The ax lay on the floor. It was only an ax. There was no severed hand growing cold on the table like a leftover piece of meat. Striker gave herself another minute to reacclimate.

Something scurried out of the chimney.

"Not again," she whispered. She couldn't believe it moved so fast. She tried to recall what the onboard ornithologist had said.

Everyone knew penguins ate fish, but were they also scavengers, eaters of the dead?

Striker knew it was up to her to protect the thing lying in the corner under the blanket. The merciful act would be to track down the invader and put it out of its misery once and for all. She could practically hear Percy telling her where to aim and not to close her eyes at the last second or she'd miss. As she reached for a fire poker, the sound changed.

Striker froze.

Something was crying. The noise small and soft and human.

It was everywhere at once, like the song a seashell makes when you hold it to your ear, its music filling your head, only now there was no distance between her and the sound of an infant crying, the baby no longer in the room next door. It was right there in the cabin. A presence rising like water in the dark. She could feel it, the sense that someone was standing over her shoulder, their breath cold on her neck. She knew if she stood there any longer, a hand would reach out and touch her arm.

"What do you want?" she whispered.

"Same as you," rasped the painfully hoarse voice of the haggard young man she'd encountered in the window. "To be counted among the forgiven."

She didn't wait to hear more. She ran out the door and kept running, intending to run all the way back to the beach, but her foot caught on something and she fell, landing on what she knew was anything but solid earth.

Striker sat in the snow on her haunches waiting for her head to clear. Thanks to the flight down from JFK, it had been more than twenty-four hours since she'd taken her meds. The little yellow pills were supposed to keep the blood vessels in her head from constricting. The pills weren't a cure-all but they seemed to help. On them she experienced fewer blackouts. Her doctor had said the same medication was also prescribed off-label for depression and other darker conditions. When Striker mentioned it to Riley, she'd felt a shiver ripple up her spine. "He wasn't talking about *me*," she'd explained. "Just that it has dual uses." Her friend had remained uncharacteristically quiet, not even so much as nodding.

Striker scanned the area where she'd fallen. She was less than twenty feet from the cabin. In the distance the cairns stood on the lip of the crater staring out over the world. She poked around under the snow, probing for what had tripped her up. From the sound it made she knew she'd landed on wood, maybe even a box of some sort buried in the earth. She just hoped it wasn't a casket. Please god, not another body.

The snow moved easily. It was wood all right. Her hand cleared a spot. Startled, she sank back on her knees. It was all she could see, the thing a cancer filling her vision.

What do you *want* from me, she thought. She looked up at the sky. Patiently the day stared back. Your move, it seemed to be saying. She was tired of it always being her move. When would it be somebody else's? She exhaled and got back to work.

The door had obviously been sawed in half, the bottom edge splintery and unsanded, leaving it looking more like a hatch. It was fairly simple in design. Six rough-hewn slats nailed together. A small porthole sat at what had probably been eye level back when it was full-sized. The glass now blackened as if smoked and heavily scratched.

The symbol was centered above the porthole. It had been gouged in the wood, presumably with an awl as the lines were thicker than a knife would have made. She thought of the Israelites marking their lintels with blood as a sign for the Angel of Death to pass them over. What could this be signaling?

Striker knocked just under the porthole, two long taps then two short. Instantly she felt stupid. Who did she think was going to answer? But the ground underneath the hatch boomed in response, proving it wasn't just a long-forgotten door left lying out in the cold. The earth below it was empty. It was a door that led somewhere.

It occurred to her she should wait for the group. What had she told the Dame about sticking together? Still, there could be something useful buried right there below her feet. Maps, clothing, a radio, food. Or something small and shiny she could tuck in her pocket just in case someone began to change. Just look at Kevin. They had only been without civilization for a few hours and already the guy's wife was dead.

Now that she'd cleared the hatch, she could see that her foot had snagged on a piece of rope. She picked it up and had barely started pulling when it disintegrated in her hands. "Plan B," she said. She bent down to try the brass handle directly, the metal green and flaking, but the handle—

<< Striker is standing in icy water up to her ankles as she pounds on the door. In a flash the water is up to her knees. Trash floating in it. Foodstuffs. A dead rat. The water now waist-high. Her hammering becomes more desperate. Please, somebody let me out. Fingernails clawing at the porthole. The room almost completely flooded. At the ceiling less than a foot of air. Her ears popping in the silence as if she's buried under a hundred feet of water. Lungs burning with the cold of a >>

Striker let go of the handle. All around her the earth lay glittering, every object bright with death. She stood up and wiped her brow. "I shouldn't be doing this," she said.

"Are you kidding?" she countered. "It could be a storage space full of goodies." A few hundred feet away something caught her eye.

A being in yellow was standing in the shadow of the mama cairn. The figure watching her. Even from far away, she could see a gray lump sitting on the figure's shoulder. Both the figure and the gray lump stony and mute like the landscape. Striker closed her eyes and counted to ten. When she looked again she was all alone on the side of a volcano.

She took a deep breath, grabbed the handle, and pulled, only this time she let go almost immediately. For an instant she felt herself floating weightlessly in a room flooded with frigid water, but just as quickly the door lay open at her feet, the strange hieroglyphic face down in the snow.

She was standing over a hole, the kind fishermen cut in frozen lakes. The hole barely bigger than a person.

"Too bad," said Striker, peering into the earth. "I need a light."

"No you don't," she said. "There's more than enough."

It was true. The hole was filled with the same flickering radiance that churned up from the vent in the hut. There was an inviting quality to it. She sat down on the edge and let her legs dangle in the brilliance.

You really gonna do this?

During childhood, the best part of climbing a tree had been jumping out of it. Just keep moving, she told herself. Nothing can catch up with you if you do. She leaned forward and let gravity do the rest.

The drop was more than six feet but the impact didn't hurt her ankles. As in the cabin, it felt like plunging into a roomful of people, the air dense with presence, the sensation that you weren't alone. She remembered a dog an old boyfriend had rescued from a shelter, how the dog would never step foot in the man's living room. Then one day when chatting with a neighbor, the man had learned that not one but *two* previous renters had shot themselves in the head while watching TV. Ever since then, Striker had always deferred to her sixth sense. But despite what her gut was telling her, she didn't go scrambling back up aboveground.

"They must have been stuck down here for forever," she said loudly as she surveyed the space.

"Yeah, in winter, the cabin probably got *awfully* small awfully fast."

"Totally," she concurred. "Idle hands." She realized she was yelling.

She was standing in a small grotto, the cavern carved in ice and heaped floor to ceiling with trash. Broken crates, chairs, cast-off clothes, things that looked vaguely like S&M harnesses but had probably been used to haul heavy sleds. A wasteland of personal effects. She began to pick her way through. Cracked eyeglasses, single gloves, boots, a sailor's footlocker with someone's name still stamped on the wood. And everywhere protruding in the icy floor was a sea of white lumps. They looked like the beginnings of stalagmites only they had no counterpoints hanging from the ceiling. Striker had to work to keep from stumbling on them. She wondered at the manpower necessary to dig such a space, the grotto a little more than five by ten, the room barely tall enough to stand in.

She could hear something humming like a distant air conditioner. It was probably just that seashell effect again, trapped air circulating in an audible fashion. Or maybe she was hearing the life force of the volcano, hundreds of feet away its heated gases churning.

A set of wooden shelves sparkled with glass jars, a pantheon of inscrutable objects housed within. She could tell the jars had once been labeled but the writing had faded. The place would've made a stunning white elephant room at a county fair. It was easy to imagine. Step right up and pick a jar, any jar, the barker would chant. Open it up and scare yourself silly.

In the corner closest to the trapdoor, four leathery shapes sat stacked like firewood on wobbly andirons, each the size of a large dog. Underneath the stack an oily puddle stained the ice. Striker took a deep breath and poked one of the leathery sacks with her finger. The thing was springy to the touch. She poked it again only harder. A thick yellow ooze leaked out.

It was a seal carcass.

She could barely wrap her head around it. The carcasses were more than a hundred years old, yet the fat was still leaching out of them, a century's worth of oil falling drop by drop. What would happen if someone were to thaw them out and throw them on the barbie? Would the meat become edible?

Her eyes landed on a depression in the ice. The hollow was only a few feet long but perfectly smooth as if something had melted there, the resulting trough blood-red in color. And lying in the middle of it was a misshapen disc like a loaf of bread that had never risen, the object dark and scabrous. Lovely, Striker thought. This hollow was probably the spot where the explorers had butchered animals. The oddity was likely part of a carcass the men had attempted to cure, overly salting it into a revolting mess.

Sickened, she turned toward the entrance and was about to head back up when she noticed it leaning against the far wall. She was surprised by its dimensions. The painting came up to her chin and was a few feet across, its simple frame cobbled together from old boards. The artist had probably used the canvas from the ship's sails. It wasn't like the men had needed it anymore.

Striker studied the scene. As many as forty men stood in front of a ship with its mast splintered like a compound fracture. The ship sat imprisoned in the ice, its decks visibly listing at 50°. You could tell the vessel was on the verge of being crushed. Pieces of ice had already burst through several of the windows. It made for an eerie tableau—the skies a creamy blue, the scene without shadows. Surprisingly the men looked upbeat, faces beaming like they were at the start of a great adventure. A few hoisted their arms in the air as if to say *huzzah!* Cheeks rosy with sun and cold.

He was standing in the back, his presence easy enough to spot as he towered over the rest. Striker's eye fell on him. When she'd gripped the ax and seen the cabin from another's perspective, she had felt herself to be the tallest person in the room, the others barely coming up to her shoulder.

At first she attributed the barrenness of the man's features to the painter's lack of skill. Then she realized he was wearing a mask, his face hidden behind a sheath of leather. He was too far away to see much else, the leather a smooth blank. The most reasonable explanation was that he was simply shielding his face from the wind. Even so, just gazing at him made her shudder.

Striker held out her hand. A soft breeze was blowing through the canvas. It was the source of the sound like a white noise machine. She gripped the painting's frame and pulled. It slid easily. She kept pulling, inching it out of the way, until she uncovered what she was looking for. I knew it, she thought, as it eased into view.

A tunnel gleamed in the icy wall.

Just out of curiosity she got down on her hands and knees and poked her head in. The ice was bright, the air pristine. To go forward she would have to crawl. All that talk about the fear of peering under the bed felt like lifetimes ago. She ran a finger around the entrance, felt ███ *what in the holy hell?*
She was hunched over in a long white tunnel, body surrounded by ice. A vein throbbed in the side of her head. The air smelled of feces. *This is not happening.* It was probably the single worst place in the entire world for Dark Striker to make an appearance. She had no memory of crawling in and no idea how far in she had crawled. Her

shoulders brushed the ceiling. The feeling of dividing by zero began to engulf her, heart on the edge of igniting. She heard the first faint notes of music. The fine hairs on her arms stood up like hackles.

Something else was down there. Something corporeal. She could sense it. Ages ago what had that little towheaded kid from Texas called them?

Shoggoths. Shape-shifters.

God. Why didn't I listen to him?

The tunnel began to narrow. Squeezing her. She imagined it caving in.

All the body's phobias hit her at once. Fear of caskets, fear of closets, fear of airplane cabins, fear of being trapped in an elevator for untold hours, fear of being a hundred feet underwater.

She knew if she could turn around she would see a being emerging from the brightness, the smell of blood flooding the space. It would take a small eternity but eventually a head would appear. When enough of it had been extruded, the thing would grab her foot and pull her toward it.

"Percy?" she whispered.

If she were lucky, it might be harmless like an insect trapped in amber. If she were unlucky, it was a presence hibernating at the bottom of the world until disturbed. If she were damned, the thing would rip her from the pleasant dream she had spent her whole life cocooning herself in, every one of her personal beliefs shredded in an instant.

What if you just stopped pretending?

A hand wormed up through the ice. It wrapped its tiny fingers around her ██████████████████████████████████████
██
██
██
██
██

 back aboveground and running down the volcano. The vein in the side of her head once again throbbing, a tiny supernova in the chaos. Striker didn't question Dark Striker's timing, Dark Striker leading her into the tunnel and then just as suddenly pulling her the hell out. It just felt good to be out in the open. She was beginning to realize it was true. What Ama used to say.

Being awake is overrated.

She was coming around the last bend. The whole way down she hadn't stopped running. She could already hear the commotion among the normal sounds of the island. Up ahead, a dark mound was writhing on the beach. Instantly she felt sick.

A small towel lay nearby. Someone must have left it covering what had once been his face before they went gallivanting off to wherever it was they'd gone. It wasn't enough. Not even close. Just a token of decorum. This place would not react well to half-hearted measures.

Striker couldn't tell his head from his feet. Couldn't see his body. She knew it was in there somewhere under the thrashing cloud.

A human being left out in the Antarctic elements. Exposed. What were they thinking? She began swinging her arms, wildly punching the air. She could see hints of yellow. Mostly she saw blood.

The birds were surprisingly stubborn. Why shouldn't they be? The only law they recognized was the law of the jungle. Animal law. Finders keepers.

"Get out of here!" she yelled.

Even over the roar of a thousand furious wings, she could hear someone kicking their way into the scrum, punting birds off the body. Striker felt one slash her palm. The pain strangely familiar. She punched harder. Where did she begin, where did she end? There was only this angry throng of energy. It was a dance. She kept fighting, driving the skua up into the sky, letting herself be carried by the moment.

Finally the birds were gone. The skua had retreated into the rocks on the edge of the rookery. She could see hundreds of scavengers perched on the hillside. Hooked beaks thirsting for an opening.

Striker approached Alexei's ruined face with the towel. She did her best not to look. Just rise up out of your body. Don't be present. Lay the shabby towel over what may or may not be the remains of a man. A thousand distant eyes are watching. At your feet may be a human body slashed to the bone by talons evolved over thousands of years to tear apart raw flesh. But if you don't actually look, there may be no body at all.

"Lord have mercy," someone said. That same someone was crying. "We can't treat each other like this, we just *can't*."

Striker was too tired to figure out who was weeping.

It was only after she had repelled the birds that she noticed the pile of small, light-colored stones standing out against the darkness of the sand. It wasn't a coincidence in the rocks. It was an arrow pointing to the far end of the beach.

"After you," said Striker. She headed toward where it was aiming.

An elephant seal watched her pass. She was surprised by the wiriness of the hair sparsely riddling its body. The creature was nonplused by the mauling that had taken place only a few feet away. It seemed like the right attitude.

At the end of the shore was another arrow.

"What is this?" she said. "A scavenger hunt?" She followed the arrow's direction, the land growing rocky and then curving out of sight. She didn't have far to walk.

They were still wearing their dry suits. She could see them at a few hundred feet. Each one a floating yolk. It was some kind of thermal spring. A rock pool slightly bigger than a hot tub. There were similar formations spanning the archipelago, the islands volcanic and rocky. Underwater vents scattered throughout the landscape. Striker remembered seeing photos of smiling passengers in the *Yegorov*'s brochure. Tourists in bikinis and swim trunks like they were anywhere but Antarctica.

"Come on in, the water's lovely," called the Baron.

"You guys left Alexei lying on the beach," she said. She could feel her voice growing shrill. There was that word again, but thanks to Kevin, she knew it wasn't always gendered. Her hand was throbbing where the skua had slashed her. She glanced at it. Through her glove the gash was deeper than she'd realized. The fabric sopping wet. The pain still eerily familiar, the wound as if ancient of days. From between some rocks she scooped up what snow she could and squeezed. Pink water dribbled out between her fingers. "Do you know where we are?" she said. "This isn't Club Med. The skua ate his eyes. His *eyes*. You hear me?" She tried to collect herself but she couldn't not see it. The hot mass writhing ecstatically, orgiastic. Small, hot bodies following their deepest hungers, their insatiable drives. "They ate his whole goddam face!"

The winds had picked up. She didn't know if anyone had heard a single thing she'd said. Her words floating uselessly back into land.

The only sound the rush of the waves, the music of the ocean lapping the rocks. An organ playing in the distance without affect or melody.

"What about your eyes now?" said la Grande Dame. The carefree way the old girl bobbed about in the frothy waters. Striker realized she herself was balling her fists.

Anders spoke up. The teen's cheeks flamed red, either from the sun or wind or shame. "We put a towel over his face," they said in a small voice. "We weighted it down with rocks."

"Haven't you noticed? Some of these birds have a ten-foot wingspan," Striker said. "You think a couple of rocks are gonna keep them away from dinner?"

That's when she noticed Vadim sitting in the rock pool. Considering the guy's arms had been a foot longer when they'd arrived on the island, he looked pale but otherwise okay, his arms back to normal, each one floating weightlessly on top of the water.

"And you?" she said to him. She tried to soften her tone. "You good?" She knew she still sounded angry but she couldn't help it. Her hand was throbbing.

"I am very great," he said.

"He's double-jointed," explained Anders, eager to change the subject. "Turns out his joints slip in and out super easy." The kid went on to explain that once Vadim regained consciousness, he just needed a little help sliding them back in. "My mom's a doctor," Anders said.

Striker turned her wrath on Bobbi Sue. The image of Alexei's tattered face—would it ever not be there in her rearview mirror? "A doctor? Why are we only learning this now?"

Bobbi Sue sat upright in the water. She didn't answer, the question not registering on her face. Striker noticed she hadn't loosened the seal around her neck. Because of her seated position, the air in her dry suit had floated up to the top, inflating her chest like some kind of centerfold. Kevin was seated beside her. He seemed as if he'd forgotten all about his wife in the cabin under the ratty blanket and was currently more concerned with keeping his two dry bags afloat.

For the first time since the accident, something inside Striker broke. Sometimes you have to hand over the keys and take the hint. If the day presents you with a hot spring, you say thanks and get your ass in. She climbed into the rock pool and sat down.

It felt good. The blue sky, the balmy water, no sounds of traffic, no people yelling at each other, no screaming kids, no sirens. Everything—the leopard seal, the accident, Alexei with his ripped face—had been leading up to this.

She put up her hood and lay back, let herself float. She thought of Percy, his naked body sliding over hers in the sauna. Was that just last night? The feel of his tongue on her lips, him telling her she tasted like cinnamon. Why not, she thought. Why not float away in the memory of being with Percy in the sauna until the *Yegorov* showed up and carried them back to the show? And if the boat didn't come, if she was destined to be stranded here for the rest of her time on earth, why not wallow in the memory of Percy with his strong arms and his ripped stomach touching her in the dark until the forever sun set?

"We should head up," a voice said. "If we're too hungry, it'll make the climb harder."

Striker sat up and opened her eyes. In the distance she could see something small and yellow standing on a faraway rock. She knew if she peered through Anders' binoculars, she would see Lucy and the gray rat preening itself on her shoulder, the kid and her little gray friend glaring at her or worse, grinning.

"Okay," the voice said. "Let's go."

They brought nothing with them but their dry bags. Striker didn't have much in hers. Some gum, lip balm, a second SD card and battery, plus both her cameras and phone. The nearest signal was likely five hundred miles away transmitting from some rocky crag on the tip of South America. She tried turning on each of her devices one more time but they all remained useless except for the Holga. On her phone, the screen was still frozen with the same time as her watch. 12:14 p.m. Had there been something electromagnetic about the insane winds that had killed Percy? She was glad she'd brought a vintage camera along. She wanted to take a picture of the group trudging toward the volcano single file like a scene straight out of Bergman but she knew she should ration her film. She only had two 24-exposure rolls.

Kevin made the hike with a dry bag hanging from each of his arms. The bags were made of the same vulcanized yellow rubber as their dry suits. Occasionally he would walk off a little ways for some privacy and crack one of them open. Each time he did, Striker thought she saw a light pouring out, his face inexplicably brightening.

Anders unscrewed a paddle, breaking it apart into two separate oars. They handed the Baron and their mom each a half. The Baron held his part with the paddle pointing up, the other end a stick he could lean on when needed. It wasn't great but it was better than nothing. Bobbi Sue dragged her half on the ground. When they reached the foot of the volcano, she gave it to the Baron. The old guy now plodding along with a stick in each hand, an aged king gripping his spears.

Slowly the group made their way up the slope. Striker kept expecting to arrive at the spot where Taylor had fallen, but nothing looked familiar. Back on the beach, she had asked Anders to give them some privacy as she told the other adults what had happened. She couldn't be sure Kevin or the Dame had mentioned it, the Dame because she was a narcissist and it didn't involve her, Kevin because it did. Afterward, Striker wondered if maybe she should have included the teen in the debriefing. Only Vadim showed any interest in the story. He'd given her a thumbs-up the way one might when asked for their opinion on a new recipe you were trying out, but in this context, she wasn't sure what it meant. The Baron had remained uncharacteristically quiet as if even talking about death might bring it on, all the while Bobbi Sue intently scanning the beach for her babies.

And now they were almost to the top without ever seeing the blood trail.

We must be going a different route, Striker thought. Yeah, there's no reason to lead a kid past a murder scene.

Still, if it were up to her, she'd have marched Kevin onto the nearest ice floe and pushed him out to sea. If you were hoping to kill someone, a chance like that—being hundreds of miles away from the nearest police station after a terrible accident with nobody left in charge—came around only once in a lifetime. Lucky duck. Someone like Taylor probably had a Lloyd's of London–level insurance policy plus a stock portfolio that went on for days. The guy had opportunity and motive. Wasn't that all you needed? If she found the time, Striker would hunt down a pen and some paper and write down her impressions. It might be enough to interest the police on multiple continents. After all, there are certain things you shouldn't be able to get away with no matter where you are.

Ain't that the pot calling the kettle black?

Out of the corner of her eye, she spotted a pointy rock smeared with goop. She rushed past the others to check it out, but it was only freshly coated with guano.

Finally there was the mama cairn rising on the lip of the crater, the other formations coming into view.

"Magnificent," said the Baron. "Reminds me of the Bixi at Harvard."

"Is perfect place for human sacrifice," said Vadim brightly.

The spot was just as she'd left it. The small black hut still clung to the side of the volcano, the door flung wide open after she fled in panic. She hadn't mentioned that. About a voice talking to her out of thin air. Also didn't tell the others about the tunnel in the underground room or the tiny fingers sprouting up out of the ice.

Life was complicated enough. She'd simply said there was a grotto of sorts under a trapdoor, a space full of trash and probably inedible food.

Back at the beach they'd decided to abandon what was left of Alexei to the elements seeing as how Mother Nature had already done half the job. Vadim dragged his fellow countryman's body to a distant spot and cut off the rest of his dry suit with an eight-inch utility knife Kevin had whipped out of nowhere. Nobody asked why he had it. It had to be the thing that made his face glow each time he opened his dry bag. Great! As if the idea of getting your brains smashed in with a rock wasn't bad enough. Now they had to worry about their new widower slicing an array of holes in their bodies.

Vadim bowed his head over Alexei before walking away. Only Anders asked if he was all right. The Russian simply grunted and kept moving. The teen turned to Striker and told her about something called a sky burial, which they'd read about in World Civ. The yogis of Tibet butchering a dead body so that the birds of the air might make short shrift of it. Been there, done that, Striker thought, studying the gash in her hand. Wasn't nothing spiritual about it.

Now at the top of the volcano, Kevin was the one to suggest they put Taylor down in the ice room far, far away from the island's feathered friends. Outside the hut, he took a deep breath and threw his shoulders back. Honey, I'm home, Striker imagined him saying as he entered.

"Can I have a second?" he asked. "A moment alone with my wife?"

"Da," said Vadim. "Do what doing needs."

The rest of the group waited outside as Kevin bowed his head and entered.

He's cutting off her finger so he can access her phone, Striker thought.

Almost as soon as he'd gone in, he came back out laughing. He hugged the dry bags closer to his chest. He laughed some more, the pitch rising and rising into the realm of hysteria (that word again). He stood there glued in the doorway, the others peering around him.

Only Striker managed to squeeze past. She walked around and around but it was just the one room. She stopped to gaze down the ragged hole where the hot air hissed forth but the radiance poured out the same as ever, nothing plugging it up.

The ratty blanket lay in a heap. Taylor was gone.

Instinctually Striker made the sign of the cross. She pulled out the little gold necklace hanging around her throat and kissed—

<< it's summer on Zinnia Trace, the full moon a piece of lint caught in the oaks that loom over the houses big as cruise ships. There's Striker and Ama and the other children on Zinnia gathering by the hydrant. What should we play? Red light green light? Kickball? Freeze tag? Two of the boys want to get a game of street hockey going, but the girls say no, soon the lights'll be on and we'll have to go inside plus this time of day the puck's too hard to see. So as usual it's hide and seek, you in? It's what we play every night, every night the neighborhood children disappearing one by one while our mumsies and daddies sit reclining in the den, the living room, the home office, the room with the TV and minibar, our parents with their own rituals for disappearing, tumblers in hand, letting themselves hide in the way adults hide, erasing themselves bit by bit through drink or later when the funny men on TV have gone to bed in sunny California, mummy and daddy erasing themselves through what the nuns at Our Lady call the offices of the flesh, what Evangeline's mummy who phones home to Paris once a month calls la petite mort, the little death, Evangeline's mummy telling her oldest amie in the world that she does not die a little death nearly enough

because Evangeline's daddy is selfish, yes, late night the parents on Zinnia Trace eager to disappear and forget their perfect lives with their perfect families, the Lord their soul to overtake with the deliciousness of forgetting through the body's one bliss until morning when all will arise again in Thee to go forth conquering with Thy flag in hand. Rinse and repeat.

Ama and Striker have lived on Zinnia Trace since the end of June. At the local elementary school this coming fall, there will be no one else like them in the whole building, Sonia Gonzalez the only one even close, Sonia's daddy a hero from Cuba. All the other girls with their long, shiny hair pulled back, tied up like the tails of horses. Same thing at Our Lady of the Annunciation, where Ama and Striker go each Sunday with Doug and Trish and also on Tuesdays for the special classes that teach them when to stand, when to sit, when to join hands and lift them to the sky, what to believe. Each week Ama and Striker living the story of Ruth peering from the alien corn, Ruth on her own in a faraway land. Same on the youth soccer team Ama and Striker will both play on, same in the pool where on Thursday afternoons they will learn to swim. The water the reason why Doug will take the clippers he uses to trim his beard and carefully cut the sisters' braids off, their heads shorn close, two little black lambs. Their old hair ratty and matted because when Mabel got more and more poorly feeling, she didn't have the energy to twist it, then the ravages of Trish and her white lady hairbrush plus the effects of chlorine, in Ama's case, the thirty minutes each week spent just trying to learn to float, Striker taking to it easily, Striker a little rain cloud on top of the water, progressing up the ladder from minnow to fish to flying fish and beyond, at the end of every lesson, Striker racing the boys up and down the lanes, meanwhile Ama by the side of the pool crying in that high-pitched way of hers the adults on Zinnia Trace call *shrieking* about the water being inside her head, taking up all the space, the water sloshing around in her ears, up in her nose, and where is she supposed to live, there's no room left for her until Trish and Doug decide it's not worth the *shrieking*, the therapist agreeing there might be an unknown trauma there, something about water and the face, maybe abuse, it's not in the file but who knows? Striker knows, knows that's just Ama with her funny little original way of being, her sister an open book. If she wants to shriek, she shrieks, why shouldn't she? And so now it's Striker alone at the YMCA on Thursdays, Striker in the locker room with the other shiny little girls like the one who circumspectly asks Striker why her skin is like that, is she dirty, the girl wanting to understand what she has never seen before, skin like soil. That last year with Mabel the apartment in the small brick house growing darker and shabbier, the flowers choked with weeds, the curtains crooked. After the haircuts, Doug's clippers nicking Ama's scalp, the braids lying on the bathroom tile like trash, Doug and Trish pleased with what they've done, so pleased they will start showing *The Wiz* on a continuous loop in the playroom as the therapist recommends, telling the girls they're beautiful, you're beautiful like Dorothy, just look at you and your beautiful head of hair like nobody else on this street in this school at this church in this pool in this town in existence.

But that is yet to come. This is Ama and Striker's first summer on Zinnia Trace, their first weeks in the big yellow house the size of ten barns. Everything new. The way their clothes smell. The ugly foods they eat. How they have to come in when the streetlights turn on. The way the street has lights that stay on all through the night until the sun comes back. The two sisters have never been around so many shiny people who walk like ducks. Who move around believing whatever they touch is important. Their children the same. Little ducks with stiff legs, nothing fluid in their movements, no grace, no pouring yourself back and forth the way the women did where Ama and Striker used to live before Mabel got stiffer and stiffer, Mabel on the floor unmoving. Here the people expect the universe to open for them like the doors to the mall when you step on the black pad. Only the chosen allowed in.

How did Striker end up here?

Oh yeah. Summer nights on Zinnia Trace. Hide and seek. The children circle up, put their feet in. One of the older boys begins the work of counting off, tapping each foot with his finger as he chants:

My mother and your mother were hanging out clothes.
My mother punched your mother right in the nose.
What color blood came out?

The song ends on Striker's foot. She knows it's a trick. All summer long she has watched and listened as these strange children say the strangest things when asked the color of blood. Orange, blue, purple, green. Have they never seen blood on asphalt, Striker thinks, blood on a doorjamb, blood beading on a man's lip, trickling down his chin?

"Red," she says.

R-E-D spells red and you shall be the one.

A small blond girl sighs, whines that she always gets tapped. Are you playing or complaining, the older boy says. The girl sighs one more time and turns her face toward a tree as if kissing it, and begins to count.

One. Two. Three. Four—

"Come on, Ronnie," says Ama, pulling her sister's arm. Ama is eight, Ronnie six. The children scatter like birds. Children like Ama and Ronnie don't live on Zinnia Trace. Until they do. For starters, there's a circle at the end of the street where the road ends, which means you barely need to look out for cars. Ama and Ronnie run and run, searching for the perfect spot. The houses big as entire apartment buildings where Ama and Ronnie used to live, buildings with whole families, the people with hundreds of years among them. Here the houses have three or more garage doors that roll up like blank faces at the push of a button. The yards bigger than the dusty parking lot where Ama and Ronnie used to play, these yards like fields, like what's that word Trish and Doug use to describe the part of the backyard beyond the stream? The meadow. Trish and Doug saying don't go into the meadow. The meadow is off-limits.

Ronnie hopes Ama isn't taking her into the meadow. At night, the meadow with its tall grass, its alien sounds. Ama is crazy enough to hide in the meadow among the unnerving animals the two sisters have never seen before, the rusting car where teen couples come to put their hands all over each other, gaze deep into each other's eyes and pretend they can see themselves there forever. The meadow where Ama ran and hid for an hour after they came home from swimming because the teacher had finally had it and threw her in, the teacher a teenager, a boy with shaggy blond hair who said she was wearing a life vest so nothing too terrible could've happened anyway, and afterward everyone frowning and making Ama feel bad about the *shrieking* instead of the kid, who was smiling when he did it, Ronnie saw, the small smile on his lips as he launched her dark and shrieking sister into the air.

When they find the spot, the smell is bad, real bad, Ronnie's eyes watering from it. Why does she know things her sister doesn't? Like how to hide the unrecognizable food Trish is constantly slopping on their plates. How to stash it in a napkin and then go to the bathroom, flush it down the toilet. That Mabel isn't coming home, that they're not going back to the place they used to live across the street from the pickup store and the Dominican restaurant where the music played in that language that itself sounds like music. They are not going back. This is their life. They still have the green T-shirts from Catholic Charities that they wore to that party and now they live with Doug and Trish. Why does Striker know this and her sister doesn't? Those green T-shirts their tickets to this heaven which will give them everything they never knew they wanted if only they play the game and watch and listen and imitate, merge.

Ama wants to play the game. When she speaks, these people smile, the space between her two front teeth like a permanent wink. But Ama doesn't have the thing Ronnie has. The inner voice that tells her the rules. The one person Ronnie will disregard the rules for is her big sister Ama. Even when Ama is wrong, which she usually is. Even when Ama doesn't understand the game, how it works, how you win, or what you get if you do. Ronnie knows Ama needs her little sister to believe in her and the game inside Ama's head. Where water can displace who you are if too much gets in. Where these people and their bizarre food are something you can beat. You can win. You can. I promise. Ama is determined.

"Climb in," says Ama and points to the ultimate hiding spot. It doesn't look like a place anyone should be. "That's why they never gonna find us," says her sister. Ama is two years older. Ama is always right. The gap between her teeth shining in the dark.

The streetlights come on. The stars shift in the sky. Doug and Trish are walking through the neighborhood full of big, faceless doors calling for them. The panic rising in their voices. Trish with her hair long and tightly permed, her hair that wants to be curly and fun like Mabel's steel-gray hair that she used to tie up in a special hat every night. Trish crying. Neighbors coming out to help. The little girl who was It and stood kissing the tree is also crying because this is her fault. She found everyone else but the two jumble bunny sisters. That's what her father calls them. Jumble bunnies. One bedtime when she asked her mother what the word jumble meant, her mother thought a moment and then said messy, like when things are mixed together and you can't tell them apart. Yeah, that's it, that's the reason why the It girl can't tell one sister from the other. Both of them the same shade of dark, the same ratty braids, teeth flashing like coins, their voices fast and then slow and all over the map when they talk, not straight ahead and clean like everyone else because they're jumbled, the two sisters mixed together, mixed up. The It girl wishes her father would call her a jumble bunny. She likes the word bunny, it sounds like something soft and cute—only when he says it, his voice sounds mean, like he gets when he comes home from a day at court and they know not to laugh too much. Either way, the jumble bunny sisters are missing. Now the It girl will never be It ever again.

Then Ama is telling Ronnie it's part of the game. People calling and calling for them to come out, come out wherever they are. People starting their searches with the area swimming pools, in the dark, the water throwing quivering shadows up in the air. It's a trick. Ronnie staring hopefully at her big sister like the time Mabel was lying on the floor and Ama said she was doing those new exercises like the people do on TV. Ronnie wanting to believe. That they'll win this game, that Mabel will rise up off the floor, that Doug and Trish will love them, everyone will love them, at Baskin-Robbins their cones will be as big as the other kids', there'll be afternoons of miniature golf and invitations to the other children's birthday parties, the other kids' parents not watching them, following them through the house when they have to use the bathroom, the moms careful to put the knife far away from where Ama and Ronnie are sitting after the moms cut the cake.

Later, Ama will say it's a new world record. Nobody has ever gone as long as they did. It's almost midnight by the time they're found. Ronnie knows it's late because when they come home, that man in the jacket is on the TV making people laugh, though Trish is crying, Doug yelling, *shrieking*, yeah, it sounds like shrieking if you ask Ronnie. "Why didn't you come when we called?" Through her tears Trish throwing them in the shower though Ama hates showers, hates the way the water gets in her ears, like a cat, it makes her crazy, the feel of the water where it shouldn't be, get it out! get it out! Trish screaming it's late, we don't have time to fill the bath. Scrubbing and scrubbing the stink out of them. Screaming why would you hide there? Why would you do that? What is wrong with you?

Yes, it's a new world record because it's almost midnight when Mrs. O'Leary spots the two of them in the backyard and scurries inside to tell her husband. "Those two coons are buried up to their necks out back in the compost pile," she says. She puts on a pair of shoes and goes out to find that poor young couple, Trish and Doug, who think love is enough and haven't the foggiest idea of what they've gotten themselves into.

Ama is right. The compost pile is the last place anyone would ever look. Among the coffee grounds and eggshells and cantaloupe rinds and a summer's worth of waste from the O'Learys' two dogs. Nobody will see us in there, says Ama. It's the first rule of hiding, of disappearing off the face of the planet. Go where you blend in. Claim the bit of earth no one else would ever want. Make peace with it. The place people fear. The spot filled with decay, shit, death, oblivion, from which springs the arduous work of rebirth, that's it, that's what's happened here, the body of that young, auburn-haired tech titan who got her head smashed in while with her husband and has now disappeared but nothing truly dies, Ronnie can hear her older sister's voice on the Antarctic wind. Ama saying that lady ain't gone, she's just off somewhere no one will ever look, she's being reborn shiny and new, all of them are changing right before your very eyes, every last one, it's all for their own good, they'll come back like nothing you ain't never seen before, so watch yourself or you will >>

Striker let go of the gold cross around her neck.

The cabin was empty. No Taylor in sight. She walked back outside with nothing but more questions.

They were seven bright yellow lemon drops standing on the lip of a volcano. The Texan and Child, the Baron and the Dame, the Fantastic Plastic Russian, and Everybody Hates Kevin plus her. The group gathered around the fisherman's hole. As always, they were waiting on Striker for answers.

"It's like a million suns are pouring out of there," said Kevin.

"I think the ice is acting like a mirror," she said.

"Okay, but how do you dig a space that big in frozen ground?" he asked. "It's like frigging cement."

"Is ancient crater formed by flying rock," offered Vadim.

"Come again?" said the Baron.

"He means a meteor," said Anders.

"Da, that," said the Russian. "Is full of extraterrestrial crazy-making microbes. Proof is penguin is craziest of birds." Because of his accent, Striker couldn't tell if he was kidding.

"Why is there even a door here?" asked Anders.

"Precisely," said Kevin. "Look around. If you aren't keeping things *out*, then what exactly are you keeping *in*?"

"Good question," said Striker. "You ask me, it was the door to a brig."

"Excellent," crowed the Baron. "We now have ourselves a fully functioning society."

"What's a brig?" yawned the Dame.

"Brig is like jail," said Vadim, matter-of-fact. "It big sucks. No window, no air for fresh breath." He began to kick snow onto the door as if to rebury it. "Brig lowest part of ship. Deep below waterline. If ship springs big leak, brig people never come out. Nobody helps them." He sounded like he'd experienced one firsthand.

"Even on a ship, you need a place to store people who don't play nice," added the Baron.

"*Na zdorovie*," said Vadim, smiling agreeably.

"How do you know where this door came from?" asked Bobbi Sue listlessly. "It could've come from anywhere."

Striker wasn't about to mention her vision of living out exactly what Vadim had just described, the frigid water gripping her lungs. Instead she pointed with her foot. You didn't have to look too hard. The door was tatted up with carvings. Names, dates, groupings of lines, mysterious hieroglyphs, doodles. It was the graffiti of imprisonment. She was just glad the eerie mark that was following her around was hidden on the other side, face down in the snow.

"Check this out," said Anders. They ran a finger over a small etching of a stick figure wielding a crude ax and running after others, one of the figures with lines gushing from its throat.

"Yes yes," said the Baron. "Ancient man was quite the *artiste*." He walked up to the mouth of the hole and peered into the light.

"But the supping hour is upon us," he said. "There was mention that this place might contain vittles." He looked around. "Who wants to go?"

"Do we think my wife's down there?" asked Kevin. His eyes grew big but stayed dull and flat. "Like, she regained consciousness and wandered off?"

Duh, thought Striker. She hadn't even been thinking about food. Taylor had to be down there, right? Hunched over among oodles of junk with the worst headache ever. Nothing else made sense.

"I'll go," said Anders.

"You most certainly will not," said Bobbi Sue.

"Mom."

"No."

"I'm not great in tight spaces," said Striker. "I found that out last time." Thankfully nobody asked for details.

"Fine," said la Grande Dame. "What do we have for light?"

It was obvious she wouldn't need it but Kevin cracked open one of his dry bags. He held it close to his chest as he rummaged around and pulled out a flashlight half the size of a pen. When he turned it on, its beam was dazzling, a light so sharp it could cut steel. He demonstrated. Twist this ring, and you could diffuse the light. He cast the beam on the wooden door, made a wide circle, the circle every bit as bright as the focused beam had been. The flashlight was *high* high-tech. You probably couldn't buy it in any store.

He handed it to the Dame. Nobody remarked on his not volunteering to go. The guy wasn't cut out for it and they all knew it, even the teen. They let him believe that by providing the flashlight, he was doing his part.

"What else you have in magic bag?" Vadim asked. Kevin ignored the question.

"Anyone care to come?" asked the Dame.

"I would, my love," said the Baron, "but you know." He tapped his chest with a finger.

"What?" said Kevin.

"My heart is—" Presumably he was searching for the right word, but it came across as bad theater.

"Fickle," said la Grande Dame.

The Baron didn't fight the description. He simply nodded.

"I will come," said Vadim. "Am very good in *tight space*." The double entendre sailed through the air like a wedding bouquet for anyone desperate enough to catch it.

"What'll you do if you find Taylor?" asked Anders.

Nobody said anything. Were they thinking about what kind of state she'd be in? The chick had already seemed high-strung enough without a traumatic brain injury to boot.

"We'll bring her out," said the Dame. "Of course we wouldn't leave her down there." The Baron saluted her answer. She threw him a withering look, then briskly disappeared into the hole.

Vadim sat down next and got in position. Already his legs had disappeared in the light.

"A question for you," said Striker. "What's *prizrak* mean?"

For a moment his face tensed, like someone crumpling up a piece of paper and then changing their mind and smoothing it back out.

"*Prizrak*? Where you hear?" he said.

She thought of the moment back in the ice field when the very dead Alexei wasn't dead long enough to utter the word before slumping back down into deadness. "Doesn't matter," she said. Instantly she wished she'd asked Vadim the question in private, but what was done was done.

Vadim made sure the zipper was fully up on his dry suit. He smiled wider. That's all he ever seemed to be doing. Every time she snuck a glance, the guy was gazing at the horizon with a maddening grin like someone who had pulled the wool over innumerable sets of eyes.

"*Prizrak*," he said. "Ghost." Then he waved and leaned forward, falling like dead weight straight into the hole. They listened for the sound of his feet hitting the bottom but nothing doing.

"What do we think?" monotoned Bobbi Sue.

"Five minutes tops," said Striker. "There's not a lot to see." She purposefully hadn't mentioned the tunnel in the far wall. Maybe the Dame and Vadim wouldn't notice it. Who knew? It was possible Dark Striker had knocked over a shelf, toppled a pile of crates, the tunnel once again hidden behind a mountain of junk.

"What if they're down there more than five minutes?" asked Anders.

Nobody answered. Not because they didn't want to, but because nobody had any answers.

For once Striker didn't instinctively check her watch. She didn't need a device to tell her more than five minutes had passed even if the sun said otherwise. Had the others noticed how the day had stopped, their shadows never growing any longer? It was unsettling. At the actual pole it must feel like walking outside time, Striker thought. Every moment the same, the light never changing. It made for an interesting thought experiment. In a world without time could you ever make a mistake? Could you harbor regrets? Without time was it even possible to have a childhood?

Her butt was numb from sitting in the snow. If only there were a hot spring nearby. She could pretend she was Swedish and shuttle back and forth between the elements. Temperature stress was supposed to be good for the heart. What about regular stress, she thought. The past several hours had put all their hearts through the wringer. That old saying was wrong, the one about what doesn't kill you makes you stronger. From what she'd seen, what doesn't kill you, doesn't kill you. Maybe next time it would.

Bobbi Sue and the Baron had disappeared inside the cabin. Somehow Bobbi Sue was starting to go even bluer in the lips, the Baron not much better. Striker shielded her eyes as she peered into the hole. Was it just her imagination or was the damn thing getting brighter?

"You hear that?"

"It's my stomach," said Anders sheepishly.

"Oh." She relaxed and went back to thinking about that first summer with Trish and Doug. There were nights she'd wanted nothing more than to be gone, hoping Zinnia Trace was something you could rub from your eyes like sleep. Ama was never able to navigate that alien world. It's not that hard, Striker would say. Just do what they do. It was such a long time ago and yet it remained baked into everything she did, the way she moved and talked, Zinnia Trace forever staining her mind. Like her use of the word *shizer*. It was the expletive her *opa* used to say, Doug's father from Bavaria. The old man cursing at the dinner table and Trish and Doug letting him get away with it because it was in German.

Truthfully she didn't remember much about the days *before* Zinnia Trace. Her old life was mostly a blank. Therapists said it was due to her young age and the candyland quality of the new existence she'd been dropped into, everything shiny and bright. The only image Striker could remember of Mabel was her grandmother slumped in the ratty old chair with her feet soaking in a dented bucket, how each night Ama told her their grandmother was part mermaid and needed to regrow parts of herself. As an adult, that was what Striker resented the most, the fact that all she had left of the world she was born into was a vision of a beat-up bucket. It was an old story, possibly the oldest. People wanting to know where they came from. On ancestry.com, Black people had to work twice as hard for the smallest scraps. Losing your autonomy often resulted in losing your history. Striker often wondered who she and Ama had been in the *before* place, if they'd had radically different personalities, been on track to become completely different people.

Something fluttered down out of the sky. Gracefully it landed on the hatch. The bird waddled over to the lip of the hole. It peered down into the light as if gauging the situation. Finally it looked up at Striker, its missing eye red like a sore.

"Agreed," she said, getting off the ground and stretching her limbs. "Time to get off our butts." She rummaged through her options. Let's be real. Bobbi Sue was never going to let Anders go. Bobbi Sue and her Wandering Uterus couldn't be trusted. The Baron was pretty much worse than useless. Kevin? She had no idea what made that guy tick.

The math wasn't in her favor. There was no one else to go. Two people, maybe three, were wandering around beneath her feet, and despite what her watch said, time wasn't stopping for any of them. Honestly, going down into the hole to find the Dame and Vadim was nothing compared to what she'd already lived through. The hardest stuff was behind her. Coming-of-age on Zinnia Trace. Keeping an eye on Ama. The thing in the tiny room under the stairs that she couldn't bring herself to recall. The smell of rotten food. Someone playing Christmas music on an organ.

"I'm gonna need a rope," she said, and headed into the hut to wrangle one up.

The Baron lay on one of the beds, Bobbi Sue squatting by the vent over a pot heaped with snow. They had both taken off their dry suits. Like some kind of zombie, Bobbi Sue sat stirring and stirring, the expression on her face one of profound emptiness. At least someone had wiped the guano up off the floor.

Striker found a length of rope hanging from a hook. It was in remarkably good condition, the rope still coated with wax. "I'm headed down to have a look," she said.

"Some things are best left alone," said the Baron. He shifted around like a dog trying to wear a depression in grass, the bedstand creaking. "My wife ain't no babe in the woods," he added. "And neither is the Russian." He rolled over and stared at Striker. Why were people constantly *staring* at her? There was a gleam in his eyes. "Think of it this way," he said. "Could be those two need a little *privacy*." He winked. "Not unlike what happened in the sauna between you and the human formerly known as Percy."

Striker stepped back as if she'd been shoved. She glanced over to see if Bobbi Sue was shocked by his insinuation, but the Baron's observation didn't seem to register with her. She remained stuck on autopilot, the sound of her spoon mindlessly circling the pot. The Baron had already turned back toward the wall (or had he never rolled over in the first place?). Striker was left clenching the rope, pulling it tight between her fists, with each tug unleashing a small snapping sound.

"If I'm not back in fifteen, close the hatch and put a weight on it," she said though she wasn't sure who she was talking to.

"I didn't catch that," said Bobbi Sue, finally looking up from her pot a whole lifetime after Striker walked out the door.

"If I tug three times, start pulling nice and easy," said Striker, wrapping the rope around her waist and then cinching it to one of the belt loops on her dry suit. "If I tug more than that, pull like hell."

"Got it," said Anders. The kid was a rock, someone she could count on. Kevin, while the owner of a bottomless bag of wonders, wasn't the person she wanted in charge of the rope her very existence dangled from. Should worse come to worst, she trusted Anders to feel the tugs and get it right.

"I still don't understand why we're outfitting you for war," said Kevin. "Didn't you say the space is the size of a pantry?" He shook his head but nevertheless pulled out a long silver tube. A small smile warped his face. He demonstrated how, like an x-acto knife, if you pressed down and slid the button, bit by bit a blade nosed out. Fully extended it was longer than her hand. It was a different knife than the one he'd lent Vadim to cut poor shredded Alexei out of his dry suit. How many knives had the guy packed? This one gleamed in the sunlight, its edge surgical in its precision. "It's self-sharpening," Kevin bragged. "Each time you deploy and retract it, the casing whets the blade."

"Yikes," said Anders.

"Yeah," said Striker. "What made you think you needed that down here?"

"You want it or not?" he said.

She held out her hand.

"They probably just got turned around," said Anders.

"In a *pantry*?" exclaimed Kevin.

Striker sat down on the ice, her feet dangling in the hole like bait. She took a deep breath. "Probably," she lied. "There's a lotta junk down there. Maybe one of them got caught on something." She imagined Vadim sniffing out the source of the hum coming from behind the painting. He was definitely the type to take a peek, the Dame rolling her eyes while he disappeared into the wall. Eventually the old girl would go in after him if only so she could hold it over his head later, yet another story added to her repertoire about the time she'd saved a man's hairy ass from himself.

As she sat on the lip of the hole, Striker could already feel her heart starting to complain. Fucking *shizer*. She took another deep breath, tried to rally her body and mind around what needed doing, but the two weren't jiving. In all honesty, they'd always had a tenuous relationship.

"Are you seaworthy? Can you harbor the lot of us?"

Striker jumped, startled.

It was the voice of the starving young man she'd seen reflected in the window.

"Hurry," he whispered, voice raw as if from weeping.

Striker slid into the hole like a deep-sea diver plunging into a whole other dimension.

Once again she was standing under the trapdoor. Who could say how much time had passed since the first go-round? She glanced back up and took a mental photograph of the pale blue sky. In a few hours it would be midnight, yet the heavens would stay the same shade of day. Anders peered over the edge, shielding their eyes. Striker flashed the teen a thumbs-up though she knew the kid couldn't see it.

"Back in a jiffy," she called, giving the rope a tug.

Just as she'd feared, the grotto was empty. The same glass jars glowed on the shelves, the seal carcasses still dripping oil. Striker tried not to look, but her eyes snagged on the shriveled disc sitting in the bloody hollow, the crusty mass foul yet fascinating.

The painting lay face up on the ice. She hadn't remembered the ship listing at such an angle. It was practically lying on its side, everywhere sheets of ice bursting through its decks. Among the crew, only one man held his arms triumphantly up in the air. The others looked worn and resigned, suspicion clouding their faces.

A towering figure stood front and center, the man's face obscured by a leather mask. Where his mouth should be were two yellow teeth, a patchy beard stubbling his chin. Striker shuddered. What kind of deformity could he be hiding? Or was it something else? The man looked monstrous, his presence a hole in the center of the painting. Darkness poured out of the eye slits. An ax rested on his shoulder.

Striker bent over and peered inside the tunnel. The cool breeze felt cleansing. She should have warned the Dame and Vadim. If they had known, maybe they could have resisted. *Coulda shoulda woulda.* She got down on her hands and knees. Piece of cake, she thought. I'm halfway there.

A few feet in, the walls gleamed a milky blue. Ice on ice on ice. Ice all the way down. She tapped a spot with her knuckles. It was harder than concrete. Kevin was right. How had stranded explorers carved this passageway? It would've taken years and the very best equipment. Drills tipped with diamonds. One of the naturalists onboard the *Yegorov* had mentioned that millions of years ago during the Mesozoic, Antarctica had been tropical with ferns and palm trees and colorful fish. But that was geologic eons ago.

"Guys?" Striker called out. Nobody answered. Her voice ricocheted through the tight space, a boomerang thumping her hard in the solar plexus. Even on her hands and knees, she had to hunch.

Up ahead she could see where the tunnel unexpectedly widened. Everywhere the sound of glass tinkling. Quickly she shuffled ahead on all fours. When she reached the opening, she skidded to a halt.

The ceiling was riddled with icicles. It was like looking up into a forest of chandeliers, their tips sharp enough to pierce metal. Down the length of each shaft, the ice had crystalized, creating beautiful patterns like undersea coral. In the light the icicles flashed a deep indigo. It meant they were old, ancient of days. The sound of their chiming the very fabric of time itself. She could hear them rattling in the air flow. Too much movement too fast, even the quivering of her heart, and one could come crashing down through the center of her skull.

Striker thought of St. Teresa, the Spanish mystic. It was confounding what she could recall from Zinnia Trace. The nuns at Our Lady always referring to the saint with a dreaminess in their eyes. The saint said to have been lanced over and over with a golden spear by the archangel himself, the pain so sweet it made her moan. Striker surprised herself by remembering the word the class had learned for what had happened to St. Teresa. Transverberation. To be run clean through with God's love. For a full week after class, her sister Ama had walked around claiming she was being transverberated anytime she hurt herself. Ama dramatically clutching her chest after skinning her knee and crying *I'm being perfected*, then asking for a hug.

If one of the icicles should fall, would there be that same sweetness for Striker? A sword of ice delivering a pain so inexorable that like the saint it would make her spasm, her body forever impaled to this spot like a butterfly pinned under glass. The sudden, terrible knowledge of God. The subsequent ecstasy. Part of her couldn't help but long for it.

On the other hand, if she turned around now she could tell the others whatever she wanted. That part of the grotto had caved in or that Vadim and the Dame had eaten something poisonous from one of the jars. Nothing was stopping her from being that person.

Typical.

Look what I'm up against. Some of the icicles were several feet in length. Even if she wanted to slip underneath the canopy of spikes, she'd have to get down on her stomach. She'd be forced to inch herself along. What if she got stuck? Her body heat melting the ice just enough to slick the surface and form a fluid skin the thickness of an eyelash, then in almost the same instant the watery layer refreezing but with her stuck in it. Wasn't that how ice skates worked—the pressure of the blade melting the surface just enough for movement. Only in her case she wouldn't be moving fast enough not to get trapped. If it happened, she would die. Her body perfectly preserved. The tattoo of Polaris on her lower back eternally pointing north. Ten thousand years in the future, the descendants who survived sea rise would find her floating in a watery nest, her dry suit long since disintegrated. Nothing left but a mass of bones and grinning teeth in a place once rumored to have been frozen solid.

Her knee came down hard on a frozen lump. The air suddenly smelled like a cesspool. Something was coming up behind her. She could feel its breath on her feet. Her throat swelled as if packed with bread. This time it would be a child, the one who had died in the *Yegorov*'s plunge pool two seasons back, the child's face bloated from drowning.

Striker closed her eyes. Tried to conjure up the blue sky, Anders peering over the edge. Summer nights on Zinnia Trace, the face of the full moon from Ama's bedroom window.

Our Father who ain't in heaven.

The ceiling began to rumble as though an elevated train were passing overhead. Tens of hundreds of thousands of icicles shivering.

Come, Lord Jesus, bury us in ice. Forgive us our sins, as we never forget those who trespass against us.

After four decades on earth, Striker gives herself over to the old ways. Holding her hands up in the air the way she and Ama used to do in Catholic mass at the moment the priest consecrated the Eucharist. Two little Black girls in a sea of white. Hands held high as if under arrest. Hands held higher in ecstasy. Amen. Everywhere icy blue needles pouring down, the sound like frozen rain shattering the ▮▮ as someone was calling her name.

Striker opened her eyes to pitch black. She couldn't even see her hands. She ran her fingers over the rough sides of whatever was confining her, the space barely bigger than a closet. The gritty walls felt strangely abstract, undulating like a giant paramecium. *This definitely ain't ice.* A uniform heat filled the darkness. Had the others finally gone and done it, throwing her in the brig?

The reality sank in. She was thousands of miles from anyone who might come running, anyone who cared. If she were being honest, did she even have people like that in her life? So many bridges burned. Too many times she'd slammed a hand up in someone's face. I hate cages, she told every new therapist. I just wanna be free. Careful what you wish for, honey, one of them had said.

"You ready to come out?" said the voice.

"I promise I'll be good," Striker answered.

"What was that?"

Someone was pulling on a section of the stony wall. A piece of it popped out. Striker stuck her head through the hole and breathed in the fresh air. Her poor eyes! The light was blinding.

Anders stared at her suspiciously. They were holding a leather-bound journal, their finger marking their place in it. Nearby, a wooden stool sat low in the snow.

"You sure you're okay?" they said.

Striker began wriggling her way out. It was slow going. "Why wouldn't I be?" she asked.

The teen considered the question. They chose their words carefully. "Jane and Vadim said you collapsed a few feet from the entrance. That you were just sitting there." Pause. "Staring at some painting."

"Me?"

"Like, catatonic." The teen sat down on the stool and pointed at her wrist. "We found your medical alert bracelet. My mom said that medication's nothing to sneeze at, that it's for schizo—"

"I take Clozapine off-label for migraines," she said. "But yeah. It has other uses."

"My mom said coming off Clozapine cold turkey—"

"I'm good. Let's drop it."

"Whatever," said Anders. "You just seem a little wobbly."

"And why were they even down there so long?"

"Inventory. Jane said they were figuring out what was what."

Striker felt annoyed that it made sense. She pulled her legs out one at a time and stood up before stepping back to study the massive rock formation she'd just crawled out of, the rock dark and shaped like a limbless person. A few hundred feet away she could see the hut perched in the shadow of the giant cairns.

"What *is* this?"

Anders lowered what they were reading. They spoke slowly as if talking to someone who didn't speak English. "Again, it's a fumarole tower. They form when the ground gets super hot and the steam comes shooting straight up through the dirt." The kid shifted uncomfortably on the stool. There was something of the academic about them. "I guess most fumarole towers go cold after they form, but some stay warm. It's like Mother Nature's sauna."

"How do you *know* all this stuff?"

"Didn't you go to any of the onboard talks?" The teen sighed. "Guess you didn't have parents dragging you to that stuff."

"I was there," Striker said. "Probably should've taken notes."

"My mom won't let me go in," said Anders, nodding at the structure. "She's worried it might collapse." The teen traced a circle in the snow with their foot. "I told her the explorers probably used it a hundred years ago and the thing's still standing, but right now I really gotta do what she says."

The kid didn't need to explain. Anders was all Bobbi Sue had left.

"That's a good plan," said Striker. "Everything's gonna be okay." She didn't know why she'd added this. Even as she was saying it, it sounded false.

Anders graciously nodded, accepting the platitude. "Everybody else has been in except Kevin. He said it looks like a human oven."

"By the way, I knew that, about this tower and shit," said Striker, lying. "I just got a little fuzzy from the heat and not eating."

"But we *did* eat, granted it was mostly broth," said Anders. "You should probably drink some more."

The ocean was the same cloudless blue as the sky, white bergs floating past like drops of time. The sun felt hot on her face. It was crazy. This was Christmas Eve in Antarctica. The air had to be in the upper fifties.

"You're right. Maybe I should." She was turning to head for the hut when it came floating in on the wind. The same sound as always.

A newborn baby was crying somewhere out in the wilderness, its cries accompanied by a church organ. Then the winds shifted and the sound deepened. Striker realized it wasn't the same keening she often heard playing in her head. This was real.

It was the sound of a person, an adult in distress crying for help.

"You hear that?" she whispered.

"Hear what?" Anders said. They had folded up the stool and started back with her toward the shelter.

"It sounds like someone—who's not here?"

"Jane and Vadim headed down to the beach. My mom and Kevin are puttering around the cabin. Robert's asleep." This last part was barely audible. "Honestly I'm not sure he's okay. Aren't most old people on lots of meds?"

"Jane and Vadim went to the beach?" Striker said. She almost laughed. It sounded like a euphemism for something naughty. Like her night with Percy in the sauna by the plunge pool only feet away from where a child had drowned.

"Why's it matter where they went?" asked Anders.

If I had a kid, would they be like you, Striker wondered. There was actually a lot she liked about this new generation. Collectively they didn't know it but they were going to be okay.

"It's just good to know where folks are," she said.

"No, I get it," said Anders. "It's not like we have a group chat going."

The two walked on in silence though she could tell there was something else on the teen's mind. A handful of gentoo penguins ambled by, headed in the direction of the fumarole tower. What the hell, Striker thought. The birds seemed like they were out on a casual hike, a group of friends out mountaineering for the day. Anders must have had the same thought.

"You have a big friend group?" they asked.

"Me?" said Striker, caught off guard. "I'd say it's about right."

The teen gave a slow nod. "Have any *white* friends?"

Ah, there it was.

Toward the end of their girls' night out, Striker recalled Riley telling the whole table that the reason Casey and Scarlett liked to hang out with them was because chilling with Black people made white girls look liberal. A few of the other women groaned, but Riley dug in.

"Seriously, who remembers back on Match.com when you could type in your racial preferences?" There were slow nods around the table, people unwilling to fully commit as they were unsure where this was headed. "Remember how many dudes checked that they were down to date every race *except* Black?"

"What's that got to do with this?" someone asked, subtly gesturing in Scarlett and Casey's direction.

"All I'm saying is two kinds of dudes checked *yes* to dating Black girls," said Riley. "The ones hoping for some freaky, down-home jungle fever, and the ones who wanted to look woke." She tipped her drink back but the glass was already empty. "Like on Facebook when the whole world started posting those dumb-as-fuck black squares. Let's face it. Virtue signaling is the new black. Amirite?" The table started to clear as people began asking for their checks. "What? Too soon?" said Riley. She glanced over at Striker and winked, raising the empty—

The penguins were already out of view. Lucky them. Striker tried to imagine what it would be like to have a group of besties who were incapable of speech. It probably made climbing a volcano with no discernible knees a lot easier.

"Yeah, I have plenty of white friends," she said.

"Like, *too* many?" Anders asked. They were almost to the cabin. "Forget it," they said. "I'm just being dumb."

"Forget what?"

The kid gazed off down the volcano. "Just sometimes I feel like I'm weighing them down. Like, I'll never *get* what it's like to be Black—how could I? So maybe they'd be better off, you know." The teen stopped and tried to smile.

Shizer, thought Striker. "Why would your friends be better off without you?"

They had arrived at the cabin. Anders knocked the snow off the bottom of their feet. "Because how can I ever apologize *enough*?"

Striker decided the fastest way to end this conversation was to bunt. "You know what my motto is?" she said. "Cut yourself some slack."

The teen sighed. "That's what my SAT coach always says." Anders pulled the door open. "Seriously. I will if you will."

Good advice is good advice, thought Striker, but as she walked into the cabin, she couldn't think of a single instance when she herself had taken it.

On one of the iron bedstands, a lone figure huddled under a blanket. Either that or someone had heaped a pile of junk on the mattress and covered it up with a quilt. Just kidding! She could tell from the lumpy shape it was the Baron. His old-man body rife with ridges and hillocks.

Two hammocks were gently swaying in the breeze blowing in through the grimy windows. "Guess my mom and Kevin must be napping," Anders whispered.

Striker couldn't blame them. It felt like good sleeping weather. She wondered if the air from the vent was stable. Did it ever fluctuate? Could it unexpectedly shoot up a burst of steam like Old Faithful, a shot of superheated vapor cooking them to death in their hammocks like lobsters in the shell? She unzipped her dry suit and wriggled out of it before peeling off her gloves.

What the hell?

The skin of her palm was completely smooth, interrupted only by a long, shiny scar in the center of it, her hand totally healed as if some hungry bird hadn't slashed it.

Anders didn't seem to notice. Maybe the teen didn't remember Striker complaining about her injury back at the rock pool. Instead, the kid pointed to a series of pots lining the floor by the vent. "The meat's inedible," they said, "but the broth ain't bad, just super salty."

Striker walked over and took the lid off one. "Remind me what this is."

"I dunno. Maybe seal?" The teen pulled a dark wad out of the broth, popped it in their mouth. "You can totally chew on it," they said. "Chewing makes you feel full. My mom says you *could* swallow it if you want to, but it might make your stomach hurt."

Striker stared into the pot. Something about the color of the water, the way it absorbed the light, told her it was nothing she wanted any part of. Still, beggars couldn't be choosey. She fished out a small piece and laid it on her palm. Once on location in Africa, she had eaten all kinds of meat including zebra, even giraffe. How was this any different? She slipped it in her mouth and started to—

<< the unearthly screams of some dying animal fill Striker's ears. The small ax raining down blow after blow as the creature tries to twist away. All she can see is blood fountaining in the cold. The thing screaming >>

She swallowed hard. The meat got stuck in her throat, but she swallowed again and the vision disappeared. "Where'd this come from?" she said, putting the lid back on.

"What do you mean? You guys found it down there. In the grotto." Anders tossed the journal they'd been reading on a pile of books and picked up another. "You're not okay," they whispered.

I've never been okay, Striker thought. "Anything interesting?"

"Just journals. Logs. Whoever was here kept track of everything." Anders flashed the book at her, the pages filled with columns and figures. "I can't tell the exact number, but a lot of people wintered in this spot. And they were here, like, for forever."

Striker pictured the icicles she'd seen down in the tunnel. Each one a dark indigo, the color of time.

"Some of this stuff makes zero sense," said Anders.

The teen handed her two journals. She flipped through the first. The script was tight but the language was definitely foreign.

> *Agus chaidh an còrr a mharbhadh leis a' chlaidheamh a tha a' tighinn amach à beul an fhir a tha na shuidhe air an each. Agus chaidh an eunlaith gu lèir a shàsachadh leis an fheòil aca.*

The second was more unsettling. In the same neat script:

RÌGH NAN RÌGHREAN AGUS TIGHEARNA NAN TIGHEARNAN.
RÌGH NAN RÌGHREAN AGUS TIGHEARNA NAN TIGHEARNAN.
RÌGH NAN RÌGHREAN AGUS TIGHEARNA NAN TIGHEARNAN.
RÌGH NAN RÌGHREAN AGUS TIGHEARNA NAN TIGHEARNAN.
RÌGH NAN RÌGHREAN AGUS TIGHEARNA NAN TIGHEARNAN.
RÌGH NAN RÌGHREAN AGUS TIGHEARNA NAN TIGHEARNAN.
RÌGH NAN RÌGHREAN AGUS TIGHEARNA NAN TIGHEARNAN.
RÌGH NAN RÌGHREAN AGUS TIGHEARNA NAN TIGHEARNAN.
RÌGH NAN RÌGHREAN AGUS TIGHEARNA NAN TIGHEARNAN.
RÌGH NAN RÌGHREAN AGUS TIGHEARNA NAN TIGHEARNAN.
RÌGH NAN RÌGHREAN AGUS TIGHEARNA NAN TIGHEARNAN.
RÌGH NAN RÌGHREAN AGUS TIGHEARNA NAN TIGHEARNAN.
RÌGH NAN RÌGHREAN AGUS TIGHEARNA NAN TIGHEARNAN.

It went on and on, page after page filled with the same one line.

Striker gave the book back. "Guess somebody had a lot of time on their hands."

"I think some weird stuff went on down here," the teen said. "You see that creepy mask?" They pointed to the basket where Bobbi Sue had tossed it.

"It was probably just for sun protection," said Striker.

"Someone wrote in his journal that there was a religious nut among the crew," Anders said. "Supposedly the guy wore it as some kind of penance. You ask me, it's very Hawthorne-esque."

Striker didn't bite. "Live and let live."

It probably wasn't the response the kid had been hoping for, but they shrugged and moved on. "Tell me when you're ready to go," they said.

"Ready to go where?"

"I'm not dumb," said the teen.

"Keep your voice down," said Striker. "I never said you were."

"You think someone's in trouble."

"Someone's *always* in trouble. *I'll* be in trouble if you come."

"What if you need help?"

"What would your mom say?"

"Long as we aren't headed down the hole, it's cool," said the teen. "Plus my mom's harmless. My *dad* was the one—"

Striker could feel the sudden sadness well up in the teen. It was a small room. They were practically crawling over each other. It wasn't hard to sense. She felt the teen push the emotion down and stamp on it like putting out the last embers of a fire.

Anders went over to the shelves and dug through a basket. They found what they were looking for and handed it to Striker.

"It's what the early explorers wore. You can still read the Burberry label," they said. "It's made out of canvas. You gotta wear it over other clothes to stay warm, but it'll be easier to move around in than the dry suit."

Striker slipped the Burberry on over her fleece. It was filthy, smudged with countless hundred-year-old stains. The air outside was heating up, a Christmas miracle. She could probably do without it, but better safe than sorry.

"I'm serious, you're *not* coming."

Anders ignored her as they continued getting ready. They slipped a hand into the dry bag attached to the low-riding hammock where Kevin was sleeping, the bottom of it practically skimming the floor, and pulled out the stainless steel knife. "Think we'll need this?" they whispered.

Striker noticed another bag locked to the empty bedstand with a bungee cable. God, Kevin was such a freak. Either that, or he really had something in there he didn't want folks to know about.

"At the very least, leave a note," she said, not answering the teen's question. "This place have any hundred-year-old pens lying around?"

"Plenty but the ink's dried up," said Anders. They tore a piece of paper out of one of the logbooks. "Don't worry, we also got pencils." They scribbled something down and left it on the table, then kept the scrap from blowing around with a rock.

Striker glanced at the note.

Gone fishing.

The kid wasn't wrong. In a place like this, who knew what they might catch?

Then she noticed the rock Anders had used for a paperweight. The rock an unearthly blue-red color that seemed to glow. She knew if she flipped it over, she'd find the eerie carving on the other side, the lines measured and exact in a way that made her shiver.

On her way out the door, Striker could feel her heart beating in her palm even though her hand was completely healed. Unlike St. Teresa, her flesh had been pierced by a winged creature but the wound hadn't brought her heart any peace. No transverberation in sight. Just an endless, unmoving wall of time and no sign of the *Yegorov*.

The hatch lay gaping open on the snow. To Striker it looked like a beam of light was shooting straight up out of the hole. Maybe it's some kind of beacon, she thought. It reminded her of one of those klieg lights you sometimes see at a car dealership, the lights flashing up into the sky to attract buyers. If it *was* a beacon, it wasn't meant to summon anyone she knew.

She reached down to close it up, then thought better of touching it. "Could you gimme a hand with this?"

"How do we know Jane and Vadim aren't down there?" asked Anders.

"Doing what?" She pictured her night with Percy in the dark of the sauna.

"I dunno. Scavenging around for more stuff?"

"I thought you said they went back to the boats."

"I did, but I don't know that for a *fact*," said the teen.

God, these people! It was like herding cats. She could hear Taylor the Tech Titan in her helium voice prattling on about *cooperation*. Chick hadn't been wrong. If you wanted to survive, you had to be willing to lean on people. Thing is, there had to be people worth leaning on.

"Get a load of that." Anders nodded at the cabin's roof.

Striker looked up. Jesus. How many scavengers fit on the roof of your only shelter waiting for you to die? Judging from the look of things, it was probably the same answer as the number of angels that fit on the head of a pin.

Infinite.

The roof was carpeted with birds. You couldn't see the wood, the whole roof rippling with wings. Everywhere scavengers of various sizes and colors sat roosting.

"Dark, huh?" said Anders.

Fear purred up Striker's spine. Didn't these beasties know there was a whole colony full of fat, juicy, defenseless penguin chicks just down the road? It wasn't the sight of hundreds of scavengers massed in one place that set her on edge. It was their otherworldly patience. Some of them groomed their feathers, others raked their talons on the wood, the birds collectively twisting their heads anytime she or

Anders did anything of interest. It reminded Striker of Lucy. The little girl with the stony face taking in whatever you'd done without comment or concern. Yeah, the silence was the worst part. When the universe watches without uttering a single word, you can feel your own self-judgement rising. Nothing it says could ever be as damning as what you yourself already think.

A bird fluttered down off the roof and landed on the hatch. The red hole where one of its eyes should be was puckered tight like a sphincter.

"Let's go," said Striker.

"Just a sec." Anders rushed back into the hut and reappeared with a pair of walking sticks. They passed one to her.

What did the Irish call them?

A shillelagh. She hefted it in her hand. She could feel where the wood thinned from being held. The sticks had probably come from across the sea, maybe from some county in Ireland. She was glad to have it. Once on location in Dublin, she had learned from a costumer that a shillelagh was both a cane and a weapon. She ran her thumb along a dent deep in—

<< Striker is stealing through the dark. The cairns towering all around her in various states of construction. She moves soundlessly, the howling wind masking the noise of her legs plowing through the waist-deep snow. A crescent moon hangs just above the horizon, the moon's yellow light reflecting off every surface. It comes to her that this could be midday, 12:14 p.m., that this is what noon looks like in deepest winter. The cold in her lungs is like nothing she has ever felt, the edges of a million knives stabbing her every breath. Something clings to her face like a second skin, frost forming around the eye and nose slits. Both her own true beard and the ginger beard of her second face softly tinkle as she moves, hair matted with ice. She turns in the direction of the wind and spits, releasing the pus that collects on her tongue as she can never shake the terrible taste of her own teeth slowly rotting in her mouth.

Someone is whispering.

"Please sir," says a hoarse voice. "Wouldn't it be more fitting if we just interred him in the chamber?"

Striker tests the weight of the shillelagh in her hand. Up ahead a hooded figure stands alone beside the tallest cairn as he looks out to sea. "Sayin's 21:15," she quietly tells her companion. "Whaen justice is done, lad, it brings bonnie joy tae the righteous."

"But he's the captain," murmurs the hoarse voice.

"Bide quiet noo an' watch while God is served."

Suddenly Striker rushes out of the shadows. In the final moment her victim turns. Hurriedly he searches the mask before finding her true eye hidden in the leather. "May whatever devil you serve have mercy on your soul," the man proclaims as she swings the walking stick through the dark and cracks it into the side of his >>

Striker pointed the shillelagh at the one-eyed bird.

"Bang," she whispered.

The bird stayed put, but on the roof the mass of its compatriots took off into the air, a great cloud of feathers shrieking uncontrollably. The downdraft from their wings like standing under a helicopter.

"I dunno," shouted Anders over the noise, "but maybe let's try not to piss 'em off."

"You think this is some normal everyday island?" yelled Striker. "You think those are regular-ass birds?"

When Anders didn't answer, Striker couldn't tell if it was because of the storm of wings or because she hadn't asked the question. Actually, it wasn't important what this kid thought. She knew the score.

They decided to walk down the volcano in the opposite direction from the beach. It was a gentler walk, the slope more gradual. This was the side of the island that took the wind. The landscape was less rocky. The remaining snow had been blown into exposed crevices, much of it melted. Everywhere the ground was shrouded with a shimmering mist. The island lay under a blanket of smoke, the unseasonable heat causing what snow there was to sublimate, move from a solid to a gas without ever becoming water. It was beautiful. The air not exactly foggy but shimmering.

"Is this where your noise is coming from?" asked Anders.

"Yeah," Striker lied. How else to explain it? The crying goes with me, kid. Wherever I go, it goes. And sometimes, if I'm *really* unlucky, it brings bad things with it.

Like last Christmas.

The four of them were skating at Rockefeller Center. Her and Riley and Riley's then boyfriend Dante and the dentist Striker was pretending she was serious with. The Christmas tree twinkling bright. The past few years her anti-migraine meds had been working wonders. Before them, the holidays had been a season when time itself became unstable, the days around her birthday ragged with holes where her mind went blank, Dark Striker walking the earth for hours. Afterward, Striker trying to piece together what had happened while the lights were out.

When the organ music started up at Rockefeller Center, Striker didn't flinch. That time of year there was an *actual* calliope up on street level, the instrument on wheels like the kind drawn by horses in the circus, its brass pipes tooting some Christmas song, the steam shooting up into the air.

It was late, almost midnight, people starting to pack it in. Striker was flying over the ice. The dentist reached for her. He was clumsy on skates, jerking himself around the rink as he tried to stay upright and not appear silly. Striker heard the first notes of "Silent Night" hissing from the dark pipes of the calliope. Suddenly the night winnowed itself down to a windowless room. The smell of rot coated her skin. The sound of heavy feet clomping overhead. Her throat swelling as if she were falling into shock.

Even now Striker shudders when she thinks of the little girl out on the ice with her parents. All night she had skated past her, each time the child smiling, the epitome of merry and bright with her long blond pigtails, her blue eyes. Then that dreadful song, the breathy notes of the calliope, and the next time Striker passed the child, she was every little girl from Zinnia Trace, the whole damn town, the one at the pool asking why she was dirty, and before she knew it the child was falling (or did Striker push her?), her small bright face smashing the ice, blood from her nose and lips, and here is what Striker pieced together later, that she looped back around and skated straight for her ("I was headed back to try to help, officer"), the child crying, Dark Striker's blades like knives, Dark Striker managing to turn at the last moment but not enough, never enough, skating over the little girl's right hand, three fingers left severed on the—

"Did you hear what I said?" asked Anders.

Striker was standing on some Antarctic island, a walking stick gripped in her hand, the wood stained at the tip where it had once bashed in a man's skull.

"I said how do you know we're headed in the right direction?" the teen repeated.

Striker pointed at the shoreline.

Something bright and red was floating among the waves. Drifting in and then drifting out. A tandem. She could see a single yellow figure slumped in the back, the figure moaning though to Striker's ears there was something accusatory in it.

There were no scavengers on this side of the island as there was nothing to scavenge, no little black-and-white birds waddling in and out of the surf. This side of the island remained barren and forlorn, the landscape rugged and lifeless. To Striker it was profoundly more beautiful.

When they finally arrived at the ocean, there was no beach. Only rocks and waves and ice floating loose in the surf. It was a small miracle the tandem had managed to get so close to shore. The stony landscape jutted up from the water like dark teeth. The ocean capped with knives, the water angry and frothing. The tandem thrown around like the silver ball in a pinball machine. Battered yet still afloat.

"I wish we'd worn the dry suits," said Anders. Striker had the same thought.

Right on cue they caught a break. High tide was winding down. One of the last big waves swept the kayak up into the air, then receded, leaving it wedged in a cluster of rocks. The boat held tight. Even as a succession of smaller waves tried to knock it loose, it remained firmly in place.

"What do we do?" asked Anders.

"Tide's going out," said Striker. "I think we just wait."

"How long?"

"Shouldn't be long now."

The two of them stood on the shore in the mist and the muggy air, watching for the water to recede enough for them to walk out to where the kayak sat lodged in the rocks. Striker imagined what an aerial shot of her and Anders standing there on the foggy coastline of a nameless Antarctic island would look like on film. Two figures in dirty smocks facing down the harshness of time. Nothing but the sound of the ocean pounding the shore as it had been doing for millions of years. What did God do with His days? The waves dull and repetitive like picking a hangnail.

She could hear the old prayer floating out of the spindrift. It was Ama's favorite. Learning it from the nuns in the humid basement of Our Lady. At night her sister sitting in the bath and reciting the prayer, the word of God shining in her gap-toothed mouth.

Hail, Mary, full of grace,
the Lord is with thee.
Blessed art thou among women
and blessed is the fruit of thy womb, Jesus.
Holy Mary, Mother of God,
pray for us sinners,
now and at the hour of our death.

"Amen," whispered Striker.

The ocean moving further and further away from her as if a miracle or a sign she was persona non grata.

"What do you do in New York?"

The teen was sitting on a rock. Striker realized she herself hadn't moved for a small eternity, her gazed locked on the kayak. She figured in another few minutes they'd be able to walk out to the tandem without getting wet. She guessed the kid had reached their limit and couldn't handle another ten minutes of silence, so now they were onto the interview portion of the competition.

"I'm a film location scout," she said. "I scope out places where a producer might want to shoot a film, sometimes TV."

Anders nodded. "So you go somewhere and take a bunch of pictures."

"More or less," said Striker. "I gotta know about the place, its infrastructure, what it'll cost to get a crew there, what kinds of permits you need, if there are any tax breaks or zoning restrictions, what the light is like at different times of day. You could say I go searching for the perfect place to stage a little make-believe."

"Who's the most famous person you've ever met?"

It was an easy question. "I once fucked one of the leads in the Marvel universe," she said. "He was married at the time, he isn't anymore, and yeah, I'd do it again."

Anders' eyes grew big as fists, which meant Striker had actually said it. Surprisingly, the kid didn't ask for details.

"What did you major in in college to get a job like that?"

"Liberal arts. I took all the useless stuff. Mostly art and English and philosophy, a little religion, some anthro," said Striker. "My parents thought it wouldn't lead anywhere but they were wrong. Wasn't the first time."

"What do they think now?"

"Now?" I don't have the foggiest idea, she thought. "My family are the people I've *chosen* to be my family, you dig?"

Low tide had almost arrived. A few more minutes and they'd be able to walk out and make their rescue. In the meantime, it felt good to talk. Talking with a gender nonconforming teen from Texas about the fact that sometimes you have to walk away and not beat yourself up about it felt surprisingly good.

"What about you?" she said. "I can't imagine living in Texas is much fun."

"Texas? My family's from Madison, Wisconsin."

"I thought your dad said he was born and bred in Texas."

"He always does." Anders paused. The kid had amazing control. Striker watched as the fire of sorrow was stamped out before it ever ignited. "He likes making that joke. My parents were both born in the tiny town of Texas, Wisconsin."

"There's a Texas in *Wisconsin*?"

"Yup. I still have cousins there. Three hours north of Madison." The teen picked up a rock and threw it at nothing in particular. "How come you had to make your own family?" they asked.

Striker glanced at her watch. She was beginning to realize she looked at it in moments she wanted to avoid. There were two ways this could go down. She could feed Anders the usual bullshit or tell the kid the truth. The universe was giving her a chance to come clean. Being stuck at the southern ass of everything meant she could unburden herself without worrying 125th Street would open up and swallow her whole.

"I just always knew someday I'd get to choose."

She couldn't pinpoint the exact moment she'd decided to never see Trish and Doug again. It had always been there, lurking behind the four faceless garage doors and the 2.3 acres. The knowledge that Zinnia Trace was temporary, an unexpected wrench in her story. When the time came, she didn't even know it had happened. It was a gradual realization, the way it slowly dawned on her that it had been months since she'd answered an email, picked up the phone. Before she knew it, it was a full year, then two. Each time she moved, not sending Trish and Doug her new address. For the first few years, they always found her, their cards and letters lining the recycling bin.

Did they deserve being cut out of her life? Probably not. But every now and then she'd see a white woman on the street, the woman wearing the same silk scarves Trish preferred, the woman's hair pinned up in the same way, or a man with the tortoise-rimmed glasses Doug favored, and Striker felt it, the old anger rising up fresh as though it had all happened yesterday.

Ama just wanted to belong. But Zinnia Trace would never let her. It was unfair to ask an eight- and a six-year-old to come be the only ones a town had ever seen. Everyone else like Ama and Ronnie were stored away on TV or in the movies where they played a sport or were led away in handcuffs, a white sheet pulled over their heads, bodies outlined in chalk. One day a judge raising his gavel and rebranding them the Ostriker sisters, simple as that.

When life became just Trish and Doug and Striker, each week the three of them would sit down to talk with a professional. In every session, Striker pretending she was somewhere far away. What have we done wrong, Trish would wail. All we did was love you.

That's the problem, Striker thought. Our grandmother died and everyone acted like she and Ama won the lottery, that the sisters should be grateful for the big house and the swimming lessons and the church camp and the bichon frise, the designer brands that neither sister wanted because for the first year when they went to visit their cousins in the *before* place, their cousins whose parents couldn't afford to take in two more mouths, their cousins would look at them funny and tell them they smelled weird and talked different. Eventually they stopped going. Understand? You picked a whole new way of being for us in a world that didn't want us the way we were. So one day when she was old enough not to need their money, enough. Basta. No more stares, no more people overcompensating, gliding over with open arms and crooning you must be Trish's beautiful daughter, look how beautiful you are, I would love to have beautiful skin like yours, no more people at church making space, giving the sisters a candle and pushing them to the front of the choir, acting like she and Ama were the Chosen Ones, the other children smelling it, the bullshit, and rolling their eyes, yeah, people either going out of their way to make sure the sisters were seen in every photo and acting like the school/team/band/organization deserved a goddam medal for including them, or the ones sidling up to them out of nowhere at the Fourth of July parade saying I don't see all that race stuff, I just see people, wouldn't you agree? Still others tacking in the opposite direction, telling the sisters to toughen up, saying it was all in their heads, the time Doug complained that Ama was too damn sensitive after the father who coached softball put his hand on Ama's knee and Doug saying you misunderstood, he was just being *friendly*, the town patting itself on the back because these two little girls were living proof that the town's perception of itself as a welcoming space was beyond reproach even if the sisters' lived experience said otherwise.

"What about you?" said Striker.

"What *about* me?" said Anders.

Striker realized she was no good at small talk. Maybe that first conversation with Lucy on the deck of the *Yegorov* had failed not because of the kid but because of her.

"I dunno. Got any favorite subjects?"

"English," the teen said.

"That's cool," said Striker. "Who's your favorite author?"

"Shirley Jackson."

"The chick who wrote 'The Lottery'?"

"My favorite's her novel *Hangsaman*."

"Hangsaman? What's that mean?"

"I guess it's like another word for the guy who runs the gallows."

"Sounds creepy," said Striker.

"It totally is," said Anders. "I couldn't even tell you what it's about."

"You gotta give me something."

"Uh, basically a girl goes off to college and loses her mind. But that doesn't really do it justice."

"College can do strange shit to you," said Striker. "Last time I saw my adoptive parents was at my graduation."

"You're adopted?" the teen asked, but then shook their head as if erasing the question, probably fearing it was rude.

"I had a biological sister, my sister Ama." Nobody knows the full story of Ama the Brave, Ama the Magnificent, Striker thought, because I have built my identity around forgetting in the name of healing. "Ama was too good for this world," she said. "We didn't deserve her, and now she's gone."

Anders picked up a rock. Instead of throwing it out into the water, they slammed it down hard right where they were standing. The echo sounding over the shore.

"They were going to try her as an adult," Striker added. "She died her first day in juvie."

The teen picked up another rock and threw it down hard at their feet. "If you don't wanna talk about it—"

"No, it's cool," said Striker. She picked up her own rock. Then she did like Anders and whammed it down on the ground, the crack sharp like a gunshot.

Wow, that felt good! Was that the loudest noise she'd ever made?

"How'd she pass?" Anders gently asked.

Striker picked up another, raised it high overhead. This time she used both hands to slam it down. Kids these days! You had to give credit where credit was due. They knew how to express themselves.

Okay then. It was easier than she thought. She picked up one last rock the size of a bowling ball. Was stunned she could lift it. She'd never told anyone the details of Ama's death, not even Riley. She was surprised she still remembered. Sometimes she tweaked the past, made up stories, conversations, events. It was easier that way. Putting words in other people's mouths. Making them into who you needed them to be. It was an old coping mechanism. It had gotten her *this* far, hadn't it? Forty years.

The sound of rock smashing on rock like worlds colliding.

"Suicide," she said, matter-of-fact. "In juvie, she swallowed a tampon." For the first time in years, Striker feels something open up in her body. The air coming in easier. She looked out over the ocean, the sky gleaming as if made of glass. "It was Christmas Day."

"Is that why you wear a cross?"

Striker nodded. "It used to be hers."

"You know it could've been epigenetic trauma," suggested the teen.

"What could've been?"

"Her suicide."

"I must have been absent that day," said Striker. "Enlighten me."

"We now know trauma can literally cause mutations, can change a baby's DNA in utero," Anders said. "Think about it. If the children of Holocaust survivors are more susceptible to certain diseases, imagine what hundreds of years of chattel slavery—"

"That's okay, I'm good," said Striker.

Her heart was starting to race. She remembered being in sixth grade and stumbling on a diagram of a slave ship in an encyclopedia under MIDDLE PASSAGE, the image crammed with hundreds of bodies packed in the airless dark. How her mind had shut down just from seeing it, her throat constricting.

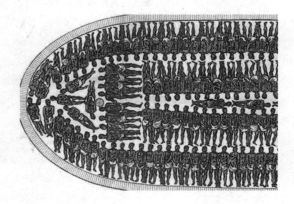

She'd needed to look at something else, anything, preferably something beautiful. Her gaze raced around the classroom. There on the teacher's desk next to a framed photo of Mrs. Bailey's family. A potted amaryllis in full bloom. The flower like an old-timey telephone, something she could whisper her secrets into.

Anders seemed contrite, sorry they'd brought it up. "Can I ask you something?" they said. Striker steeled herself. "Why do you think bad things happen to good people?"

Wow! This kid was full of surprises. "You mean like my sister?"

"Like anybody," said the teen.

"Why shouldn't it?" she said. "Life isn't cut-and-dry like some horror movie where the class slut dies in the opening minutes."

"So in your universe, being a good person won't save you."

"Never has." Just look at me, she thought. Tomorrow I'm going on four decades.

Anders took a deep breath. "It's just maybe a part of me isn't surprised this is happening."

"I need a little more," said Striker.

"Like, we are *literally* walking in the footsteps of a bunch of dead white guys. Isn't that like—" The teen paused. "Ironic?"

Striker shook her head. "Nah," she said. "It's more like kismet."

"Kismet?"

"Fate."

The teen stared out at the ocean. "Know anything about process philosophy?"

Striker flashed back to a long-ago afternoon in a lecture hall, the chilling sensation of being divided by multiple zeroes.

"You mean the philosopher Alfred North Whitehead?"

"Yup," said the teen.

"Shit, what kind of *high school* do you go to?"

"I'm in an international baccalaureate program."

"*Jesus*. In my day high school was just trying not to get pushed into the boys' bathroom. What do you know about Whitehead?"

"This place just makes me think of him," Anders softly said. "The idea that everything's relational, that there are no *things*, just processes."

"So you're okay with there being no such thing as a flower," said Striker.

The teen let out a small laugh. "A flower needs sun, rain, dirt, worms, bees, on and on. Who are we to say where a flower begins or ends?" They waved their arms around at the landscape. "This is all just one fluid moment. Like us."

"Us?"

The kid nodded. "Right this second there's no *me* without *you*."

Together the two of them sat watching the waves grow smaller. "Makes for a nice bumper sticker," Striker finally said. And with that, the interview portion of the competition came to an end.

High tide was finished. It was time to get the show on the road. Striker picked her way over the rocks. She could see the figure slumped in the back of the tandem, the form unmoving. Were they too late?

The sparkling white smoke was growing denser, tiny droplets wetting her skin. Normally she might have found it refreshing, but it felt like being pricked by a storm of needles.

"Should've brought some water with us," she said.

"We did," said Anders. They pulled a bottle out from underneath their jacket.

"Nice work." Striker motioned the teen forward, trying to honor their thoughtfulness, but she noticed their hand shaking as though palsied. It hadn't occurred to her that this might be the teen's dad. Four tandems had set out from the *Yegorov*. The Dame and the Baron each in their own, and the two underage kayakers both accompanied by a parent. It meant this was either the Texas, er, Wisconsin crew, or the brown dad and Lucy. Gently Striker took the water bottle from Anders.

"I'll see what's up," she said.

The tandem was a few feet off the ground. The man was gripping his paddle. Though she'd watched it happen, she couldn't figure out how the boat had gotten wedged so tightly in the rocks. Gingerly she reached out and touched the man's shoulder.

"Hey there," she said. She heard herself channeling her inner Grande Dame. "Fancy meeting you here." When he turned and faced her, she stifled a scream.

Blood stained the front of his dry suit like a bright red bib. Then he grinned, his face contorting in a terrible rictus. His mouth glistened like a clown's, red and dripping.

She wanted to look away but couldn't. An image of a skating rink flashed in her mind. Three little fingers lying severed on the ice.

The man was shivering, his front teeth chipped all to hell. Somewhere between pushing off from the *Yegorov* and now the man's upper incisors had completely shattered. She tried not to show her revulsion. What was left of his mouth gleamed like a vampire's. Little white shards of bone poking from the gums. His bottom lip was completely shredded where he had chewed his own mouth to bits.

"Meeting you here meeting you here," the man recited. The same affectless tone his daughter would've used. It was clear he was insane. A mental link had been severed. He turned his gaze fully on Striker, both eyes salt white. "Hand it here, wee one. It's fur yer own gude," he growled. Suddenly the sparkling air smelled like an outhouse, the rocks ████████████████████████████
██
██
██
██
██
████████████████████████ where the man was standing on the shore. His two front teeth were chipped, his lip cut, but other than that, he seemed okay, mostly dead tired, the front of his dry suit yellow and spotless. Nearby the kayak sat beached several feet above the tideline. Having a boat on this side of the island couldn't

hurt any. From everything she'd ever heard, it was never a bad idea to have multiple escape routes just in case. Only thing was, Striker didn't recall carrying it there or helping the man out of it.

"Come on, we gotta go," Anders called.

The teen was standing next to Hector, the urgency front and center in their voice. Striker realized the kid was trying not to panic. She looked down at her hands. Between her palms she was gripping a large rock. What had Dark Striker intended to do with it? Slowly she bent down and placed it back on the ground.

"What's the hurry?" she asked as she ambled over to where the two were standing.

"Are you for *real*?" said Anders. The kid didn't wait for an answer. They turned and began hurrying back toward the volcano, one arm tight around their charge. "We've been through this," they called over their shoulder. "The guy's sopping wet. He must have fallen out of his boat."

What, thought Striker. Percy said you could only last fifteen minutes max in water this cold. How was this guy still standing?

The skin on the back of her neck began to itch. She glanced back at the cluster of rocks where the kayak had been pinned, expecting to see the little girl with the fat gray rat balled up on her shoulder. For an instant in the shimmering mist, something did seem to be staring her way. It was the right size to be a child. She was about to shout to the others that she'd found Lucy when the mist thinned. She stood staring, waiting for the object to transform, reveal its true nature. But it was nothing more than one of the stones that had trapped the boat. She turned and rushed to catch up with the others.

Neither she nor Anders asked Hector about his daughter. It wasn't the time for questions. They had to get him back to the cabin, set him up by the vent with a bowl of steaming-hot broth, let him rest. Hector was stiff but he could walk. The guy moved as if bearing a heavy box on his back, hunched like he wasn't sure he was still alive. If you thought about it, he *was* carrying a tremendous burden.

Striker imagined him and Bobbi Sue standing face-to-face like two mirrors, the grief infinite between them.

They were almost back up to the top of the volcano when she spotted a trail of footprints winding around a bend. She wasn't surprised when Anders and Hector didn't notice.

"I need to make a pit stop," she said. She raised an eyebrow at Anders. "You got this?"

The teen eyed her warily but nodded. Before the two of them disappeared from view, she heard Anders say, "We gotta get rescued soon. Everyone's falling apart."

Striker turned and followed the prints through the sparkling fog. They looked like small hands had made them, the right hand missing several fingers. Instead of going straight up the volcano, the trail wound around the cone. Maybe they would take her back to the scene of the crime where Kevin had brained his wife. Eagerly she trudged along, wondering what time it was, how many meals she'd missed, what her friends were doing for Christmas back in the city. Overhead the sun sat in its usual spot.

The trail ended by a large boulder. Something was propped up against it. Its face pale and bloodless. The back of its head not visible. Its eyes were closed but Striker knew it wasn't *dead* dead. How it got there she couldn't imagine. The snow around the spot remained fresh and powdery.

"What do you want?" she whispered.

Taylor the Tech Titan opened her salt-white eyes. "Nice to see you too," she said. Her voice had dropped several octaves. Her red hair blazed, the color of fresh blood. "I want what you want. αηο θανειν θελω."

Striker couldn't tell what language it was, but she knew it was ancient. Wasn't that what being dead was all about? Instant irrelevancy. Walking the earth in a space beyond human understanding.

Speaking in riddles. Regretting what you'd done with your life. A tableau flashed in her mind of a woman perched in an iron cage, the woman older than time itself, a group of young boys gathered around to gawk.

"So what's it gonna be?" asked Taylor. "You or them?"

Something fluttered down out of the sky and landed on Taylor's shoulder. Its missing eye as if someone had taken a red-hot poker and cauterized the place where the eye had been. Taylor reached up and stroked the bird's dirty wings. She grinned. A dark gap winked between her front teeth. She stuck her tongue in the space, lewdly wriggling it in and out.

"How long you been here?" said Striker.

"I knew you before you were," said Taylor. "And don't bother sending Kevin down. I think I can manage." Her smile as if gouged in her face. "Though do ask him what he's toting around in that dry bag of his, if it makes him feel like a man."

"I try not to get involved in other people's relationships," said Striker.

"Don't bullshit me, girlie," Taylor sneered. "Really. Don't." She seemed like she might stand up.

"Okay okay." Striker already knew what the answer would be, but all the same she had to try. "Is it *really* me or them?"

Taylor shook her head and clucked her teeth. "You gotta ask?"

"It's just bizarre is all," said Striker. "I see a little bit of me in each one."

"There's the problem," said Taylor. "You never kept enough of you for yourself."

Striker hated to admit it, but it was probably an apt diagnosis. Still, her modus operandi couldn't be *that* bad. After all, she was the one who'd made it out alive.

"Is this about revenge?" she whispered.

It was the one-eyed bird who fielded this one. Its voice filling her head like the song inside a seashell.

Baby, this is about redemption.

Something landed on her forehead. When had it started snowing? It was really coming down, flakes the size of quarters. The sun was out, not a cloud in the sky, the day bright as a movie set.

Striker rubbed her eyes with the tips of her fingers. She gazed up into the blue. She hadn't known such a thing was possible.

It sat shining in the sky, its colors sharp enough to touch. She knew it was for her eyes only.

Why not? It was Christmas Eve. Showtime. Tomorrow she'd be

The Unveiling | 189

██████████████████████████████ gave the cabin door a good, hard yank, but the dang thing wouldn't budge. *Shizer*. Bits of rust flaked off as she jiggled the ancient bolt. Okay then. This time she wrapped both hands around the bar and pulled.

It was like tugging on a thousand-year-old redwood.

Couldn't the others hear her struggling out there, or had everyone skipped town on her again? She was about to walk around and slip in through the window when she heard the inner bolt slide out of its catch. The door creaked open. She thought of the mausoleum she'd encountered out on the ocean, the ice like a crypt.

The Baron filled the doorway. His face was puffy, his coloring off, but it was probably just from the geothermal radiance seeping up through the floorboards.

"We're hundreds of miles *beyond* nowheresville," she said as she entered. "Why is there a lock on *both sides*?"

"Keep out the riffraff," said the Baron.

"Then why are *you* here?" she retorted.

The door blew shut. She could hardly breathe. Did no one else notice?

Everywhere the air shimmered. Faint shapes like silvery clouds hovered around each of the survivors though the glow haloing Anders remained faint. The clearest glintings were huddled around la Grande Dame, the shimmerings thronging the old woman like mosquitoes. Though featureless, one seemed to tower a full head taller than the rest.

Striker closed her eyes, overwhelmed by the stifling sense of bodies packed in tight spaces. It's just an illusion, she told herself. Back on the *Yegorov*, a lecturer had explained how a sun dog forms when clouds filled with ice crystals float close to the earth, creating a ring around the sun. Antarctica is the land of illusion, the lecturer had concluded. All this endless white tricks the eye.

Striker took a deep breath.

When she looked again, the glintings were gone.

The way the group had arranged themselves on the furniture reminded her of the cover of that old board game *Clue*. Anders at the table with their nose in a book. Bobbi Sue by the vent mindlessly stirring the pots. Kevin swinging in a hammock, the thing sagging where his flabby ass brushed the ground, both dry bags tucked in tight beside him, a pair of rubber teddy bears. The Baron propped up on one of the beds, cleaning out what appeared to be an old pipe. The Dame in the room's only armchair, Vadim looming behind her and furiously stroking her neck.

And the newest member of the band was there too. The man she and Anders had rescued from the shifting tides. Lucy's dad. The brown one. Hector with his mouth full of rubble, or was it just his two front teeth? A sour odor wafted from where he lay shivering under a mound of blankets, the smell a mixture of mildew and an acridness Striker associated with fear.

"Where've you been?" asked la Grande Dame.

"Nice to see you too," said Striker. She was still carrying the walking stick Anders had handed her before they'd hiked down the volcano to the far shore. She leaned it up in the corner with its twin, careful to turn the dark and murderous dent toward the wall. "Anyone notice the rainbow?"

"Rainbow?" scoffed the Dame.

"I guess *technically* it's a snowbow," said Striker. "It's coming down pretty hard. Look at me. I'm covered in—"

She glanced down at her arms, but the sleeves of her Burberry were bone-dry.

In the silence, Vadim continued stroking the anterior muscles in the Dame's neck, running his fingers up and down the sides of her throat as if stropping a razor. Suddenly he grabbed a fistful of the old woman's hair and wrenched her head, the sound like wood cracking.

"*Nostrovia*, darling," the Dame sighed, patting both his hands where they lay on her shoulders.

"Yes, thanks muchly, young feller," said the Baron without looking up from his pipe. "Janey needed her a good adjusting."

La Grande Dame ran a jeweled finger over Vadim's knuckles, the emerald big as a scarab. "Anna and Hector came back ages ago," she said in a slow, thick voice. Sheesh, why couldn't the old girl get the kid's name right? "So I'll ask one more time." She pitched her voice light and kittenish, which only intensified its sinister undertone. "Veronique," cooed the Dame, "what have you been up to?"

Striker decided the best defense was a good offense. She pointed to the bed where Hector lay wheezing. "And while Anders and I were out rescuing him, what were *you* doing?" She toggled a finger back and forth between the Dame and Vadim. The memory was still fresh in her mind of the empty grotto, the two of them nowhere in sight.

"*I* was hunter-gathering with Sarah," said Vadim proudly. At the mention of her name, Bobbi Sue looked up and blinked. "We work up big appetite bringing home the bacons for dinner."

Dinner? Striker glanced at her watch. 12:14 p.m. "Anyone know what time it is?" she asked, already fearing the answer.

"Almost seven," said Bobbi Sue. Her voice was small and factual, the voice of a woman committed to keeping her distance from something painful.

"No it's not," said Kevin, struggling to get out of his hammock. "It's a little before midnight."

"Then why are we all wide awake?" asked Anders.

"Adrenaline," said Kevin. He gave up and sank back down, the fabric groaning as he moved.

"Doesn't anybody have a watch that's working?" asked Striker. She turned to the Baron. "You there. Isn't your Rolex analog?"

"Mine stopped telling time at a quarter past noon," he said, holding his wrist out for proof.

"Rolexes suck," muttered Kevin.

"So said the man who couldn't afford one," replied the Baron.

"They're like diamonds, just for show," said Kevin. "Everyone with half a brain knows they're not worth the money."

"Yeah but what time is it really?" said Striker, trying to move things along.

"Quality knows quality," the Baron replied.

"What does big friend sun say?" said Vadim.

"We're a couple of days out from the summer solstice in freaking Antarctica," said Kevin. "The sun hasn't moved all damn day."

"What about the tides?" asked the Baron.

"Yeah," said Kevin. He turned to Vadim. "You're *supposed* to be a sailor. Enlighten us."

"Tide shifts all over planet," said Vadim, still focused on the Dame's neck. "You need chart to read them. You need reference point. You have reference point?"

"I'm pretty good with time," said Anders. "In school, each period's like fifty minutes. I got a feel for it. I think it's like nine o'clock–ish."

"It's Christmas morning," rasped Hector from his nest of blankets.

Outside the windows the sky gleamed clean and white like newly washed linens. What if they were all correct? Didn't modern physics teach that time and space were now optional, some unlucky cat trapped in a box both alive and dead? The faint stench of rotten meat drifted through the room. Or was it just the odor of feverish Hector wallowing in a heap of hundred-year-old blankets?

"For Chrissake let's just open the gifts like the kid wants and then hit the hay," said Kevin.

"Gifts?" said Striker.

"Santa is big secret." Vadim held up a tiny piece of paper with something scrawled on it, then crammed it in his mouth and started chewing.

"Hey!" said Anders. "You were supposed to label your present with that."

Vadim shrugged. He kept his eyes on Striker. "Santa says you are big naughty girl," he said.

"Second that," said the Baron. From a small bag he poured some dark clumps in the bowl of his pipe and lit a match. Striker watched as he sucked rapidly on the mouthpiece. A thin braid of smoke curled up from the chamber. Instantly his eyes slitted. "Splendid," he slurred. He lay back and blew a gray ring up toward the ceiling.

Didn't his mama ever teach him not to smoke in bed?

Striker could smell it. *Incredible.* A hundred years old and it still had the same skunkiness to it. The Baron sat back up and held out the pipe. She didn't even have to ask. Game knows game. Why not? She could use a good fake laugh, everything temporarily hilarious. The only thing she feared was the terrible hunger that would inevitably arise, and the fact that there would be nothing to satisfy it when it did.

She took the pipe in both hands and inhaled down to the tips of her toes. Instantly the dread that had been massing in her chest began to slow. She was about to hand back the pipe and thank him for playing nicely with others when he turned to face her.

Both his eyes burned salt white. He put a hand to his ear. "What was that now, dearie?" he asked.

Striker found her voice. "Danke schoen," she whispered. She had never seen him without his old-man sunglasses. Each pupil veiled with a pearly film. They were cataracts. His cloudy eyes made him look like a seer, someone with knowledge of the deeper truths of life.

He smiled and went back to staring vacantly into the corner. She followed his gaze across the room. Her eyes landed on the walking stick. Hadn't she positioned it so that the dent in the wood was facing the wall? Even from where she was standing, it was plain as day.

Something dark and viscous was dripping from the dent and running down the wood. Holy shit, she thought. Can a piece of wood form a stigmata?

Of course we can, said the Walking Stick. *When we crucified our Lord, we were forever stained with His blood.*

Shizer.

Striker's inner radar pinged hard, the paranoia already ramping up. You'd think she would've learned her lesson three years back from that second location setup in Portland. Never get stoned around white people. It was going to be a long, pale night.

They were seated around the table. Striker wondered how many people had sat in this very spot, in the cloying light their faces grayed like overcooked meat. Amazingly, the hundred-year-old matches still sparked up at first strike, the room strewn with candles. She ran a finger back and forth through the tip of a flame. Every time there should be pain, there was nothing. With each swipe she left her finger in the fire a little longer, hoping to feel something, anything.

When the pain finally hit, it didn't seem to belong to her. She recalled an article Riley had texted her that said almost half of all med school students at one top-ten program didn't believe Black people feel pain the same way white people do. Judging from the look plastered on the Baron's face, the old guy was also undoubtedly floating above the clouds. You could probably set his whole body on fire and he would just stare at you and wink.

"What *are* they?" asked la Grande Dame. For once she sounded genuinely baffled rather than rude.

"Woman, what's it look like?" yawned the Baron.

Bobbi Sue set down the platter. They were bigger than Striker expected, each shell whiter than snow from having been immersed in boiling water.

"Penguin eggs," beamed Vadim. He was so proud he looked like he might start pounding his chest.

"We got lucky," said Bobbi Sue. Striker noticed the dark crescents under her eyes, the deep parentheses creased around her mouth. Somehow the lady had aged a solid decade since the last time Striker had seen her. Was such a thing even possible? "Most of the penguin chicks have already hatched, but there were quite a few eggs left that were either abandoned or never viable."

"Wouldn't they go—you know." Striker found herself searching for the right word, but nothing else came to mind. "Bad?"

"It's cold out there," said Bobbi Sue without conviction.

"No it's not," said the Dame. "It's like Boca in winter."

"If the egg isn't *too* old, it should be fine," said Anders brightly in support of their mom. "Back home we sometimes keep eggs in the fridge for a couple of weeks."

"When I was a bachelor, I could go an entire month on one dozen," said Kevin. There was pride in his voice. The mystery of why Taylor the Tech Titan ever married this dingus only deepened.

"In Sankt Peterburg, we don't refrigerate," said Vadim. "You buy egg right off shelf in grocery store. Who knows how long they sit?"

"You're from St. Petersburg?" said the Baron, his eyes softening.

"Da," said Vadim slowly.

"My my my," replied the Baron. He took a deep breath like a man standing on a mountaintop who, thanks to the alpine air, has just had the most pristine thought of his life. "When it comes to ruthlessness, there's nothing like a Russian gangster." There was no anger in his voice, just pure observation.

Bobbi Sue finished handing the eggs out. Apparently she'd spent enough holidays with relatives to know when a topic of conversation needed to be cut off at the knees. "Anders, why don't you make a toast?"

"Wouldn't a blessing be more appropriate?" said the Dame.

"I'm Jewish," said Kevin.

"And we're Unitarian," said Anders. "Our church was designed by Frank Lloyd Wright."

"More like Frank Lloyd Wrong," said the Baron.

"Shut up," said the Dame.

"Seriously, that scarf-wearing dwarf wouldn't know a sight line if it bit him in the ass."

"We don't say 'dwarf' anymore," said Bobbi Sue flatly.

"Why don't you say a prayer?" said the Dame, turning toward Striker. "You're the one wearing a cross."

It was peeking out at the neck of her dry suit. "Don't look at me," she said, stuffing it back in. "It's just an old habit I can't seem to break."

Anders was a real trooper. They raised their glass in the air. Striker didn't mention the prohibition against toasting with water. They were only a kid. Why be a negative Nellie if you don't have to?

"May love surround you, may joy gladden you, may peace lie deep within," intoned Anders. "And may your life and the lives of all those you touch, go well."

"Merry Christmas."

"Merry Christmas."

"L'chaim," said Striker.

The Dame turned to Kevin. "When's Hanukkah this year?"

He scratched his neck, mumbled something.

"What was that?"

"I don't know. I'm not a *practicing* Jew."

"*Na zdorovie*," said Vadim, a beat too late.

They picked up their hundred-year-old forks and dug in.

They all used different techniques. Vadim simply lifted his egg high off his plate and dropped it, the shell splintering. The Dame cupped it in her palm and squeezed, all while keeping her eyes locked on her husband. The Baron, meanwhile, had taken his knife and was delicately tapping different spots on the egg as if cutting a diamond. Striker hit hers a couple of times with her fork, then realized in her purple haze she was practically bludgeoning the thing to death.

Once she cracked it open, she didn't know what she'd been expecting. This wasn't tea at the Four Seasons. Still, regardless of origins, weren't eggs basically all the same on the inside?

To say Bobbi Sue had erred on the side of caution was an understatement. After Vadim busted up a few crates and packed it with wood, the stove had fired right up. Who could say how long she had boiled them? With no functioning watch to keep track of time, it was all about instinct. Each egg cooked hard as rubber. And once you peeled off the shell, the egg white was completely transparent, the yolk suspended in what looked like glass, the yolk itself a fiery orange in color.

"It's because of the cold temps," explained Anders. "The ornithologist on the *Yegorov* said penguin eggs have less albumin than chicken eggs, so they don't turn white when you cook them."

"Is that a foot?" someone asked.

"I think I got a beak."

"In countries in Asia, eating an embryonic duck cooked right in the shell is a delicacy."

"Did anyone wish me a hearty *konnichiwa* this morning?" said the Baron.

From his bed by the vent, Hector began coughing. "*Konnichiwa, konnichiwa*," he finally managed to croak.

"Is it just me or is the music getting worse?" said Striker.

In the corner near the door, the Victrola stood a little more than three feet tall and was a beautiful golden color, the box solid oak.

"You're only supposed to use a needle a couple of times max before it gets too dull," said Kevin. "They must have played them down to the nub. I put in the best one I could find." The music stretched out like dark taffy.

"St. Petersburg," repeated the Baron.

"Land of big culture, white knights, warrior people," said Vadim.

"Everyone knows Russian gangsters are more vicious than any other gang," said the Baron. "MS-13. The Blacks in South Central. The Asians out of Vietnam. They're a bunch of mama's boys compared to you Ruskies."

"That's racist," said Anders.

Ah, thought Striker. This really *does* feel like a good old-fashioned holiday meal. Christmases when she and Ama were young, Doug's brother would come over with his family. Doug's sister-in-law couldn't seem to help herself. Talking about the illegals or those animals in New York City, what they did to that poor jogger. Later in the kitchen, Mindy not even lowering her voice when she asked Trish how the grand experiment was going. Was the darker one giving her any problems? No? Well, just wait, she would say.

"Live a little, feller," said the Baron to Anders. "Then call me when you've seen some things."

Striker was surprised how fast the kid went for the jugular.

"You're what's wrong with America."

"Greatest Generation," said the Baron.

The Dame laughed. "That was your father's generation," she said. "The last of the *real* American men. And now they're dead."

"What is it with you women and the strong silent types?" said Kevin. "Is that what you want? Someone who can kill a bunch of people on a battlefield and then come home and never talk about it?"

Striker recalled a skit she'd seen on TV. A Black comedian, she couldn't remember who, explaining that after the 2016 election he was gonna take a knee and watch white people duke it out. The second time around proved 2016 wasn't a fluke. *Peace on earth, goodwill towards men* was simply a recommendation, like getting eight hours of sleep. Most people she knew got by on six, which maybe explained the state of the world. She was still too high to say anything plus the egg wasn't half bad. Several contained tiny wings, the bones soft enough you could crunch right through them with your teeth. Others held small shrimp-like creatures suspended in the yolk, each one like a fun-sized candy bar.

"There's more pemmican soaking in a bucket if anyone's still hungry," said Bobbi Sue.

"Pemmi-*what*?" said Striker.

"Pemmican," said Anders. "It's a kinda jerky. Probably penguin. Stuff never goes bad. There was a write-up about it in some guy's journal. Claimed it tasted like goat."

Striker dipped the last of her egg in the bowl of broth they'd each been given. It was nice and salty. In SoHo, people would pay big bucks for a meal like this. She turned to la Grande Dame and her flat white woman ass.

"You gonna eat that?"

The Dame slid her plate across the table, the disgust wrinkling her lips.

Anders explained that the tradition was German, but Striker already knew that. It was how she and Ama had always celebrated Christmas. On Zinnia Trace Santa didn't arrive on Christmas Day but the night before. Celebrating Christmas on Christmas Eve meant no pictures were taken before you'd combed your hair, de-soured your mouth. Why only the Germans had figured this out, she couldn't say.

The teen addressed the room. "Has everyone put their gifts on the chair by the door?"

"Seriously?" said Striker.

"We tossed our names in a bowl," Anders said. They explained how once you picked a name, it was up to you to find something to gift that person. "It could be anything," they said. A pretty stone from the beach, some breath mints you still had in your dry bag, something you discovered around the hut, like one of the hundred-year-old Victorian novels that made up the library. "Don't worry," the teen concluded with a wink. "Santa put in a few extra gifts. We got you covered."

"Has someone screwed the whatchamacalit into the whosananie yet?" barked la Grande Dame. She was back in the armchair and in need of entertaining.

"Relax, Jane," said Kevin. He held a needle up to the light, trying to gauge how much of it was left. He turned to Vadim. "First thing I ever tried playing on the vintage Victrola my wife gave me for my birthday?" He waited a spell, creating his own drumroll. "Megadeth's *Countdown to Extinction*."

"Classic," said Vadim. He put down the book he'd been squinting at. "But Black Sabbath's *Paranoid* number-one album." He thrashed his arm up and down, playing an invisible Stratocaster. "'Generals gathered in their masses,'" he warbled, "'just like witches at black masses.'"

"I feel you, brother," said Kevin. "But you can only play shellac on one of these babies, not vinyl." He seemed sad, even sadder than when his wife's body had up and vanished. "I found out the hard way," he said. "I totally shredded my Megadeth to pieces trying to listen to it."

"Fascinating," yawned the Dame.

Kevin closed his eyes, picked a needle at random from the reserve. "Okay. I take zero responsibility for this," he said, screwing the thing into place. He put the needle down on the record and cranked the handle.

The music started up. It was instrumental, an Austrian orchestra playing holiday favorites. "The Blue Danube" poured out of the vents. Striker was surprised it sounded so good.

Vadim approached the Dame and did a formal curtsey, held out his hand. The Dame gave him a long, withering look. Vadim held his ground. The Dame glared harder. It was like a game of chicken. Finally the old bird stood up. She pressed her palm to his wrist, never taking his hand directly in hers. In turn he slipped an arm around her waist. They began to move, twirling in a circle, their dancing unexpectedly elegant. Like the others, Striker couldn't help staring. The way the Dame arched her body slightly away from his, and how Vadim spun her around the tiny space, the two of them circling each other like magnets.

It was sexy. The Baron watched with a small smile on his face, holding his arms up and swaying them gently through the air as though holding his wife. Striker noticed Hector sitting up in bed, his broken teeth gleaming in the candlelight. Yeah, the Dame had definitely been a dancer, maybe even a great one. And what was Vadim's story? Maybe all Russians could dance the same way all Italians could sing Puccini. For ten minutes the Victrola transported them all to some place far away, wherever in their minds they longed to be.

Striker on Zinnia Trace balancing on Doug's toes as he shuffled his feet across the floor, the smell of the fifteen-foot Scottish fir by the French doors in the less formal living room, the tree fragrant and bright, little Ronnie laughing with each twirl, Ama shouting *it's my turn, do me!* Trish smiling in the doorway with the video camera in her hand, the sound of the greatest river in Europe pouring through the stereo's  "Striker?"

The room came back into view.

"This is for you," said Anders. The kid shook the gift like someone offering a dog a bone. Striker could already see a rectangular shape buried in the dishcloth. "Go ahead. Everyone else has already opened theirs."

She peered around the room, trying to spot the differences. Vadim with a monocle lodged in his eye. Bobbi Sue drifting around the table with a new broom. The Baron in bed with what appeared to be an iron protractor he kept aiming at various things. The Dame with a dark green bottle clamped between her thighs, the old gal clawing at the cork like a rat trying to liberate some cheese. Hector upright in bed wearing a scarf. The way he'd tied it around his neck was rather dashing.

Striker remembered the Christmas Doug and Trish had given her and Ama a whole new rec room with a pool table and foosball. Truth was Doug spent more time down there with his friends than she and Ama ever did. Growing up on Zinnia Trace, she was never quite certain who Christmas was for. It seemed like an excuse to make yourself appear generous in front of the neighbors.

"What did *you* get?" she asked Anders. The candles flickered redly in their watery jars, everyone's faces flushed.

The teen held up the severed head of a penguin, the thing's eyes bulging, the blood still tacky around its beak. "I know it's out of the ordinary," Anders said, "but I like it." They tucked the head back under their arm. "I'm gonna name him George."

"What's your favorite saying?" said the Baron, pointing at the gruesome knickknack. "Oh, I know. 'That's racist,'" he sang.

"What is?" said the teen.

"Heavens to Murgatroyd, I know something you don't," said the Baron.

The old man and the teen launched into another argument. Striker tuned it out. She could see that the penguin head was actually some sort of Victorian-era gewgaw, the thing dark and exotic with popping eyes. Most likely it had come from one of the British colonies, a souvenir a soldier had brought back to the isle. Anders seemed convinced it was just some silly little beast, but Striker had to agree with the Baron. Though the thing was animalistic in appearance, you could tell from the plush red mouth it was supposed to be human even if vaguely so.

Quietly she reached over and took the dishcloth from Anders, leaving the teen and the old man to their battle. Tied up in the fabric was a small leather journal, its cover scored with scratches.

The Dame nodded at the notebook. Somehow her voice cut through the noise. "Didn't someone mention something or other about women dressing up like men so they could follow their lover to the ends of the earth?"

"Percy," said Striker. "His name was Percy."

The old girl stopped trying to uncork the bottle. It was only a matter of time before she'd smash it open and slash her mouth to ribbons guzzling from the shards. "I guess there have always been women who need a man to be happy," she said.

Striker opened the book at random.

Doctor claims He is the only one among our party with all His teeth still anchored in His jaw though who can tell? All I can see are those two terrible incisors stitched to his leather mouth, each one yellowed as a wolf's fangs. Day and night the breath issuing from that hole is worse than sulfur.

Based on his calculations Bernard believed that in three weeks' time the first hints of Dawn should begin staining the horizon. When I think of Bernard figuring by the fire, my heart briefly warms. But I must not become maudlin. Ever since the day Bernard strode out to hunt seals with Doctor and only Doctor returned, I am without protection. I know not what I live for.

Because this journal is a True record of my Heart, I shall not keep secrets from it. Each hour I am freshly acquainted with what my Subterfuge is costing. I can see no end to It. There is a whispering among the men that Doctor is not a True doctor but merely an uneducated Scotsman with a few sharp tools at His disposal; His true training is in the art of Dentistry. If this proves correct, then the Lord has seen fit to abandon us to one who knows Little. In short, we are Forsaken.

When the moment comes and my Lie is revealed, I can only hope God sees fit to do with me what I have not the Nerve to do by my own Hand. May the Lord take Everything and Nothing less than that.

"Too bad for those ladies, no?" said the Dame.

Striker flipped through the rest of the book. Toward the end she landed on a dog-eared page. Someone had scrawled over that day's entry in huge red letters. The ink watery and without pigments, the way blood dries on paper. It looked fresh. The words jagged as lightning.

PLEASE KILL MY HUSBAND!

The Dame smiled wide. The metal studs winked in her jaw. Striker ran a finger over the red letters, the feet on the K bleeding down the—

<< A lantern throws shadows on a low ceiling rife with icicles, the whole world stabbed by shadows. Striker lies panting in the weak light. The pain is excruciating, a bright star burning between her thighs hungry to rip a path out. She can feel the hot fluids gush from her body, everywhere the smell of blood and the heat of it melting the ice.

Striker runs a hand over her shorn head, scalp riddled with scabs, the other hand soothing her distended belly. Somehow she knows her silence is a matter of life and death. She must not cry out. These past two years she and Bernard have succeeded in keeping her sex hidden from the others, but before he died, even he didn't know of the tiny sun slowing growing inside his beloved like the coming of spring. She had kept her condition from him, fearing how desperate the news would make him. She has seen enough of desperation.

Another contraction hits. Striker's body as if struck by lightning. She thinks of what Doctor says every time one of the men lies dying. *Repent ye!* Doctor in his terrible artificial face looming over the dying man with the ax raised in >>

Striker took her finger off the page. In the cabin all hell had broken loose.

"Original Position is just some academic's wet dream," scoffed Kevin.

"But what *is* it?" asked the Baron. "More liberal tripe?"

Anders grimaced. "It's a thought experiment that says people would make just laws that benefit everyone if they believed there was a chance they might be reborn as a member of an underclass. Like, would politicians be so hungry to legislate where folks pee if they thought they might be reincarnated as a trans woman?" The kid sat chewing on a strip of pemmican. "And affirmative action benefits you too. When Harvard Med becomes one hundred percent Asian, being a legacy won't help your grandkids get in."

"Would *you* accept longer wait times to see a doctor if it meant *everyone* had free healthcare?" said the Dame.

"'Land of the Free' is a *metaphor*, not a sales price," raged the Baron.

"Could someone *please* teach me what microaggression is?" said Vadim.

Striker heard herself chuckle. On the flight down to Buenos Aires, the middle-aged white guy next to her had assumed she'd been upgraded to business just because he had. The guy had been pretty innocuous otherwise, so who could say? Would he have made the same assumption about another white man? Or was the guy's Id subtly telling her that in his world, Black people don't fly business?

"Microaggression are comments or actions that consciously or unconsciously imply the inferiority of members of a marginalized community," said Bobbi Sue blankly as if reading from an HR pamphlet.

"The word 'micro' is right there front and center," muttered Kevin. "As in whatever you're complaining about is small potatoes."

"Look, the *real* reason America's falling apart isn't immigration or the price of eggs or low information voters. It's because we've never dealt with the country's original sin," Anders said. "1619."

"Is that some big celebrity's tequila?" asked Vadim. He seemed to be serious.

"1619: the first Africans were abducted and brought to A'nowara'ko:wa."

"Ano wawa *what*?"

"A'nowara'ko:wa. Turtle Island. You know, America had a name before Columbus and the slavers showed up."

"Slavery slavery slavery," said the Dame. She sat quietly twirling the gargantuan emerald on her finger. Already it seemed loose. "After two hundred years, don't you little antifas have anything new?"

"Dave Chappelle's dad was raised by his grandmother, a woman born into slavery," said Anders.

Of course, thought Striker. It was Dave Chappelle on *Saturday Night Live*.

"No way," said Kevin.

"Yes way," said Anders.

"Who?" said Vadim, but the kid was on fire.

"Think about it. If you were born in the 1940s, you'd be in your eighties by now," they explained. "Someone born in 1860 would be eighty when you were born. It means there are people alive *right now* whose grandparents were slaves."

"Dave Chappelle's a comedian," Kevin clarified. "I was at that concert down at the Hollywood Bowl where he got attacked."

"So don't roll your eyes and moan 'slavery slavery slavery' like it's yesterday's news. Where do you think the filibuster came from?" Anders hissed. "Two hundred years later and we're still apportioning seats in Congress based on some stupid compromise with slave states. Google it."

If Striker had wanted to eat overcooked holiday food and hear white people shriek at each other, she would've bought a ticket back to Zinnia Trace. Goddammit, she thought. I am not high enough for this.

From the look of things, Anders was only just getting started. "Critical race theory just says you'll never dismantle the master's house with the master's tools."

"What kind of *commie* high school do you go to?" the Baron demanded.

"Like it or not, we are *still* living in the age of the transatlantic slave trade," Anders said. The kid seemed to be enjoying themself.

"What are you *talking* about?" said Kevin.

"Americans fight about slave stuff a lot," observed Vadim.

"The purpose of the transatlantic slave trade was to commodify the Black body," said Anders. "After 1865, this country kept making money off African Americans legally and culturally through *Plessy versus Ferguson*, separate but equal, Jim Crow, you name it. We never granted Black people full citizenship, thus creating a permanent underclass that white America could keep exploiting through things like sharecropping, or when that didn't work, by *literally* blowing up Black wealth like we did during the Tulsa race riots."

"Well I, for one, didn't register for this class."

"And how are we still—" The spittle flew from the Baron's lips. "*Commodifying* the Black body?"

"Look at the war on drugs," said Anders, "not to mention the prison industrial complex. Private corporations make a profit off keeping as many people as possible locked up. Why do you think the prison sentences for crack were a hundred times worse than for cocaine?"

"Russia is still worker's paradise."

The teen continued. "There are schematics online showing the number of people you can fit in a prison block that look an *awful* lot like the drawings of Africans packed into ships for the Middle Passage."

"Can someone *please* turn up the Victrola?"

"Nothing reeks of the transatlantic slave trade more than a handful of rich white men profiting off Black men *pulverizing their own brains* on national television every Sunday. Or what about the fact that Haiti had to pay France, *their former colonial oppressor*, millions of dollars in compensation for the revenue France lost when Haiti became free, yet no country has ever paid reparations to the *descendants of slaves* but Britain *literally* paid restitution to slave owners *and their heirs* up until 2015."

"That doesn't make any sense," said Kevin.

"Exactly but it's the truth." The teen sighed, an exasperated teacher in charge of a classroom full of boneheads. "Listen. You can still watch footage from 1945 of everyday Germans being marched through the death camps. It ain't pretty. American soldiers *forced* them to look at what was done in their name. Where are *our* truth commissions? What have *we* ever been forced to *see*?"

"Why would we need to be *marched* through anything?" said a voice. "Slavery wasn't a secret tucked away behind some walls. It was a way of life."

Striker closed the notebook. "Just like today." She realized she was the one speaking. "All you gotta do is open your eyes. Employment discrimination. Underfunded inner-city schools. Black people murdered in the streets by cops. White landlords not renting to you because your name's Quashida. What are we gonna march people through? A *McDonald's* so they can ask themselves why it's mostly Black and brown folks ringing up their Filet-O-Fish?"

Silence. The group sat looking at her as if she had ten heads.

"What's that got to do with the difference between yams and sweet potatoes?" Kevin finally asked.

"It doesn't," said the Dame. "She's cracking up." The Dame turned to Bobbi Sue. "Funny. I would've put money on you being the first one to lose it."

"Jane," said the Baron. "Methinks perhaps the gentlewoman is not the heavy hitter she might think she is when it comes to herb." He took another hit off the pipe.

"Thanks for explanation, guys," said Vadim. "Next time *Yegorov* cook bakes potato sweet pie, I will eat."

Striker realized she was inhabiting a totally different planet.

It didn't matter. Something was massing outside in the sunlight, tunneling up out of the ice. What had Billy Bob said a million years ago about the stories these islands had to tell if the planet ever saw fit to thaw them out?

Someone had given birth out there in the grotto, deep down in the cold and the winter dark. The revolting disc like a loaf of crusty bread wasn't a baby seal or a giant mushroom or even alien in origin.

It was afterbirth, a human placenta.

Striker could still taste the woman's fear. She knew what the woman had been afraid of. She herself had eaten the egg of a partially formed penguin, then turned and asked for another. There was nothing a human being wouldn't devour. We are a species capable of killing fifty thousand fur seals in a single week, she thought, of selling human beings to the highest bidder, of separating children from their mothers *even now*. Around the turn of the last century, some poor lovesick woman had shaved her head and swaddled herself in wool and canvas. But the interminable winter couldn't hide what that woman was inevitably becoming.

There was a sudden knock at the door. On the Victrola, the needle began skipping.

"Look at that." Vadim pointed to the walking stick. "It's bleeding, da?"

In the candlelight, the Stick did indeed appear wet and red.

Kevin got up to investigate. He tapped his finger in the ooze running out of the dent, smelled it before putting the finger in his mouth.

"Sap," he said. "Tastes like an IPA."

The knock sounded again. On the table the water jumped in every glass. The windows began rattling.

Nobody moved.

Striker could feel the skin of her chest bruising as something beat its terrible fist on the wood. She thought of the long-ago philosophy class that had sent her into a panic, all of existence suddenly divided by zero, the other students quietly scribbling notes. Every head buried in the sand. Living as if they'd never die. The professor asking questions like who were you before you were born? His questions causing Striker's mind to go blank.

The door clattered in its frame. With one strong gust it blew open. Snow streamed into the room. Outside the night was white as bone. Striker had to shield her eyes.

Something was standing on the threshold, the thing barely bigger than an infant. Awkwardly it hopped forward. A single red point burning like the tip of a lit cigarette.

It was the one-eyed bird.

Willkommen, shouted the Walking Stick.

The Baron let out a great big belly laugh. "Did someone order takeout?"

"Vadim, grab the net," Kevin whispered, pointing to one hanging on the wall.

The bird peered around the hut. Suddenly it shot into the room. Striker threw her arms up over her eyes. She was the one it had come for, the one with all the secrets. The bird tore past her face, a new rip glistening in her cheek as ████████████████████
██
██
██
██
██
██
██
██
██
██
██

"Hey."

"Hey?" said Striker.

"You wanna dance or not?" asked Anders.

"Me?" said Striker. She looked around. The group was staring at her. Vadim standing in the middle of the room with his hand held out.

"Yeah," said Anders. "Don't worry. He'll lead. All you gotta do is follow."

"I think I need some sleep," said Striker. She handed the teen the journal she'd been gifted and made her way to an empty hammock.

It was only when she pulled the hammock wide so she could lie down that she found a sack of what looked like skin. It was the size of a person and mostly bald. During a talk onboard the *Yegorov*, a lecturer had mentioned that turn-of-the-century explorers were constantly battling to keep their reindeer sleeping bags dry. In bitterly cold conditions, warm air would get trapped inside the bag and form condensation, the men soaked in their own body heat.

Delicately Striker pinched the thing between two fingers and tossed it on the floor. Sleeping in it would be like crawling inside someone else's skin. She knew it had come from a reindeer, but the sleeping bag was eerily smooth. She curled up in the hammock and glanced one last time at her watch. 12:14 p.m. She was still high but at this point what could it matter?

"Why is she so tired?" someone whispered. "We've only been here a few hours."

"Do the math," someone else countered. "It's been more like—"

Striker tuned out the argument that was just getting going, letting the weed or fatigue or both carry her away

to the Yegorov. Finally! She's back on the boat and not a moment too soon.

Odd footprints ramble over the deck. Some track in circles, others walk through walls. Each print perfect and flat and redly wet as if stamped by a child's bleeding hand.

Somewhere a church organ is playing. It's a Christmas carol. Holy infant so tender and mild. Shizer, *not* that *one. The description of the baby Jesus as though He were a basket of wings, a little sumthing sumthing to tide you over.*

Then she's standing in front of the Yegorov's sauna door. Slowly she pulls it open. Inside sits a tiny, forlorn pool filled with saltwater gleaming black as oil. A body bobs face down in the shadows, its back inked with a chain of lights. It's Polaris, the North Star, the tattoo exactly like the six stars Striker has inked on her own back, an invisible compass steering her through time.

Within the dreamscape she's hungry to know what prolonged submersion in saltwater will do to a human face. Silently she approaches the edge of the pool and reaches out.

In the water the corpse rolls easily onto its back. Suddenly the body opens its swollen eyes. Between the front teeth is a gap wide enough to fit a pencil.

"Hello, Ronnie," it gurgles. Something thick and wet bubbles from its peeling lips. "Merry Christmas!" An icy hand shoots up out of the water and latches onto her neck.

Striker needs both hands to pry the spongy fingers off her throat. She can tell it is only a warning. If it had wanted to, the thing could have crushed her windpipe within seconds.

The corpse flashes one last smile, then rolls over and resumes floating face down. This time Striker sees it loud and clear. Inked at the base of the creature's neck, the mark she can't seem to outrun.

She feels the skin tingling on the back of her own neck just as a voice begins to shout—

"Let him have it, young gun," shrieked the Baron, the bloodlust peppering his words. "Give him a taste of his own medicine right in his manhood."

Wearily Striker opened her eyes. Vadim and la Grande Dame were standing on the other side of the room. From her hammock she couldn't tell if the Russian was holding the Dame's arm against her will or if the old girl was looking to accompany him somewhere, maybe dance one more song. Why can't these people just let me sleep, she thought.

"Your woman is liar," said Vadim. "I am not man who needs to go where I am not invited."

"Let go of her," repeated Anders, legs akimbo, both hands gripping the small black hole drawing all eyes to it. Striker knew it wasn't a prop.

"You not understand adult games, girly boy," added Vadim, shaking his head. He was still holding the Dame's arm. Slowly he brought it to his face, making as if to kiss her hand. At the last moment he torqued her wrist and licked the giant emerald nested on her finger, crudely dragging his tongue over the gem's myriad facets.

The Dame ripped her hand away. "Men are children," she announced, then furiously rubbed the jewel on her thigh, polishing it back into perfection. The old gal showed zero interest in clarifying whatever had happened between her and the Russian. The titanium posts in her gums worrying her lip as she worked her magic.

"See?" said Vadim. "Is all big act." He winked and started clapping. "Brava. For wife, *jealous* husband easier to lead around by big rich nose."

Anders stood their ground, the little black hole quaking in their hand. If you thought about it, how could something so small inflict such carnage?

Murder, sang the Walking Stick.

"I mean it," repeated Anders. "Leave."

Vadim laughed again. "And go where, little lamb?"

"Christ," said Kevin. "I kept both bags locked up."

"Anna," said Bobbi Sue.

"Mom, just because the school didn't lift a finger when it happened to me doesn't mean it didn't happen."

"I *believed* you," said Bobbi Sue. "It's just—"

"I saw." The teen nodded at the Russian. "He put his hand down there without asking and then wouldn't stop."

The Dame shook her head but remained silent. As Striker saw it the chick was in a bind. Attesting to the Russian's innocence would mean admitting to being a player. If anything, her husband the Baron seemed strangely aroused.

"What you don't understand, little potato," said Vadim. "Words ruin adult fun."

"Get out."

Vadim shrugged and did as Anders said. The group watched as he opened the cabin door. Striker stretched in her hammock before standing up. *Sheesh. Can't a body catch some shut-eye around here?*

She'd been having the weirdest dream, but in reality, the current drama was even weirder.

Outside the sky glimmered bright as noon. The teen marched the captive out to the hatch gaping wide in the snow.

"Now get in," Anders commanded. The little black hole shook in their fist.

"At least give him his jacket, Anna," said Bobbi Sue.

"Why bother?" said Kevin. "It's like frigging spring out here."

"Down there is not up here," the Dame pointed out.

"Extreme cold is *exactly* what the doctor ordered for a case of criminal randyness," said the Baron in ecstasy.

All the same Bobbi Sue disappeared inside the hut and came back out with Vadim's things, shoving them in his arms.

"Not ship, not submarine, not killer whale," explained Vadim as he calmly suited up. He took a deep breath. To Striker, he seemed to grow ten feet with every inhalation. "Face it. Was bomb," he said. "Nuclear bomb." Behind him the sky shone bloodless and pale, the sun without heat or color, a titanium star stuck a few degrees past noon. "*Yegorov*, gone, beloved North America, gone." He finished zipping up his parka. "I am strongest man left on earth. When you need me—"

He put his hat on at a rakish angle and disappeared into the hole. Striker had to admit the guy had a flair for drama.

If they hadn't already been standing around outside, they might have missed the tiny white triangle floating on the blue.

"Talk about a Christmas miracle," said la Grande Dame.

"I prefer *deus ex machina*," said the Baron.

"Shut up, Robert," said the Dame, but there was a discernible note of relief in her voice.

Kevin seemed weirdly glum. "I *suppose* we could borrow their radio," he said.

"They might even be happy to anchor in our little bay until help arrives," said the Baron. Already there was a little more color in his old-man face though it might have come from throwing the Russian in the hole.

"Vadim could paddle that in under fifteen minutes," said the Dame.

"Agreed," murmured Bobbi Sue. "He's the only one fast enough to catch up with it."

"We just sent the guy six feet under with extreme prejudice," said Kevin. "*You* wanna be the one to go ask him to bail our asses out?"

Details, details.

The general consensus was that the boat was some kind of high-end sailboat, not exactly a yacht but close. The Baron went one step further, pulling out his maritime bona fides and spraying them all with his seafaring wisdom.

"You ask me, that beauty rides like a vintage Hallberg-Rassy ninety-eight-footer. The Swedes know how to build 'em," he said. "Those things practically sail themselves."

"I thought you were from Omaha," said Kevin. "Now you're a seaman?"

"What, a man can't travel?" the Baron retorted.

"You're not at the helm," said Bobbi Sue. "How can you tell how it rides?" Somehow all this talk of boats was bringing her back to life.

"If you'd ever piloted a Hallberg-Rassy, you'd know," said the Baron, the condescension coloring his voice.

"We live within hours of some of the best sailing in the US," said Anders. "Michigan and Superior. My mom and dad sail a Hanse forty-two-footer out of Sturgeon Bay in Door County, the Cape Cod of the Midwest."

"No disrespect, young 'un," said the Baron, winding back for the pitch, "but the Great Lakes are a bathtub compared to the Pacific."

Bobbi Sue ignored the comment. "All I know is that boat's closer to sixty," she said, "and you'd be crazy to come down here in a vintage sloop with no autopilot. Yeah, you *could* have a Hallberg retrofitted to make the journey, but folks who own the vintage boats aren't the kind who like to modernize."

All Striker wanted was a lounge chair with deep cushions, a nice cold mai tai, and to sit back and enjoy the view. Nobody had remarked on the beauty of the day. Was it possible the others couldn't see it, the whole lot of them stumbling around with scales on their eyes? Everywhere the terrain glimmered as if frosted with a pearliness. The boat floating easily on azure waves.

The group was going nowhere fast as they continued to bicker. Bobbi Sue *Sarah, goddammit! Her name's Sarah* shook her head and headed into the hut. She reappeared with a bowl of jerky she'd been soaking. "Pemmican?" she said, offering the group sludgy bits of cardboard. The chick's hostessing skills were nonpareil.

"What about the extra eggs?" asked the Dame. Striker took it as a good sign the old girl was hungry. The appearance of the sailboat was having a positive impact on all of them. Like Kevin's high-tech x-acto knife, the Dame's humanity was inching out bit by bit.

"We should ration them for later," said Sarah.

"Later?" scoffed the Baron. "*Later* we'll be eating the other white meat."

"*Pork?*" asked Bobbi, er, Sarah.

"No, people," said Kevin under his breath. Too bad for him but in such pristine air, sound traveled freely. His words came out loud and clear as if he were speaking directly into their heads. Great! The guy who'd packed a loaded gun for a simple kayak outing had cannibalism on his mind.

The other white guy realized his mistake. "I meant the other *other* white meat," the Baron said. "Poultry." He squeezed his wife by the shoulder. "We have opposable thumbs. I say we use them." To demonstrate, he made a pistol with his fingers, shooting Anders in the face.

"Guys," said Kevin. "Our boat's on the move."

Shizer! They didn't have much time.

"How many miles we think that is?" Sarah asked.

Striker took another peek through the binoculars. She was pretty good at this sort of thing. Often she needed to be able to judge distances for a principal cinematographer. She had come of age before all the laser tapes and digital gizmos. On set, she'd often wow people with her accuracy. She was usually right within a tenth of a mile.

"Not quite three miles," she said. "2.8." The Dame looked at her approvingly and nodded.

"What are we gonna do once we get there?" asked Anders.

"Asking for help is the easy part," said Kevin. "We gotta get there first."

It came on abruptly. The group was standing in a spot that hadn't hosted human habitation in a good hundred years, and suddenly it smelled like a city dump. Striker wondered how long it would take for whatever bad mojo was gunning for them to arrive.

"I'll go with Vadim in one of the tandems," she said.

"What if he tries to manhandle you?" asked the Dame. There was genuine concern in her voice.

"The guy wants to get rescued as bad as the rest of us."

"What about what he said?" asked Sarah.

"You mean that the Ruskies dropped the big one?" said the Baron.

"If it happened, I don't think you can drop just one," mused Sarah.

"Like potato chips," said Kevin. Nobody laughed. "Sarah's right," he said. "All that stuff's run by algorithms. One drops, they all drop."

"Can we just focus on this?" asked the Dame.

For the first time since Percy's death, Striker could hear a faint whisper of panic in la Grande Dame's voice. *Our girl's name is Jane.* A light sweat glistened on the older woman's upper lip. Jane, thought Striker. The name made her seem vulnerable. Had she *always* presented that way, her caustic demeanor masking an obvious brittleness that Striker had used as an excuse to cast her in the one-note role of villain?

"Vadim was about to get dropped in a hole by a kid," she said. "The guy was bluffing." She did her best to look like she believed it, but all you had to do was open your eyes. Everywhere the colors seemed off. Fiery but with a hint of something else, maybe something atomic? And what was going on with the temperature? It was growing warm enough that soon they'd find themselves wishing Kevin had packed a deodorant stick in one of his dry bags.

"Fine," said the Baron. "Let's dig the bastard up."

He spit out the pemmican he'd been chewing on. Striker couldn't say why but she buried it in the melting snow with her foot.

They circled up around the hatch.

"Vadim?" called Striker. "You down there?"

No response.

"Poor baby's hiding," said the Baron.

Striker knew she was the only one with a shot of getting this done. Vadim would throttle the Baron if given the chance, same for the old girl. He also wouldn't be overly keen on having a heart-to-heart with either the teen who'd held a gun on him or the teen's mom. Kevin might have been his heavy-metal bro, but Kevin was weak and a loose cannon. They couldn't risk Vadim talking the guy into some crazy plan, like shooting all of them in the head and then feasting on their flesh until spring, when they would sail out into the watery blue yonder and take over the globe, a Golden Horde of two, the last real men on the planet.

"Okay, lemme go talk to him." For the third time in forever, she sat down on the lip of the hole. It's all in my mind, she consoled herself. There's nothing down there but a Russian and a stack of frozen seals. Despite what her watch said, it was probably officially Christmas, the day her sister had died in juvie twenty-five years ago. As she slid down into the light, she could hear voices talking aboveground.

"Should we have given her a weapon?"

"Too late now" was the last thing she heard.

Striker surveyed the grotto. The air smelled musty and close. The only light was the thin shaft trickling down from the opening. Standing in the gloom she knew there was no tunnel. This space had never been crazy bright like an operating room. Somewhere she had read that for a tree to touch heaven, its roots must first reach down to hell. That's all this icy cavern under the scarred wooden door ever was. A hell of the mind. A place to frighten yourself silly with shadows and possibilities and regrets. A hall of mirrors reflecting your inner life back to you.

"Vadim?" she called. "Can we talk?"

Great. The guy was hiding somewhere behind a mountain of garbage, whimpering about being the strongest man on earth yet stuck down here with the trash.

Striker began to pick her way through the heaps of refuse. In spots the junk scraped the ceiling. Uneven shelves, foodstuffs hardened into unrecognizable shapes, cracked lanterns, century-old down pillows now calcified stiff, a pianoforte with half its keyboard missing. The floor was still studded with icy knobs. Striker noticed part of a toothbrush poking up out of the white. If a man got scurvy and lost his teeth, he probably didn't have much use for it.

It was her craving for a mai tai that spurred her on. The sailboat will be fully stocked, she told herself. They're on an around-the-world voyage. They'll have it all. Expensive rum, little colorful umbrellas. Ice, real ice, cubes of it, not the towering blue stuff that seemed to stalk you wherever you went.

"Vadim?" she called out again.

An old fear colored her breathing. But I'm not alone, she told herself. Vadim's floating around here somewhere. Still, another part of her couldn't keep from picturing a larger presence nearby that dwarfed the both of them. The thing waiting for her to come sniffing around a corner and walk straight into its web of decay and madness.

She found him behind a pyramid of splintered tables. He was lying in the red hollow melted in the floor. Nearby the hundred-year-old placenta lay tossed on a broken chair. It was the spot where some poor woman had birthed her lover's baby just feet from a cabinful of starving men. The woman's scalp laced with cuts from shaving her head, voice hoarse as she tried to pass herself off as one of them.

Striker's first thought was that he was dead. *Dead* dead. Vadim's pallor ghoulish, skin mottled like an old bruise. Just to be sure, she prodded him with her foot.

He opened his salt-white eyes and grabbed her ankle.

She spun around and took off running.

Head-on she smacked into a pile of crates. It toppled over. A broken violin fell out, smashing with a discordant clang on the ice. Where was the entrance? How had this tiny room suddenly become so big?

Figures she'd never seen before began to emerge on every surface. In the walls, on the ceiling, in the floor. Images like looking in an icy mirror. Everywhere she turned gaunt and hollow-eyed men glared from the shadows of their ragged anoraks. Beards straggly, faces burned by cold. Their numbers seemed to multiply. Two of the men waved shillelaghs. Several were missing limbs. One man looked to be missing both arms. The man snarling at her intently.

She watched as the tallest man in the group began punching his way through the ice. Cold chips shot through the air. The man's face was sheathed in leather, two yellow fangs slick with spit. She could practically smell his rancid breath. The figure wasn't using his fists to break through. He was wielding an ax, his face a void. Expressionless.

Striker knew she was running in circles. She would never get away. The sound of her panic bounced off the walls. Turning corner after countless corner. She could hear the ice splintering. Everywhere the sound like glass breaking.

She rounded yet another corner and saw the worst face yet. The shriek on the face like death itself. Mouth a black hole of despair. Eyes colorless. Lips shrunken, black twists clinging lifelessly to the patchy scalp.

A hand landed on her shoulder.

"You came for me?"

She had no choice but to turn and face it.

"You need me," sighed Vadim. He seemed tired but otherwise healthy, all his impishness drained away. "Why, I not know, but okay." Striker realized they were standing below the entrance. He leaned over and intertwined his fingers. "You think this maybe heaven?" he asked. He spoke while working something out in his mind. "I think yes," he said. "We are dead. We just need to believe we are. Then comes big peace."

She stepped into the web of his hands, felt the thrust as he boosted her back up among the living.

And so she was out on the Southern Ocean paddling hard toward a mai tai, the possibility of a few ounces of smooth Jamaican rum all the motivation she needed even if her hands wouldn't stop cramping.

Before she set out from the beach, Jane had awkwardly approached her. The penguins scurried about like small black-and-white traffic cones, but the old woman navigated her way through. At first, Striker didn't know what she wanted. She took a step back as Jane entered her personal space. The old woman held out her arms. Oh, Striker thought. Half-heartedly she let herself be embraced.

"Good luck," Jane whispered in her ear. "You can do this."

"Thanks, Jane," Striker said. She realized it was the first time she'd said her name.

The sailboat was growing closer though there were moments she had her doubts. It was hard to tell how long they'd been chasing it. Like the sun, the few existing shadows seemed stuck in place. If the boat slipped away, Striker knew the group would only have the long, slow trek into hunger and madness to look forward to, that plus whatever else those two ingredients cooked up.

Out on the ocean with no sense of time, she felt herself grow wistful. Ama used to lie in bed on nights with a full moon and talk about traveling to the great white hole in the sky, babbling on about how long it would take to get there and what the sisters would find once they did. "Ice cream," she'd say. "That's why it's so cold." Having snuck out of her own room, Striker would bed down with her sister and listen to her sugary dreams, the two of them safe and happy on their own planet. "We can do it," Ama would say, pointing out the window, the gap between her teeth somehow twinkling in the dark. "We just need a way up into the sky." At her sister's nudging, Striker would sit up on her elbows and peer out into the night. "See?" her sister would say, pointing off in the distance at Our Lady of the Annunciation with the copper cross like a sentinel keeping watch over the sleeping town. "It's the same distance as the church." And each time as Ama predicted, there was the full moon drifting just above the steeple, the moon and the copper cross within inches of grazing each other.

Now Striker had found it. The way up into the sky. Everywhere the water like velvet stretching to the horizon, the Southern Ocean a giant infinity pool. From her kayak there was no difference between the sea and the cosmos. If she paddled hard enough, she could slip the bonds of earth and launch herself into the heavens.

She was surprised Vadim wasn't much further ahead. Possibly he was growing weak from the lack of food. Or maybe she herself was getting stronger. Every few minutes Vadim would turn and call over his shoulder. *Push!* And she would dig deep, lengthen her stroke, unsure of where her inner reserves were coming from, wondering how they'd make it back to the island or if it was an open secret that they were never meant to. Like Robert Scott and his men pushing on to the Pole knowing full well all was lost, that Amundsen and his dogs had already been there and back. Scott's team trudging on in agony through the unforgiving whiteness, skin blackened as though charred by fire. The way the objective changes when you realize there's no returning. The journey becomes its own reward.

She and Kevin were trailing in a second tandem but still close enough to hear Vadim's exhortations. Though the sailboat was their goal, she was discovering she didn't need a mai tai to see this through. With each stroke, she could feel herself winnowing down, every unimportant thing falling away, her mind quieting, body jazzed like she could paddle all the way to New York and back. Admittedly it was a little uncanny. She'd never felt so alive, as if the kayaking group had just pushed off from the *Yegorov* only minutes before.

Up ahead, Vadim paddled languidly over the ocean. "Big push," he called.

The air felt fresh on her skin, the universe vast and shining and intimate. He didn't need to tell her to push. She was already halfway to the moon.

They were breaching off the starboard side of the sailboat. She could hear Percy's voice in her ear, his excitement at witnessing a wonder of nature.

"Right whales," she said, channeling their dead guide, "or I guess they could be humpbacks."

"What about orca?" asked Kevin. There was trepidation in his voice. For much of the way out, the guy had kept a hand buried in his dry bag. He was probably clutching the THING, acting like he was some kind of bodyguard. Who was he kidding? Vadim was lifetimes ahead of them, soaring along in a separate boat, plus what could the Russian possibly do out there in the middle of nowhere to deserve a slug in the back? She really just needed Kevin to help paddle and stop playing rent-a-cop.

By her count there were at least five funnels jetting in the air. "I don't think orcas spout that high," she said, remembering a clip she'd seen of killer whales zooming around their prison-like tanks at SeaWorld.

"Da, spout too big for orca," called Vadim over his shoulder. Thanks to the atmospherics, they could hear him despite the distance. "Is blue whale. Biggest beast to ever exist on planet."

It had been decided that the three of them would head out on what the Baron dubbed *our little errand*. Striker and Kevin would be in one of the tandems, Vadim in the other. They could use the extra space in the second boat to bring back supplies. While the three of them chased down the sailboat, the others would stay behind and build a fire, covering two bases at once. Though the three of them had been paddling for what felt like days, Striker still didn't see any smoke staining the skies. Each time she turned to look, it was getting harder and harder to tell which speck of rock was theirs. She was just grateful for the smooth ride out. At times she found herself wondering if this was truly Antarctica. The deep blue water flat as a lake.

Strangely, it was Sarah who had insisted that Kevin come along. "I did my residency on a psych ward," she'd whispered. "He fits the profile."

"What profile?"

"Of someone who's got nothing to lose," said Sarah. "That's when people are at their most dangerous."

At this point didn't they *all* have nothing left to lose? "So you think he's better off in a tandem with *me* than here with you guys?"

Sarah made a quizzical face. "There'll only be four of us," she said.

"Don't forget Hector."

"Precisely. We aren't exactly the strongest bunch. I'd go," she added, "but I have to stay and watch out for Anna. There's a lot of healing going on in that one," she murmured.

Striker decided she didn't need to know what Sarah was talking about. "Does Kevin even *want* to go?" she asked. The two women glanced over at him. He was windmilling his arms around like a swimmer limbering up for a race. Striker sighed but didn't argue the point any further.

Before heading out, the three of them each choked down a penguin egg.

"There'll be food aplenty onboard," said the Baron. "Any yachtsman worth his weight in gold will have hordes of vittles." He clapped Vadim on the back. Striker was surprised the Russian didn't deck him one. "You'll see. There'll be cans of beluga from bow to stern."

"What's he going on about?" asked Anders.

"Caviar," said Jane.

For some reason, Striker imagined boarding the sailboat only to find the pantry stocked with cans of Ensure. The image made her laugh.

"What?" said Kevin, but she shook her head.

Up ahead Vadim was almost within striking distance. Kevin pulled his hand out of his dry bag and squirmed around in his seat, trying to scratch a spot on his back.

"Hey there," he called out. "At dinner, did I hear you say you spent time in Ukraine?" Vadim didn't answer. Kevin tried again only louder. "Hey," he yelled. "Were you in Ukraine?"

Why bring that up now, Striker thought.

The Russian merely turned his head in their direction. "Push," he called, before taking off at a breakneck clip.

Striker realized he hadn't been exerting himself. The guy had energy for days.

"Dude was totally in Ukraine," said Kevin, as the two of them watched him burn rubber. "Bet he did some bad shit there."

"Like what?" said Striker. "It's a fucking war."

"So?" said Kevin. "You can still break the law. They're not called *war crimes* for nothing."

"How's that compare to bashing someone's head in with a rock?" Instantly she relaxed, safe in the knowledge that she hadn't actually said it though if she had, so what? The guy had it coming.

"All I'm saying is he's a bad hombre, as in bad to women," he said. "It's written all over his face. But whatever," he concluded. "We need him." Kevin hugged the dry bag a little tighter in his lap. "Until we don't," he added under his breath.

Vadim was nearing the sailboat. It was still on the move but slowing, the keel gliding along as if drawn by a magnet. It looked to be headed for a circular island up ahead with tall black cliffs rising dramatically up out of the water. There was a narrow break in the rock face, an opening like a gap between two teeth where the ocean entered. The space looked barely big enough for a kayak let alone a sixty-foot sailboat. Striker couldn't tell what the opening even led to. It could be a small inlet leading nowhere, a sore spot where the ocean had worn away the rock. Entering would be a leap of faith. If the entryway narrowed, you might not be able to maneuver your way back out.

She thought of the journal she'd been gifted for Christmas. How badly would you have to love someone to follow them into hell? A hundred years ago there was no way back from here, no turning yourself around and simply sailing for home.

Suddenly the boat slowed. Its main sail began to fall slack. She could hear loose ropes flapping wildly. Sarah had said that on these fancy boats, an onboard computer was likely running the show. It seemed like something had pretty seriously malfunctioned. The top sail sagged like an empty bedsheet. Then Striker realized what was happening.

The sails were coming down, retracting as the vessel decelerated, the canvas folding up on itself.

"*Da iti ta!*" shouted Vadim.

He had reached the boat and tied his kayak to it. Now he was scrambling up the back ladder. Striker watched as he strode to the front, seemingly unconcerned with making noise and rousing anyone. Boldly he stood at the helm peering out toward the gap in the rock face. Was it even going to fit? A pale blue light settled on his skin. It looked like the glow from a computer screen, but then it deepened and grew more otherworldly, Vadim on the edge of transitioning into another realm.

"Come come," he yelled, his voice growing faint as the boat nosed into the gap. Striker could see there was no room for error, the fit like a hand in a glove. "Hurry," Vadim called. "Water—" but then the sailboat slipped into the breach and disappeared.

"You can let go of your manhood now." Striker wondered how much of that she'd said. Either way, it did the trick. Sheepishly Kevin pulled his hand out of his dry bag and started paddling.

Up ahead the island loomed like a fortress. She pictured their kayak slipping inside the rock face and finding themselves in a land of the lost where giant pterodactyls soared through the clouds, the waters studded with prehistoric fish. Or maybe the island was more like *South Pacific*, home to women in grass skirts balancing baskets of breadfruit on their heads, their long black hair rippling in the sea breeze.

As they drifted closer she began to notice the eeriness of the spot. The waters around the island were glassine, the air unmoving. Kevin pointed out another oddity.

"Where's the white stuff?" he asked.

It was true. Not a single iceberg could be seen bumbling along. Nothing about this spot screamed Antarctica. An emptiness clung to the landscape as if life had turned its back on this island.

Just minutes before, Vadim had been standing on the sailboat peering into the breach, his face aglow. Now there was no sign of him or the boat, only the electric blue light pouring out of the opening in the rock face.

"That ain't natural," whispered Kevin.

"Man has a very narrow sense of nature," said Striker.

She had been on plenty of movie sets. If you set up the kliegs in a certain way, you could create an impenetrable wall of light. The same thing happened in live theater. Actors standing on stage unable to see beyond the footlights. Most of them preferred it that way. It made them less nervous. Striker took a deep breath as their kayak slipped into the fissure.

Inside, the rocky corridor was a gamut of blue. She could feel her teeth instantly whiten, bones shining through her skin. It was hard to gauge where it was coming from. It seemed to be pouring up from the water itself, the ocean as if electrified. The further in they paddled, the worse the visibility became until it was down to mere inches. She was having trouble seeing her own hands.

"Say something," she called out.

"It's like I'm being erased," said Kevin.

She was no longer sure they were still moving. Now and then she could see the sheerness of the cliff walls. Each time the rock face broke through the blue, the cliffs seemed closer, narrowing. She was surprised the sailboat had fit.

"In a couple of days we were supposed to visit Deception Island," said Kevin. "Maybe this is it."

"The prospectus didn't mention anything about being blinded."

The itinerary had described Deception Island as a sunken caldera where the volcanic cone had collapsed enough to let the ocean in. The collapse had left the island shaped like an atoll with a rocky outer ring and an inner harbor heated by geothermal vents. She recalled flipping through pictures of happy tourists in bathing suits shrouded by wisps of steam curling off the surface of the ocean. In none of the photos were the people obscured by so much blue they couldn't see their neighbors let alone their own hands.

Slowly the color of the air softened. The day regained its normalcy. The blue was indeed radiating from the water. Striker thought of an afternoon she'd spent floating in the Blue Grotto in Capri, the gondolier singing "O Sole Mio." Even there, it was only the ocean shining a blue bright as heaven. The cave itself had remained as it was, dark and craggy.

Finally the tandem floated into a wide harbor.

The sailboat was anchored in the middle, Vadim's kayak tied up to the back. Striker dipped her hand in, watched as it instantly disappeared. There are so many ways to be erased, she thought. On this trip I've encountered practically all of them.

Then something burst out of the water right next to the kayak. Kevin jumped out of his skin. Instinctually his hand shot deep into his dry bag as if whatever was in there could save him.

He was floating on his back. Just a pale white face, the rest of him effaced in the blue water. "Is maybe twenty-three, twenty-four degrees."

"Celsius?" asked Kevin.

"Go tie up," said Vadim, ignoring the question. "Take off everything. No worries. Peeksies not possible here." Quickly she and Kevin crawled up on deck.

The Baron was full of shit. Sarah had called it, the sailboat about sixty feet in length though its opulence was stunning. No one appeared onboard to greet them or challenge their right to be standing on this multi-million-dollar craft. For the moment Striker didn't dwell on the oddness of this ghost ship navigating pilotless through the waters of the Southern Ocean. Instead, she stood gazing out over the bay, soaking in the wonder of the mesmerizing color.

Where was Percy when you needed him? Oh, that's right. He was dead. They would have to do their best without him.

"It's an algae bloom," said Kevin. "You know, like red tide."

"Where is red?" said Vadim from the water. "Show me red."

"I meant it's the same principle in action," retorted Kevin.

Striker knew if it were wintertime and the skies were dark, it would be so beautiful you would never want to leave. "Bioluminescence," she whispered.

"Da," said Vadim. "Plankton. One trip last year we find big patch. Marine biologist says very rare. Largest feeding ground on planet earth."

Striker unzipped her dry suit. She went around to the other side of the boat and peeled off most of her clothes. A few minutes later the two men heard a splash.

Kevin remained onboard. "Have fun getting out, dipshits," he said, as he disappeared down a hatchway. "Don't come crying to me if you end up a frozen popsicle like Nicholson in *The Shining*."

That's not how the book ends, Striker thought, but whatever. She knew it wasn't fear of the cold that was keeping Kevin out of the bluest water on earth. Striker had known guys like him. It was the doughiness of his body, his belly pale and bloodless like a dolphin's. She wondered how long it had been since his innermost flesh had seen the sun. Why let shame keep you from having a good time? On Zinnia Trace she had seen white humanity's bottomless hatred of their own bodies up close and personal. Women holding themselves back from a dip in the pool because it required the shedding of their everyday armor called clothes.

"Any masks up there, maybe some goggles?" she called.

He didn't answer. He was probably rifling through the owner's belongings, pawing through their medicine cabinet, their underwear drawer, practicing a little unfettered voyeurism in his search for the truly useless, like new needles for a 1908 Victrola.

Vadim popped up next to her. Already she had learned not to startle. The color of the water was so saturated it appeared solid, like a brick of blue clay. Striker lowered her face into it. Within seconds her heart began to pound, the feeling like being buried alive in the sky. With her luck she'd dive and hit something, her face colliding with an old pylon or worse. She wondered how Vadim managed it. How did he know how far away he was from the surface? Maybe days, weeks, in a windowless brig had taught him to navigate by landmarks other than sight, a kind of echolocation birthed from imprisonment.

For now he lay on his back spitting water up out of his mouth. He turned to her and grinned. For a long time they held each other's gaze.

Striker knew what he was thinking. She was thinking it herself. You, me, this boat—get it? All this could be our bubble bath. And Kevin? It's not like anyone back on Gilligan's Island will miss him if he fell overboard with something industrial and heavy tied around his foot. What had Sarah said? The guy had nothing left to lose. Dudes like that were dangerous—just look at the culture. Maybe Sarah had *really* been saying she wanted him dead. Striker imagined the good doctor scribbling something out on her prescription pad. *Take two slugs to the back of the head and call me in the morning.*

And what about the others? Did this endless blue even *care* about the group left behind on the volcano? It could be just the two of them, her and Vadim, riding out the season in mahogany luxury here on this rich man's yacht, the sky and the ocean one seamless jewel.

Vadim grinned harder. Yeah, he was definitely thinking it. He was a sailor and a strategist and a Russian who had either hightailed it out of the motherland or served in the festering pit that had become Ukraine. The guy knew better than anyone that a chess board is made solely for two. They could pull up anchor and sail whenever they wanted. If the winds were right, the next port of call might be Cape Town, somewhere the sun would kiss them all over.

"You hear that?" she said, but Vadim had disappeared again. She gazed out across the bay. It was the sound of tools at work, a steadfast hammering. There was something weirdly musical in the noise. She decided it was probably just some lonely bird drilling into the stony walls for its own inscrutable reason.

Eventually Vadim resurfaced. He held up a hand. "Wrinkly like elephant scrotum," he called, wiggling his pruny fingers.

The look that had passed between them remained suspended in the air. The day smelled of possibility and callousness, of putting yourself first. Striker had never had a problem with every man for himself. Every man for himself led to long nights in hot tubs with married men. All the same she wasn't one to bite first. Besides, she'd developed a sore spot for the kid. *You said sore. The phrase is "soft."* If Striker left the kid trapped on an island with their mom and a pair of serpentine geezers and crewed up to St. Barts, would she be able to face herself in the mirror every Christmas or would the holiday become that much worse?

All these years you seem to be sleeping just fine.

"Time to head in," she agreed.

Vadim yelled out, "Naked lady boarding!" Everywhere only the sound of water lapping against the boat's hull.

Striker takes a deep breath, the air filling her belly. What does she have to lose?

She dives deep, her feet rising up out of the water like a tail, head face down in the solid blue, letting herself get lost in it.

Down, down, down.

Everything blue, her eyes filling with sky, lungs on the verge of bursting.

Then some inner mechanism kicks in that won't let her go any deeper. Her body is a buoy that will only take so much, heart beating in her neck.

Involuntarily she breaks upward, airlessness drawing the body back up to what it needs. She feels herself split open the blue surface, gasping.

Did she even *want* to go deeper, all the way down to the end?

Maybe. It wouldn't be the worst way to go.

Two fluffy towels were lying by the ladder. One was white and blue and said MYCENAE on it, the other mint green, the towels plush as minks. Striker felt a greediness rise in her animal. She grabbed both, wrapping her twists in one and drying herself with the other.

She was pulling on her fleece when Vadim came crawling up the ladder. He climbed on deck and let out a roar. It was primal and masculine and distinctly Slavic. Something bearlike about it. He didn't ask for a towel. Just stood in his soaking wet boxers dripping in the summer sun, the water running down the ridges in his glistening muscles, thighs stippled with several unsophisticated tattoos. Striker could tell he had been his own artist. You had to have a lot of time on your hands to do that to yourself. You also needed a high pain threshold and a need to prove to yourself that you were still alive despite everything you'd been told. She imagined him sitting in the dark with a broken ballpoint pen, the results irregular and ugly.

Vadim noticed her staring. He laughed his big bear laugh and grabbed his crotch. "There space here for new tattoo," he said, as he disappeared behind the wheel house. "One of your face."

"Gross," said Striker.

"What is gross?" he called.

She didn't reply, unsure of whether or not either of them had spoken.

Their first stop was the alcove housing the communications equipment. Striker felt her heart sink. "Jesus," she whispered. Vadim put his hand on her shoulder.

The radio was smashed up and strewn all over the floor, cables and wires like ganglia sprouting from the wall.

Kevin appeared. "Someone didn't want our boy calling for help."

A crowbar lay in the broken glass. She bent over and picked it—

<< Striker is smashing up the room. The crowbar sails through the air. A jolt fires up her arm each time it breaks something. She is practically dancing. Glass and plastic and destruction clouding the day, metal casings left badly dented. An unfettered glee surges through her body. She is singing at the top of her lungs. Something atonal and heavy, rebellious. She has never felt so >>

The crowbar clattered on the floor. Striker rubbed her arm, her wrist sore from bashing at instruments designed to survive a hurricane.

"You all right?" Kevin asked. She nodded. "Okay then. Follow me."

He led them to the master berth. It was pretty swank but even in a sixty-footer space was an issue. A thickly padded maroon strip ran horizontally around the room. Striker realized it was for purchase, a bumper to keep you from battering yourself into the walls during rough seas. The queen-sized bed had a padded headboard the same red as everything else.

She could tell the padding was intended for safety and not kink. Still, there was something else going on in the berth. She couldn't put her finger on it but chalked it up to money. The room had a stentorian feel to it. Everything fusty, shellacked with a veneer of a turn-of-the-century gentlemen's club, velvet and brass and big, shiny rivets, what Riley would've dubbed *robber baron chic*. It was an odd combination. A first-rate, modern-day vessel with old-timey décor.

"Kate like me," said Vadim, lightly beating his chest. He was standing in front of a mirror screwed into the wall. "Well-built."

"Who's Kate?" said Kevin.

"This Kate," repeated Vadim, running a hand over the mirror. Striker could tell by the sound of his finger tapping the surface that it wasn't real glass. It was a smart move in case you ever made contact with it headfirst in high seas.

"The boat's named Kate," explained Striker. "It's painted on the back. I couldn't tell what flag she's flying."

"Antigua," said Vadim.

"Someone gets a gold star on the nations' flags quiz," said Kevin. "Also I hate to break it to you, but I don't think that's bioluminescence out there."

"What?" said Vadim distractedly. He was looking over a small stainless steel case about the size of a woman's evening clutch. "Then what is it?"

"What if I said you all took a dip in some radioactivity?"

Vadim laughed. "Big word, little man."

"I may not know a lot about radioactivity," sneered Kevin, "but I've seen plenty of bioluminescence. In Fiji. Snorkeling. And I can tell you." He paused for effect. "That there outside? That. Ain't. It."

"Come again?" said Striker. *Shizer*. Was she starting to feel itchy?

"You only see bioluminescence at night," Kevin explained. "And it's more like sparkles. Millions and millions of tiny sea creatures glowing up a storm. An entire bay wouldn't glow like this. This?" He nodded out toward the water. "This is artificial dye number two, like Blue Hawaiian Punch."

Vadim shook his head. "I know radioactivity," he said, though he didn't elaborate. "If water radioactive, me and her not standing here now."

"Then why is the water so warm?" Kevin countered.

"It's an extinct volcano," said Striker. "There's gotta be underwater vents."

Kevin didn't give up that easy. "Why no animals?" he asked. "No penguins, no birds of prey."

"There's no beach," said Striker. "Where are they supposed to nest?"

"Is too hot for birdies," said Vadim. "Life down here like me. We prefer cold."

Striker could tell they hadn't convinced him, but every minute she and Vadim remained upright, Kevin's theory seemed more and more far-fetched.

"Anyhoo," he concluded. "While you two were out playing Flipper, I found some things."

He dumped a rubber pouch on the bed. ID, money, tickets, a USB stick plus a handful of tiny ziplocks filled with individual portions of what looked like flour. Based on the available evidence, Gordon Baker, a citizen of both the US and Antigua, was living his best life. According to his passport, Gordon Baker was a sixty-four-year-old Libra who had been out at sea for at least five months, having flown from New York to St. John's back in June. The boat itself was registered to a Marsha Baker of Scottsdale, Arizona, but there was no passport for Marsha among the papers. No Marsha Baker plane ticket, no insurance cards, no photos, no videos, though there were soon plenty of images of Gordon Baker being Gordon Baker.

Kevin twirled the USB stick in his fingers. He slid the drive into a laptop. It came up under the name *Antietam*. "If this guy's still alive, first thing I'd tell him is always password protect."

After the first twenty seconds, Striker figured out what was going on with the décor of the captain's berth. *Well this is some bullshit*, Riley would've said before pouring the contents of a high-end bottle of cologne on the bed and ashing a lit cigarette on it.

"Yup," said Kevin. "Dude likes him some serious cosplay."

"Cosplay? What is this?" asked Vadim. "Some American thing?"

Kevin and Striker looked at each other. Striker shook her head. Nuh-uh. Not today. She wasn't going to touch that one.

"Cosplay is people dressing up in costumes and then letting their freak flag fly," Kevin offered. Not bad, Striker thought.

Vadim nodded. "This freak flag?" he said, pulling a hoop skirt out of a drawer followed by a pair of pantaloons, which he laid down on the bed next to a high-end leather riding crop. Kevin nodded. "But what is costume supposed to be? Russian peasant?"

Striker felt herself drawn into this terrible conversation against her will.

"It's antebellum."

"Ante what?"

"Antebellum," she said. "Gordon Baker likes him some antebellum shit." She pointed to what was playing on the laptop. A dark-skinned woman was dressed in rags while a white woman in a ball gown watched as Gordon Baker did his thing. "Antebellum," Striker said for the last time. "The days before the War of Northern Aggression. And turn that shit off." *Shizer*. Even at the ass of the world, there was no escaping history.

Vadim was still confused.

"The American Civil War," Kevin said. "North versus south. It would seem our host likes pretending he's a slave owner and diddling the merchandise."

"Merchandise?" said Striker.

"I was being facetious."

"Well don't." Suddenly she felt sick. She was pretty sure it was due to the appearance of the riding crop coupled with Gordon Baker's shining pate bobbing up and down as the darker woman serviced him and not thanks to her recent dip in the possibly radioactive blue lagoon. "So where do we think the swashbuckling Gordon Baker has disappeared to?"

The two men stood watching the video, angling their heads when needed to help see better. As a concession, Kevin turned the sound off. Poor beasts. For the millionth time in her life, Striker felt fortunate not to harbor a Y chromosome among her genome.

"I can't believe you guys are watching that. What about us getting rescued?"

"What about it?" said Kevin, distractedly.

"Does that thing have internet service?"

"Yes and no," he said, still on autopilot. Something in the look on his face. Not like Vadim, the Russian with a genuine curiosity to see what kind of ending the threesome would arrive at. No, there was an emptiness lurking in Kevin's eyes. *Guy has nothing left to lose.* It was like the floor had dropped out.

"I opened his search history," Kevin said. "There's no more Wi-Fi, but we can see his final searches." He stopped the video. "You *sure* you wanna know?"

"If it involves a Rosa Parks fetish, then no. Everything else? Bring it."

Kevin opened a new search window. He angled the screen toward her. Something in his face told her she should drop it. The most beautiful water imaginable was mere feet from where she was standing, the ocean a perfect bath. Nothing was stopping her. Just walk back up the stairs and jump overboard. Live out your remaining days like a mermaid in paradise.

There were no open pages, only a long list of websites. It went on and on. Striker realized she had stopped breathing.

"Hold arms above head," commanded Vadim. "Now in through nose."

But she couldn't. "This cannot be happening," she said. "It just *can't*." She rushed back up on deck. For the second time since boarding, she peeled off all her clothes and dove in headfirst, pylons or rusting shipping containers be damned, even welcomed.

The walls of the caldera ringing the harbor were unforgiving in their verticality. Still, Striker managed to find the one spot where the sea had worn away a few feet of rock. She crawled out of the weird blue water and lay down. It felt delicious. The black sand retained the heat in a way white sand never would. There had been heated tile in the master bath on Zinnia Trace. In the winters, she and Ama would lie on the floor in their pajamas and giggle in the unexpected warmth. Striker closed her eyes. Here the quiet was deafening. Kevin was right. There was something wrong with this place.

"Okay for me too?" said a small voice from the water.

"Go for it," said Striker. From the somber tone of his voice, she could tell Vadim hadn't swum up hungry to start any shenanigans. She listened as he settled on the black sand, the back of his head almost touching hers. For a long time, they lay soaking up the sun. "You okay?"

"I feel big shame," he said.

"Well don't," she said. "All those searches on the laptop for surviving a nuclear war? It doesn't mean anything actually *happened*. And if it *did*, we don't know for a *fact* it was Russia."

"Get real. Who else?"

"Listen," she said. "Gordon Baker probably had a thing for war. Maybe that's what turns him on, pretending he's the last man on earth."

"Okay, but why there no Gordon Baker here?"

What was it about white men and self-destruction? She had seen it on too many movie sets to count. Directors burning every bridge they'd ever built in the span of a single afternoon. Actors blowing up their careers, by the film's last shot, getting dropped by both their agents and their friends. Some guys couldn't see the long game, didn't understand there were lives out there beyond their own. That was why the short little man with the overly Botoxed face in Moscow could be willing to pull the plug on everything.

"I ask again. Where is Mr. Boat Captain?" said Vadim. "What? Kate says, 'Enough of sex party,' sails on ahead without him?"

Striker tried gaming it out. Mr. Boat Captain probably liked to sail his pride and joy into some unsuspecting port, then ply the internet's streets for ladies willing to help him put on his show. Maybe this time his ship had sailed into the wrong port and a pair of burly associates of the ladies had decided to put an end to Appomattox. Afterward, these same burly associates had cut Kate loose. Striker knew that scenario wasn't likely judging from all the rich-guy stuff still onboard. Okay then. How about this?

"One night he was solo partying too much and lost his balance. Simple as that."

Vadim remained quiet. The next time he spoke, his voice was soft.

"In Ukraine, I saw men *decide* to die," he said. "Nobody picks beautiful place full of sunshine. Men are dogs. We crawl off into dark shadows, into bottomless hole. Men pick dying over living when they see no future."

Striker didn't respond. She could tell he was no longer lying on this black sand beach.

"I spend eight months in prison camp," he said. "Before Ukrainians capture me, us Russians shoot themselves in feet, in hands. Some trust others to shoot them anywhere unimportant for believableness. Like your Vietnam. Men wanting to go home." She could feel him trembling. "Ukrainians are our brothers. Why fight them?" He sighed. "I give you secret. Me, big strong Vadim? I am coward. Any gunshot is not for me, on purposeful or not. So I hand my beautiful body over. I give up, I surrender, white flag, hands up. We hear Ukrainians don't have infrastructure for prisoners. If you surrender, you stay one week, one month, maybe two in camp, then both sides do prisoner swap and you go home. So me and my mate, we raise white flag. We walk to them and say, 'Comrades, war is bullshit. Please show big Ukrainian mercy.'"

He tells her everything. The beatings, the tasers, the military phones they would use if they didn't have a taser lying around to shock them with. Each night the sound of new prisoners screaming as they were grilled for intel about the latest battlefield strategies. Nobody complained. Sometimes they were allowed to watch TV, make a little pocket money working for local businesses. They all knew on the other side of the line, the Ukrainians had it worse. The ones imprisoned in Donbas were likely having jagged things shoved into their bodies, car batteries hooked up to their balls. The Ukrainians hurt men like him when you first entered the camp and maybe a few times after that, but their hearts weren't really in it. Not like the Russians. He knew the Russians were limitless in the bad things they were doing. On the battlefield he had seen Ukrainian teenagers being led away into the night, girls *and* boys. He told himself it was the decades—no, the *generations*—of powerlessness, of living like serfs while the West moved on to brighter, shinier things. Some men thrilled at the chance to finally be omnipotent, even if that power came from terrorizing children. Most men weren't built like that. But the ones who were?

War made them kings.

"You gave yourself those tattoos in the prison camp."

"Da," he said. "I write poems on myself." She could tell from the tone of his voice he was smiling. "Anna Akhmatova, best poet of Russia. Osip Mandelstam, a Jew. You wouldn't understand," he said. "Their truths cannot be translated." She was about to ask him to read her something, give her one tiny taste, but then he was far away again.

"That rich old lady from *Akademik Yegorov*? She lies," he insisted. "I never hurt woman or child." Striker could tell he needed forgiveness, needed her to say yes yes, I understand, but the longer she stayed quiet, the more he crumbled. "In Vovchansk, what I could do?" he implored. "Night after night Ukrainian screaming begins. I never know where it is coming from. Then screaming stops." Striker held her hand out in case he wanted to squeeze it. But he didn't.

"Each night when screaming starts, 'What?' says my commander, 'you never hear wind howling?'" Vadim's imitation of his superior sounded strangely American. "Little Veronique," he said. "You won't believe but silence is worst, worser than anything. Worser than knife, worser than rope, gun. In silence, you *become* nothing. Knowing you *did* nothing. Just lay on god's cold earth and tried to sleep." He rolled toward her. "What Ukrainians did to me in prison camp was small peanuts compared to terrible silence I hear nights among my brother Russians."

I've known silences like that, she almost said.

His finger landed on her back. He began tracing a path on her skin. She could feel his heart beating through his fingertip. He came to the last dot in her tattoo.

"Is North Star," he said, tapping it with his finger. "Every sailor's friend."

"When lost, it'll lead you home," she explained.

"What is this?"

At the base of her neck, she felt his hand gently brush aside her twists.

A shot of electricity needled up her spine. She knew the pattern his finger would make even before he finished tracing it.

"A and V," she said. "Ama and Veronique. My sister and I used to use a ruler to draw it on all of our stuff."

"Ah, was some kind of game."

"No, to prove it was ours."

"Why it needs proving?"

She gave a small laugh. "Because we lived in a place where the locals didn't expect people like us to have anything."

"Having things is overrated," said Vadim. He patted her shoulder and rolled away. She could hear the shift in his gaze again, his eyes somewhere in the past. "Having things means protecting things."

The only thing she'd ever had worth protecting was Ama, and at that, she had failed spectacularly. Later, swimming back to the boat, she realized in all the most important ways, Vadim was miles ahead of her even though he was trailing a few blue feet behind in her blue wake.

Back onboard, Kevin had heaped a stack of supplies by the yacht's zodiac. Gordon Baker might be truant, but the tender was still sitting on the back deck. Even Striker knew most sailboats the size of Kate would have some kind of secondary craft. On a big boat, the tender was meant to shuttle passengers into port from a mooring out on the water. If Kate's zodiac was still onboard, it meant her owner had disembarked in one of two ways. Either the guy had boarded someone else's tender, or he'd abandoned ship by going over the side.

"I can't believe there's no spare radio," Striker said.

"Silver case downstairs is radio," said Vadim.

"Then why haven't we tried it?"

Vadim shook his head. "What is rush?" He was walking around the zodiac, punching the inflatable in a few choice spots with his fists. Striker watched his inspection. Though it was warm now, she knew what effect cold temps could have on equipment. Even to her untrained eye, the zodiac gleamed like someone had just readied it for an outing, the thing plump and rearing to go. "We take silver case back with us," he said. "Maybe bring nice wine from wine rack. One for each of us on island. Then we power up and listen."

Suddenly she understood.

He was afraid.

What good would it do right this second to find out what they were up against? It was better to brace yourself for news like that. Mix yourself a mai tai. Maybe crack open a can of nuts.

"You think it's weird the zodiac is launch-ready?" she asked.

Vadim nodded. "Big weird," he said. "Gas line is connected to engine. Nobody stores gas tank with gas line still attached."

"So what?" said Kevin, appearing from below with another load of stuff. "Dude wasn't in his right mind."

"Little boat is just right, not too soft. Air boats stay optimum one day, two in cold weather. I think owner-man only just went bye-bye." He finished his walkaround with a series of playful jabs at the zodiac's gunwales as if channeling his inner Rocky Balboa, then headed down the stairs.

"What if the guy's off scuba diving?" asked Striker.

"See any orange flags floating around?" said Kevin. "We watched this thing sail in. The guy's definitely not here."

He was carrying a crate. It was mostly foodstuff, though Striker could see the laptop case and a few DVDs. Dude probably had the zip drive tucked away in a pocket for a rainy day.

"You two have a nice powwow out there?" Kevin said in a low voice. Striker knew what he was hinting at. While she and Vadim had been parked on the beach, he'd probably picked up the binoculars, scanned the harbor hoping to find the two of them in flagrante. That was how guys like him saw the world. Everyone else was off having fun and he wasn't invited. His whole life spent below deck burning up with envy.

"Only the shadow knows," said Striker.

"What is happening? Why we move all this?" said Vadim, reappearing. He was wearing a tracksuit he'd scavenged from the captain's berth. The pants were too short on him, but the material gleamed, the white racing stripes running up the arms and legs lending him an air of rakishness. He looked like some kind of tycoon or a full-fledged Russian mobster. Man, the Baron's gonna have a field day with this one, Striker thought.

"Waddya mean why are we moving all this stuff?" said Kevin.

"I am sailor," Vadim said. "You are crew. We raise sail, pull anchor, steer our big, beautiful sailing boat back to island like Santa Claus returning from war." He picked up Anders' binoculars and strung them around his neck. A pair of mirrored sunglasses sat on a shelf near the wheel. He rubbed them on his cuff then slid them on, handed his old ones to Striker. They were much too big but she put them on anyway, her eyes finally shielded behind polarized lenses.

"This thing has a motor," said Kevin. "Why not just power it up?"

"Why waste precious gas when air is free?" explained Vadim. "We may need petrol later for bigger important use."

Striker left the men to it. She was hoping to find a tracksuit of her own down below like the one Vadim was sporting. "Back in a jiffy," she said, before disappearing.

She had just found a white one, a Karl Lagerfeld pure as the driven snow, and was pulling on the pants when she heard what sounded like feet stamping the wood overhead, scuffling around for purchase. They were probably trying to move something heavy, too heavy even for them.

She didn't hurry. They were grown men. It couldn't be anything urgent or they'd call her. As expected, the Lagerfeld was way too big but tracksuits were the most forgiving of clothes. All you had to do was roll up the sleeves or the bottoms on the pants and voila! You were back in business.

Suddenly a strange noise filled the air. Striker had to admit it wasn't unpleasant. Up on deck the men must have hit something metal, making it resonate. It brought a smile to her face. She turned to fix her hair in the faux mirror screwed to the wall. Instantly she froze.

In the reflection the little girl in the yellow dry suit stood with her mouth open. The rat sat cleaning its claws on her shoulder. The tuning fork the child had pilfered from Paulet Island was ringing between her fingers. Slowly the note faded out. Lucy tapped the fork on her front teeth. Again the sound pervaded the room.

Striker spun around.

There was no one there. She turned and peered in the mirror.

Now the little girl was holding the leather riding crop. Playfully she flicked it at Striker. In her affectless voice she began to speak in a language not English. It was all so confusing. In those first hours on the *Yegorov*, what had the girl's dads said about where she was from? She didn't know how, but Striker could understand every word.

> *During the frightening years of the Yezhov terror,*
> *I spent seventeen months waiting in prison queues*
> *in Leningrad. One day, somehow, someone "picked me out."*
> *On that occasion there was a woman standing behind me,*
> *her lips blue with cold. Jolted out of the torpor*
> *characteristic of all of us, she said into my ear:*
> *"Could someone ever describe this?" And I answered: "I can."*
> *It was then that something like a smile*
> *dawned on what had previously been*
> *a void.*

It was one of the poems inked on Vadim's body.

"Anna Akhmatova lost two husbands to Stalin," the child said. "Her son spent years in a Russian gulag." The little girl sat down on the bed's dark red duvet. Her feet dangled off the edge. "She was Ukrainian." With the riding crop, she cut a Z in the air, then smacked the pillow. A spray of feathers erupted in the air. "You believe that story he fed you?"

Striker turned from the mirror. The little girl and her rat were gone, the cabin filled with small white feathers. She stood watching them settle on the furniture. Suddenly she noticed the total silence echoing overhead. Her ears popped as though she were a hundred feet underwater. She thought of the special room in Midtown, how easy it would be to drift off into nothing. She gave her head a hard shake and raced up on deck.

Kevin was gazing up the mast. His face lit with wonder. Then he saw her staring at him and his eyes grew large. "Help," he stated.

He tried again but with more conviction. "Help!" he shouted, pointing.

Striker ran over to the controls but had no idea what anything was. The whole time Kevin just stood there watching.

Vadim was slowly being pulled up the mast. His face the color of raw meat. The sunglasses had fallen off and shattered. She couldn't *not* see his eyes, two big, discolored eggs. The binoculars he was wearing had somehow gotten caught in the pulleys that raise the sail. The day filled with the clamor of the mechanization blindly performing its task. It was shocking to watch a grown man being lifted so easily. If the sails were wet, they might weigh hundreds of pounds. Taking Vadim along for the ride was probably a piece of cake. But how had he managed to get tangled up in it?

Striker kept pounding on the console. What else could she do? His feet kicked the empty air, his hands gouging at his neck where the binocular strap dug into his throat. She didn't look. She wouldn't look. Even as he slowly settled into stillness. By the time the mechanism reached its conclusion, his body hung limp atop the mast like a flag on a windless day.

A seabird came and landed a few feet from Striker. The bird carefully folded its wings, its one good eye never blinking. Like her, the skua was somehow both a witness and an active participant. She just felt grateful for its presence.

That strange phrase—*it was all a blur*—was starting to mean something. Now skimming over the surface of the Southern Ocean, she couldn't remember how they'd managed.

Together she and Kevin had loaded everything into the zodiac—the food, the first aid kit, the electronics that were probably already dead. Next they lowered the inflatable over the side and tied the two red tandems to it. Striker was surprised Kate didn't have a tender with an electric starter, but she pulled the cord and on the first attempt the engine roared to life. As she steered the inflatable back through the flaming blue corridor and out to sea, she wondered what they'd find out there. Would the whole earth be on fire, the ocean boiled away? She kept her hand steady, tried even harder not to think about what they were leaving behind.

The zodiac shot out of the breach. The light of the jewel-blue paradise faded behind them as if a spell had been broken. In those last moments onboard the stranger's sailboat, she and Kevin had taken great care not to glance up at the terrible flag casting its eerie shadow on deck. Striker realized she was still holding her breath.

They were more than a mile away before she saw the first bergy bit sullenly bobbing along. Even the ice seemed to know to leave that eerie blue island alone. The heat from the caldera probably extended some distance, the island surrounded by a chain of volcanic vents that kept the wildlife at bay. Or maybe it had all been a dream. Maybe Vadim had found his heaven.

Off on the horizon she could see a small braid of smoke staining the sky. She was surprised by how far they had kayaked. She was relieved they didn't have to paddle back.

As kids, she and Ama had puttered around on lakes in the White Mountains in a series of small boats with outboard motors. There was really nothing to it. She knew to move the tiller left to go right, right to move left, how to turn the throttle to speed up or slow down. The motor was tuned up, smooth and quiet, no plumes of smoke shooting out of the casing. Judging from the engine's effortless handling, someone had recently added the right mix of oil to the gas, readying the boat for an escape. She was just glad everything worked.

The ride back to the volcano was exactly what the doctor ordered. It felt good to be out on the water. The ocean was calm, the salt spray gentle on her face. She needed a long moment to try and cleanse her mind. What would she tell the others?

I was downstairs. I found a tracksuit. It was white. Karl Lagerfeld. A little too big around the waist but so what? I slipped it on. The feel of the velour utterly delicious. I imagined pairing the outfit with a gold chain and box braids and heading out to Washington Heights for some spicy

Dominican food and a night of dancing. Then I heard footsteps overhead. The feet moving in a tight ring. Like they were jockeying for position, trying to gauge the best angle to lift something. There were no shouts, no calls for help. Nothing. Just the sound of feet scraping in a circle. So I finished getting dressed. I went back up. I didn't hurry. I was still basking in the softness of high-end velour, in fantasies of being home among people like me.

She knew she wouldn't mention what she had seen in the mirror. The white feathers clouding the air. The little girl with the flat voice holding a leather riding crop and speaking in Russian.

"That was *crazy*, huh?" said Kevin. He shook his head. It was the first thing either one of them had said since abandoning the sailboat. He sounded like a man coming down from a high. The yellow dry bag sat in his lap. Periodically he buried his hand in it for what she could only assume was reassurance.

"What was crazy?" said Striker. She kept the zodiac aimed on the curl of smoke. Honestly she knew what he meant. But she was determined to make him earn every second of this conversation. It shouldn't be so easy.

"I said that was some crazy shit."

"I still don't understand what happened," she said.

"Like I do," he said.

"You were there."

"So? I don't know sailboats. I'm a gadgets guy."

"Tell me again only slower."

"What for?"

"Just tell me," she said.

He sighed. "I was tightening the clasp on one of the cases when I thought I saw something, like a seal. Behind me I heard this funny squeaking noise, but I figured it was just the sail going up, that the pulley needed oil." He shook his head. "I kept looking over the bay, trying to find what I'd seen. I was about to ask him for the binoculars. Jesus." He winced. "I thought he was kidding around. Like, pretend dancing. Guy's a goof, no?"

She didn't pull any punches. "Why didn't you do anything?"

His hand was back in his dry bag though he was staring off at the sky. "I didn't even realize what was happening until he was like a foot off the ground."

"So why didn't you help?"

He grew quiet. She imagined his fingers fondling whatever was in his bag, starting to squeeze. "Is this about Vadim," he said, "or are you asking me about—" He paused. "That other thing?"

"What *about* Taylor?" she said.

"It just feels like you've already made up your mind," he said. "Same as last time."

"Not my style."

"What do you want me to say?" he said. "Fine. I panic. There. You happy? I'm a panicker. Panic is what I do. Shit goes south? I freeze. Boom!"

She didn't like the way he was staring at her. Like he might lunge. But she couldn't stop now. They were actually getting somewhere. She kept pushing. Vadim was dead. It was probably Christmas Day. She had nothing to lose.

Like you never panicked before.

"Admit it," she said.

"Admit what?"

"You smashed up the radio."

"I did *what* now?"

"You don't want us to be rescued, so you smashed it all up."

"What's my plan?"

"Beats me," she said. "All I know is if we ever get off this rock, you'll be arrested for the murder of your wife."

He laughed. "Even if that were true, you got zero witnesses and your crime scene's thousands of miles from the nearest courtroom. Plus, where's the body?"

Striker didn't back down. "Her injury says it all," she said. "Any decent coroner could call it just from the depth of that hole you left in her head. Rest assured I took lots of photos." She kept her hand steady on the tiller. Did he know it was a lie, that she couldn't even *find* the crime scene a second time? "Even if you aren't arrested, there's enough circumstantial evidence to cut you out of her will."

He stood up. She'd never realized how big he was. Only an inch or two shorter than Vadim but without the muscle. She shimmied the boat back and forth. It worked. He struggled to keep his balance and fell back down.

"I didn't kill Vadim but if I did?" he said. "Guys like that who prey on other guys' wives—they disgust me."

"He disgusted you?"

"What?" said Kevin, genuinely puzzled. "I said your crazy woman driver shtick is gonna send our food into the sea." He pointed at a row of crates. The buckle on one had come loose in the wind.

Keep it together, Ronnie.

She could still see Vadim's body dangling from the mast, the two of them hustling around in its shadow, desperate to be gone.

"And for your information, Taylor was no angel," said Kevin. "Take it from me. The last six months we had an open relationship."

Striker recalled how lovey-dovey he'd acted after they'd first shoved off from the *Yegorov*, him playing with his wife's hair, his hand rubbing her knee.

"You do anything with it?"

"With what?" he said.

"With your freedom. Get any side action going? Or was that the problem?" She couldn't stop. She knew this time the conversation wasn't just in her head, and that there was a limit to it, a line that couldn't be crossed without something breaking. "Maybe Taylor liked what she found out there, all that hunky new freedom. A man who wouldn't *freeze up* when it counted."

He didn't answer. His eyes were locked on the blue sky, combing the heavens for something.

"This trip was supposed to save our marriage," he finally said, gritting his teeth, "and she didn't even want to come. Two years ago *I* was the one on top. It was *me* pulling in seven figures."

"Times change."

"What happened to everyone's sense of humor?" he said. "I hadn't even posted on that forum in almost five years."

"Didn't you get the memo?" she said. "On the internet nothing ever dies."

"I'm not a racist!" he yelled. The word hung in the air. "They were just *jokes*," he said. "For Chrissake, nobody got killed."

There was an interminable moment of silence. Her ears popped.

"So you lost your job and got branded with a scarlet R," she said. "And now you're what—an independent consultant? Part of the gig economy?"

"They didn't even have the *balls* to out-and-out fire me," he said. "Probably knew I had a solid First Amendment case if they tried." He shook his head. "No, they were real smooth about it. They rolled out this big gun from HR. Told me it was time to make room at the table, and what had I ever done to create a more *inclusive* space? 'Uh, besides make you a shit ton of money?'"

Warily he kept his eyes on the sky. "'We have a new corporate strategy,' they said. 'We're happy to have you stay on, only you'll be back out on the floor, and oh yeah, at a fifth of your former salary.'" He looked deflated, like he'd been pricked with a pin, all the hot air hissing out. "Then they turned around and packed the place." She could hear the bitterness in his voice. "Now it's all brown and foreign-born."

If he'd been hoping for even a modicum of understanding, he'd just blown it. "I bet the stock value's gone sky-high," said Striker. "Admit it. The place's on fire now with new ideas."

He laughed. "Fat chance. It's all one big revolving door," he said. "They hire these new people for the optics, but when it doesn't work out, they kick 'em to the curb."

Though she didn't want to admit it, Striker actually felt herself relating. Riley called it the Great Blackrush of 2020. In her line of work, Striker had watched as all the major studios and media companies were chomping at the bit to get their hands on Black creatives, every new series thirsting for a Black showrunner. But when you never had a proper pipeline in place, a truly equitable ladder where the cream could rise to the top as they learned the ropes, you ended up with folks at the table who didn't fully understand the trade through no fault of their own. She'd heard the same thing was happening all over the place, in historically white fields like advertising and publishing. Basically corporate white America was setting a generation of Black and brown folks up for failure. And they were patting themselves on the back about it, blind to the fact that the systems they were shoring up really needed dismantling. Telling themselves through it all that they'd done good.

But despite the Great Blackrush, there was always the other side of the coin. "Just admit it," Striker said. She was surprised how easily the words came out. "You don't want us to exist."

Kevin took his eyes off the sky. "Wow," he said. "Where'd you come up with that?"

"You don't think so?" Something inside her was heating up. Out there in all that gleaming emptiness, it had never felt more clear. "A Black person lands a decent job, and what does the Twitterverse say? They gotta be a DEI hire."

"Most of that's Russian bots."

"Okay. An interracial family pops up in an ad for breakfast cereal, and forty percent of the country loses its shit."

"How's that my fault?" Already he'd gone back to searching the skies.

Striker recalled the whole online ruckus over that terrible ad campaign for some luxury car company featuring a bunch of beautiful people flouncing around but no car. As if just casting Black actors in your commercial made you woke. Didn't people realize they were gradually moving toward a society where a Black person couldn't be cast in anything let alone wield any sort of power, Blackness nothing more than a symbol onto which the audience could ascribe their own worldview?

Waddya mean "moving toward"? Baby, we've arrived!

Striker was still trying to work out if she and Kevin might actually have a common grievance about the myopia of corporate America *hell no* when he shot up out of his seat.

"Get off me," he was yelling. "Get it off!"

He picked up his dry bag and began swinging it blindly in the air. Madly he twirled around flapping his arms, bouncing from side to side, falling down and then springing back up.

Striker slowed the zodiac, trying to maintain control of it.

"Sit down," she screamed, "you're gonna tip us!" But he stayed locked in his frenzy, spinning in circles, arms up, trying to knock something out of the sky.

A shot rang out.

He slumped to his knees.

A door opened in the back of his head. Red stuff gushing from it. He fell backward, face up. The gunshot right through the eye. His heart was still beating, gore rhythmically pumping out of the wound. He was still trying to breathe. She could hear it, each bloody rasp. The blood filling the bottom of the boat. It was coming toward her, running into the inflatable's drainage system. A bright red stream flowing toward the lowest point in the zodiac. He stopped moving. It was then she saw what he'd been trying to drive off.

Sitting at the other end of the inflatable was the one-eyed bird. The thing perfectly still like a hood ornament. Striker gripped the little gold cross hanging around her—

<< In the basement of Our Lady of the Annunciation, the air is hot and clammy as an army of dehumidifiers do their best to keep water from forming on the ceiling. Soon the little ones will file up the back stairs to the portable risers the deacons have set up in the sanctuary where the children's choir will sing their little hearts out like Ama and Ronnie used to do on Christmas Eve when they were small and cute and malleable, which means easy to pick up and cart out when the shrieking set in, not the surly teenagers they have become who want nothing to do with Our Lady of the

Annunciation, especially tonight when Sam Bly is back in town from his first semester at Wake Forest and some of the other kids from school are gathering out by Hammond Farms to pass a bottle. No, this night Ama and Ronnie have been tasked with helping to make sure the little ones don't put their robes on backward, their wings neat and straight, that no one is chewing gum, that the girls who want it are given a small dab of cream blush on their pale, bloodless cheeks, the boys' hair run through one last time with a comb.

Ama is in surprisingly good spirits. She moves among the children, singing "Jesus Loves Me" under her breath, a song Sister Abigail says feels too, er, uh, *boisterous* the way she sings it, too full of the meatier passions of the world *you mean life* especially in the way it pours out of Ama's mouth, hips like honey, eyes closed in ecstasy, the moment just between her and some special someone the same way Ama's hero Whitney Houston sings it on *The Bodyguard* soundtrack, gorgeous soulful Whitney, Whitney who never hides the power of her instrument, inhabiting every square inch of it, her voice always informed by the spirit of the true church, the one where people have bodies and desires and testify about a Lord they aren't ashamed to be bursting with.

It's been almost ten years since the sisters came to live on Zinnia Trace. A decade since the two hid in the compost heap. Ten years of adapting, of obfuscating when necessary, of figuring out how to make this place work for them, of keeping the shrieking to a minimum by keeping it on the inside. For Ama, singing her way through Zinnia Trace has been a calming balm. For Ronnie, that same balm has been the stories she silently invents about this place and the people who inhabit it.

Tonight Sam Bly is back. The prodigal son has returned. Ama is shining in a way that makes the older women blush. The gap between her front teeth like a lock in search of a key. Even Ronnie must divert her eyes. All these months the sisters holding their secret close to their chests as they always have. The way these two can hide all sorts of things, but they can't hide anything from each other.

*Jesus loves me—He who died
Heaven's gate to open wide.
He will wash away my sin,
And let the child come right in.*

And so it's time. The little ones are rising two by two up into the navel of the church under the dreaming eyes of these teenaged sisters, the stairs wide enough for each pair of cherubim to hold hands.

When the first stirrings of trouble begin lowing in the basement's dank air, Ronnie knows it's the same rumbling Mary must have felt all those years ago in the desert night. She looks to her sister. Like Mary, Ama is shining so hard her inner light is what brightens the >>

Striker let go of her sister's gold cross and killed the boat's engine, the Antarctic air preternaturally still. Only an arm's length away sat the rapidly cooling heap that was once called Kevin. At the other end of the zodiac, the one-eyed skua stood folding and refolding its wings. Striker wondered what part of her psyche had summoned this unwavering beast. The bird some kind of feathery gunslinger with the infinite patience of a buddha.

Another wave crashed over the side. The lid popped off a crate. Some of the things packed inside toppled out. One of them bumped her foot. Striker reached down and picked it up out of the dark stuff sloshing around her ankles.

It was a bottle of Yoo-hoo, the drink brown like something decanted from the bottom of a river.

The universe has a funny sense of humor, she thought. She considered breaking into uncontrollable laughter, but if she did, would she ever be able to stop?

Overhead, the sun stayed stuck beyond time. Striker rinsed the bottle in the ocean and twisted it open. She could see a series of waterspouts erupting on the horizon. *Like the fountains at Caesar's*

Palace. She tried to remember her last trip to Vegas, tried to recall what musician had been in residence, what she'd done while there, who she's slept with, if it had been any good. It didn't work. The thing was still foremost in her mind, this thing she was trying to forget. The gore still swirling around the drain, her yellow booties a ghastly shade of orange.

She was desperate for anything to break the silence. My kingdom for a single word, she thought. She swallowed hard, hoping to find her voice. Ama was the real singer in the family but Striker wasn't half bad. She both was and wasn't surprised by what erupted from her mouth.

Silent night, holy night.
Shepherds quake at the sight.

"How long you gonna sit there?"

"Long as I want," she said. "I don't see any signs around saying no two-hour parking."

"Well, when you decide to come back to Planet Earth, our friend with the newly aerated head is still gonna be here doing his best impression of a floor mat."

"Why you gotta be like that?"

"Like what?"

"All sarcastic and shit."

"You gonna complain now? Remember all those times this sarcasm got shit done?"

"What I remember is all the shit it got us *into*."

Silence. She could no longer see the small fountains jetting up in the distance. She wondered how long a whale could go without breathing. Please don't leave me, she thought. I need you.

"Uncle," she finally said.

Still nothing. The voice remained silent. There was nothing else to do. Striker tipped back the Yoo-hoo and drained it. The sugar hit her in the chest like a chocolaty fist.

"Apology accepted," said the voice. "First things first. Didn't you learn nothing from me? Always start by counting your blessings."

"My blessings?"

"At least homeboy didn't go shooting no hole in your craft."

"Amen to that."

"Second: Homeboy got anything on him you might want?"

"Such as?"

"Such as that magical yellow bag of his. Personally all this time I been waiting for his ass to pull out an ironing board."

"That would mean I have to look."

"Newsflash: it's not like I can."

"Okay okay." She closed her eyes and took a deep, centering breath.

"Just do it already. We ain't got all day."

"I'm looking I'm looking."

Striker opened her eyes.

The one-eyed bird was brazenly standing on the dry bag as if staking its claim. Daring her to come and get it.

"So what? You used to play softball."

"That I did," Striker said softly. She hefted the empty Yoo-hoo in her hand, gauging how fast it might fly. Who was she kidding? She lowered the bottle, took a deep breath, and leaned forward on the exhale, grabbing at the bag.

The bird didn't budge. Instead, it sat down on the shredded yellow rubber like it was nesting.

Striker tugged but the dead man's hand wouldn't slip out. His fingers were buried in what was left of the bag as if it were a mitten. She pulled harder. The action sent his body tumbling toward her. She panicked, tried to keep him from falling on her. In the struggle she found herself gazing on what was left of him. It was worse than she'd expected.

He was grinning at her. A big shit-eating grin. The upper right quadrant of his face blasted to kingdom come. Striker imagined a pizza where the toppings had slid off. His face a wasteland of grease and ooze and red nothingness.

"Let go, goddammit," she whispered.

"I seen worse."

Striker couldn't argue with that. Together they had both seen worse. Something small and hot, like a loaf of bread wheezing on the concrete floor, the voices of angels singing from on high, the smell of the redness all over her.

For the first time in a long time, she realized she was angry. At Kevin for being stupid enough to wave a bag holding a gun at a demon bird. At Vadim for going and getting his fool self run up a rich perv's mast. At Zinnia Trace for making her the kind of person who let herself be talked into leaving a dead body hanging thirty feet up in the air and getting the hell out of there. *Not our problem*, Kevin had said, and she'd listened to him, silently agreeing, and kept her eyes locked on the deck, avoiding the shadow the body was casting on the two of them like a pox on both their houses.

Seeing Kevin's ravaged visage, she felt her anger dissolve. She sat back and let herself stare. Looking is a kind of love. Who had told her that? Not that she loved this man, this person who had probably killed his wife, smashed up all the sailboat's communication equipment, slipped the binocular strap into the sail's pulley system, and happily watched as the Russian was ratcheted home to his orthodox lord. We reap what we sow, she thought, some of us more than others.

Gently she leaned forward and took hold of his arm. This time she kept her eyes on the ruins of his blasted head. His hand slid smoothly out of the dry bag, his ravaged face still grinning at her. The bird hopped back and took off into the sky.

She remembered how the two of them had motored away from the sailboat. She had glanced back one last time like the wife of Lot itching for trouble. At the top of the mast, there had been an imperceptible movement, the smallest twitch as Vadim's leg spasmed. He's still alive, she thought. The horror of it locked around her lungs. Reflexively, she'd gunned the tender for the passage out. Once back on the open sea, she told herself it had been an illusion, the sun playing tricks on her weary eyes.

"Okay, we got what we wanted," said the voice. "Time to dump his ass." Striker didn't answer. "You know I'm right. Ain't nobody waiting for him back at the volcano."

She tossed the dry bag in a crate and braced herself against the side of the zodiac, put her feet up on his chest. As she pushed Kevin overboard, the red wasteland that was once his face winked. Joke's on you, it seemed to be saying.

This time Striker didn't look back. She knew if she did, she'd see a bright yellow object floating on the ocean like a broken yolk. For once, the one-eyed bird was nowhere to be seen.

She picked up the ruined dry bag. The rubber smelled bad where the gunshot had blasted a hole in it, but Kevin's manhood was still in there. She hugged the bag close to her chest, felt a glow come over her. Was she already becoming like him? Or thanks to Zinnia Trace, had there always been a part of him in her, a part that was always ready to blame everyone else?

"Okay, now we getting somewhere. Home, Jeeves."

"Don't tell me what to do." She cut the engine and laid back. If you stared long enough, the darkness sloshing around in the bottom of the tender gleamed like claret or an aged merlot. But Striker was already asleep.

When she woke up, it felt like she was back in the earsplitting silence of Midtown. The only sound in existence was the soft thud of her heart. As always, the sun sat a few degrees from vertical. In all directions the water lay shiny and smooth, a sheet of unstamped silver, the ocean so still she couldn't be sure the zodiac was moving. The islands remained fixed on the horizon, growing neither closer nor more distant. Even the thin column of smoke Striker was aiming for appeared static, the smoke unwavering as if captured in a photograph. It all brought to mind a silly sci-fi movie she'd seen where the main character comes into possession of a magical remote control. At the touch of a button, the character could make time stop, allowing him to stroll freely around town as everyone else remained frozen mid-act.

"I broke the world," said Striker.

"You break it, you buy it."

"I'm starting to feel unreal," she said.

"Starting?"

A dimple appeared on the surface of the water. She watched as a ripple radiated out from it, the ripple growing bigger and bigger until it slipped under the zodiac and disappeared. A second dimple emerged on the other side of the tender. Something was kissing the surface of the water from below, the glassy sea quivering concentrically. Others appeared. The area around the inflatable silently filling with these moments and their echoes. It was beautiful to watch. The water rippling as though it were raining but not a drop was falling from the sky, the ripples hypnotizing as a lava lamp.

"Start the engine."

Striker didn't move.

"You gotta get out of here."

She could feel it under her legs. Something was knocking on the bottom of the zodiac. Two long taps, then two short. She scrambled to her knees and pulled the engine cord. The thing stayed dead.

She knew what it would be before it even surfaced. The way it sliced the ocean open like a long black knife. She was floating in a boat full of blood. She wondered if the creature could smell it.

A dark fin began to circle the tender. The zodiac jounced around as the thing swam donuts around her, the water churning. More fins surfaced. The ocean filled with the sound of their mewling, like demented cows.

They were orca. Somewhere she'd read they were as smart as humans. She knew they were toying with her. If they wanted to capsize the tender, it was as good as done. She had read about a pod of orca ramming sailboats off the coast of Spain after one of the females in the group had been harassed by boaters. The species was beginning to lose patience. Antarctica was theirs. She pulled the cord again but the engine didn't fire up.

One edged in closer. It opened its ponderous jaws. She couldn't believe its size, the beast long as a small bus. She could see its pink tongue waggling from side to side, its tongue an animal unto itself, mouth lined with razor-sharp teeth. She knew the species sometimes hunted other animals just for sport. One bite would puncture the zodiac. Within minutes she'd be in the water. As if reading her mind, the leader swam up and put its mouth on the gunwale. It sat gumming the boat, daring her to stop it.

Striker picked up a can of chili. She threw it straight at the animal's snout. With sharks, you were supposed to drive the bone in their nose up into their brains. She picked up the laptop, hurled it as hard as she could. It was like tossing pebbles at an elephant. Her only hope lay buried in the yellow dry bag with the ragged hole shot through it.

An unfathomable intelligence flared in the orca's great black eyes. It was grinning at her, laughing. She thought of the long-ago albatross convulsing on the *Yegorov*. Was there a similar curse surrounding the killing of a whale? On a practical level, the gun's recoil might blow her out of the boat. She'd injure the animal but it'd be nearly impossible to kill it with just one shot. She'd have to keep firing and firing until the clip was empty. If she didn't, she'd only make it and its kind angrier.

"It's either you or them."

Was that the story of her life?

The animal is less than a foot away, sinking its teeth deeper into the rubber. Striker's hand shakes as she takes aim. Percy would've told her the trick is to keep your eyes fully open even beyond the moment when you pull the trigger. If you don't, you'll miss. But Percy is dead. She doesn't know how she can possibly keep from flinching, considering

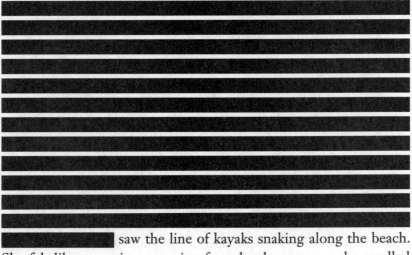 saw the line of kayaks snaking along the beach. She felt like a warrior returning from battle, was sure she smelled like one too. The front of her dry suit spattered with gore, her skin freckled with somebody else's face.

And then there were five, Striker thought.

Six. You forgot the brown dad.

The tide was in. She drew on the ancient muscle memory of how to beach a boat with an outboard motor, running the zodiac in until she could see the rocky bottom, then cutting the engine and tipping the motor up out of the water before hopping over the side and pulling the inflatable up on land. It maneuvered easily, the boat empty. Only a silver case lay floating in the bottom.

It was done. She had come back with nothing but a radio that most likely none of them knew how to use. Even the sunnies Vadim had gifted her on the rich man's boat were missing. She walked back into the ocean up to her knees and rinsed her face, rubbed the blood off her dry suit. The rubber remained stained, the dark spots the only proof any of it had happened. Already her calves were numb though the water wasn't nearly as cold as she'd anticipated. She looked around at the endless nothingness and let out a gut-blasting scream. Between the cries of the penguin chicks and the pounding surf, she couldn't even hear herself. The universe went on doing as it had been doing. She picked her way out of the ocean and lay down on the rocks, closed her eyes.

Something was sitting on her chest. A small, dense weight like a foot. She bolted upright and the thing scuttled off, flapping its flippers as it waddled away. She remembered the penguin that had coughed on her whole lifetimes ago back on Paulet. If that bird had been sick, how long would it take for her to come down with whatever it had? And what would her symptoms be? Her mind growing soggy, softening into a red mush?

She got up and peered into the zodiac. Seeing the blood slosh back and forth made her stomach heave. Why now, she thought, as she doubled over. Why not back when she'd actually been staring at both men's ruined corpses? The one with his face turning purple, eyes big as rotten apples, and the other with all his features blasted off.

The vomit came quick and easy. Instantly the surf washed it away. She was surprised by how much came out, that there was still a whole meal roiling around inside her. It felt like ages ago since she'd eaten. Or had it only been a few hours? She heaved one more time, thankful it was gone in the waves before she even saw it.

"You done?"

She wiped her mouth on her sleeve. "Almost," she said. "Gimme a minute."

She willed herself to pick the radio up out of the wretched soup in the bottom of the zodiac. She washed the case in the ocean before heading up the beach. Her eyes were on fire. She kept her gaze down off the sky. She noticed the booties on her feet. They would never be lemony yellow again.

Overhead the sun gleamed, an immobile white hole. She recalled a YouTube clip she'd seen of an astrophysicist claiming time is a byproduct, an entanglement produced by the mind. Time only exists because we believe in it, the scientist explained. The subtle illusoriness of everyday existence was beginning to seem obvious. All these years how had she missed it?

The white arrows drawn in stones were still pointing the way. Finally she rounded the promontory and found him floating in the water. She could tell he hadn't been expecting anyone. His old-man clothes rumpled in a pile. The murderous walking stick propped up among the rocks.

"Careful," the Baron said. "Word on the street is hot tub usage may result in premature death."

Striker set the radio by his clothes, then sat on the edge and slid in. "Do I wanna know?" she said.

Weakly he paddled around on his back. "I'm ethically obligated to tell you someone got cooked in one of these here things."

She gave her face another scrubbing, wanting to make sure she wasn't still spattered with evidence. "Cooked?"

"Anders says the temps could spike without warning," he said. "Guess our trusty vent isn't so trusty." For the first time since she'd made his acquaintance, the Baron sounded vaguely human, the sardonic bite gone from his voice. She chalked it up to fatigue. Already his face appeared thinner, cheeks gaunt, the skin loose around his throat. "The kid read about it in one of the journals," he said. "Claims any second now we could be boiled alive."

Wait. Had he actually called Anders *Anders*? She realized she had never heard him say the teen's name.

"How often we think that happens?" she said.

"Dunno," he said. "My understanding is a hundred years ago a party of sailors met an inglorious end that way." He lifted his head and smiled at her. "I can think of worse endings," he added, then lay back down. "Where's Kevin and Vadim?" he asked. There was real concern in his voice.

Striker began floating in the rock pool waiting for the earth to send a blast of avenging steam ripping through her flesh, her body's meat blasted right off the bone. When nothing happened, all she said was, "There wasn't any caviar."

The Baron nodded understandingly. "There are very few true gentlemen left in the world," he replied.

The sun stayed pinned in place but they kept floating. Striker figured it was just as easy to die there as anywhere. Even as a child, she had thought drowning wouldn't be a bad way to cash out. There was something romantic about it, the way the ocean forced you to surrender. Fighting it would only drag you down faster. She lay floating, letting the water take her wherever it would.

Okay then. How about some truth?
Truth?
Yeah. Truth is you thrived on Zinnia Trace.
Me?
Hell yeah. You ate it up!

Striker couldn't really argue with that. Little Ronnie had squeezed every last drop out of the lemon for all it was worth while that very same lemon had destroyed her sister. *It's like I never left,* she thought. She may have walked away from Zinnia Trace, but she had packed up its worldview and taken it with her. It was in the minerals that formed her bones. A feeling of entitlement. A sense that if the police ever came knocking, she'd stare the officer square in the face like Trish had done on numerous occasions, too many to count, telling the officer not to lecture her about her driving and just give her the ticket already.

"Ama stayed true to where we came from. But me." Striker searched her memories. "I *became* that place. A Black woman with a white mind." All around her the Southern Ocean nodded in agreement. It was why she'd had no fear about traveling to Antarctica. The earth was hers. She'd learned that on Zinnia Trace. "Who knew white privilege could include someone like me?"

"You say something?" asked Robert.

"Negative," she said.

Striker watched as the old man splashed a penguin that had waddled up to the edge of the pool. Suddenly it all made sense. His hiring one of the Russians to ferry him around in a tandem. How thin he looked. The marijuana still potent because it wasn't a hundred years old. It was freshly harvested—he'd brought it with him.

Robert Foley was dying. She could see it in the looseness of his skin. Maybe it was cancer or some problem with his heart or one of the million other calamities that kill people. It was obvious the old man wouldn't live to see another Christmas. Striker felt her own heart crack open a smidge.

She lifted her head off the water. Smoke was rising from the top of the volcano. It wasn't some tiny fire the others had built to help her find her way back. It was too big for that, the smoke billowy and white. It could even be the start of what Percy would've called a seismic event, the volcano waking up. She was about to say something when Robert pointed down the beach.

"Who's that?" he said.

The two of them watched as the zodiac came screaming around the bend and shot out into the ocean.

"Weird," she said. "Looks like Hector. The third dad."

"Ah, the lawyer with unusual views."

"Like what?"

"That something in the ice is driving us all nuts."

Striker tried to act casual as if she had nothing riding on his answer. "That's pretty kooky," she said. "What do *you* think?"

"I think this is *exactly* who each and every one of us has always been," he replied.

She nodded toward the zodiac. "Where do we think he's headed?"

Robert shrugged and lay back in the water. "Home."

The tide was high, the rock pool white with froth. Each incoming wave battered the shore, sending spray ten feet up in the air. Striker had lost all sense of time. She was learning you could live without it. When she tuned in again, Robert was reading a book. How he kept it dry was a mystery.

"For real," she called from her side of the hot spring. "We should probably call it a day and head back up."

"I'm on the last page," he said.

She sat up on the edge of the pool, happy to let the sun warm her. She wondered if he'd agree with her assessment that it was almost 70°. *Shizer*, that can't be good. She pushed it from her mind and thought instead about the killing spree one of the *Yegorov*'s historians had detailed in a talk. The lecturer explained that upon arriving on Elephant Island, Shackleton had allowed his crew to bludgeon to death anything that moved. Penguins, flying birds, seals. She wondered if the men had left the carcasses to rot or if, after they worked off some steam, they'd gone back and salvaged what might be eaten. Thing is, when you smash something dead with a piece of wood over and over, chances are what's left doesn't make for good eating. Still, it was a case study in productive cruelty. It was probably something they studied in business school or at West Point. When letting your men become savages is in a commander's best interests.

Robert lowered the book.

"I'd give it six out of ten stars," he said. "Eight if you like happy endings." He waded over to a spot where the rocks acted like steps but didn't climb out. "In case you were wondering," he said apologetically, "but I'm all out of Mary Jane. It was nice while it lasted."

"Does it—" Striker wasn't sure how to phrase the question. "Help with your symptoms?"

"Is it that obvious?" When she didn't answer, he sighed. "Don't tell anyone but I've *always* been a smoker. Even before this." He gestured down at his withered body.

Look at that. Y'all have something in common.

"The Supreme Court's terrible ruling last summer has only made it worse," he said. "Now the police have the right to search you just by claiming they *smelled* it." Robert shook his head. "It's downright fascist."

Why's everyone suddenly got their panties in a wad about fascism? America's never been great for everyone.

"And if there's one thing I hate more than anything, it's overreach," he added. He gazed off at the horizon. Striker wondered how far he could see, the film on his eyes eerily pearly. "Though I suppose it's human to overreact in the name of justice. Take my Janey, for example."

Silently it landed a few feet away on the rocks. "We should get out," Striker said in a low voice. The bird cocked its head, appraising her with its one good eye. "Like now." She pulled her legs out of the water and stood up.

Oblivious, Robert went back to bobbing on the surface. "I love that woman," he said. "That's why I did what I did." A wave crashed over the rocks. He shuddered but kept on going. "Afterward I gave her her space," he said. "And that monster emerald on her finger. How could I not? I'd denied her a child of her very own, even if it was for her own good." Striker could tell he was mostly talking to himself. "Thing is I've kept her in the dark all these years," he mused. "Nothing builds a wall between two people like a secret."

You can say that again.

The bird fluttered over to the edge of the hot spring. It hopped down into the water and began washing itself.

"Why hello there," Robert said. "Won't you be my neighbor?"

A foul smell filled the air. "Please," urged Striker. "Climb out before it's too late."

"She thinks I don't know she gave up a child," he said, "a son when she was much too young to be anyone's mother. But a man like me doesn't take a woman into his milieu without knowing these things." Lazily he backstroked to the center of the pool. "She was in her late thirties. I was almost sixty with three grown children." The bird dipped its head, sending water rolling down its back. "It was right as we were getting married. The kid had the nerve to insist *she* had contacted *him*." Righteousness darkened his face. "The boy was a liar. He came crawling out of the woodwork for money. I managed to intercept the little bugger, send him packing faster than you could say—"

The bird lifted off the water.

"Robert!" shouted Striker, but the old man's mind was still at work, still meandering through the memory of the time he'd saved his wife from meeting the son she didn't want.

"I told him to never darken our door again, that she didn't want to see—"

The steam was scalding. Even watching from the edge of the hot spring, Striker felt like she was standing on the surface of the sun.

The old man's skin began to bubble. Oil seeped from his flesh. It floated on the surface, the froth greasy. The air filled with the stench of cooked meat. Overhead a storm of birds formed. Striker turned and was about to run when his hand shot up out of the water. The flesh hung off his wrist in bloodless strips like bracelets.

"Help." There it was. Soft but clear. How could he still be alive?

Striker grabbed the walking stick. The wood quivered in her fists, but she held it out. Somehow he grabbed on. She tried to lift him but she almost lost her balance. The surface of the water roiled as if teeming with faces. Things bubbling in the foam.

Robert Foley wasn't trying to pull himself out. Something was looking to pull her in.

It's either you or them.

She let go of the stick. His hand fell back into the boiling water. Striker grabbed the radio and ran, kept running, up the volcano and into the clouds. She would never stop. The voice forever echoing in her head. *Help.* It had sounded like an elderly man crying out in the final pain-racked moments of his life. It had also sounded like a chorus of desperate voices demanding she rescue them at any cost. E pluribus unum. *From many, one.* She was wrong about water. It was one of the worst ways to go.

The air thickened. Sweat pearled down her back. Everywhere a mugginess like swimming through bisque. Overhead the sun sat motionless in a sky leached of color, the day a hot silvery glare. Striker was halfway up the cone, the ground spongy. The island was thawing at a breakneck clip. She glanced back down on the coastline.

Where the hot spring had once sat nestled in the rocks, giant plumes of steam were now shooting straight up out of the earth. Along the shore heated water from undersea vents was colliding with the cooler air, the clash in temperatures creating an impenetrable fog. It was pouring up out of the ocean, a thick white mist blanketing the beach. Ferociously it sparkled, the air gleaming as if embedded with needles. She watched as the vapor erased the landscape, extinguishing all sounds as it crept up out of the sea. Instantly it snuffed out the ruckus of the penguin colony, the silence as if the rookery had never existed.

A second vaporous cloud was inching down the slope from the mouth of the volcano. She wondered if this was something worse than fog, maybe the same poisonous gases that had wiped out Pompeii. The two mists were on course to collide right where she was standing. Striker hadn't been in the city on 9/11 but who hadn't seen the videos of waves of ash racing through the streets, people instantly powdered pale as corpses?

Any second now the dueling fogs would wrap her tight in a single white fist. She took a deep breath and held it. It seemed to take forever. Just as she was about to breathe, the hot mist slammed into her from both sides. She couldn't tell if her eyes were still open. The fog had erased everything. The day an endless white. She tried to recall any nearby cliffs, spots where even the smallest miscalculation might send her tumbling over the edge. She kept moving, stuttering up the cone step by slushy step, testing the air with one outstretched hand like an insect's antenna, the other clutching the radio.

Her palm grazed something cold. The fog muffled her scream. Tentatively she ran her fingers over the smooth surface, tracing a familiar pattern.

She was in the forest of cairns. The monoliths were perched along the crater's rim. If she had gone any further, she would've tumbled in. She imagined herself standing by the mama cairn, the formation towering over her with its massive blue-red boulder anchoring it to the earth. Please let this be right, she thought. Blindly she turned herself around.

In her head she could still hear the shrieks of the skua as they dive-bombed the hot spring. Some of the birds swooping and rising with hunks of steaming meat in their beaks, scorching their gullets, others miscalculating and skimming the frothy surface of the boiling water, their dying shrieks ricocheting off the landscape.

The terrible scene had reminded her of an astronaut movie she'd scouted for years ago. One of the researchers had shown the team slides of the carbonized body of the Soviet cosmonaut Vladimir Komarov, his remains just a handful of shiny rocks. How the shoddily built capsule he was flying in had burned up upon reentry. The worst part of the story was that it was an open secret. Everyone knew he would never make it back alive though nobody breathed a word about the ship's slipshod construction, afraid of what the party bosses would say. That was the *true* nature of horror. It needed your full participation. You climbing in the capsule and pulling the hatch shut of your own free will. Why had any of them ever come down here to the ass of the world *voluntarily*—the Robert Scotts, the Shackletons, happily signing themselves up for dehydration and hunger, bodies blackened by unimaginable cold, the madness of a single night six months long.

Those boys are like the chicken that crossed the road. They gotta know for themselves what's on the other side.

So why am I here, she wondered as she stumbled through the mist.

Maybe you ready to cross over.

Under her feet the earth seemed to rumble in agreement.

Finally the cabin emerged through the haze. Striker had to stand back. Hot air poured out between its loose boards, the day wavy with heat. She didn't want to think about it but there was nothing else to think about. Had Anders, Sarah, and Jane been cooked to death inside the hut just like the Baron, their skin falling off the bone?

Then just as suddenly as it had appeared, the cabin was gone. In a flash, the hut exploded. A fiery blast filled her vision. The dense fog smothered the noise of the explosion. A wave of superheated air swept her off her feet. Check me out, Striker thought as she went sailing through the haze in a rain of debris. I'm flying. She had all the time in the world. The moment stretched on and on.

Midair she tried to recollect how the stuntmen did it, throwing themselves down flights of stairs or out of speeding cars for multiple takes. She remembered one old dog she'd bedded once or twice, the guy a legend in the industry and crazy sexy in a vintage leather kind of way. He constantly referred to the numerous scars snaking over his body as the Interstate, was always urging her to *ride it south*. One night after a particularly circuitous tryst, he told her the ultimate stuntman secret.

"Resistance is what kills you," he growled. "It's why the drunk driver survives the crash but the person he hit dies."

"How do you *not* resist?" she'd asked.

He grinned at her, one of his front teeth missing. "Very carefully," he said, patting his stomach as if their sex had been a feast.

Just before she hit the earth, she gripped Ama's gold cross in her—

<< Striker is lying in bed. Her head is ringing as she opens her eyes. Gently she taps the god's eye hanging from the ceiling, watches it twirl. Trish's mother lovingly crafted each of its seven panels. It has only ever needed the lightest touch to set it going. Nights as a child Striker would often fall asleep under the small blue-and-white vortex.

The wooden toy chest with a lion carved on the lid still sits under the double windows. Were she to open it, the toys would be long gone, the chest crammed with the trappings that mark her teenaged years. Clothes, old issues of *Seventeen*, a Mötley Crüe CD, boxes of Dark and Lovely, half-full packs of Marlboro Lights, a few Magic Eyes, their pages dog-eared, each book's visions circled in pen. The first time she sees a unicorn emerge from a sea of blue and red squiggles, it feels like solving a great mystery. "See, there's its horn," she tells her sister, and Ama nods vigorously then points at a nonsensical place where the unicorn doesn't appear, pretending to be in on the secret.

As a teenager Striker never asked Trish if she could replace the toy chest with something less childish. Standing on it makes you tall enough to reach through the windows and grab onto the hundred-year-old oak that grows beside the house. From there it's an easy climb down to the ground. How many times have she and her sister crawled out that very window? Toward the end Ama making her descent practically nightly.

Next door in her sister's room, clothes and shoes and handbags lie scattered on every surface along with *Ebony* magazines, tools to twist and rip dreads, candy wrappers, a CD of Bob Marley's *Legend*, Ama's stash of loose condoms left out on her desk. As always, her sister's bed is stuffed with an old sleeping bag crammed full of towels. In these final months Striker suspects Trish and Doug know Ama isn't sleeping in her room but are too tired to fight anymore.

For old time's sake she lies down on Ama's bed and gazes out the window. Even from Zinnia Trace, she can see Our Lady's steeple with the copper cross. Above it a gibbous moon hangs on the verge of impalement. She gets up and glances through the titles on her sister's mostly empty shelves. *For Colored Girls Who Have Considered Suicide / When the Rainbow Is Enuf*; *Their Eyes Were Watching God*; *Philip Hall Likes Me, I Reckon Maybe*; *Catcher in the Rye*; *It*; *Beloved*. She can still hear Ama's bewilderment when she learned that the same author had written both *Philip Hall Likes Me* and also *Summer of My German Soldier*. But I thought she was like *me*, Ama complained. You can still like the story, Trish said, but Ama never picked up the book again.

Striker leaves the room and heads down the curved staircase, turning on every light the way Doug does. Doug always claiming he likes how the house looks from the street when fully illuminated, the home even more imposing and regal. She secretly suspects he is afraid of the dark as he will turn on each light in the pantry even if just popping in for a bag of popcorn.

It's crazy how much space there is. The den, the family room, Doug's office, Trish's hobby room, the TV space off the kitchen, the formal and informal dining rooms. It goes on and on, the sweet scent of amaryllis lacing the air. The family only ever uses a quarter of the house, maybe less. The fifteen-foot Scottish fir stands in the everyday living room, not the one used for entertaining, which has its own twenty-foot tree. During this, their last Christmas together, the four of them will open each gilded box tucked under the fir before heading out to midnight mass. Doug will even gift Striker a camera that doesn't need film. After what happens, the three of them will never touch their presents. Trish softly weeping anytime she stumbles across the scarf Ama gave her in her scarf rack, the silk printed with tropical fish.

In the portico the grandfather clock chimes the hour. Striker will have to hurry if she doesn't want to be late. Her first night on Zinnia Trace, Doug had to stop the clock so that her sister could sleep, Ama convinced the house was haunted.

Outside the air smells pristine. The cypresses lining the drive glitter in the moonlight. A languid snow falls. She almost forgot how each year Trish and Doug set up a holiday crèche on the expansive front lawn. The thing tasteful and modern, the figures of the Holy Family abstracted rather than lifelike, the barnyard animals mere silhouettes and gestures.

Doug bought this crèche to replace the one that got vandalized two years after she and Ama moved in. One morning as he left for work, Doug discovered that someone had spray-painted the face of the Baby Jesus black, the paint as though they'd carelessly scribbled on it. By that afternoon, the whole crèche had been replaced, surveillance cameras conspicuously positioned. Doug never mentioned it to the family, telling Trish he thought the crèche needed an update, but Ama and Striker knew. They heard about it on the playground from the younger siblings of the vandals but only after they promised not to tell. The story spreading that at a house party someone dared someone else to do it, said they even had the paint in their car. Ama was pleased. "Somebody wanted to make the Baby Jesus look like us," she said happily as the sisters walked home. Years later Striker learned the truth. The teens lied, looking to take credit for someone else's work. A grown man had done it. One of the dads from the girls' under-ten soccer team. The man always volunteering to substitute coach when needed.

It doesn't take long to walk the half mile to the intersection of Main and Birch. The downtown like something out of a Norman Rockwell, the streetlamps draped with icicle lights. Several famous movies have been shot in the gazebo, the productions hungry to capture the town's distinct air of Americana.

At Our Lady of the Annunciation, every shade of light pours through the stained-glass windows, the church like a prism. Once inside, Striker dips her fingers in the font. Nobody sees her as she glides like a bride up the center aisle, the parishioners evenly parted. These are the people she has seen every Sunday since childhood. The Phillips, the Flynns, the Castronovos, Mrs. Hagerty at the head of her ten-person brood. Striker knows Trish and Doug will be sitting on the end in the second pew on the left. They are such creatures of habit.

She passes her adoptive parents without looking as the first pangs of fear sound in her chest. After all this time she is afraid she has misremembered. In her mind Trish and Doug are forever young and hopeful and a lot naive. She doesn't blame them for what is to come in a few short hours. But now if she were to gaze at them directly, all that could change. Perhaps on this, her sister's last night on earth, she will find their pale faces haggard and drawn with the strain of loving her and Ama. It's a foundational part of the story, that Trish and Doug Ostriker were just two hapless dreamers who got in over their heads. She needs to believe this, otherwise it's too much to bear. The thought that someone tried to love you and that it ruined every good thing in them.

At the front of the church, Father Chester stands at the altar holding the chalice aloft. Of all the priests who cycle through the diocese, he is the one she likes best. At the close of each service, he reminds them, "The mass is never-ending. Go in peace." She has always wanted to believe that the sign of peace the congregants wish each other spills over into the world. Thankfully the children's choir is floating up the stairs and filling the risers behind Father Chester with the rustling of their wings. Silently she slips through the exit behind the chapel and trots down the stairs, leaving Doug and Trish and the entire congregation safely ensconced in their dream that love is omnipotent.

In the basement of Our Lady of the Annunciation, the air is hot. An army of dehumidifiers are doing their best though several of their pans need emptying. Why the room should be equatorial in the middle of winter is only one of several mysteries. The tables are riddled with little coats and bags, wet boots, a tray of sugar cookies, half-full cups of juice. In the classroom to the left, Striker sees where she and Ama used to sit when they were sent here to learn about this puzzling religion with its preternatural happenings—a basket of bread feeding thousands, the dead coming back to life, an innocent woman giving birth to no one's baby, a man on the brink of killing his own son until the boy is replaced with a ram.

Then begins the Christmas pageant she has come through hell and highest water to play her part in. The organist hits the opening chords. The music is breathy, a pointed reminder that an organ is essentially a wind instrument. Striker finds her mark. There was never really any possibility she'd be late. She is the star of this show. Tonight the windowless bathroom under the stairs in the basement of Our Lady of the Annunciation is where the true Nativity is taking place. She has traveled through twenty-five years of darkness to stand in this very spot.

On the floor drops of red sparkle like garnets. She follows them to the bathroom door, the wood tatted with the carvings of generations of bored children. She raps on the door with her knuckles. Two long, two short knocks. It's the way she and Ama let the other know it's them.

Upstairs the children have started to sing. Their song reminds her to be quiet, to keep her mouth shut no matter what lies behind this door. To bear it all as she and Ama have always borne it. Silently, grace optional. And so she twists the knob and enters the most transformative night of her life. The sisters remain oblivious to her presence. Neither speaks. Tonight she is the specter.

In this room there is so much love. So much fear. Endless pain. Striker is surprised and saddened by how young these sisters are. The only sound is of distant children singing along to the reedy breath of an organ.

Silent night, holy night
Son of God, love's pure light
Radiant beams from thy holy face
With the dawn of redeeming grace
Jesus Lord at Thy birth
Jesus Lord at Thy birth

Finally it's done. The sisters sit marveling at this being their silence has created. Its pinched face dark as a heart, its sides heaving in and out like bellows. Their grandmother Mabel used to say true looking is a kind of love.

"See," whispers Ama, her face streaked with blood. "It's blue and red all at once," but all Striker can see is the strange film covering its pupils, its eyes gray, almost salt >>

Ama's gold cross slipped out of Striker's hand.

"It's you," said a small voice. "I knew you'd be back."

The teen was curled up on a stack of crates. The grotto looked the same as ever. Cast-off junk, rags, shelves lined with jars, the floor studded with combs, pocket watches, rings, strange white knobs frozen in the ice.

Sarah stood next to her child wearing a T-shirt she'd made by ripping the sleeves off her own thermal. Striker tried to hide her revulsion. All the way up to her shoulders, the good doctor's arms just bones wrapped in skin, her upper arms as thin as her wrists.

"See? She didn't forget us," Anders mumbled.

Striker's first thoughts were of the aftermath of war, refugees streaming across borders, each gaunt face plastered with a thousand-mile stare. Bruised hollows gleamed under the teen's eyes, their head seemingly too big for their body. Striker wondered if they could even still walk. In the time she traveled to the sailboat and back, the teen had become skeletal.

"Find any food?" Anders whispered.

"How long have I been gone?" Striker asked. She put her fingers on her own face, tried to feel if the skin around her eyes was loose.

Sarah began moving a chair from one wall of the grotto to the other. Once she'd reach the opposite side, she'd put it down, then pick it up again and head back. "You went somewhere?" she said.

Striker couldn't help but think of her again as Bobbi Sue, her uterus loose, mind quietly turning to mush.

"We should go," she said. "The island's heating up. It won't be long before this place caves in." Already she could hear the ceiling cracking.

"They kept eating it," Anders blurted out.

"*What?*"

"I only ate it because we're already damned," offered Bobbi Sue listlessly. She put the chair down. "Plus I have to stay alive. For *them*." In the gloom, a pair of figures seemed to shimmer by her side, the air sparkling. "What would my babies do without me?" she said, but when Striker looked again, the glimmers were gone.

"You and your highfalutin principles," sneered Jane at the teen. The old woman was still fiddling with the unopened bottle of wine she'd been gifted for Christmas. "Like a goddam newborn. Can't even hold up your own head."

"Robert won't eat it," the teen shot back.

Jane stopped clawing at the cork. "Say, where *is* Robert?"

Striker tried to keep her voice steady. "He wouldn't get out of the water," she said, and left it at that.

Something flashed in the old woman's eyes. Her whole face winched into a single grievous point. But then she sighed and the pain was gone, a cloud passing over the sun.

"He was hoping to die down here." She went back to clawing at the cork. "Lucky bastard."

That ain't your friend Jane talking.

It was true. La Grande Dame was back. Compared to Bobbi Sue and Anders, the Dame was the least emaciated but ravaged all the same. Her face drawn, skin sallow, cheekbones sharp as blades. Her once-luscious hair hung limp. Each time she spoke, her gums flashed, the flesh inflamed, the two titanium posts barely visible in the swelling.

Striker swallowed a scream.

The edge of the old woman's hairline was bordered by one long, continuous gash. Slowly the incision was widening. Blood trickled down her neck. It was the goriest of scurvy's symptoms. The reappearance of old wounds. The Dame's face was coming apart where once it had been razored open and nipped and stitched back together. Striker wondered what other injuries were resurfacing. A dreadful aura flickered about the old girl. The air around her body shimmered as if her soul had come loose. Striker imagined an army of spirits swarming the old woman, mosquitoes looking to feed.

"What did you guys eat?" she whispered.

"And whose fault was it?" said the Dame.

"I didn't *know*," cried Anders.

"Know what?" said Striker, the unease building in her chest.

"The pemmican," said Bobbi Sue. She spoke lightly like a girl picking daisies in a field. "Those long strips of jerky, the ones I softened up in water."

It started to rain in the chamber, fat drops dripping from the ceiling. "Pemmican was originally invented by First Nations as a high-protein food that traveled easy," said Anders. "They made it from shredded meat mixed with wild berries and fat." Facts seemed to comfort the teen. The kid rattled off a list about how Native Americans learned to seal the mixture into pouches of uncured bison skin. As the skin dried, it shrank, essentially vacuum-sealing the stuff, making the pemmican last forever. Striker wondered if Anders had perfect recall. The kid reciting verbatim one of the lectures an expert had delivered on the *Yegorov*. "In Canada, there was even a war called the Pemmican War. Pemmican was almost as valuable as fur." Anders lay still. "You ate it too," they murmured.

Striker thought of the strange broth from which she'd pulled a tiny wad of meat, the way the water absorbed all light. She could still feel the quarter-sized lump of flesh lying in her palm, then the sensation of biting down on it, the vision she'd seen, the day filled with blood.

"The explorers who were stranded here before us? They were bad *bad* men," said Anders. "There was even a baby here," they whispered. "A newborn."

"How do you know?" said Striker.

The teen looked her in the eye but there was a deadness in their stare. "I read it in the journal you got for Christmas," they said. "A woman stowed away on the HMS *Bonaventure* to be with her beloved."

Striker thought of the hoarse-voiced specter who had first spoken to her in the cabin. "What happened to her?"

"Maybe she was a little crazy?" said the teen. "She starts off loving her husband but by the end she seemed to be in cahoots with the ship's doctor. The guy took over after the captain vanished."

The Dame licked her lips. It was a new tic. She probably didn't even realize she was doing it. "Well I for one don't look a gift horse in the mouth," she said. Pink fluid was beading on the tip of her nose. "You wanna play vegan? Go ahead and die."

The walls of the chamber began to vibrate. "We gotta get out of here," said Striker. The grotto was starting to flood.

"This place is filled with the bad they did," said Anders. The teen curled up tighter on their crate. "We've been sheltering in their evil."

Striker stepped on something hard, the whole floor studded with lumps. Now that the ice was melting, she reached down and pulled. The thing came up easier than she'd expected. She turned it this way and that, trying to see it better.

It was a long white bone. Her eyes landed on a series of tiny, crescent-shaped indents patterning its surface.

Startled, she dropped it back in the water.

They were teeth marks.

The four of them heard it at the same time. The sound of engines.

Striker positioned herself under the fisherman's hole. She kicked the grotto's walls and scraped out a series of hollows, creating a chain of hand- and footholds. Quickly she clamored up the wall. She had the sensation something was trying to hold her back, a weight tied to each of her legs. But she made it out.

Back aboveground, the fog had thickened. She couldn't be sure she was returning to the same world. She turned and pulled the others up after her. They were so insubstantial—there was hardly anything to them!—like harvesting food from the earth. It was so easy, maybe *too* easy. She wondered if she'd pulled anything else up with them.

The roar was coming from every direction. She might have mistaken it for a scrum of helicopters except she had ridden in choppers countless times, always with a long lens hanging from her neck. No, the song of a helicopter was more uniform in nature, a constant thwacking. This was a high-pitched whine that dipped and rolled, a boat engine navigating over waves. It was likely the fog was distorting sound again. She couldn't tell how many boats were racing toward them. It could be one, it could be fifty.

"Whoever's coming could still be a long ways off," she said.

"We're over here," yelled Anders.

Striker rotated in their direction. She looked up at the sky. Even through the haze the white hole of the sun hadn't budged. She didn't need to look at her watch to know it would always be 12:14 p.m.

"We should link arms and hike down to the beach," said Bobbi Sue. "My babies will want us to be there when they land."

"Don't be stupid," said the Dame through the mist. "You wanna end up like Taylor with your skull smashed open on the rocks?"

"Who?" said Bobbi Sue.

"They'll find us, Mom," said Anders. "The kayaks are right there on the beach."

"Can *you* see the kayaks?" countered the Dame. She seemed to be undermining her own argument.

"Let's just sit tight," said Striker. She took a step toward their voices and slipped. The terrain was rapidly changing. "See?" she said. She lifted her foot. The sucking sound like an exaggerated kiss. It took real effort to pull her leg out. No way in hell did Bobbi Sue or Anders have the strength to free themselves from muck like this. Besides the ground, what else was thawing out?

A loud pop rang through the haze. The hairs on both of Striker's arms stood up.

"Success!" cried the Dame.

Striker stood listening to the Dame's long, uninterrupted swallows, wondering what a hundred-year-old Antarctic wine tasted like. It was probably thick and vinegary, the old woman's eyes tearing as she pounded it down.

Suddenly the engine roar cut out. In the silence, the Dame lowered the bottle. Striker felt her ears pop, pressure building behind her eyes. There was no way a flotilla of rescue craft could synchronously cut their engines like that. It meant there was just one boat. If it was Hector returning in the zodiac, the thought of what he might have dredged up out there in the white-hot fog made her stomach clench. Hector like a cat dragging its broken trophy home. And if whoever had just landed *wasn't* Hector—

"Aren't you holding a radio?" said the tired voice of Bobbi Sue.

In the fog it took Striker a minute to realize the doctor was talking to her. "I am but god knows how to use it."

"Give it to Anna," said Bobbi Sue. "She's good at finding channels."

"Let's hope the battery works," said the teen.

Striker inched through the mist to where the kid was standing, stopping when she hit two open hands. The teen took the radio out of the case and brought it up to their face.

"It's a Cobra," they said. "I'll do a scan and see what's what." Expertly the teen powered it on and began surfing the channels.

"Think you can find the *Yegorov*?" asked Striker.

"A radio like this, you can only talk to other boats if they're close by," explained the teen. "Depending on the atmospherics, we could get lucky. Maybe we'll hit one of the stations out of the research bases, or one up in Argentina. But if we do, all you can do is listen."

Striker held her breath. A time or two the radio landed on the steady hum of a test pattern. Suddenly what sounded like some South American country's national anthem came through crystal clear. The four of them stood waiting for an announcer to come back on with the news. But once it finished, the song started over again straight from the top.

The teen didn't give up. Striker was beginning to think it was pointless when a faint voice pierced the mist. The station was weak. The group edged in closer.

"I think it's coming out of Mawson, the Australian base," said Anders. They sounded like their old pedantic self. "I know the call number. I saw a chart listing all the Antarctic radio stations in the bridge on the *Yegorov*."

Shizer. The kid really was some kind of memorizing genius.

Despite the low volume, the voice was strident. Striker had to agree the accent was probably Australian.

. . . has said there are many rooms in His father's house. But you can trust there's no room for the fornicator. No room for the coveter. No room for the abortionist. No room—

"Turn it off," she said.

"But we only just—"

"Atone! Only by the blood of the lamb are we saved," said the voice.

Anders powered it down.

The four fell back into silence. The day hung white and thick. Through the mist the only sound was of heated air geysering up from the bowels of the earth.

Time either passed or it didn't. Overhead the white-hot smudge remained stuck past noon. Though she was standing upright in the swirling mist, Striker couldn't be sure she was awake. Her mind felt slushy. She remembered the name for this kind of disorientation.

White torture.

Of course!

She had read about it in the holiday newsletter Amnesty International mailed out begging for year-end gifts. All the global baddies used it. Iran. Venezuela. In a somewhat mitigated form, George W. Bush's United States. Basically you stuck someone in a white room and deprived them of everything. You dressed them in white, fed them a daily diet of white rice served on a white plate, the guards padding the bottom of their white shoes to muffle the sound of their walking on the white floor. White lights were installed on the white ceiling in such a way as to render the white room shadowless, every white surface rounded and smooth, barren of texture. In Caracas they called it La Tumba. Throw someone in the Tomb and all you had to do was sit back and wait. Months. Years. Decades. Their brains softening into a white paste, the prisoner's whole world a void. Striker could still remember the words of one man who had been white tortured.

They get what they want without having to hit you.

Thankfully the teen broke the monotony.

"After all that stuff happened, I said I didn't care," said Anders. "But I do."

Striker knew the teen was addressing their mom. She would've happily wandered off and given the two some privacy but there was nowhere to safely wander to.

"I just wish you'd see me for who I am." Somewhere inside the teen a plug had been pulled, all the dirty dishwater draining out.

"We asked you again and again," said Sarah. Her voice was shaking but for the first time since the accident, she sounded stable. "'Tell us who you want to be,' we said, and you said it was all good. Anna or Anders. Take your pick." Striker listened for the sound of Sarah reaching out for her child, but the two voices remained at a distance. "You told the therapist you weren't sure. You said you identified as both." Her voice was growing soft. "We wanted you to still have Anna in case you decided Anna was who you wanted to be. We didn't want to take that life away from you."

"I didn't lie," said Anders. "My name, my pronouns—I truly don't care. What matters is I can *tell*, I can *feel it*. You don't *like* this." Striker knew the thumping sound echoing in the fog was the teen beating their chest. "Admit it. You don't like *me*."

"Of *course* I like you," said Sarah. "I love you. You're my child."

"So why don't you *act* like it? Why do you hate me so much?"

"I don't hate *you*," whispered Sarah. "I hate *me*."

From out of the quiet, something began to rumble. It wasn't thunder. It was the island itself.

"You are the bravest person I know," said Sarah. "You never settle, even when settling would make things easier. Me? Every time I had a choice, I compromised. I never put me first."

"Boo hoo," slurred the Dame. "I squeezed out a baby at fifteen. Left the silly thing at the hospital and never looked back. We're women. We do what we have to do."

"Stay out of this," warned Sarah.

"My sister had a baby Christmas Day in the basement of our church," Striker said. She could feel the words issuing out of her mouth, the action of speaking utterly out of her control. "Nobody knew she was pregnant. I was there, I saw it breathing on the floor. She zipped it up in her backpack. Then we stuffed my sister's underwear with towels and she snuck off to a party and buried it."

"See?" said the Dame. She paused. Apparently the bottle wasn't empty yet. The fog filled with the sound of the wine sluicing down her throat. "Twenty years after I gave birth to a son, I hired a detective to track him down." A pungent smell wafted through the mist. "Surprise surprise. Little fucker didn't want a damn thing to do with me."

What had the Baron said? Nothing builds a wall like a secret. Their whole marriage the Dame had never told him she'd had a baby, and on the eve of their wedding, he had kept her from knowing her only child, gifting her instead with an emerald fit for a dowager.

"Anders?" said Sarah. Her words were tinged with dread. "I have something I need to tell you."

"I already know," said the teen. "I knew this whole year. Mrs. Winters, the guidance counselor, told me. You and Dad never filed a report."

"I didn't want that for you. Your whole senior year spent fighting."

"Let me guess," the teen said wearily. "You did it for my own good." They gave a sharp laugh. "But it was *my* decision to make. You guys love me but you fucked—"

They all heard it at the same time. A voice suddenly cutting through the fog.

"Mommy?"

"Mikey?" Sarah whispered. She pivoted toward the sound of footsteps. "Mikey!" Off she went, rushing blindly into the mist.

"Mom!" shouted Anders. The teen raced after her.

There was a terrible noise louder than thunder. Striker slapped her hands over her ears. A chunk of earth ripped away. It plummeted into the caldera. None of them realized they'd been standing so close to the rim. Another thunderous crack sounded. The air shook.

Then the mist receded long enough for Striker to see every detail. She had never noticed how much Anders looked like their mom. Both their smiles favoring the left sides of their faces, a small cleft adorning each of their chins. Neither of them screamed as the earth disappeared under their feet. Instead, they both locked eyes on Striker. The moment almost gentle. A kind of ballet. The ground split open. The two went tumbling through the whiteness. Sarah locking fingers with Anders. Her other hand reaching uselessly for Striker. The fog sealed back up. Even after the earth stopped rumbling, Striker kept her palms clamped over her ears.

"You can stop cowering now," said the Dame. "They're gone." The old woman jiggled the wine bottle, trying to gauge how much was left. Striker could see something was wrong with the old girl's face. It kept shuddering, various expressions flitting across her skin like some sort of glitch.

The haze glowed, the day fiery though for all Striker knew, it was deepest night. Tendrils of mist climbed the air, rising as if from a witch's brew. It was coming. She could feel it in her gut. Any minute now the fog would coalesce and form something unspeakable, the horror of the last twenty-five years finally taking corporeal shape. Wasn't that what she'd been expecting all this time? Her past walking the earth.

And God said let there be light. And the light revealed the horror.
Then something *did* step out of the mist.
The little girl looked healthy. There were no signs of dehydration, exposure, hunger, extreme fright. Something fat and gray sat balled on her shoulder.
"Where are your dads?" barked the Dame.
"She doesn't really talk," said Striker, relieved she wasn't the only one who could see her. Still, it was a good question. Where had she been? And where the hell was Hector?
Wherever he was, Striker knew in that instant he was staring at her and nodding, his eyes burning her skin. She thought of their long-ago conversation back on the *Yegorov*. The way he'd sized her up. Now at the end of everything, he was calling on her as an ally, a fellow traveler in the white mist. *Look after her*, he was saying. *Keep her safe.* "What makes you think I can?" Striker whispered.
She couldn't tell if the fog was growing worse or if her eyesight was failing. One minute she would see Lucy standing clear as day in her yellow dry suit. Then something would shift and the child would disappear in clouds of white. Striker had been too long without sunglasses, her retinas burned from too much seeing. She couldn't be sure if it was snow blindness or the elements or something more sinister.

"The truth shall set you free," mused the Dame. The old girl had plopped herself down on a new outcrop that hadn't been there only minutes ago, the rock still steaming from the heat of its birth.

"What was that?" said Striker.

Blood was beginning to stain the front of the Dame's dry suit. Two red bullseyes forming on the front of her chest. "I said, and then there were three. Jesus Christ. Pull yourself together." The wine had loosened the old girl's tongue. "Two's company, three's a crowd," she roared. "A three-ring circus. Three wise men. Three in the pink, one in the stink."

"There's a child here, for god's sake," but when the Dame didn't hit back, Striker wasn't sure either of them had spoken.

The old girl lifted a hand to her mouth. There was a sound like cloth being torn. The smell of stale blood wafted through the mist. Striker felt her stomach heave. She could hear the tiny clicks as the Dame's jaw worked overtime. Even through the fog the old woman's titanium stumps flashed, two silver bullets.

"You're *still* eating it?" whispered Striker.

The Dame got up off the steaming rock and faded into the mist. Her voice floated through the fog. "I wouldn't have to if you'd brought us back something decent to gnaw on."

The word *us* sent a shiver through Striker's veins. She went to put a hand on Lucy, hoping to keep the little girl close, but the child had disappeared again in the haze.

"You know damn well what happened here," called the Dame. "Don't act like you don't." Before she vanished, Striker had seen a series of faces ripple over the Dame's, heard the polyphony of voices in her words. Through the mist the old woman and several dozen others spoke in unison. "We're all the same, just waiting to be rescued."

"I'm not taking them back with us," said Striker.

"As if you have a—" The Dame and her many voices cut out.

There was only one place she could be. The damn thing had yet to collapse. Maybe it never would. Maybe the grotto was simply cleansing itself, waiting for the next round of visitors to arrive, beings it could infuse with the horror of what had happened on this island, the bloody hollow dented in the floor fully thawed.

The Dame was right. Striker did know what had happened down there. Maybe she had known ever since her very first vision in the cabin when she'd picked up the ax. The silver blade lopping off the sick man's entire hand though only the tips of a few fingers were frostbitten. The grotto wasn't just some storage pantry. It was a graveyard. The long white bone she'd pulled from the floor hadn't belonged to a seal or even a whale. Limb by limb the men had killed each other off. They had pared each other down like dying trees, the severed parts thrown in the hoosh. In his soiled leather mask the doctor keeping himself and his lackeys alive by mutilating the sick and the unyielding and blaming it on frostbite or infection. Hacking off an entire arm or leg at the first sign of injury though the patient might have fully recovered with the right care. And all the while the doctor acting as if the men should be grateful for his intervention. With each surgery telling the unlucky patient in his thick brogue *it's fur yer ain gude, aye*. The silver hatchet rising hungrily in the air until the hand that wielded it was the only hand left.

How many times had Striker and Ama been told some decision was for their own good? Learning to swim. Going to church. Moving to Zinnia Trace. Anytime the world tells you something is for your own good, a road your life could have traveled gets erased. After that, you can never know what might have happened. All you can do is keep going.

The fog thinned just enough. The child hadn't gone far. She was standing only a few feet away on a ledge overlooking the crater. Her face stony as ever. Striker felt her own legs shake as she approached the edge. She had to move fast while the child was still visible.

"Lucy," she whispered, extending her hand. "We have to go." Only the beating of her heart infused the moment with a sense of time.

The rat pressed itself flat on the girl's shoulder. It looked like it was gearing up to pounce. Finally the child reached out and took Striker's hand. It was surprisingly warm. Striker realized the little girl was the first person she'd willingly touched since the accident. She was startled by the comfort it gave her.

"Merrily merrily merrily," sang a voice. "Life is but a dream."

The Dame stepped out of the fog. Her skin shimmered, her whole body bursting with an unearthly light. Striker knew it wasn't the ocean she was hearing swelling in the distance. It was the sound of the old gal's heart sloshing behind her ribs. The organ enlarged and swollen, the thing brimming with water. The old-fashioned word for that was dropsy, wasn't it? Of course. As the island thawed, Jane Foley was filling up. The Antarctic dead were seeping in through her pores, hungry to be carried home. She was almost to capacity. They were drowning her and she didn't even know it, an army of icy wraiths shape-shifting all over her body.

The Dame stepped closer. Her form flickered. Face after gaunt face rising to the surface. Suddenly the features of a young man stabilized on her skin. Instinctually Striker shielded Lucy with her body.

The man was small in stature and rail thin, his stick-like arms outstretched. The man's hair shorn close, his scalp nicked and scabby.

"Please," he said, voice hoarse as if he'd been screaming.

It was the woman who had stowed away at the turn of the last century to be with her beloved. "We've been waiting," pleaded the woman. "Our only hope of home is you."

Suddenly they were all visible, the mist teeming with their spectral forms. As many as forty men dressed in rags, beards ratty and gray. They were the dead of the island, the ones who'd been stranded and left desperate. A menacing figure stood at the front of the group. The man a full head taller than the rest. His face smooth and without expression, his eyes barely visible behind the slits in his mask. The leather stippled with blood.

It was the doctor. The man who had performed surgery even when only a bandage was called for, hacking off arms and legs, butchering the sick and even the healthy who questioned his authority.

"Kin ye draw oot the leviathan wi' a hook? Or his tongue wi' a cord ye let doon?" he declared. A terrible smell issued from his mouth. Spit glistened on the two yellow teeth sewn in the leather. "Kin ye pit a hook in his snoot? Or bore his jaw through wi' a thorn?" The man was obviously insane, the mask his only vestige of being human. It disguised the gaping hole in him. All things divided by zero are zero. Striker knew if her own mask ever fell away, she would find herself wedded to the void. Like everyone she'd ever encountered, she'd been wearing it so long she didn't even remember tying it on.

The wraiths were closing in. The specters didn't seem to walk so much as glide. An army of Antarctic dead moving with the mindlessness of glaciers. It was her they wanted and not the child. Already the woman who had disguised herself as a man was within arm's reach. She grabbed Striker's wrist, her grip like being kissed by both fire and ice.

"Please don't leave us here," said the woman. Striker ripped her hand away. The woman's mouth twisted into a snarl. "If it wasn't for us, you'd already be dead," she growled. "We gave you shelter. We fed you."

Striker knew what it would mean to merge with this broken woman. She would be left with only a distorted version of herself. The Antarctic dead were slavering to become corporeal again. They needed a host. They needed her. They wouldn't be denied. Maybe it wouldn't be all that different from life on Zinnia Trace. Being stuffed with other people's stories, their beliefs.

Suddenly the army of wraiths folded back into the fog. La Grande Dame strode forward gripping a shillelagh. The old gal strolled along like a woman out for a Sunday promenade. Dapperly picking the walking stick up and placing it on the pitted earth. "So many terrible things happened here," she said as she circled Striker and the little girl. "And just think. This used to be the most pristine spot on earth."

"But *we* did this," said Striker. "Whatever this is?" She waved around at the glittering landscape. "We carried it down here inside of us."

"Speak for yourself," scoffed the Dame. Without warning she hurled the empty wine bottle through the fog. It whizzed past Striker's head and smashed on a nearby rock. Voices began to echo in the mist.

"Veronique." The woman who'd been concealed as a man stepped forward again. Striker could see the woman's face shining through the Dame's, the woman interposing herself on the Dame's body. The vision gave a sad smile. "When Doctor came for it, what else was I to do?" Striker felt her heart tremble. "I was weak and alone," the woman said. "The only one who walked by my side was the Lord and in my hour of need the Lord stayed silent." The woman disappeared in a thick band of fog, the Dame along with her. Her words echoed through the haze. "He said it was best for everyone," the woman lamented. "He told me it would be like—"

Doctor's voice filled the mist. "*Jesus feedin' scran tae the wee masses. Blessed are they that are hungry, for they'll be filled up.*"

The word was out of Striker's mouth before she could stop herself. "Monster," she whispered.

"How *dare* you?"

The Dame came charging out of the fog. She loomed ten feet tall. The stick gleamed in her hand. They were shape-shifting all over her skin. Her face distorted with faces. She had become porous. There was nothing solid left of her.

Why had Striker ever thought of her as *old*? It had been the silvery hair. She was young, decades younger than the Baron. He had said as much while floating in the hot spring. There was even a possibility she was barely fifty.

Striker gripped Lucy's hand and turned to run. A sinkhole roared open at their feet. She managed to pivot. Their only hope was to head directly into the fog and cloak themselves in it. But she couldn't even see her own legs let alone a path of escape down the volcano.

"An' Ham saw the nakitness o his faither an' telt his brithers," intoned the Dame. "An' Shem an' Japheth took a cloak, an' laid it oan baith their shooders, an' went backwaird, an' covered the bare bits o' their faither. An' Noah wauked up, an knewed whit his younger son had dune."

Striker had never understood that Bible story. White Christians had used it for generations to justify their treatment of Black people. How did Noah's getting drunk and passing out warrant Ham and his descendants being cursed into chattel slavery?

It doesn't.

The mist was working against her. Striker crept along feeling the earth with her toes. At one point, she turned and pulled the child closer as she held a finger to her lips, signaling for quiet.

Only it wasn't Lucy's hand she was holding.

Striker couldn't even scream as the woman with the shaved head drifted out of the fog. The woman didn't say a word, just opened her mouth. A white string appeared between her lips. It was too awful but there was nothing else to do. Striker reached out and pulled.

An amaryllis bloomed from the woman's mouth. The blossom like a white trumpet. "Little ones to Him belong," cooed the woman as she rocked an invisible baby in her arms. "They are weak but He is strong."

A chorus of voices filled the day. There was Trish and Doug calling that summer night long ago, begging the sisters to come home. There was the little girl at the pool, asking why she was dirty; the teenaged swim instructor's laugher as he tossed Ama in the water. The old nun with the rheumy eyes telling the sisters about the urges the devil plants in every young girl's heart. The nun warning them that if the girl should give in and throw herself down at Satan's feet, her body will no longer be hers.

The Dame's voice carried the loudest. "How do you live with yourself?" she crowed. "At least I left my son at the hospital."

Striker felt something burning the skin of her throat. She touched the little gold cross to—

<< Everywhere the sound of children singing in the midnight hour. Outside the snow falling cold and blameless. Striker and Ama are sneaking back down to the basement room under the stairs, the humidifiers roaring like a storm. The human body is amazing. What normally takes hours, even days, can happen in thirty minutes when a teen girl is desperate enough. And all too often she is desperate enough. Teen girls giving birth at the prom, in the toilet at a gas station, in the silence of her room. Afterward willing herself to get up and walk, go back to her life.

And later that day when the knock arrives at the door of the big white house at the top of the hill on Zinnia Trace, the two sisters are lying in bed. One sister quietly singing to herself while far away in a beautiful dream. The other sister fearful and cunning, a gash in the palm of her hand where her sister accidentally slashed it as the two worked to cut the umbilical cord.

Quickly the bloody towels are found. Striker can't look Trish and Doug in the eye. So many voices are coming at the two sisters, so many questions though no one is listening. No one ever has. They already know how this story ends. It was written before the sisters even arrived a decade earlier when everyone was assigned their roles to play.

Places, everyone!

And so it happens. Her sister is led away. Ama refuses to be seen by a doctor. Says take me straight to juvie, begins to shriek in that way she has. The pitch so high it gets inside your head and you want it to stop, will do anything it says to make it stop, and so they do. Within hours Ama is dead. No one even checks her body. They are all so sure about who she was and the nature of what happened.

The little blue-red loaf lying on the floor. The umbilical cord full of blood running up into >>

"I had a baby," Striker whispers. "I abandoned it Christmas Eve. Told my sister it was *our* baby, her and me. Ama and Veronique forever. Told her we had to get rid of it. Said it was for our own good, that we had to look out for each other because no one else would. She didn't say a word. Just scooped it up and played her part. She was arrested and taken away, where she killed herself. Nobody ever suspected."

Striker braces for the crushing wave of sorrow to break over her. After that interminable night, her grip on reality loosened. From then on she shaped her life to fit the story the world believed. Striker the model daughter. Ama the sister voted Most Likely to Fuck Up. But after Ama's death, it was too much for one psyche to bear, so Dark Striker came and went as needed, more and bigger swaths of her life swallowed by fantasy and projection and then unexpectedly this white continent offering itself up like a mirror in which travelers like Shackleton and Scott and even Striker might finally encounter their true selves, the ice a vast fun house reflecting her life back to her, the things done and the things she did in the name of surviving.

Striker is alone on an unnamed island somewhere in the Antarctic peninsula, the sun unflinching, and she is coming to realize she can barely see, eyes burning as if rubbed with salt. Slowly, silently she searches the haze for Lucy, not even daring to call out. This must be how the child's fathers felt, the kid constantly ghosting them. But now isn't the place for fun and games. The Dame is somewhere out there in the hot white mist and she's not alone. The air eerily sparkling. Every soul that has waited more than a hundred years for deliverance is pouring its way into the old girl's bloodstream, her heart as if infested with worms. Striker knows now what the old woman saw out there on the Southern Ocean when the winds picked up and sent a kayak crashing through Percy's skull. From out of the void Jane Foley heard the long-forgotten dead calling her to be their vessel, saw their faces in the waves. Wherever she is, her strength is becoming inhuman. The last dregs of her soul are losing out to whatever is thawing in the ice.

Terror coils in Striker's belly. Everywhere voices capering on the wind. Even in her blindness, figures appear in the vapor. The faces of starving men in whom the desperate animal has been revealed. After everything she's done, she can hardly blame them.

The fog begins to shimmer. On its surface scenes appear like a film on a movie screen. Tableaux of bloodshed and murder. A man hacking another man's fingers off over a discrepancy in the size of his bowl of hoosh. Everything falling apart with the unexplained disappearance of their captain. Men crawling around on their naked bellies in the Antarctic night roaring madly at the moon. When the first cries of a baby come issuing out of the earth, the pandemonium is indescribable. Skeletal men pouring out of the cabin like ants and racing toward the grotto, those still capable of it drooling.

The Dame shoots out of the mist. The old lady lifts the stick in her newly massive hand. Striker can see the blood rippling all over her body. Some of the wounds are ancient. Some new like the one on her bottom lip from gnawing on her own flesh.

"I'll ask one more time," says the Dame. "Who did you hurt to get here?" But when Striker turns to face her, the place where the Dame was standing is empty.

As a child, Striker learned from the nuns that in order to be saved, you have to see Christ's face in everyone you meet. Already she can feel the shillelagh smashing through her skull. But don't they also have to see Him in *me*, she thinks.

"Hullo there." The old girl reappears, gripping a shattered bottle by its neck. "Care for some wine?"

Striker backs away but the Dame pops up behind her.

"You know what your problem is?" The old woman leans over her shoulder and caresses Striker's cheek with an icy finger. "Everything about you is wrong." She disappears again, a chimera in the wind. Where the Dame touched her, the skin on Striker's face is blackened with frostbite.

Striker feels herself being herded toward the edge of the crater. More than once the walking stick comes smashing into the side of her head only to vanish at the last second, her skull kissed by a blast of icy wind. A weariness settles over her. There is nothing else to do. She sinks to her knees. She doesn't know what is wanted of her and is tired of guessing. Hands up. Hands behind your back. Lie down. Up against the car. What's your name? Shut up.

The Dame strolls victoriously out of the fog. "You shouldn't have come here," she says in her patchwork of many voices. "You don't belong." With both hands she raises the shillelagh one last time high overhead. "You should have tried harder to get along," the chorus that is the Dame sings. "You shouldn't have been you."

Suddenly the winds shift. The island fills with the sound of rending. Bone from bone, rock from rock. The clamor crescendos until it's unbearable, an event pregnant with seismic force. All Striker can think is the island is finally sinking into the sea. There are no winners. That's what early twentieth century explorers discovered the hard way. Dominion over the earth begins with dominion over each other, but ultimately it's a false power. It leaves you with nothing on which to build your church.

The Dame and her many faces look confused. Striker closes her eyes and listens, quietly raising both hands in the air.

There. Under the clang of total destruction. A single note. Clear and bright.

Something falls out of the sky, the object massive as a bank vault. It lands squarely on la Grande Dame's head, sending the person once known as Jane Foley to the ground.

Not a drop of blood is spilled. Only water gushes out of the body as though it has sprung a leak. Two yellow teeth and a tattered scrap of leather lie in a sour-smelling puddle. Quickly the earth soaks up the fluids.

The murderous rock that fell from the heavens is an uncanny blue-red in color. A symbol carved on its surface.

As the fog begins to dissipate, Striker finds herself kneeling in the shadow of the mama cairn and staring at the blue-red giant forming its base. Overhead something catches her eye.

Atop the rickety spire of rocks, a one-eyed bird sits preening its feathers.

Then Lucy steps out from behind the pillar. Each stone in the tower appears misaligned. Playfully the child runs her fingers over the bottom rock. Lightly she raps on it with a tuning fork. At the sound, the cairn quivers. Lucy taps it again. The column shifts back into place.

And so Lucy holds out her hand. Striker takes it and together they walk out of the thinning mist and down the far side of the volcano. The child is her shepherd.

Now that the fog is breaking up, Striker knows it is her own eyes and not the white mist obscuring her vision. How each of us only sees what we expect to see, the world conforming to our beliefs. But now that her sight is ruined, everything is perfectly clear. No more misconceptions, no more fears. The earth shakes and leaps under her feet. Everything coming alive.

On this side of the island, there is no penguin colony. No four-ton seals roaming the beach. Nothing but water and melting ice and the sea like a road stretching in every direction. Striker sees the kayak she and Anders freed Hector from years before, and there is Hector lying on his back beside the zodiac, his unblinking gaze fixed on the heavens.

Lucy closes her father's eyes and kisses his nose. He looks peaceful, a man who has accomplished what he set out to achieve. The child tucks something small and gray in the crook of his arm. It's a stuffed animal, a rat with an orange bow tie, its two buck teeth permanently grinning. This object of love will be Hector's headstone.

Then Lucy does what needs doing. Striker is her baby. The child is surprisingly adept. On the stony beach she leads Striker to the tandem, places her in the front of the boat. A burning rock goes flying past, its origin either celestial or volcanic. The sky is raining fire, the sun a few degrees past either noon or midnight. Sulfur and brimstone. The sounds of a great blast. Poisonous gases shoot up into the air. Trumpets. Nothing can sleep forever. We are interconnected. My father's mansion contains many rooms.

How much of our personal narratives are even true? All of Striker's trysts and dalliances with men, none of them ever amounting to much—are they the daydreams of a lonely woman or memories of actual encounters? And is Riley a real flesh-and-blood person, or just the Black ride-or-die friend Striker has spent a lifetime wishing into existence?

Didn't she always know it would end like this? How could it not? A house divided will not stand. All her stories catching up with her at once. She just didn't think she'd take the whole universe down with her.

Lovingly Lucy hands her a paddle. Striker accepts it and looks straight out toward the horizon. Wasn't it only minutes ago she pushed off from the *Yegorov*, the albatross convulsing on deck?

The kayak wobbles gently as someone seats themself in the back. Once the person is in, Striker inhales deeply and pushes the boat out into the Southern Ocean. Already she can feel her boatmate's breath on the nape of her neck. She thinks of the myth of Orpheus. How he turned around too soon and was forced to watch as the ghost of his wife disappeared back into the dark.

Striker knows it isn't Eurydice in this tandem with her. Most likely it's Lucy, the Morning Star. The little girl with some unworldly knowledge of where to find help.

If Striker is damned, it's the icy dead seated behind her, an island's worth of souls with their personal histories slowly drowning her. As punishment for the things she has done, she must be their deliverer, the past a country she can never transcend.

But if she is blessed, it's her sister paddling behind her, Ama with her gap-toothed grin from ear to ear, and together she and Ama are going home for some good food, good music, rest, a little justice. Striker knows if her sister is the one sitting just over her shoulder, at some point Ama will say:

"Remember that time we told Trish about our cones at Baskin-Robbins being smaller than everyone else's and she told us *don't be silly?*"

The words will bring a smile to Striker's face. Only Ama could think of ice cream at a time like this, all over the blistering ocean growlers hurtling past the sisters like blue comets.

Then it will come to her. The worst thing in the world. The thing that terrifies her most of all. It isn't full-frontal insanity. It's this long-forgotten truth, like transverberation piercing her in the heart.

"I remember," Striker will say, the agony dawning in her voice.

"You know the next day she drove down there and ripped them a new one."

Striker will feel the tears starting to rise. "I know," she'll whisper.

Ama will sit smiling, trailing a finger in the water. "Trish and Doug were always doing stuff like that," she'll say. "Fighting for us behind our backs. Putting on a brave face because they wanted us to believe we were just like everyone else."

Striker will nod. The golden pain rising like sap in her veins. Remembering how she never saw that teenaged swim instructor again after he threw Ama in the pool. Remembering the first moments of Ama deep in the pale blue water before her sister even knew what happened. A brief moment of unabashed wonder in Ama's eyes. Then her small body of its own accord carrying her back up to the surface.

ACKNOWLEDGMENTS

The toast on page 198 was the Reverend Ed Lynn's closing words at the Northshore Unitarian Church in the 1980s.

The definition on page 207 of a microagression comes from Merriam-Webster's online dictionary.

On page 221 the line about a tree touching heaven is a reworking of a quote from Carl Jung.

The Anna Akhmatova excerpt on page 247 is from her poem "Requiem."

The history of pemmican described on page 283 relies on Jason C. Anthony's *Hoosh*.

Deepest thanks to early reader Chele Isaac for her insightful comments throughout the book's many drafts, and to Kelly Parks Snider for listening as I talked it out. Thanks to my brother Sean for his thoughts about sailboats, though he would've preferred a more gruesome death involving getting one's face chewed up by the engine (heh!). I would also like to acknowledge the Bogliasco Foundation; Rowland Writers Retreat and my fellow fellows there, who were generous in sharing their thoughts on the things that scare them; Macdowell; the T. S. Eliot House; and the University of Wisconsin–Madison for support in writing this book.

REFERENCES

Anthony, Jason C. *Hoosh: Roast Penguin, Scurvy Day, and Other Stories of Antarctic Cuisine*. Lincoln: University of Nebraska, 2012.

Blum, Hester. *The News at the Ends of the Earth*. Durham and London: Duke University Press, 2019.

Monteath, Colin. *Antarctica: Beyond the Southern Ocean*. Hauppauge, NY: Barron's Educational Books, 1997.

Moss, Sarah. *The Frozen Ship: The Histories and Tales of Polar Exploration*. New York: Burbage, 2006.

Wilkes, Ally. *All the White Spaces*. New York: Atria, 2022.

The character of Robert Foley was named by Bob Wally as part of a fundraiser for the Worcester, Massachusetts, Public Library. (I'm sorry, Bob, that "Martha" didn't make the cut.)

Books I am indebted to for their tone and narrative suspense include Shirley Jackson's *Hangsaman*; *Lord of the Flies* by William Golding; the Inimitable One, Stephen King's *The Shining*; and of course, the OG dark tales storyteller, Nathaniel Hawthorne:

> "When the friend shows his inmost heart to his friend; the lover to his best-beloved; when man does not vainly shrink from the eye of his Creator, loathsomely treasuring up the secret of his sin; then deem me a monster, for the symbol beneath which I have lived, and die! I look around me, and, lo! on every visage a Black Veil!"

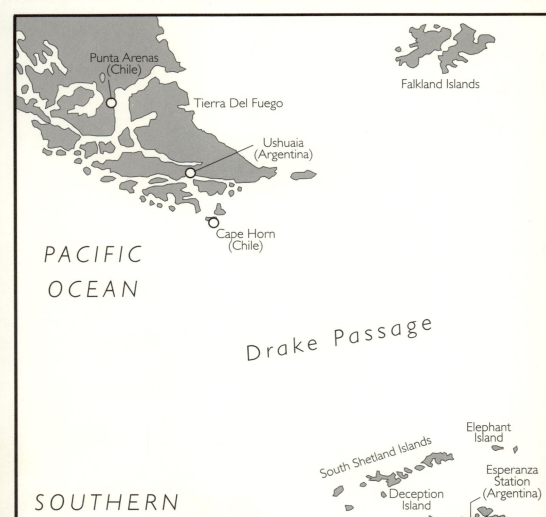